# THE FIGHTING MAN

'An exciting novel that is full of inside knowledge ... It's time for Gerald Seymour to be recognized as ranking right up there with Graham Greene' – *New York Times*

'Unstoppable momentum' – *Daily Telegraph*

'Moving and gripping. Seymour's characters are all beautifully drawn. The dialogue is so real you can hear it and the plot is as tight as a drum. It is tempting to say that Seymour is at the height of his powers ... He just gets better and better' – *Today*

# HAVE YOU READ . . . ?

## CONDITION BLACK

In the final months before Saddam Hussein's invasion of Kuwait in 1991, the only man who stands in the way of the total collapse of the Middle Eastern situation is a young FBI agent hot on the heels of a deadly assassin working for the Iraqi government.

## HARRY'S GAME

A British cabinet minister is gunned down by an IRA assassin. The police trail goes cold, and undercover agent Harry Brown is sent to infiltrate the terrorist organisation and uncover the killer. It's a race against the clock, and one false move will be enough to leave him dead before he reaches his target.

## THE UNKNOWN SOLDIER

In the depths of the Arabian Desert, American and British counter-terrorism experts are desperately searching for one man. If they fail to find him, he will re-emerge in a teeming western city, carrying only a suitcase that will wreak havoc and devastation when detonated.

## THE WAITING TIME

On a winter's night at the height of the Cold War, in a small East German town, a young man is killed by the secret police. All the witnesses are terrorised into silence. But Tracey Barnes heard the shot that ended her lover's life, and she will wait for as long as it takes until there arises the opportunity for revenge.

# ABOUT THE AUTHOR

Gerald Seymour spent fifteen years as an international television news reporter with ITN, covering Vietnam and the Middle East, and specialising in the subject of terrorism across the world. Seymour was on the streets of Londonderry on the afternoon of Bloody Sunday, and was a witness to the massacre of Israeli athletes at the Munich Olympics.

Gerald Seymour is now a full-time writer, and six of his novels have been filmed for television in the UK and US. THE FIGHTING MAN is his fourteenth novel.

For more information about Gerald Seymour and his books, visit his Facebook page at
www.facebook.com/GeraldSeymourAuthor

*Also By Gerald Seymour*

Harry's Game
The Glory Boys
Kingfisher
Red Fox
The Contract
Archangel
In Honour Bound
Field of Blood
A Song in the Morning
At Close Quarters
Home Run
Condition Black
The Journeyman Tailor
The Fighting Man
The Heart of Danger
Killing Ground
The Waiting Time
A Line in the Sand
Holding the Zero
The Untouchable
Traitor's Kiss
The Unknown Soldier
Rat Run
The Walking Dead
Timebomb
The Collaborator
The Dealer and the Dead
A Deniable Death
The Outsiders
The Corporal's Wife

GERALD SEYMOUR

# The Fighting Man

HODDER

First published in Great Britain in 1993 by HarperCollins Publishers

This paperback edition first published in 2013

1

A CIP catalogue record for this title is available from the British Library.

Book ISBN 978 1 444 76027 9
eBook ISBN 978 1 444 76028 6

Printed and bound by Clays Ltd, St Ives plc

Hodder & Stoughton policy is to use papers that are natural, renewable
and recyclable products and made from wood grown in sustainable
forests. The logging and manufacturing processes are expected to
conform to the environmental regulations of the country of origin.

Hodder & Stoughton Ltd
338 Euston Road
London NW1 3BH

www.hodder.co.uk

*To Gillian, Nicholas and James*

# THE FIGHTING MAN:

## *Introduction by Mark Urban*

There are a good many things about the hero of this volume that may at first strike the average reader as improbable. And I am not referring to the odd coincidence of his sharing a name with someone who became prime minister after Gerald Seymour wrote it!

No, the issues surrounding this Gordon Brown are more to do with why on earth would someone who had been an SAS officer really engage in such a dangerous, hopeless mission, without pay and with every chance of ending up in an unmarked grave? Aren't the people in Britain's Special Forces supposed to be brighter than that, more stable?

Well, I have never served in the SAS or SBS (its Royal Marine sister unit) but I do know quite a few people who have. These men have poured out a lot of anecdotes to me over the years, helping me to write a couple of factual books about these normally secretive units. Let me give you a few details of real men that might offer some insight into the fictional Gord Brown.

Soldier A, driven by the pursuit of excellence to the point where he felt even the SAS could not satisfy his standards, resigned and disappeared. Contemplating suicide, he was eventually found and helped after a police search.

Soldier B, like Gerald's hero, served in Iraq during the 1991 Gulf War, where he fell foul of the hierarchy, being 'RTU'ed' or Returned to Unit. The SAS is full is highly competitive alpha males – and a posting there often ends unhappily, with recriminations.

My last real-life case, Soldier C, had left the forces and was working with me and a BBC team covering a revolution. Several times he confided in me his sympathy for the rebels, his conviction that they needed better training and leadership, as well as the fact that he would consider coming back, on his own, to help them once our assignment was over.

Scanning the news archives, you will find a number of examples of former British Special Forces soldiers who turned up in odd places, helping mount coups or train resistance fighters. Many had hired themselves out as mercenaries, some had ideological reasons. However it is fair to say that what unites characters like these is a relish for action and adventure, 'the refusal', in the words of one SAS friend, 'to respect boundaries'.

As Gerald transports his hero into action, he highlights this essential truth, writing, 'he would have admitted it, couldn't have hidden it, the excitement consumed him'. Gord Brown was dealing with a surge of excitement that had welled up, 'as it always did whenever he flew forward to combat'.

Passing the selection tests for the Special Forces requires enormous drive, stamina and focus – so much so that you can argue that most of those who get through are not 'balanced' people to start with. The experience of soldiering in this rarified and dangerous atmosphere leaves some of them addicted to risk.

Add these factors together and you understand some of the reasons why many of these men meet untimely deaths. There are those who have perished doing extreme sports, others in obscure foreign conflicts, and some who cannot deal with their inner demons anymore end up taking their own lives.

They are often solitary characters too – leaving a trail of broken marriages, estranged friendships and lost jobs in their trail. Many find that life after Hereford or Poole is a series of disappointments. This isn't a destiny that unites all of these one-time warriors, of course, many of whom go on to live fulfilling lives, but it does seem to consume a surprising number of them.

These were the sorts of characters that Gerald and I discussed when he was writing THE FIGHTING MAN. Gerald is the sort of writer who insists on authenticity, whether that concerns the flight performance of the Antonov An-2 biplane or the feel of Guatemala City's shanties.

The result is a compelling thriller and an excellently plotted page-turner. But it is also a vivid study of a fighting man, one of those who ran out of road with the SAS, and hazarded his life on an apparently hopeless mission in a far-off land.

Mark Urban
London, 21 April 2013

# PROLOGUE

He saw the cockroach scurry across the tiled floor, and ignored it.

His father saw the cockroach and swiped at it with his stick and cursed because the creature had found the cover of a chair.

He sat at the table and turned the pages of the morning's newspaper. He heard his father's hacked cough and then the shuffle of the shoes on the tiles and the beat of the stick that supported him. The cockroach had reached the angle of the tiled floor and the walls and headed for the safety of the divan bed. The bed was not made yet, and the floor was not washed down, and the walls of the room were scarred with damp and the paint had flaked. It was a room that no woman cared for, home for a father and his son. Behind his shoulder there was a grunt from his father and then the closing of the inner door and then the slamming of the heavier outer door. At the same time each morning his father grunted and went out through the doors and there would be the awkward footfall of the injured leg down the staircase that led to the street.

He rolled the newspaper tight enough to make it a weapon. He went catlike across the room. He never spoke of the cockroaches in the room to his father. With a sudden movement, he pulled the divan bed away from the wall. It was as if he believed that to have spoken of the cockroaches would have seemed to be a criticism of his father. They floundered, their security taken from them. He would never criticize his father, not after the life that he had lived, not after the suffering he had endured. He beat the cockroaches with the rolled newspaper until they were pulped and smeared on the tiles. Their home was a two-bedroomed apartment in the Campeche quarter at the south end of the Old City, with a kitchenette annexe behind a curtain off the day room where he slept, and a shower and lavatory on the landing beyond the outer door. He pushed the bed back against the wall; the ant columns would dispose of the broken cockroaches.

He unrolled the newspaper, threw it back on the table so that it hid the used cups and the dirtied plates. There were bloodstains across the speech of the minister that celebrated the harvest of cut sugar cane.

He went to the window.

They were waiting for his father at the café. They were the other old men, the exiles. They sat where they always sat in the mid-morning to await the arrival of his father. They were at two tables pushed together and in the centre was an empty plastic chair that was ready for him. He saw the fat stomachs and the muscleless arms and the bald heads that were discoloured by the sun. They would be counting through their money so that each had enough for two cups of thin coffee and a packet of cigarettes. They were the dreamers.

His father would have stopped and talked in the ground-floor hallway with Marta, nearly blind and a little deaf, who guarded the staircase with fierce devotion, and who pinned each morning to the chest of her black dress the medal she had been given as recompense for her husband's death in the revolution. He wrinkled his nostrils at the stench of the gasoline fumes. The street outside their apartment now carried all the traffic from the wider parallel route that was closed to permit the slow rebuilding of a sewer. He saw his father come onto the pavement and wave his stick as a farewell behind him. The noise of the street flooded through the open window. It was that morning of the week when he collected up their shirts and vests and underpants and socks and washed them, scrubbing clean the threadbare cotton.

His father was about to negotiate a crossing of the street. They were standing for him, the men around the tables of the coffee house, because he was their leader. He smiled, as he smiled each morning when he saw them stand as straight as their backs would allow to greet his father. Old men's dreams. He turned away. The washing was in a basket beside the chest in which the two Makarov pistols were locked, along with his father's camouflage uniform and the boots that still carried the long-ago-gathered mud. He heard the screaming of the traffic horn.

He was drawn to the window. He stumbled the last three strides. He stared down into the street.

His father was in the middle of the road. It was as if his father was marooned on an island in a river, and waved his stick at the bus that careered towards him. He understood. His father had needed the stick for three years now to take the weight from an arthritis-ridden knee. The driver had lost control of the bus, one of those shipped in from Hungary many years before.

He heard the warning shouts of the men from the coffee house and then only the blare of the bus horn.

He ran.

He bundled open the inner door of the apartment and the outer door. He charged down the two flights of the staircase. He bullocked past old Marta who knew nothing. The sunlight of the pavement caught at his face. There was the crash as the bus came to rest having scraped two parked cars. He saw his father.

He would have thought his father a big man, but the impact of the bus wheel had shrivelled him. His father lay in the road near the rubbish-filled gutter, so small and so still.

The face was whitening with the pallor of coming death, the breath was short spurts. There seemed to be no pain. He knelt by his father and slipped his arms under the knees and around the shoulders. Some of those who had waited at the tables were yelling at him that his father should not be moved, and he heard and ignored the call that one had been sent to find a telephone to ring for an ambulance. Down the street he saw that others were prising open the door of the bus driver's cab. He carried his father, so small and so still and so lightweight, across the

3

street and across the pavement. The crowd opened for him. When he glanced back he saw the boots and fists raining on the driver of the bus.

Up the staircase, his father's feet hitting the unpainted iron-work of the stair rail. Through the opened outer door, and through the inner door, and across the day room and through the door of the room where his father slept.

They came behind him in silence, the cronies of his father. He laid his father on the tousled sheets of the bed. He crouched by the bed and held his father's hand.

It was the room of a life gone by.

On the wall above the bed was a picture in colour, taken from a magazine, that showed the stern jowl face of Leonid Brezhnev. It was the room in which his father had wept into his hands after hearing on the radio of the death of the Party. On the table beside the bed was a photograph in a cardboard mount with a facing of yellowed cellophane of a group of men in combat fatigues and carrying automatic rifles. It was the room in which his father had spread the maps that were torn at the creases, and planned the return to his homeland. On the chest beside the open window was the black and white sketch drawing, framed in dulled silver, of a woman large with middle age who carried a girl child astride her hip and who held the hand of a young teen-age boy. It was the room in which his father made a display of flowers each year in a water-filled jam jar for a fast-dug grave beyond the defence ditches of a faraway village.

He heard the wail cry of the approaching ambulance locked in traffic.

It was where it ended. It was where the life of a fighter slipped. It was where an exile had dragged out the last years of betrayal. It was where the dreams alone ruled. The breathing was regular now and the eyes rolled slowly as if to find the source of comfort that held his bony hand. They were behind him, the old men who had fled with his father when the gunships had destroyed the village, and quiet as if they dared not break the spell of peace as a son held a father's hand. The feet of the ambulancemen

4

clattered on the flooring. He didn't look over his shoulder, he shook his head. None of them, the old men, had the courage to intervene. It was the slipping of power, the exchange of authority, command ebbing from father to son. He heard the voices behind him tell the ambulancemen that they were not needed, that the victim of a road accident was beyond help. They were only foreigners, it was not important to the ambulancemen whether they left with their stretcher empty.

The words were few.

'You must go back . . .'

There was phlegm at his father's lips.

'. . . before it is too late you must go back . . .'

He took a dirtied handkerchief from his pocket.

'. . . you must take back what was taken from us . . .'

He wiped the mess from his father's mouth.

'. . . fight fire with fire . . .'

He held tight to the hand.

'. . . it is dead here, finished. You must go back and they will follow you because you are my son. The masses will follow you . . .'

He sensed the supreme effort.

'. . . you will need a fighting man. Without a man who knows how to fight them you will have no possibility, none. Take a man to be close to you who can fight, a man who understands the mind of our enemy. Make them cry for mercy as you march through the villages and towns and cities, and give them nothing . . .'

He heard the failing whisper.

'. . . I will watch for you. Fire with fire . . . Take a fighting man . . .'

After the silence, gently as he would have touched a girl's body, Rodolfo Jorge Ramírez closed the lids of his father's eyes. He stood upright. It was what they had dreamed about, all of the old men who followed his father into exile. He was twenty-three years old. He turned to face them. There was the authority in his voice.

'I will go back. It is what my father wanted. I am the son of my father. The masses will follow me as they followed my father. I will return.'

He could see it in them, in the shift and hesitation of their eyes. They had been too long in exile, ten years less a month, too long dreaming of a return across the sea to the village in the triangle of the mountains. He was the son of his father. They were fat, nervous, without spine. They pleaded to be led, to find again their youth. He stood beside the bed on which his dead father lay. None had the courage to tell him that time had moved and that the past was spent. They looked into the certainty of his features.

'I will go back.'

# I

They might as well have brought the taste, smell, of the dead fish into the bar with them.

The taste, smell, was as strong as when they had reached the bar a little more than two hours earlier. The draught from the poorly fitted windows and the beer swilling in their mouths had failed to remove it. The atmosphere of dead fish was around them and through them. If there had been other customers in the bar then the landlord might have suggested, only suggested, that they should go and wash up first and change from their work clothes. He'd kept his peace because they were his only drinkers on a foul night. The rain was in from the west, sometimes merging with hail when the wind strengthened. The rain, and sometimes the hail, and always the wind hit at the windows and wet rivers ran down the wallpaper below them to the newspapers that were folded to catch the damp. There was supposed to be a man coming in to fix the window frames and replace the rotten wood, the landlord would say each evening as he bent to place the newspapers on the floor, and he'd been saying that since last winter. They were both of them on their fifth pint of beer, extra strong, high alcohol content, and the bigger of the two men took a whisky chaser with each of his pints. They weren't loud drunk. They were miserable drunk. They had come straight from the cages of the salmon farm across on the far side of the loch. They had been out on the heaving walkways round the cages, working with flashlights, sometimes bothering to use the safety harnesses and sometimes not, and they had come to the bar with their trousers wringing wet where the sea water came in above their boots, and with their hands still slimed with the fish scales. The scales, the bright life gone from them, had peeled onto the table where they sat close to the fire and they left them, dull and opaque, flotsam amongst the stained beer mats. The problem was double bad. There was the increase in the lice, immature and adult, that fastened to the bodies of the caged fish. And there was the effect of the chemicals that they poured into the pens to kill the lice and which stressed the fish to death. Too many dead fish sliding into the dead hole at the bottom of each cage. Too great a number of wasted fish, too much wasted money, too many wasted hours. They didn't have to chew on the consequences of having so many fish dragged by the suction tube out of the dead holes below the cages. It was bloody damn obvious . . . The farm was up for sale, the owners who had once thought it was a pretty little investment to finance a salmon farm in the Highlands and Islands had lost their patience and nerve. No buyer in sight, the market saturated. The business was going down the dead hole as fast as the young farmed salmon that could not take the predatory lice and the stressing chemicals.

The fire was going well. There would always be a good log fire as long as the man who had promised to come and fix the windows stayed away. The wind came some of the time with a thin whistle through the gaps in the frames of the woodwork. The wind was enough to shift the curtains on the window nearest them, flutter what had once been heavy velvet. They were hunched over the table. Neither had spoken for a full quarter of an hour. They lit cigarettes, they drank, they dragged on the cigarettes, they slumped, they squashed the glow from the cigarettes into a filled ashtray.

There was the sound of a car on the gravel beyond the window, going slowly, as if feeling its way through the darkness of the storm night. The shorter man looked up. It might have been his training to have been aware of a stranger's car. A local would have powered into the car park and snapped to a halt. For years he had been taught to be aware of what was out of place. No strangers came to a bar late on a bad night before the holiday season. His eyes seemed to clear. He looked past the head of the stag mounted above the wide fireplace with the fur manged at the neck, and past the smoke-darkened glass that protected the stuffed salmon that had been wild and caught thirty-eight years earlier and that encouraged the futile sportsmen who travelled up from London, and past the wide wing span of the preserved golden eagle which had lost most of its tail feathers at the party three New Year's Eves back. He saw the turning lights between the moving drapes of the curtain.

The bigger man, the one with the whisky chasers, who called himself Rocky, muttered, 'What you going to do?'

The shorter man swerved his eyeline back from the lit curtains. 'Look for something else.'

Rocky snorted. He was from Glasgow. His accent was harsher than that of the men and women who had lived from birth in the cottages and bungalows beside the lock. 'That'll not be easy.'

'I think I know that.' He heard car doors slam shut, and then the sound of the car pulling away fast.

'You'll have another, 'course you will. Nothing to do but get pissed up . . .'

The shorter man nodded. He seemed not to care whether he had another drink or not. His nostrils wrinkled at the smell of dead fish and he wiped his tongue hard round the inside of his mouth to try to lose the taste of dead fish, without success. He was watching the door into the bar.

His training was always to watch a door for the entry of strangers, but the training was for a life that no longer existed.

Rocky lurched to his feet, noisily lifted up the empty glasses. 'You're a miserable sod, don't you know . . . ?'

The shorter man watched the door.

It was seven days since they had left the Campeche quarter of the Old City of Havana. It would be their last place of calling, and if they were turned down again then they would be flying back to Cuba in failure. One of them, the one who led down the dark corridor of the hotel that ran past the reception to the door of the bar, slipped into his small wallet the receipt from the taxi driver. They were blank-faced, none of the three of them showed an expression of anticipation nor a fear of further failure. For each of them it had been a huge journey, beyond the limits of what they could have imagined before the funeral. They had gone the day after the burial of the man they had followed into exile so long before. And each of them, because they had been told it individually and then together by Rodolfo Jorge Ramírez, understood that they had been chosen for the mission of importance because older men, travelled men, *Ladinos*, had doubted the possibility of what they were charged to achieve, and wrung their hands and murmured the excuse and sidled away. The one who led, who spoke English the best, paused in front of the door that was marked 'Bar'. They were each dressed in the same style, narrow shoes of thin black leather, white shirts and gaudy ties, and suits that seemed too large for their bodies. Each wore a wide-brimmed hat . . . They had flown from Cuba to Madrid, and been rejected. They had taken a second aircraft, sat stiff and belted in through gales and turbulence, to Frankfurt in Germany, gone to the address given them, and again been rejected. They had gone by coach to Louvain in Belgium and sat in an office that was decorated with photographs of smiling white men in combat uniform who carried machine guns and rifles and posed beside the bodies of dead black men, and again been rejected. They had taken a ferry boat across grey seas to England, and been sick before landfall, and had made their way to London, and been laughed at before they had again been rejected. Making their way out of the door of the London office they had been called back, and a name had been scribbled on a piece of paper and the name of a village and the name of a nearest town. They had thought, each of them, that after the rejection they had been played with by the broad-shouldered man with the paratroop emblems tattooed below the hair on his forearms.

But they had still taken the name of the man, the name of the village, the name of the nearest town.

A train had carried them through the day north from London to Scotland. A smaller train had brought them from Glasgow to

Fort William, through bare mountains that were shadowed in cloud and rain and dusk.

A taxi had driven them on narrow roads from Fort William to the village, to a darkened shed beside a quay where the water whipped in storm waves. The taxi driver had been good to them, and taken the piece of paper with the handwritten name and knocked at the door of a small house and shown a woman the name and been given directions. The headlights of the taxi had found a caravan building, blacked out, and again the driver had found the nearest house and smacked his fist on the door and repeated the name.

The three men had sat, squashed close, in the back of the taxi, and seen the gestures through the rain running on the window.

They had been dropped at the hotel. They had paid, they had taken the receipt.

It was the last chance. The bar door was closed in front of them. They had travelled to Madrid and to Frankfurt and to Louvain and to London to find a fighting man. It was the last chance or it was failure.

The door opened. Because Rocky was at the bar, because the bulk of Rocky's body was not between the door and himself, Gord's hand fluttered with a trained instinct towards his belt. Just instinct. At his belt there was no pistol, no holster. His fist rested on the damp denim of his jeans and dislodged more of the dried fish scales.

Gord saw them come in.

As if to a signal they took off their hats. They stood inside the bar. Their features were a uniform. Dark hair cut short, wide-set ears, flattened noses that looked as if they were pressed against glass, long mouths with strong lips, high and forward cheekbones. Gord thought they might have come from a production line. Each of them was short in height but with the power of barrel chests. The tan on their faces was milk mixed chocolate. They stood, each of them, inside the bar with their hats held across their privates and they looked around them with slanted eyes.

The accent was Spanish, thick English and taught. It was the one at the back who spoke. 'Please, Mr Brown? Mr Gordon Brown . . . ?'

Rocky swayed at the bar. 'Who's wanting him?'

'I was told that here we would find Mr Gordon Brown . . .'

There was the mischief look in Rocky's eye. The small boy, the big bully, fun in the schoolyard. 'Well, you've found him.'

Gord chuckled to himself, dry. A hell of an awful day in the middle of a hell of an awful week. He anticipated sport. He eased back in his chair and readied himself for the show. Rocky put the filled glass in front of Gord, then turned to face them. Gord thought that he deserved to be amused.

The one in the middle, who would have been the smallest, not more than two inches above five feet in height, said, 'We are from Guatemala. We are from the old village of Acul which is in the Ixil triangle region of the Quiché district. We live now in the city of Havana. Rodolfo Jorge Ramírez has sent us to find you, Mr Gordon Brown . . .'

The one at the front, an inch taller and older because he had grey smears in the black hair, said, 'We want the help, Mr Brown. We want you to march with Rodolfo Jorge Ramírez when we go back to the triangle . . .'

The one at the back who carried a small attaché case, imitation leather and cheap as they come, dribbling with the rain, said, 'We have come to find a fighting man, Mr Brown, one who will know the mind of our enemy. May we talk with you, Mr Brown . . . ?'

'Be my guest,' Rocky slurred.

Gord watched. He wondered what sort of place was Acul, what sort of village . . . They ignored Gord, as if he didn't exist. They made for the furthest corner of the bar, and they stood in respect until Rocky had slumped down on a chair. Gord heard occasional words, the ones that were hardest on their tongues and which they seemed to speak the loudest. Once Rocky looked across at Gord and winked hard. The words that Gord heard were 'atrocity' and 'genocide' and 'massacre' and 'revolution'. Gord knew a little of Guatemala. He hadn't been to the Jungle Warfare School in Belize that was less than fifty miles from the Guatemalan border, but he'd known those who had, and it had been their job to learn the capabilities of the Guatemalan forces. He knew the reputation of those forces. From what he'd heard, 'atrocity' and 'genocide' and 'massacre' were not out of place, but 'revolution' was. That's what he'd heard, way back . . . The smallest sat straight upright in front of Rocky and spoke as if he had learned by heart the proposition, and Rocky couldn't help himself and spurted as a reaction half a mouthful of beer and chaser onto the table, and the one with the grey smears in his hair wiped the table with the sleeve of his jacket. Rocky was giggling into their faces and they showed no shock, none of them. The one who had the attaché case opened it and lifted out a heap of photographs, and Gord craned from where he sat to see them. He heard the peal of Rocky's laughter, and he thought from what he could see across the room that the photograph on the top showed the naked body of a woman, and he thought he could see the scar marks on the body.

The baying now of Rocky's voice. 'Why not? Piece of cake, right? Walk straight in there? Bang, bang, bang, all over. We've won, fuck the bad guys. Count me in . . .'

He thought they realized. Surely they would have known by now that they were used for fun, an amusement and a sport. He felt shame.

He stood.

He had humiliated himself.

Gord said quietly across the room, 'Go home, Rocky . . .'

He was three inches, minimum, shorter than his friend, he was fifty pounds lighter.

'. . . Just take yourself off home, Rocky. Game's over.'

He saw the puzzlement on the big man's face and then the annoyance flickering at his mouth. Gord stood his ground with his hands easily on his hips.

13

Rocky went. He left a third of his big glass full on the table and a half of his chaser glass, but he went out of the bar and Gord heard him slip in the corridor and fall and then heard the vivid curse from the outer door when the weather would have hit him.

Gord went to the table where they sat.

'I apologize . . . I'm Gord Brown.'

Each of them shook his hand. He cringed. They showed no anger. He asked them to show him their photographs. He was sobered by their dignity. He took Rocky's chair, pushed aside Rocky's drink, scoured the table with his handkerchief.

The top photograph was pushed towards him by the smallest man. A woman lying naked in her own blood on the steel trolley that had been pulled out from a refrigerated compartment in a morgue. Her arms were crossed in death to preserve the modesty of her breasts, but one hand had been severed at the wrist. A small square of cloth had been placed over her groin. The pale skin of the body was marked by contusions and slashes and bruises. Gord breathed hard.

He moved aside the top photograph. He saw a picture of a man laid out on a dirt floor and some of his face was obscured by the kneeling shape of a woman, and the focus on the camera had been sharp enough to record the tears on her cheeks. The shirt of the man had been opened to display the wounds that Gord reckoned were the work of a knife or bayonet. There was a bullet entry wound in the centre of the forehead. He felt the vomit rising in his throat, he had only drunk that evening and had not eaten.

There was the image of a child's face, close up, rigid in death. He could not look away because he had played a game with these people, made his fun and amusement and sport from them. He owed it to them to hold the photograph in his mind. The eyes of the child had been gouged out of blood-dark sockets. The ears of the child had been sliced off. He could see because the cadaver's mouth was open that the tongue of the child had been cut short . . .

He turned away. He was sick onto the floor.

From behind the bar the landlord watched him, said nothing.

Another image was slid in front of him.

He vomited again, his evening's drink and his lunchtime's sandwiches and he could taste the flesh of dead fish.

A photograph of a fresh-excavated grave with bodies half retrieved from mud and a woman pointing to a corpse and men standing around leaning on long-handled spades . . .

He knew where they were kept. He went from the table and out across the bar and down the corridor to the scullery beyond the hotel kitchen. He ran water from the sink into the bucket and he took the mop back with him. They sat in their silence as he sluiced the floor around the table. No word from the landlord at the bar. It was Gord's work. He poured Dettol from a plastic bottle onto the linoleum of the floor, dosed it so that the smell of the vomit and of the dead fish was overwhelmed. He took back to the scullery the mop and the bucket and the disinfectant, and threw the contents of the bucket as far as he could into the night. He came back to the bar and sat in his chair.

'I'm Gord Brown, what do you want of me?'

The dawn came in a grey haze off the sea waters of the loch. He walked the white sand of the beach. Where the incoming tide had not covered them his footprints showed the trek he had made back and forth from the rock cliff to the west, in the darkness, to the black mass of the seaweed field to the east.

The wind took the top from the waves, flecked clear white against the shadow distance. What did Gord Brown stand for? He had been told of an Indian people suffering under the boot of the military.

The cloud was sweeping fast from the shoreline across the road to the base of the mountains beyond. Where was the life of Gord Brown going? He had been told of a young man charged by a dying father to return to his own and to take with him a fighting man who would understand the mind of an enemy.

His anorak billowed open from the soaked shirt clinging to his chest. Was Gord Brown looking to a future? He had been told of the proletarian masses who waited only for the call to rise up in arms and of a victory that was inevitable.

Each time that he turned now at the extremity of his walk he could see them. They stood on the wind-stung sedge grass between the beach sand and the road in front of the hotel. Before they had gone from the bar to negotiate accommodation with the landlord, and he had come down to the sand to walk away the night hours and contemplate the proposition, they had talked to him in a language that was half damn funny and half damn pathetic. Funny and pathetic because 'proletarian masses' and 'revolutionary struggle' and 'power of the people' were old slogans, buried. But it was the dignity, sincerity, that was hard to mock.

They stood beside the road in the front of the hotel and waited on his decision.

If they had come a week earlier, before the fish had slid stressed into the dead hole . . . What did Gord Brown stand for?

If they had come six weeks earlier, before the farm had been put onto a stagnant market . . . Where was the life of Gord Brown going?

If they had come three months earlier, before the first signs of the sea lice on the underbellies of the salmon . . . Was Gord Brown looking to a future?

If they had come before he would have heard them out, smiled, shaken their hands, and told them to go lose themselves on the way to Acul village of the Ixil triangle region in the Quiché district, or anywhere.

He was, had been, a fighting man.

He was thirty-four years old. He wavered. He could stride to the west of the beach and climb the granite rock stones and go back to his mobile caravan home, he could slide across the sea-weed mass to the east and go to the caravan and lock the door and strip the clothes from his body and sleep till it was time to go back to the farm and start up the suction pumps that drew the wasted fish from the dead hole . . . It was three years since he had seen a beaten people and turned his back on them, left them to the mercy of an army's firepower.

He walked towards them.

It was ridiculous.

When he was close to them he saw that their faces showed no surprise that he came to them. It was as if they had not contemplated rejection.

Gord said brusquely, 'What are you paying?'

The smallest man said, 'We have no money.'

Scornfully, 'You don't pay?'

The man with the attaché case lisped, 'What is the price of freedom? What is the cost of honour?'

Softly, 'You reckon I come cheap?'

The oldest man smiled. 'Mr Brown, you would have our gratitude.'

It was five days since he had been able to see the summit of Sidhean Mor, where the eagles flew, where he had climbed the previous year to be close to the nest where the big birds reared their young on an escarpment ledge. He would have liked to have watched them again, the big birds. He could not see the steep slope walls of Sidhean Mor.

Gord Brown was death on the move. He had worked all the previous day and into the evening, and then he had drunk and thrown up, and then he had paced the beach through the night. Nothing seemed to him now to be ridiculous.

He started to walk towards his mobile home and the three Indians from Guatemala trailed after him.

The landlord of the loch-side hotel had been awake for more than an hour.

His dog had woken him, yelped for attention from the kitchen, and he had heard the outer downstairs door of the hotel being opened, the bolts being ground back. He stood at the west-wing window while his wife slept behind him. He had thrown on a sweater and his heavy wool dressing gown, and he used the binoculars that he kept beside the window to watch most mornings for otters in the seaweed at the eastern end of the beach. He had been able to see them, the three of them, standing on the grassline between the road and the beach, and he had been able to follow the restless pacing passage of Gord Brown across the sand. In the bar he had been able to hear little, but the landlord had the wit to know that a proposition had been put by these stunted little beggars from wherever to the man who played at being a fish farm labourer. He had seen Gord walk over to them, talk briefly with them, and now he watched as Gord led them away to the right to where the mobile home was parked in the old stone quarry. If he had thought his wife knew more about Gord Brown than he did himself then he would have roused her, but she didn't; none of them in the village knew about the outsider who had come to live amongst them fifteen months back, other than that he had a past. The landlord knew that Gord Brown had a past that was obscured because the man steered every conversation away from his life history before he had come north and west to the peninsula that jutted towards the islands off this Scottish coast. The villagers, and he counted himself among them, rated themselves as having a rare talent at probing any blow-in's history, and all would have admitted quite total failure with Gord Brown. Not rude about it, not aggressive, just determined that the past was private and staying that way.

The landlord would have said, if he had been asked, that he had come to respect the quiet Englishman. Typical of him, what he had done in the bar. Thrown up, not the first and he wouldn't be the last, in the bar – but the first and last to go out into the kitchen and get a mop and a bucket and a bottle of disinfectant and sluice away the mess. He had never had trouble with the Englishman and he had noted the strength last night when Gord Brown had told big Rocky that the fun time was over, and big Rocky was capable of putting men into hospital and had gone like a lamb, and Gord's voice never raised. Gord had reached the mobile home. In the vision of the binoculars the little guys hung back. The landlord focused again on Gord Brown. The contours of his body were shown under the wet clinging trousers and shirt, no spare weight. An easy roll on the balls of his feet as if work and the absence of sleep were something he could cope with. The landlord wouldn't have known what was a good-looking man, but his wife had told him that there had to be a good and concrete reason for a man with those features to be without a woman. Dark hair was flattened back on his scalp. The eyes were clear, the ears were neat. There was a weather tan to his cheeks. Good teeth that were looked after. He could see the stubble, through the magnification, on a jaw that was powerful . . . Gord went into the mobile home.

The landlord would have admitted it, wasn't ashamed of it, that he would have given a week's takings to have known what proposition had stirred Gord Brown to miss his bed when he needed it. He considered how, some time and some day, he might find out. He would speak to the post. The post was sister-in-law to the driver who delivered orders from the store in the village. The driver went rough shooting with the policeman. If the policeman got to hear then it would come back to him along the chain of the driver and the post. But the post wouldn't be with him that morning for more than an hour.

Gord came out of the mobile home . . . He carried a black and bulging bin liner bag. The landlord saw Gord drop the caravan's keys into the message box beside the road. The rims of the binoculars were pressed hard against the landlord's eyes. Gord opened the passenger door of the Nissan pick-up and the smallest of the little beggars climbed up and inside. Gord picked up one of the others, the only one who carried a bag, and lifted him easily into the open back of the pick-up, and the landlord fancied that he heard, carried on the wind, shrill laughter, and then the last one went the same way, and Gord threw the bin liner bag in after the two of them. The landlord watched Gord drive the red and mud-spattered Nissan down the road past the hotel and round the corner, gone from sight. Gone without fanfare. As far as the landlord remembered from fifteen months back, he had arrived without fuss.

He went away down the corridor to the guest rooms, to the room where the door had been left open. Last night, late, he had spent more than twenty minutes getting out two collapsible beds and bringing sheets and pillowcases from the airing cupboard. He'd insisted on it, two collapsible beds and the double bed, for the three of them. Little beggars, dirty little beggars, because only the double bed had been slept in.

There had to have been a past. If there hadn't been a past then Gord Brown would never have driven away with them.

'. . . Fight fire with fire . . .'

The fast train hammered south.

He understood fighting fire with fire because it had been talked of by the embarrassed young officer, searching for neutral ground, safe talk, who had been charged with minding him when he was confined to quarters in the base camp at Dhahran before the flight back to England. They had spared him close confinement, but he was never to be out of the sight of the minder when he was eating, lounging, sleeping, crapping. The minder, an infantry officer who had come out to Saudi too late to join his unit for the big push into the Iraqi desert, had rabbited one evening about the shortage of flame throwers experienced by his battalion when they had hit the concrete defensive positions of the Republican Guards. The infantryman had said that what he had been told by those who had been in close-quarters combat was that flame throwers would have been the answer to the defensive machine-gun positions, that they'd been held up while waiting for an armoured squadron to give them the punch needed to silence the machine guns. It was more than three years back and Gord could still remember the chatter of the infantry officer, and the nervous young man's pleasure at finding acceptable conversation.

He had driven the Nissan to the centre of Glasgow, left it parked on a double yellow line underneath a sign that threatened clamping and towing. The carriage clattered at speed through a station, blurring the faces of those on the platform who waited to take the slow stopping train behind.

He was far back in his seat. The flame throwers that Gord had been told about were all old Soviet stock. He had good retentive memory, had been blessed with it since a child. The sort of soldiering he'd done, before the Gulf and ignominy, had been an endless series of courses, the stacking of knowledge as a way of keeping men from boredom. The word turned in his mind, ignominy, and it hurt deep. It was the word that had been used by the Discipline Board, unofficial . . . All the flame throwers that he knew of were Soviet made. The principals, the most recently manufactured, were the LPO-50 and the TPO-50. He could recall the instructor's session, tipping rain outside, a blackboard hung with photographs and plans of the working parts, in a camp lecture room. The LPO-50 was worn on the back supported with a shoulder harness, good for street fighting, range of fifty metres with something to spare. There was the heavier cousin, the TPO-50, that was mounted on a two-wheeled cart, a big bad beast that threw thickened fuel close to 200 metres. Good dirty weapons . . .

A slow streak of advancing fire. Gord dozed. His eyes blinked. There was a flame flash in front of him. The smallest lit a cigarette. The fire was moved into the face of the one with the attaché case, and then was passed across the central table to the oldest who sat beside Gord. The triple cloud of smoke wafted towards him. They seemed to think it funny, and each of them was grinning and there was their reed chuckle. The cigarettes were bloody hideous and it was foul smoke. He laughed himself. They grinned wider and chuckled louder and spurted the smoke over him again. He was laughing because he had bought his rail ticket, standard class and single, on his plastic, and in four or five weeks the bill from the plastic company would be pitched by the post into the box in front of his caravan home, and it would rot there because sure as hell Rocky wouldn't be picking up his debts. There was his note in the box to Rocky, along with the caravan's keys and the Nissan's spare keys, and his instructions that Rocky should sell the pick-up and dispose of what he had left behind in the mobile home, everything that wasn't in the black plastic bag on the rack above him, get what he could for them and binge the lot in the hotel bar. Rocky wouldn't get much for the Nissan, not after he'd paid off the clamping or the towing fee, not with the bodywork rust, but there would be enough for him to drink himself stupid.

His commitment was made. Gord Brown did not expect to be coming back to the sea loch and the failing fish farm. He had turned his back on the eagle nest on Sidhean Mor . . .

If he wasn't coming back then Christ alone knew where he was going.

He drifted close to sleep. The flame was in his mind, careering forward towards the slits of a machine-gun nest. There were no doubts to confuse him. The hesitation had been settled in the dark hours on the beach. Too long since any bastard had come for him in respect. They were the best he had, three little devils with suits that didn't fit them and hats that were down across bright eyes, but they had come to him from necessity. It was good to Gord Brown to feel wanted. Their smoke was across his face, inside his mouth, up his nose, seeping into his closed eyes. He had yearned to be wanted.

The train jerked to a stop. The crowds on the platform and then the concourse swam around him. He thought that anyone there, if he had told them the business he was at, would have told him he was lunatic, just as big Rocky and the landlord would have told him, if they'd been offered the chance.

Wrong, the whole damn lot of them.

Their names were gibberish to him. He gave them the names of the three best men he had known. Francis and Vernon and Zachary. They had been with him in the Land Rover, too bloody long ago, *Eff* and *Vee* and *Zed*.

Gord stopped on the concourse and set the black bag down. He kicked aside a discarded fast food pack and opened the top of the bag and lifted out his scarred boots and rummaged until he found what he searched for. The passport was given to Vee. All of them looked at the photograph, tight-faced and glowering and blinking at the flash, and there was the shout of their laughter. He told Eff where he would see them the next day, and he slapped Vee on the back and felt the strength, and he tweaked the cheek of Zed and saw the friendship light in the man's eyes.

It was because they had come for him, and wanted him.

# 2

The clerk was busy that evening, as he was every day and every evening of his working week, in the private world that was his filing system. His territory was a small annexe area by the entrance to the long rectangle basement room that housed the Record Section. The clerk was the master of this basement territory, and watched over it with all the keen spite of the wild cat jaguar in the magazine photograph that was stuck with adhesive tape to the plaster wall above his personal desk in the annexe. Every officer who came to the Record Section, no matter how senior, even the colonels and the brigadiers and the general himself, was required by the clerk to wait at the iron barred door for admittance to this part of the basement and to show his personal identity document, and to sign himself in, and later to sign himself out. No matter how senior the officer, he was obliged to leave his attaché case on the floor beside the wastepaper bin and the legs of the table that held the shredder machine. It was the empire of the clerk. The Israeli advisers had put in the IBM computer system, but the clerk dictated how much information was fed onto the disks, and the great majority of his material was still stored, as it had been for the last decade, in the cardboard box files on the racks that divided the basement room into narrow and high-sided corridors. The power had come in gradual degrees to the clerk, and now he revelled in the knowledge that he was indispensable to the smooth running of the G-2 section of military intelligence. He arrived at his desk a little before seven each morning and he never looked up and switched off the lights before eleven each evening, and if there was a crisis and access was required in the black small hours of the night then the clerk would have come in response to the call within five minutes. Only five minutes for him to throw on his fatigues and ride the empty streets on his motorcyclette from the room that he rented behind the McDonald's on 1 Calle and 4a Avenida. It was accepted by those who used the files in the G-2 section tucked away without prominence behind the Palacio Nacional.

The clerk knew the smooth-faced lieutenant by the name of Benedicto.

The attaché case of the lieutenant was set on the floor beside the wastepaper bin and the legs of the table that carried the shredder.

The clerk assumed that the name of Benedicto was a cover. The lieutenant only came to the basement area late in the evenings, never wore uniform.

Behind the clerk was the scraping sound of the vacuum flask being opened, and the scent of ground coffee. He turned away from the photographs that covered his desk. He had them in two piles. One for the faces that he could identify, and one for those he could not. It would take back-checking, research, for him to be able to put names to all the faces of the men featured in the photographs. He glanced at the hunched, concentrating features of the lieutenant.

Sometimes the clerk shaved before he came to the basement, sometimes he was not troubled. It was his mark of independence, as a humble clerk who earned less than five hundred quetzals a month, that he could appear in the Record Section unshaven and have power over the manicured officers with their smells of lotion and talc.

The clerk thought it would have taken the lieutenant at least twenty minutes each morning to shave around that thinnest of moustaches on his upper lip.

The clerk saw, and there was little that slipped his attention, the clear lines of the scratch marks on the right forearm of the lieutenant. Not for him to pass comment . . . but he noted them, the scratching of the nails of a man, woman, driven beyond despair by pain.

It irritated the clerk that he could not identify three of the faces of the mourners. Twice he went to the corridors between the file racks, and manipulated the stair steps into position and climbed, awkwardly because of the old injury, to gather back-files from upper shelves. He would brush the cobweb skein from the files, shake clear the small spiders and stamp on them, and take the files to his desk. The files that harboured the small green spiders contained a dossier bank on the population of Guatemala, and of those in exile, of far greater quality than the disks of the IBM computer installed by the Israeli advisers. As long as he ruled the basement, the clerk would maintain that balance.

Another file was laid quietly on his desk.

He looked up and into the calm of the lieutenant's eyes. He had never been told but it was obvious to him. The lieutenant was an interrogator. It was late in the evening. The Cherokee Chief station wagons would be out and tasked and cruising for the lift. A suspect would be brought to a safe house. Of course it was necessary for the interrogator to prepare himself for his work.

The lieutenant was looking over his shoulder, down to the yellowed sheets of paper from the files, down onto the new photographs that had come that afternoon from Havana.

He liked the boy. He respected the lieutenant's attitude to work.

The clerk's forefinger, taken away at the upper joint, jabbed at the photograph that showed a coffin on a trestle at a graveside. He peered into the lieutenant's face and smiled.

'The end of the old whore Ramírez. It was taken eight, nine, days ago, from Havana . . . You had heard, lieutenant, of the whore Ramírez . . . ?'

It was good coffee that the lieutenant brought in his flask. He could smell the quality. He saw the shaken head.

'. . . From Acul, from the Ixil triangle. He was a *Ladino*, he ran a hardware shop in the village. He was the big man there. He reckoned himself the leader of the Indians in that village. There was a poison in him, and he spread the poison through the villages around Acul, right to the towns of the triangle. A cunning

26

old whore because he had learned the matter of defence. The army came to destroy him, but not with enough force and could not take the village. He was successful against the campaign of Victory '82. In the campaign of Firmness '83 he was again permitted to survive. It was not until Institutional Re-encounter '84, when the Kaibiles were used against the village, that he was defeated. The village of the whore was the last in the triangle to be taken. It was a big battle, a day and most of a night, the whore had taught them to fight well. It was where my leg . . .'

The clerk grimaced. It was always in the evenings when the wasted muscles around the shrapnel wound had stiffened that he felt the greatest pain. It had been a small mine, made in the village, positioned off the road in the cover beside a track, well sited. It was the rusted nails in the mine, scattered by the explosion, that had torn into the calf muscle of his right leg and caused the secondary gangrene. It was where he had lost the tip of his right-hand forefinger.

'. . . He is still remembered, a little of the poison remains. He went into exile. He went to the clown fantasy land of Cuba. I have it here . . .'

The clerk flicked at close-typed pages, some corrected with ink, of a file half covered by the twin piles of photographs.

'. . . It is said that the old whore dreamed only of returning to the triangle, that he sat in the cafés in the Campeche quarter of Old Havana and played the game of fighting his way back to his village – just the dream of an old whore. You know how it ended, the dream? Not at the head of a column, not in the jungle in the Petén, not in the mountains of the Cuchumatanes – it ended when he was hit by a bus that had lost its brakes, when he was crossing the road to go for his coffee with the other fools who believed he would take them back. I suppose it was possible, in the shithouse of Havana, to believe that one day he would return and that the Indians, dumbfucks, would follow him again. He had a good funeral . . .'

The lieutenant's breath played on the back of the clerk's neck. The lieutenant's hand rested loosely on the clerk's shoulder.

27

'. . . All the old men who went into exile with him were there, look at them, raddled, wrinkled, hair gone, all cretins. There are just three that I can't locate. Too old, too changed. I tell you what I think, I think it would be a worse death to be in exile in Havana, than to face the guns of the Kaibiles. Look at them, if they were in the Petén, in the jungle, they would be gone in forty-eight hours. They are pathetic . . .'

The lieutenant reached forward and pushed away the corners of photographs so that one was left clear. The clerk shrugged.

'. . . His son. That is Rodolfo Jorge Ramírez. There was a daughter but she had already gone, she is in Europe. The wife of the whore was killed. The whore took his son with him when he fled. They went in the last light of the second day of the battle . . . Yes, a good-looking young man, I don't mind saying that. Perhaps now that he is free of the chains of the old whore he will go to Europe to his sister . . .'

The lieutenant poured what was left of the coffee into the plastic beaker of the clerk, and picked up his attaché case from the floor. The clerk shuffled after him, dragging the damaged leg, and cleared him through the outer barred door of the basement. Not for him to ask the business of the lieutenant now that darkness had fallen on the city, not for him to remember which file had been begged by the lieutenant for study. He slammed the door shut again. He called cheerfully to the lieutenant's slim back.

'It was a real war then. Not this shit of today. There was a time when it was thought they might win, the communists, might actually march into the Plaza Mayor, right to the Palacio Nacional. You know, all the flights, every day, to Miami, they were full then . . . a long time ago. Good night.'

Just the sound of light footsteps slipping away up the basement's staircase.

He cackled his laughter. He was afraid of none of them, not the generals nor the field commanders nor the interrogators, all of whom would recognize the gold-dust value of the material he had assembled.

The clerk returned to his desk. He packed up the file of a father who had died in exile and tied a length of string twice round the file and knotted the end of it. From the drawer of his desk he took a new file cover and slipped the photograph of the young man at a funeral into it, and he wrote carefully on the outside of the file 'RODOLFO JORGE RAMÍREZ'.

The silence of the basement was around him. His company was the files of the dead and the living. He drank the coffee that had been left for him.

He rang the bell.

The doorway was beside the shop's window.

There was a mist off the harbour but the rain had stopped. The narrow street was deserted. Gord shivered. He rang the bell again, and was rewarded. A light came on behind the curtains drawn across the sash window above the shop front. There was a sign in the window, written in biro on cardboard, stating that the shop would be reopening in Whitsun week. The window was empty and the shelves in the interior gloom were bare. The sign above the window was Torbay Crafts, and flaking. He had come off the slow train that brought the mail and the newspapers from London, catnapped for two hours on a platform bench at Newton Abbot, and taken the first train of the morning on to Paignton, and then a taxi. He had walked twice round the harbour, seen the fishing fleet prepare to sail, and then climbed the steps to the street and the shop with the accommodation above it.

He had been there once before, another dawn, the visit before he had flown out to the Gulf. Twelve hours' leave, and most of it spent getting to and from Torbay.

Gord was there, on that bloody wet doorstep, because he had thought that it was what his father would have wanted.

There was the lock being turned. Not the opportunity to bring his mother flowers, nor a present.

A man in the doorway. The man had grey thin hair sprouting uncombed and he wore a vest under a woman's dressing gown that was fastened only at the waist and below long spindle legs he wore a pair of crushed carpet slippers. The sleep was becoming anger on the man's face.

'What's your bloody game then . . . ?'

Gord stood in the clothes of the fish farm, and of the bar beside the sea loch, and of the train to London.

'. . . What time of the bloody day do you reckon this is?'

Gord didn't know his mother had a live-in, but then he hadn't seen her, hadn't wanted to, since he had come back from the Gulf.

Gord saw his mother in the shadow behind the guy. She was in a tent of a nightdress.

'Hello, Mum.'

There was her embarrassment, and the introduction. He was Bill, he was the lodger. He helped with the shop. Not Gord's business if his mother was shacked up. Not for him to query, from a high horse, why the lodger needed to wear his mother's dressing gown and be on hand to help in a shop that had been closed for seven months.

He told her that he was going away.

'You could have telephoned . . .' said critically.

He told her that he didn't know when he would be back.

'You didn't have to just pitch up . . .'

He told her that where he was going he would not be able to stay in touch.

'You joking – how long since you were last "in touch" . . . ?'

He told her to look after herself.

'You got a funny way with words, you think you can just pick people up, drop them. Damn you, you're your father's son . . .'

It was two hundred miles to be there and it would be two hundred miles back. He didn't ask himself inside for a cup of coffee and it wasn't offered. He had not been asked where he was going, and why, and when. He wouldn't have told her. He turned away. He headed off down the narrow street. He had gone because it was what his father would have expected of him. He heard her call, perhaps frightened, perhaps in late good will. He didn't stop. He didn't wave.

30

He went down the steps leading to the harbour. He had to watch his feet for the dog shit and the broken bottles. His sister was somewhere in the north of England and teaching at an inner-city primary school and likely still to be wearing a Campaign for Nuclear Disarmament badge, and she was contemptuous of him. His mother had made room in her bed for a guy who was, certain and sure, fleecing off her the money she'd made when she'd sold up in London. That was her business and only hers, and she had no room in her life for him.

It was only for his father that he'd come.

The last public goodbye to his father had been the memorial service at St Bride's, the hacks' church in Fleet Street. They'd been in the pews behind him, the old muckers of Theo Joseph (TeeJay) Brown, and they'd have been glancing down at their watches and working it out, how long until they could get outside and light up, and how long until they could get into the pub and start the rounds of doubles. They'd sung out of tune, off scale, and he'd blessed them because he'd heard the nose-blowing of the old bastards close to tears. There had been the hacks and the florid-faced men in their dark suits from Regional Crime Squad and Flying Squad and Drugs Squad, and there had been barristers' clerks and the solicitors who wouldn't have been happy to share a bench with a detective. The lesson read by the chief sub who'd started on the same newsagency as TeeJay, and the address given by the last editor to fire him. Gord had never been able to reckon out whether his father would have approved of the service; sure as hell, wherever he'd gone, he'd have been cursing that he'd missed out on the piss-up in the pub round the corner afterwards.

Gord Brown had no other business to detain him.

He would fly with the men who wanted him.

So goddamn alone, and lengthening his stride, hurrying to get to the taxi rank beside the bus station.

When Colonel Arturo heard of the shooting dead of the two *subversivos* he ordered that the bodies should be brought down to the village for display.

He watched from in front of the small whitewashed church that was close to the military compound as they were carried by the Civil Patrollers, brought down from the tree line that clung to the rising ground around the cleared area where the new community of Acul was settled. He could recite the statistics, because each time that a gringo bastard came down from New York or Washington or Los Angeles to write a lying and distorted article then it would be picked up and reprinted in the edition of the *International Herald Tribune* that he would find in the officers' mess of the *estado mayor*. All of the senior officers attached to the Military Headquarters read the *International Herald Tribune* in the mess. The statistics that were always used stated that 100,000 civilians, what Colonel Arturo called *subversivos*, had been killed by the regular army and paramilitary forces. But they were harder now to obtain, the bodies of *subversivos*, because the war was won, the shit enemy was deep in the jungle, high on the mountains, and beaten. The shit enemy was little more than a nuisance . . . He had been told that these two men, down from the high ground and scavenging for food, were of the Ejército Guerrillero de los Pobres, the group that still festered in the remotest country of the Ixil triangle. He raised his stub field binoculars, saw the procession enter the far extremity of the village.

With the war won it was good to take the opportunity to remind the people of the Model Village in the Pole of Development, the new housing programme where Indians could be supervised and controlled, of the protection that they received from the army and their own men who served in the Civil Patrols. He thought that he would make a speech, impromptu, and perhaps suggest to the captain who commanded the village garrison that a small fiesta, plenty of drink for the animals, should be held that evening. Once inside the perimeter line of the village, the bodies were taken through the side streets, the dirt strips that ran between the lines of tin-roofed houses. Up the Calzada de Libertad, down Avenida República de China, along Avenida Soldado Guatemalteco. It was correct that as many of the villagers as possible should see the bodies.

He had come to Acul that morning because the place was set in the history of his military service.

The bodies were carried into the open plaza in front of the whitewashed church. A Civil Patroller was at each end of the long and bent poles, taking the weight on his shoulder.

Ten years earlier Colonel Arturo, then a major, had commanded the assault company of the Kaibiles that had taken the former village of Acul.

The ankles and the wrists of the two *subversivos* had been knotted together with rope, and the poles had been threaded under them so that the bodies hung down and swayed in the motion of the carrying and the heads that were mud-smeared and bloodstained rolled with the movement.

Colonel Arturo had been decorated by the President of the Republic for the assault on the former village of Acul. He wore the ribbon of the medal, with others, on his camouflage combat tunic.

The bodies were dropped in front of him. He told the captain that all the villagers should be brought to the plaza, compulsory. He said that the bodies should be stripped naked. It was necessary to make a show.

He had heard, that morning, of the death of the old whore Ramírez in the communist nest that was Havana. He had thought it would be of interest to him to see for himself how the news was accepted in the village . . . A hard battle it had been, casualties in his company, and the old whore Ramírez had organized good defence lines . . . it had been the air strike that had finished the resistance . . . no prisoners surviving . . . he could remember how he had cursed when he had found finally that the old whore Ramírez was not amongst the men herded into the church of the former village of Acul . . . there had been the smell when the fire had taken hold in the church, the smell was still with him.

He could see across the plaza that the priest had come to stand and watch him, challenge him, surrounded by women and condemning him with silence. He hated the priests. The villagers were pushed forward by the Civil Patrollers. They should come close to the bodies, spit upon them, laugh at them. Because the bodies were naked he could see the way that the ribcages jutted. They were starved up there in the mountains. Colonel Arturo knew all the textbooks, he knew about denying the fish the freedom of the sea.

Colonel Arturo stood on a wooden box. He was protected by the guns of his escort.

'They are the kind of scum that destroys your crops or steals what you have grown. They bring violence to your village. They make life bad for you. Show what you think of them . . .'

He stared out at their faces. Dirty sub-human faces. There were pigs and dogs searching for food scraps among the homes behind the crowd. Expressionless faces gazing back at him. He saw the defiance of the priest. When the order was shouted to them, then more of the villagers came forward in file and ritually spat upon the bodies. He asked the captain, low voice. What would they think of the death of the old whore Ramírez? The captain shrugged. How would he know? Who would tell him? Colonel Arturo felt a small sense of failure and that was rare for him.

Later the bodies would be taken down to near the river and buried. They would be buried not from respect, but in shallow graves that were far enough down for the dogs and pigs to be unable to maul the remains.

His failure was that he had learned nothing of what they thought of the death of a man in Old Havana.

And he thought that he would learn nothing more in the two hours that he would be in the Model Village before the helicopter returned to ferry him back to Guatemala City.

They would be late for their table and that didn't please him.

Benny had sat at the bar for more than twenty minutes now, was well down on his second gin, knew none of the older men around him, and had little to do but fidget and wait. Benny came to London twice a year from the Adventure Training School in mid-Wales that he owned with the bank manager, and each time that he came he alternated with Sebastian in paying for lunch at their mutual watering hole. It was a place that was not mentioned outside the company of members, an address that was never written down and a telephone number that was unrecorded. They were mostly old-timers who gathered in the middle of the day at the Special Forces Club, veterans nostalgic for the North African campaign or the Malayan Emergency . . . Sebastian was sitting near the window, huddled with a chappie who looked short of a bath and a shave and a haircut and a visit to a tailor. Benny had come in, prompt to the minute for the schedule, seen Sebastian in company and been casually waved away. Strange bloody company that Sebastian was standing him up for, and the chappie even had a plastic dustbin bag, that was filled and knotted at the top, under his legs. He glanced at the barman, gestured with his eyes towards the man with Sebastian, and there was a wry smile, and then a raised thumb that said, No call for panic, vetting is positive. He relaxed, eavesdropped on haphazard conversation. Silly of him, to have considered that an 'undesirable' would have made it across the doormat in the hall. The talk around Benny was the same as half a year before, and half a year before that. The talk didn't change . . . What should be done in Ulster. What should not be done in Bosnia. What should have been done in Iraq. What had been done in the Falklands . . . About bloody time. Sebastian on his feet, and shaking the chappie's hand, and seeming to wish him well. Benny turned to the barman, ordered the Campari soda that was Sebastian's drink. Too right, about bloody time. He saw the chappie shamble out through the door.

'Sorry about that.'

'Charitable work? Bringing tramps in off the street?' Benny grinned.

'Actually, no. I don't suppose you knew who it was . . . ?'

'I pass.'

Sebastian, whom Benny thought quite the funniest man that he knew, had no humour just then. Rather bloody stern-faced.

'After your time, but before I came out. Poor smell it left at the time. If he hadn't been so pig-headed . . .'

Benny queried, 'Not the fellow who . . . ?'

' "Bullshit Brown", the very same. Not much of a label for a guy to be lumbered with. "Bullshit". I don't mind it being known, but I fought that geriatric committee here to keep his membership . . .'

'I heard it didn't have to happen.'

Sebastian, retired fourteen months back with the substantive rank of major, now a security adviser to any sheik or emir or prince with a hefty enough cheque book, snorted. 'All he had to do was apologize, grovel for a few minutes, would have been forgotten. Obstinate beggar, he wouldn't. Did you know that he was even in for a medal, gallantry, not the "stand and stare" brigade. The citation was torn up. To put it mildly, he wasn't well used.'

Benny called for another gin, and a second Campari soda. 'So, what was the germ of the heart to heart?'

'Bit bloody odd really . . .'

'What?'

'Came to me because I used to be in Belize, last posting, well you know that . . . I was up on the Guatemala border. Mossies, malaria, the shits day and night, awful place. He wanted to talk about Guatemala . . .'

They ordered. They would be called when the table was ready.

'What the hell for, Guatemala?'

Sebastian grimaced. 'Wanted a run-down, capability of the Guatemalan armed forces.'

'And . . . ?'

'I gave it him . . . best fighting outfit in Central America, probably better than anything in Latin America. Very tough, quite ruthless, heavy motivation. We took them seriously enough when we thought they might come into Belize. Not that well equipped, but just ruthless. I did my best to warn him off. You see, he wasn't chattering about going out there and advising, lecturing, the government forces. Too bloody easy for "Bull-shit". He was talking about joining up with some guerrilla group. I gave it him straight, I said he was out of his tiny mind . . . They really are very good, the Guatemalans, and arrogant. They've just about won their little war and they got that far with no American help, hence conceit. I warned him, but I don't think he was listening by then. It's the problem of "Bullshit's" life, never knew when to step back. I told him that the Guatemalan army would mince any little group with holes in their trousers. He told me to listen to the radio . . .'

Their table was ready. A waiter gestured for them to follow him.

Benny drained his glass, spluttered on the gin. 'It was true, wasn't it? Brown told that Yank jerk he was talking bullshit?'

'Too true, but brigadier generals don't exactly like that sort of chat . . . So, how's the old world treating you?'

'Can't complain . . .'

They headed for the dining room.

'. . . poor old Brown.'

'Forget him. If he goes into Guatemala, within a month he'll be dead. Worse than dead would be captured. Best to forget him. I'd give him a month, maximum, not a week or a day or an hour longer. If he's lucky, dead . . .'


The helicopter that had swooped low over the former village was long gone.

The high grass that had been beaten down by the rotors stood erect again.

The former village was a place of sadness and avoided by the Ixil people now housed in the Model Village of Acul. Ten years since the battle, and the grass had grown high, and the weed had flourished, and the small maize fields that had been worked by the women were lost to sight. The remnants of the former village would have been clearer from the air, but at ground level, if a man had tried to push his way through the vegetation, there would have been little to see that showed what had once

37

been home for a thousand people. The roads of the village, where the pigs had grubbed along with the dogs and hens and ducks and turkeys, were gone under the undergrowth's advance. The plaza in the heart of the former village, where the men had played the marimba on fiesta evenings, was buried by dense green foliage.

The soldiers and the Civil Patrollers would have chased away the people if they had tried to come back to the former village.

It was not necessary . . .

The church, that had been of white adobe, remained, high outer walls rising above the sprouting trees and bushes of flowers and steepling grass. The roof was gone but the tower that had held the bell was still in place. The outer walls and the tower, daubed each year in white under the supervision of the Father from the Jesuit order, were stained black from the fire that had destroyed the church. Nearby, close to the back entrance, visible neither from the ground nor the air, was the head of the well. It was because of the well, and what it held, that the men and women who had survived the battle of ten years before would not return to their former village. It was into the well that the burned bodies from the church had been tipped. The well shaft was dug too deep for the living to retrieve the dead, and the soldiers anyway would not have permitted it.

Across the open space from the scorched front facade of the church was the shape of a compact building that had been constructed of concrete blocks around an inner courtyard. The building had been destroyed by explosives and the vines that were alive with a mass of rich red flowers obscured most of the inner and outer walls. The building had been the general purpose and hardware store to the former village of Acul, once the home of a *Ladino* of mixed race, and of his wife who was trained in nursing, and of his daughter, and of his son who was Rodolfo Jorge Ramírez. Where the walls could be seen, below the height of where the windows had been, the spatter of the bullet marks was visible. The building had been the last strongpoint in the former village.

Surrounding the village, where they would have been seen by the passenger in the low-flying helicopter, were the defence ditches, now bedded with green . . . Only one path still led to the former village, and it came close to the defence ditches on the south side. The path was clearly trodden but seemed to end abruptly in the wilderness growth. Overgrown now and overwhelmed were the old graves. On one grave, covered over by the grass and undergrowth, fresh-picked flowers had been placed, and when those died more flowers would be brought, and laid where they would be seen neither from the ground nor the air.

A place of death, and of memories.

A place of silence after the low-flying helicopter had powered away, a place of close-kept secrets.

Gord paid off the taxi and walked into the terminal.

Before looking for them he went into the lavatories and again rinsed the rawness of his knuckles in a basin filled with water as hot as he could bear it. An hour earlier he had scrubbed his fists in the toilets of a pub in central London.

He wiped his hands, winced at the keen pain.

They had told him of the man they had been to see in London, and how they had been mocked. They had told him, phrasing with care the story, of the sneers of the man who sold mercenary contracts. They had told him of the way they had been called back, dogs to heel, to be given a name and an address. Gord understood. Another bastard having fun with them, and getting amusement from sending the flotsam trio on the goose chase to Scotland, and them taking the train north because it was the last chance to avoid failure. They had told him enough . . . He had gone to the office of a man who placed mercenaries where there was a bid and a percentage . . . It was nineteen months since the dismissed colour sergeant of 2 Para had tracked him and propositioned him and been told to go put his tongue up his arse. Gord understood. They had been sent to Scotland because the man had been certain enough that they would have been sent packing, double fast. Big laugh . . . He had smashed the office, spilled and mixed the files, and he had beaten the face of the one-time colour sergeant and taken the grin from it.

Gord's hands hurt, and he felt the better for it.

He went to the telephone rank and dialled a number from memory and heard the bleeps of an answerphone, and rang off.

He saw them.

They were with a fourth man, tall and elegantly dressed, suit and light raincoat. The fourth man was Latin, and glanced twice at his wristwatch. Gord came forward.

Relief on all their faces, because he had shown. Surprise on the Latin's face, because he had come as they had said he would. Introductions made by Vee. Gord reckoned the Latin, Cuban, would be from the Military Attaché's office. Not the Attaché himself, bloody hell no, not the top man getting his hands dirty. He assumed that the Cuban Military Attaché would be routinely trailed round London by the watchers of the Security Service. They gripped his hand, each of them. He felt the rough calluses of working hands hold his tightly. No, they couldn't have known that he would show . . . The Latin passed him back his passport, and there was the puzzled questioning in his eyes . . . Gord smiled at him, didn't help him. He flicked the pages of the passport and came to the visa for Havana.

No doubts. There was no future for him.

No hesitation. There was nothing to keep him.

They were the ones who had come for him . . .

'Let's go then.'

Zed gave him his ticket. He went through Emigration separately from them. They had forty minutes before take-off to Madrid.

No other bastard did, but they valued him. He was wanted.

What he saw, what took his eyes first from the road ahead, was the dog pulling at the arm of the body.

Foot onto the brake, and the clamour of a horn behind him, and another, and a cacophony. He could accelerate or he could swerve to the hard shoulder.

A man threw a stone at the dog. The dog howled, released the arm.

Cars and a truck swept past his Chevrolet wagon. He looked at other drivers and none seemed to have seen a dog pulling at the arm of a body. The first flight in the helicopter was gone from his mind. The dog had backed off, tail arched under its sunken belly. The excitement of the first flight was lost . . . For Christ's sake, it was a fucking dog at a fucking body beside the fucking road. He pulled over.

He dropped down from the driving seat, slammed the door behind him. The traffic was spearing past him, like no other driver cared.

The man who had thrown the stone at the dog stared at him in hostility. Seemed that he hadn't noticed the other people standing around and near the body. There were men and women and children, and beyond them were the low roofs of the shanty town that was built on the ground falling away from the highway. They didn't look at the body any more; he held the attention of all of them. It was fast, the highway behind him. His assumption was made, the assumption he would have made back home in St Louis, a guy trying to cross a six-lane highway, and not making it across, and the bastard who'd hit him not stopping, leaving him at the roadside for the fucking dogs.

Tom Schultz had learned the language, at State's school in San Diego.

'Can I help? – I'd like to help.'

When he took a step forward, towards the body, they moved away, all of them, like he was a danger to them.

There was a siren far down the highway and closing.

No expression for him to gauge on the faces of the men and the women and children who backed off from him. He went to the body. The dog had already torn the shirt back. The waist of the trousers was halfway down over the buttocks. There was one shoe in place, a second shoe was a half-dozen paces away. He bent to look more closely at the body. He could see the bruises on the back and on the buttocks. He thought the poor bastard

41

would have nearly made it across the six lanes, been running when he was hit, lost his shoe as he'd been tipped onto the rubbish-strewn side of the highway. The siren had cut behind him.

He stood and turned.

He saw the fire engine, and the men climbing down slowly. There was a police car behind the fire engine, and only one of the crew stepping out. He stood back. He knew the procedure for traffic fatalities, didn't know it well but he knew the basics of it. The crewman from the police car had not produced a notebook. Two of the fire engine team had reached the body and they spilled it over, turned it onto its back. A man, young, Latin. One had hold of the arms and one had hold of the legs. Tom Schultz watched. The body was dragged, bare buttocks scraping the grit stone and the rubbish at the side of the highway, towards the fire engine. There was a square of paper fastened to the shirt. He read. He could only make out the largest written words, '*El Buitre Justiciero*'. He read it as the 'Hawk of Justice'. He saw the wounds. He had done the homicide course. He knew a knife wound, and he knew a bullet wound. There were knife wounds in the upper chest and across the cheeks of the face and there was a blood mass in the groin. He saw the ants in the blood. There was a bullet wound in the centre of the forehead. He knew how to read the signs, because that was a part of the course at Quantico, and there was a powder stain at the entry that meant a close-quarters shot from a hand gun. The body had been tortured, then executed. No fucking commendation for Tom Schultz for recognizing fact.

The body was thrown through the hatch into the back of the fire engine. The fire engine drove away. He heard the door slamming on the police car. He saw the small crowd drift away, scramble down the steep fall towards the shanty town.

He looked back to the ground where he had first seen the body. Just the side of a highway that was loose stone collecting garbage.

When he was back in his Chevrolet wagon, glancing a last time at the place, the dog had crept close again to where the young man had been and sniffed the old blood on the ground.

He was the new guy in town. His fingernails ground at the scar tissue at the side of his face, where the stubble didn't grow. Just taking a ride back from the military side of La Aurora airport, where he had flown the Huey bird for the first time since getting himself to Guatemala City. Just the new guy in town . . . He concentrated hard on the traffic all the way into the embassy compound.

On another course, at headquarters in Washington DC, he'd been lectured that he wasn't paid to make judgements on the set-up where he was posted . . . Great, and the lecture had been shit.

He showed his pass to the marine and took the elevator up to the third floor and strode down the corridor, and punched the security code and let himself into the cramped office space that housed the Drug Enforcement Administration agents.

'Hi, Tom, go well?'

'No problem, the bird handled sweet.'

An Iberian airliner slammed onto the runway at Havana International, jolted Gord Brown awake.

# 3

They were surrounded by tourists as they came off the bus and into the terminal.

Germans and Spaniards and Portuguese and Italians, the tourists were the faithful, travelling for a conscience holiday to Cuba before the worker state went under. They had the light in their eyes, the way pilgrims were, he supposed, when they first came close to the Almighty. Gord didn't have religion, and it was only what he supposed. And he didn't have politics either, had never voted in a British election, but the light in their eyes was adoration. There was not much that he believed in, not politics and not religion. Before the 'ignominy' he would have reckoned that he believed in himself, his own qualities and his own capabilities, and since the 'ignominy' he had believed in nothing – until three Ixil Indians from Guatemala had come to the hotel beside the sea loch.

A way was forced through the crush for him by Eff and Vee and Zed. Rats up a drainpipe and going there fast. They pushed and heaved and used their knees and elbows, manoeuvred him to third place in the queue at the passport desk, and grinned at him. The black plastic bag was squeezed against his legs and was ripping apart. He had taken the bag into the airliner's cabin and ignored the protests of the stewardesses that it was too large. The concourse was dismal. Only three of the row of passport desks were occupied. There must have been a bad storm because there were damp stains on the roofing above him, and the holiday posters on the wall were curled from moisture. He offered his passport.

The official's shirt was grimed at the collar. The man hadn't shaved, not for that shift and not for the shift before. The fingers that took the passport, slowly and as if a favour were being given, were dirty under the nails.

Spoken slowly, a struggling American accent, 'What is your business in Cuba?'

He'd assumed, why not, that he would be met, no immigration and customs, taken through as if he was important. Gord gagged.

'To enjoy myself . . .'

'Enjoyment is tourism, this is not a tourist visa.'

'It's what I was given.'

The official studied the passport, looked for meaning in the stamps and handwriting of the visa. Gord looked round. Vee shrugged, not his fault. Eff rolled his eyes, nothing could be done. Zed hung his head, took personal blame. He was beckoned to follow. He left the three of them behind him. He was shut in a small room and it was twenty-five minutes before the door was opened again. The doorway was crowded. The official sourly gave him back his passport and a man in a laundered uniform of better-quality material hissed spite into the ear of the official, and there were three more men, older, in slacks and shirts hanging behind. He smiled sweetly at the laundered official, hoped the bollocking was severe, and was taken to the customs benches. He tipped out his plastic bag onto the table surface. Underpants and vests, dull green shirts, a pair of camouflage trousers, thick woollen socks, a pair of old hiking boots. There was a cloth sack, drawn tight with cord at the neck, that clattered onto the table and he opened it to show the bottles and the sprays and the packet of pills. The customs woman would have had her fingers into the bottles and sprays and pills if the laundered official hadn't snapped at her. The laundered official turned away, stalked off. Gord stretched on his toes and looked back and couldn't see Eff and Vee and Zed.

There were the three men around him. He heard a jargon of names, said fast, too quick for him, and he could not bother himself to stop them and tell them to do it all again, and slower.

Funny guys . . .

Zeppo had wide braces that held tented trousers up to the width of his stomach, hung over a good gut.

Harpo was the tallest and the ceiling banks of lights shone on the perspiration of his hairless scalp.

Groucho smiled with steel-capped teeth and wrung together the palms of wet hands.

The way he imagined it, wasting the in-flight hours, he would be met by fit young men. Right, the young men would be heavy with crap and the ideology of the armed struggle, but they would be ready to learn from a fighting man. They went out into the blackness of the night and he carried the bag, wouldn't let Groucho get his hands on it. Harpo spoke fair English. Harpo said there was a power cut and that the airport had its own generators. He was ushered into a car that he rated as veteran, more than thirty years old, a Pontiac, big enough for a small bus. He sat in the back with Zeppo and heard the wheeze of hard breathing. Before they turned out of the airport they went past a bus stop and Gord saw Eff and Vee and Zed far down a queue. He asked Harpo, why were they not riding into Havana, why were they waiting at the bus stop; no answer. He asked how often there were power cuts in the capital city; no answer . . . Few cars on the broad avenue, and those that he did see were as old as the one in which he rode, all chrome and wings. Groucho was driving, and needing to concentrate because of the cyclists that loomed from the darkness and wobbled away from their path as they swept by. Harpo had lit his own cigarette and passed another to Zeppo, and not offered a smoke to Gord, and neither had asked him whether he'd had a good flight . . . Good bloody start, Gord, useful bloody beginning. He closed his eyes. Not much to keep them open for in a Havana power cut. He thought that he disliked all three of them, disliked them most because they had left the Indians, Eff and Vee and Zed, at the bus stop.

The car stopped. Doors slammed. The entrance to a hotel of concrete walls, and he could see the candles burning inside the windows.

There was shouting from Harpo at the cash desk, and pleading from Groucho, and Zeppo banged the width of his fist onto the desk. Gord thought they were negotiating the rate. The foyer of the hotel was marble-floored. He carried his plastic bag up three flights of stairs. No marble left over for the corridor. A shit awful cramped little room, and the sheets smelled stale. The window onto the street was open and blew darting shadows from the low candle that Zeppo lit.

They closed the door of the room on him, and he fell onto the bed, and none of them had hoped he felt welcome, and none of them had wished him a good sleep. Faith sinking. From the thin pillow he followed the line of the crack that ran ceiling to floor on the wall in front of him.

He had always been volunteered before. Never had a staff officer ask him – Want to go? Don't bother if you don't want to. Could be a bit rough down there. Pass it by if you'd rather – if he was inclined to take the military flight to Belfast, or to Germany, or south to Dhahran. Soft old life it had been, where the decisions were made for him . . . It had been Gord Brown's choice to listen to Eff and Vee and Zed.

The listening might just have been a mistake. He lay on the bed and wondered how long the candle would last.

She drove the Land Rover off the street and parked close to the main entrance to the city's judicial mortuary.

She helped the two women and the man down, and squeezed tight on the older woman's hand. She called to the dog, tethered in the back of the vehicle, that she would not be long.

It was the third successive morning that Alex Pitt had taken the mother and the father and the sister to the judicial mortuary. It was the only place to search for the 'disappeared' student. She was nine months in Guatemala and had slipped already into the local vernacular. She thought in the terms of the language of the city in which she lived. It was Guatemala's own word, given with authority to the rest of Central and Latin America; a missing person was a 'disappeared'. The disappeared was a student at the University of San Carlos, from the mathematics faculty. There had been witnesses to the lift. The student had left the campus late and told his friends that he intended to walk along the main road back towards the city, and that he would try to hitch a ride. Two other students, on a motorcycle, coming later, had seen the big station wagon pull up alongside the walking student. The two other students had seen the men jump from the station wagon, grab their friend before he thought to run, heave him inside. The two other students had seen the station wagon drive away into the night.

She was taller than any of the family. She was sturdily built, powerful in the hips and shoulders. If she had taken the trouble to mind it then the flow of her hair, ripe wheat blonde, would have been attractive, but she wore it uncombed on the nape of her neck, bound with an elastic band. She was good with the language, should have been because she had the grades at school and in the first year of the university course, and she talked softly to the mother of the disappeared all the way into the flat-roofed, single-storey building. The dog, the tethered German shepherd, barked in frenzy from the interior of the Land Rover as she led the family into the mortuary.

Each time she came she had to catch her breath.

The forensic doctor, almost a friend, had told her that in the bad black days they had received an average of a dozen bodies each day, so many that they were stacked on the tiled floor; now they took in a body every other day. Each body would be held, refrigerated, until it was collected by a family. She didn't know whether she would have had the strength to come to the mortuary in the bad black days.

Whispered voices.

A cradle pulled back.

The shrouded shape revealed.

The technician who smoked dropped his cigarette to the floor and stamped on it. The family were braced and Alex held the hand of the mother and the hand of the sister. The technician lifted the shroud from the face. She saw the bullet hole in

48

the centre of the forehead. The sister crumpled. She heard the father whimper and sensed that he turned away. It was the mother who had the control. The mother reached forward with her free hand and pulled back the shroud. The bruising and the stabbing and the burning on the hosed body were clear against the skin pallor. She felt the hand tightening in hers, and the nails digging in the flesh of her hand.

Before she had come to Guatemala, Alex Pitt had been lectured at the training seminars of the Peace Brigades on what she would see and how she should react. She thought that nothing at the seminars had prepared her for what she would find.

She swallowed hard. The trolley was slid back into the steel cupboard. The technician lit another cigarette.

The mother was staring at the closed door of the cupboard.

A high voice. 'Can something not be done . . . ?'

The forensic doctor gestured with his hands, hopeless. 'They have immunity.'

'When will something be done . . . ?'

The forensic doctor went to the drawer of his desk and he took out a see-through cellophane folder. He held it in front of the family. He showed the family the message of the Death Squad, the Hawk of Justice . . . Alex Pitt made the arrangements, as she had done before, for the collection of the body for burial. After she had taken the family back to their home in Zona 4, dropped them, kissed each of them in turn, seen the car with the smoked windows at the end of the street, she drove to the Zoo Park. She stopped off the road, in the shade of trees. She wriggled into the back of the Land Rover, and she huddled against the tail door and the weight of the dog was across her legs and she held the body of the dog against her, and took comfort from the warmth of the dog.

The dog, its weight and its warmth, was her weakness. Alex Pitt, serving with the Peace Brigades in Guatemala, believed sincerely and with passion in the Bible of the turned cheek. She despised violence, but the dog was the symbol of protection and retaliation. The pretence of her colleagues was that the dog was her company, and it was the small lie in her life.

When she had blown her nose hard, when she had wiped her handkerchief across her eyes, she hugged the dog a last time, then climbed forward into the driving seat.

It was a hell of a good machine, the Land Rover, with 103,000 miles on the clock, but then she had been taught well how to keep a vehicle on the road that should have gone to the scrap yard. She tried to whistle something of a tune, to close her mind from the body of a student who had been 'disappeared'. It was necessary for her to have regained her toughness before she returned to the Peace House.

'When will something be done . . . ?'

Haunting her . . .

Driving away from the Zoo Park, each time she looked into the centre mirror, she saw the car behind her with the smoked-glass windows, holding back but following.

'It will not be what you *require*, Mr Brown,' Zeppo said.

'It will be what you *request*.'

'What I was trying to say . . .'

'We know what is available,' Harpo said. 'We know what can be taken.'

'I had merely drawn up a list of the necessary . . .'

'We are able to write ourselves,' Groucho said. 'We are able to make our own list.'

He had barely slept. Gord had drifted off just before the dawn came, and he had bites all over his body from the bed. He had gone downstairs and into the hotel's dining room and waited more than an hour to be served with thin coffee, good orange juice, and bread rolls. He had gone back to his room and ripped the sheets off the bed and taken them to the window and shaken them outside as hard as he was able. He had gone out into the corridor, not asked, but taken the mop and bucket from the two gossiping room maids. He had scrubbed the floor of the room and of the small shower and lavatory cubicle, and done the walls afterwards. He had made his bed, then returned the mop and bucket to the room maids. He had sat on the bed with paper and pencil and drawn up a list of what he reckoned would be needed for the launching of a revolution. He knew about revolutions. If he hadn't watched, eye witness close, the failure of a revolution, the slaughter, then he wouldn't have told a brigadier general, starched up in best uniform, that the brigadier general was talking bullshit.

He tore up into small pieces the sheet of paper on which he had written his list.

The list, front side of the paper, had been assault rifles, machine guns, heavy mortars, rocket launchers, military explosives and detonators, and a TPO-50 wheel-based flame thrower.

He dropped the pieces of paper onto the floor that he had scrubbed. The list on the second side of the sheet of paper had been portable communications radios, combat rations, anti-mosquito sprays, anti-malaria tablets, field dressings, basic surgery equipment. Consigned to the shining floor . . .

'Please yourselves.'

No, he had not expected a red carpet, nor a band, nor a little girl in a party frock to offer him a bouquet of flowers, no. Yes, he had reckoned that his expertise would be respected, too damn right, yes.

Harpo said, 'It was not every member of our group who thought it necessary to bring a foreigner to Havana. We understand fighting, we are capable.'

Zeppo said, 'We do not need a foreigner to tell us what we must take. We have fought on the mountains and in the jungle. We are veterans of warfare.'

He said nothing. He kept his eyes on the torn pieces of paper on the floor. They let themselves out. Groucho looked back at him, furtive, before closing the door. He sat again on his bed.

It had not just been stupid, it had been a mistake . . . There was something his father used to say to him, something about making footprints on life's path. It was the sort of thing his father used to say when he was drunk. It was necessary to make footprints, leave a mark. The last time his father had come home and had to be helped from the taxi and talked about footprints, with Gord back on a forty-eight-hour leave and waiting half the night to see him, had been after the last sacking. Good story his father had told, told it well for all the drink. The new computer system in the newsroom, and the old hack had been on the familiarization weekend a month before to learn state-of-the-art technology, and a pissed-up finger had pressed Delete, lost the whole of a hell of a story, lost a big one, and the print run about to go, and no copy. His father, the way he'd told it, had ripped the VDU from the desk cables, not been able to open the windows because the newsroom was state-of-the-art-technology air-conditioned. His father had thrown the VDU straight through the plate-glass window, and the newsroom was on the ninth floor. His father had been fired, gone down the pub, and come home to tell his son of the need to make footprints. His father had been dead a year later ... Gord thought that, in Havana, he walked on concrete. No footprints, no marks on life's path.

He dragged open the door of the wardrobe, had to pull it hard because it was warped on the hinges. He lifted out the black plastic bag.

He heard the knock at his door, faint.

He saw the rips in the plastic bag. He would need a new plastic bag if he were catching the flight home.

The knock at his door was repeated.

It had been a mistake.

'Yes?'

In the open doorway, Groucho cringed, and kneaded his hands together.

'What do you want?'

'There is so much that you have to comprehend, Mr Brown.'

'I think I comprehend pretty well.'

'Please, hear me.'

Gord said, 'I doubt there is much to say.'

'Please ... It was a fantasy that was lived here. The fantasy was that we would return to the villages of the triangle, that is the place in the Cuchumatanes between the towns of Nebaj and

Chajul and Cotzal. It was only fantasy. We had followed Ramírez in battle, and we followed him in exile. He was dying, perhaps delirious, perhaps his last joking. He told his son, Rodolfo Jorge, that he should return and fight and win. Right to the funeral there was the argument, none of the old men would go to Europe as Rodolfo Jorge demanded. It was why the Indians were sent . . . How can there be any more fantasy, now that you have come? You are a fighting man, I assume it. After the fantasy is reality. To be in exile is comfortable. There are some who would wish that you had never come . . .'

Groucho knelt on the floor and began to pick up the small pieces of paper that had carried the list.

He had the plastic bag in his hand. Gord said briskly, 'I think I should go home. I think that is best.'

'I was a professor of history. My special area of research was the Conquest. I have not been comfortable. I want to walk again in the corridors of the university. I want to teach again at San Carlos. I want to know a life, in my home, where my students are not disappeared, tortured, killed . . . Please, Mr Brown, do not go home.'

'It has to get better, and soon,' Gord said.

They had escaped the third floor of the embassy.

Lunch was served in the American Club. It was the first lunchtime since Tom Schultz had arrived in Guatemala City that hadn't been Cokes and fast sandwiches, eaten at the desk, taken during a meeting. It was the Intelligence Analyst's birthday. Five of them, all eating the same, all chewing into rye bread and salad with Stilton dressing over the crab and prawn and tuna. Tom thought it good to be out from the third-floor offices that were always dull grey gloomy because of the shield of heavy mesh wire bolted outside the glass windows. Tom and the Intelligence Analyst and the Chemist and the Treasurer, and the Southern Command Liaison who was regular army and down on secondment from Panama, all with Stilton dressing and crab pieces and half-prawns and tuna shreds on their shirt fronts and ties. They sat away from the door and had arrived early enough to take a table where they weren't hemmed in. They could talk their own talk, clear of the American Chamber of Commerce loud-mouths.

Gentle talk, spoken quiet, and Tom learning the ways of the men that he would work with. All equals, and all with their specialized field. The gentle talk was of a new airfield that was used for refuelling by light aircraft carrying the cocaine powder from Bolivia, on via Colombia, through Guatemala, up into the Caribbean for a sea drop to a fast launch; gentle talk of the new capabilities of the vacuum machine that had been made available to them by headquarters that could suck micro-particles from the interior of an aircraft and tell a chemist not only that coca compounds had been there, but where they'd come from; gentle talk on Washington's bitching at the money being thrown at the Confidential Informants and the headaches that gave a field station treasurer; gentle talk about when the paper could be shifted to get the black boxes, the parabolic saucers for satellite communication, from SouthCom. He wanted to belong. Might just be getting there. None of them had cared to question the cause of the wide scar running down the right side of his face from his ear to the jawbone. They did what every man and woman did, what he was getting used to, they stared at it and looked away. He thought he might just be getting there because the glances, furtive, were less frequent than on the first two days inside the office area. He needed to belong. Tom's own gentle talk was of the UH-1H, the Huey bird, out at the La Aurora base, and what he reckoned he could get in distance and speed from her.

He'd found they worked a dozen hours a day, and it was good to be wound down.

'Hi, you're Tom . . . ?'

Talking night flying, night navigation over jungle . . . He turned.

'. . . Good to have you with us.'

There was the hand of friendship thrust at him. In DEA talk, the slightly built man, thinning hair, quiet eyes, light suit, was the Country Attaché. He shook the hand of his bossman, found the grip firm.

An open smile. 'Hope you haven't learned their table habits. Christ, my kids eat neater . . .'

Laughter round the table and the paper napkins grabbed.

'. . . Sorry I wasn't around when you came in, we'll catch up when the food's been scrubbed off you. Well, guys, Washington sends its love, wants to know when we're going to stop sleeping and do some work . . .'

Tom had heard about him. Everyone on the third floor had had their piece about the Country Attaché away at a meeting at headquarters. Green Beret in Vietnam in the last years before the scuttle. In position undercover in Tehran when Desert One had fiascoed and taking two weeks to walk out and over the Iraqi border. Joined the Drug Enforcement Administration. Big in Bolivia before getting the Guatemala City posting. Everyone on the third floor said that he knew how to lead a team.

'. . . Guys, I think you'll remember from the first meeting, Colonel Mario Arturo, new military liaison for us. Be providing the firepower back-up when we need it. In harness from tomorrow . . .'

The man was short, squat. His jacket was too tight for his chest. He was the intruder. He straightened, he stood for a moment at attention, then ducked his head. The mood of gentle talk over lunch was changed.

It happened too fast.

Tom Schultz was caught, not thinking the way he should have.

'. . . Colonel, I think you met everyone else at last month's briefing, except our new flier, Schultz, Tom Schultz . . .'

He was caught, and he wasn't thinking, and he just seemed to see the cold, the contempt, in the little bastard's face. He had taken the colonel's hand.

'Very pleased to meet you, Mr Schultz. I hope you are enjoying the hospitality of our capital city. What have you seen so far of the delights of Guatemala?'

'Well,' Tom said loudly, 'I'd say top of my sight-seeing has been a dog trying to run off with the right arm of a body. Most interesting thing about the body was that it had been knife-slashed, cigarette-burned, beaten, shot in the head . . .'

They were three feet apart.

'. . . Second most interesting thing was that the police who picked the body up made no attempt at the basics of homicide investigation. Third, the "Hawk of Justice" left their calling card . . .'

He dropped the colonel's hand.

There was silence around him. Every table quiet. Waiters frozen.

The Country Attaché whipped, 'Something I want to show you, Schultz.'

He was led from the room. The Country Attaché's foot smacked the swing door open. Into the corridor. Back against the wall. The Country Attaché's finger jabbing into his shirt, beating on the stain of the Stilton cheese, his voice never raised.

'Don't ever give me shit like that again, Schultz. Don't come in here and play smartass with the locals. We live here and we work here, and we can't live and work without their help. Got me? We are dead without them . . . I don't want Amnesty shit, and I don't want Americas Watch shit. Our job in Guatemala, never forget it, is to block what we can of cocaine heading for home. End of story . . . Human rights? Not my concern, not yours. What they do to each other is their business. What they're telling me in headquarters, sorry they didn't find the time to tell you, is that crack cocaine's price on the streets at home is going through the floor, supply outstrips demand, we're flooded with the fucking stuff. The paper I listened to yesterday morning said that the quality of American life, life itself, is being destroyed at all the strata of our society . . . That's my priority. The man you played games with is a colonel from the Kaibiles, that's the best they have in counter-insurgency. That's the sort of guy that can get things done. Understand me right, I don't give a fuck for the politics of this place, I don't give a fuck for bodies at the side of the road . . . I care about how much, what quantity of, cocaine I can intercept on its way home. We want this government because, after a fashion, piss awful fashion, we can work with it, and getting up these people's noses is not my way forward. If you don't like it then you can take the plane back, like tomorrow. Do you hear me, Schultz?'

'I apologize.'

'I don't know whether it's because you had your face chopped about, but I don't take guys with attitude problems. I take team men. You understand me? For your apology, thank you.'

He was smarting as they went back into the room. He sat again at the table. The colonel was listening intently to the Intelligence Analyst, and his eyes never met Tom's. They all knew around the table that the new guy in town had had his ass kicked, and hard. He had opened his fat fucking mouth and killed a birthday party.

His fingernail scratched at his face scar. God bless America.

'This is just crazy, you know that, crazy . . .'

Gord waited for Groucho to translate. Gord said, side of his mouth, 'I don't want his opinion. I want the list.'

The Cuban had his pen at the paper. The first page of the newly prepared list. He slashed. The PK 7.62mm general purpose machine gun with bipod mount stayed. The PKMB 7.62mm tripod-mounted general purpose machine gun was erased. The M-1937 82mm mortars stayed, not the M-1943 120mm mortars.

'What you get is what I don't want. Crazy . . .'

'Tell him', Gord said, 'it is necessary for me to have what is on the list.'

He heard the snigger behind him from Zeppo. Harpo sat alongside the table with his arms folded across his chest. They would not intervene, no help from either of the bastards. Gord thought it was only because, yesterday, Groucho had seen him with the black plastic bag that he had won some action.

57

The old version AK-47s stayed, the number was halved. The replacement AKMs were inked out.

They had wasted all the morning in the hotel while Groucho had paced and waited for the authorization to be telephoned through. Harpo had slept. Zeppo had crunched boiled sweets. When the authorization had come they had driven in the big Pontiac out of the city, on slow roads, past worked crop fields. They had crossed two vintage steel bridges, and seen vultures circling high. They had been an hour driving before they had reached the army camp. Half an hour's wait in the guard room, forty minutes' wait in an office. Gord had said to Groucho, Zeppo and Harpo that this was the biggest foul-up he had known, and he had known some. And where the hell was super marvellous bloody Rodolfo Jorge Ramírez? And that if this was their concept of urgency then they'd be better, much better, staying at home and scratching.

The Cuban officer seemed not to give a damn for them.

Explosives, ticked. Detonators, ticked. The RPG-7 40mm rocket launcher, some. The RPG-75 73mm rocket launcher, none.

Communications radios, no. Field dressings, yes. Basic surgical equipment, query. Tablets, pills, sprays, ointments, no . . .

'You get no radios because I don't have any that work. You get field dressings because I have half a warehouse of them. I don't know if I have the surgical instruments. Medicines, they don't send us them any more, our old lost friends . . . You are lucky that you have never had the delight of Russian friends . . . This, no.'

The Cuban's finger lay on the writing that spelled out TPO-50, the bottom of the list faithfully copied out by Groucho.

'I have to have it.'

'No.'

'I want it.'

'You don't have it . . .'

The sticking point. He would have the flame thrower or he would quit. It was the flame thrower, alone, red oil fire going forward, that deflected him from the certainty of his mistake.

'Why not?'

The Cuban spoke first. Groucho translated. 'You are a soldier, I am told you have been in your regular army. You are a man I would like to respect. Myself, I have been in combat. I was two times in Angola. The army of South Africa is hard. I fought on the Cuvelai river, and at the Benguela airport. I know what it is like to fight beside shit . . . What I do not know, someone like yourself, professional, why do you wish to help these shit people?'

Gord saw the anger flush at Zeppo's jowl. He said quietly, 'I want the flame thrower.'

The Cuban shrugged. He put his pen again through the writing that spelled out TPO-50. 'I tell you, frankly, I have two. My instructions are to provide you with surplus and with what is obsolete. That mark of the flame thrower is neither surplus nor obsolete. You do not have it . . .'

Gord cut him. 'Then I quit.'

'Of supreme indifference to me. And supreme indifference to me if you go into Guatemala with these shit people, where you will not last a week, where you will be killed, and for nothing.'

Gord scraped back his chair, stood. 'Thank you for your time.'

'It is best that you quit. Go home, go where you belong. Perhaps I give you a favour.'

It was a back-hand drop shot that took the set and the match.

There was thin applause around the court.

The girl bounded forward, skipped the net, and shook her opponent's hand.

He had been reared to be formal, it was the way of their society. He did not kiss his fiancée's cheek, only shook her hand with grace. She always won when he competed with her at tennis. The young man ushered his fiancée through the wire gate of the court, led her to her father's table. The young man, who used the codename of Benedicto, pulled back a chair at the table for his fiancée to sit on. He thought she was a spoiled little cow.

His fiancée called casually across her shoulder for a drink to be brought her. Her father was a big man, not athletic, groomed grey hair swept back on his head, and rich. It was because of the wealth of the family that the junior officer was prepared to contemplate marriage to the daughter that he thought was a stupid and ignorant bitch . . .

The drink was brought by a waiter, not acknowledged. His fiancée, the little cow, the ignorant bitch, was busy with her mother, the new dresses that had come from Europe to the boutiques on 6a Avenida.

For the junior officer it would be a good marriage, financial security. The family owned thousands of hectares of cleared ground in the Northern Transverse Strip of the Petén region. The war was dying, the enemy forces were scattered, there was little work left for an interrogator. When he was married, when he came out of the army, he would have no need to work again. It would be a good match, even if she was spoiled, ignorant, and had not yet lost the child fat on her hips.

He talked with his fiancée's father about the price of beef in the United States and what the McDonald's chain was paying now per kilo. A full hour he listened to the drip whine of complaint at the fall of the beef price in the United States, until, God-given relief, the family swept away from the Guatemala Club in their Mercedes limousine that was headed and tailed by the privately hired armed guards . . . small mercy, he had been spared talk of the cost of the guards, the danger of kidnapping . . . He waved at the retreating convoy, as if the light fled his life, until the dust obscured it.

He drove back to his desk at G-2. His desk was clear.

The war had withered.

It had been a mistake. Mistakes, in Gord's creed, were time wasted.

He had taken a taxi to the city centre. He had used the plastic to buy the ticket. More shame that the first flight out, that evening, was the bloody Aeroflot to the west of Ireland. He had taken a taxi back to the hotel. He had enough money left over, because he had changed his few sterling notes with the kids out behind the kitchens at the back of the hotel, for one more taxi to the airline office, and for the bus to the airport. Not enough money left for a drink on the flight . . . tough, because it was Aeroflot . . . It had been a mistake.

He was quitting because he was not wanted, because Rodolfo bloody Jorge bloody Ramírez had not done him the courtesy of showing.

He was turning his back on a mistake, right thing to do.

He had turned his back before. He had walked out on the Shia people of Karbala when the tanks had come south from Baghdad, wrong thing to do. Still the pain in him from walking out on the Shia people, behind the barricades, armed with rifles, waiting to face tanks. Still the pain, for the Shia people, as keen as it had been when he had faced the American brigadier general on the airstrip at Dhahran.

But no pain now, because it had been a mistake.

The ticket was on the bed.

He heard the shouting from down the corridor, from the stairwell.

Beside his feet was the black plastic bag which he had repaired with adhesive tape begged from the Aeroflot staff, filled again.

He heard the slow squealing from the corridor, unoiled metal on metal.

The sound stopped outside his door. Gord had stiffened. He sat upright. It was his instinct to feel immediately his vulnerability. He had no weapon. There was a light knock on the door. He had only light trainer shoes on his feet, he would break his toes if he kicked hard in them. The light knock was repeated. His right hand was rigid, extended; he could kill with a blow from the heel of his fist. He went silently to the door. One movement, the unlocking and opening of the door.

They swept in.

There was the bubble of their laughter.

There was the shriek of their fun.

Gord's hand dropped.

They poured into the room. Eff and Vee and Zed, each of them carrying the identical tubes. The tubes were three, four feet long. They were painted dull green with the nozzles forward. There was a young man behind them and he wheeled the cart into the hotel bedroom.

The young man said, 'It's what you wanted . . . ? It's what you asked for . . . ? You wanted the TPO-50. You required the flame thrower.'

Gord gazed into the youth of the face.

The young man said, 'I tell you, Mr Brown, it was not meant for taking up the stairs . . .'

Dark hair sleeked and combed to a parting, hazel eyes, close-shaven over a flawless skin that could have been a girl's, white teeth showing in the grin.

'. . . I am Jorge, Mr Brown. I am Rodolfo Jorge Ramírez. I apologize to you for my rudeness in not having before made the time to see you. Please accept my apology.'

The opened ticket was on the bed, the filled plastic bag on the floor.

Not his way, Gord stumbled. '. . . It doesn't matter . . .'

'I heard, Mr Brown, that you had been to the offices of Aeroflot . . . in my opinion, from what I have been told, I would prefer to go in, one engine lost, cratered dirt strip, contested landing, to Guatemala – rather than fly Aeroflot across the Atlantic – just what I have been told . . .'

He had his composure again. Gord said, cold, 'I accept your apology. I also accept that I made a mistake. There's not really much more to talk about.'

Gord saw their fun drained. Eff and Vee and Zed held the tubes loosely.

'May I talk, Mr Brown?'

'You can do what you like.'

'Can we not be comfortable, Mr Brown?'

'I have one hour until I need to go to the Aeroflot office.'

The young man squatted on the floor. Gord sat on the bed.

Eff and Vee and Zed cradled the tubes and stood in line against the wall.

'I learned my English at the school. You will excuse me if it is not adequate . . . My country, Mr Brown, is a military camp. The regime in Guatemala survives by terror. To speak for freedom, the rights that are second nature to you, is to invite the attention of the Death Squads. To fight for freedom is to invite the retaliation of the army. In my country, Mr Brown, freedom belongs only to the generals, and the politicians to whom they have given power . . .'

Gord listened. Rodolfo Jorge Ramírez talked the detail of the armed forces of Guatemala. The structure, the deployment, the firepower. He glanced at his watch. Time running.

'. . . My country is divided in many ways, Mr Brown. It is divided by privilege and opportunity so that a ruling oligarchy, a tiny minority, controls the vast majority of the wealth. There is division in health care, division in education, division in human rights – and there is the division of racism. The subjugation of an ethnic majority is at the heart of my country's nightmare. The ethnic majority of Guatemala are the Mayan Indian people. If the majority were to receive their share of the wealth of Guatemala then the privilege of the minority would be threatened. Do I speak like a communist, Mr Brown, or do I speak of a fairness that is natural to you? The Indian people and their culture have suffered a consistent programme of genocide, of torture, of abuse, of displacement . . .'

Gord had heard it before. He had heard it in the souk and the mosque and the coffee houses of Karbala, before he had walked out, before the tanks had attacked.

'. . . My father and mother were what is called *Ladino*, they are of Latin descent, but they chose to make their lives amongst the Indians of the Ixil triangle. My father was trusted, did not cheat them. My mother was loved, nursed them. The war came, my father was a leader. He was a humble man, he would have claimed no genius, but he understood the common sense of war. He led a rebellion. For two years that rebellion was too strong

63

for the military. After two years the military came with air strikes and helicopters and the Kaibil battalion . . .'

Gord had imagined it before. The armoured columns over-running the barricades of the Shia men and women that he had walked out on. There was a darkness in the room.

'. . . On the second evening, after my mother had been killed, after the ammunition was exhausted, after he had been squeezed back to our store and our home, the last strongpoint, the military broadcast on loudspeakers that all the men who surrendered would be safe, except for my father. It was his decision. The decision lay with him for the rest of his life. He took me, I was thirteen years old, and he took his oldest and most trusted friends. In the darkness it was possible for a few to slip clear. All the time that we ran I could hear his weeping. When we were a few miles away, on higher ground than the village, we saw the fire of the church of Acul. All the men that surrendered were burned alive, Mr Brown. We lived . . .'

Gord knew what had happened in Karbala. He had heard it afterwards. He knew of the executions by shooting and by hanging. He knew of the terror that had been brought to the city by the security teams that had followed the tanks.

'. . . I promised my father that I would return. I made the promise to him when he was close to death. I want to go back to Guatemala, Mr Brown, and I want to drive out the bastards who could herd men into a church and set fire to it. I want to go back, Mr Brown, and root out the bastards who serve the army by day and the Death Squads by night. I want to go back, Mr Brown, to restore the dignity of an Indian society that had a civilization five hundred years before the birth of Christ. I believe that in my country there is a people that will follow me . . .'

Gord looked at his watch, saw the lines of the luminous hands. The Aeroflot would be boarding.

'. . . I want you at my side, Mr Brown. I hope that I have my father's common sense, but I have no military training. I want your skill and your experience and your knowledge. The people will follow us, the regime will disintegrate, it is corrupt and rotten and it will fall. I don't know what you have in your home country, Mr Brown, what you have that is more important . . . It might still be possible, just, for you to catch your flight . . .'

The young man had taken him, and he could recognize it. He was the moth brought to the bulb, the nail slapped against the magnet's face. Something about the voice and something about the humility and something about the optimism. The Aeroflot was lost. It was not his way to clasp a man's hand, nor to hug his shoulders, but his commitment was made to Jorge who had captivated him.

Gord said, quiet, 'You did well to get the flame thrower.'

The chuckle from the floor in the gloom of the room. 'The flame thrower, that was nothing, it was the two aircraft that were difficult.'

Something that his father had said, something about making footprints.

Under arc lights the crates that held the weapons and the boxes of ammunition, and the frame of the TPO-50's cart with the fuel tubes were loaded onto the two aircraft.

There were ten of them who would fly.

# 4

They flew in radio silence, without navigation lights, and hugged the sea surface. No bogus flight plan had been transmitted to the air-traffic controllers of Tegucigalpa or Managua or San José or Guatemala City.

There were squall storms blowing in from the south-west, and the meteorological forecast had determined the fast departure from the airfield east of Havana. It was assumed that any flight plan received by radio in Honduras or Nicaragua or Costa Rica or Guatemala would be monitored by Southern Command at the Quarry Heights base camp in Panama and fed on to the Drug Enforcement Administration and Customs teams in the Central America region.

The storms would kill the ability of the radar screen slung across the Caribbean by the DEA and Customs agencies to identify the two aircraft. In silence and darkness, the two aircraft designated as Echo Foxtrot and Whisky Alpha flew at their maximum cruising speed of 120 land miles an hour. Set against them, to be avoided, were fixed land-based radar installations, the airborne radar of the E-3 AWAC system mounted in the fuselages of the Boeing 707s, and the aerostat balloon-floated radars. All were vulnerable to poor weather. The airspace of the Caribbean was under continual surveillance as part of the billion-dollar programme to track and interdict narco-trafficking aircraft making the fast run from Colombia and north to the transshipment points.

They were the old workhorses of the Cuban air force. They were the miracle of maintenance care and the inventiveness of the ground technicians who scavenged and cannibalized and

66

improvised now that the spare parts from the Soviet Union and Poland had to be paid for with cash currency. Two old aircraft, flown by two pairs of old cockpit crewmen whose careers had long ago become stagnant, wheezing and coughing and lurching across the sea space of the Caribbean waters.

They had left behind them the dull lights of the Isla de la Juventud, crossed the line of twenty-one degrees latitude, headed out over the Yucatan Basin where the depth of the water below them was in excess of 4000 metres. They took a course to the west of the British-administered Grand Cayman, too far distant for the lights of Georgetown to be seen by the navigators, and then on above the Cayman Trench. The aircraft flew over the line of eighty-four degrees longitude, and again the navigators' fingers, illuminated by their pencil torch beams, pointed to the pilots the crossing of eighteen degrees latitude. They would turn west again close to the empty pimples in the sea mass that were the Swan Islands. The fuel situation would be desperate. Each pilot relied totally on the skill of his navigator.

The aircraft were Antonovs. They were the An-2 Colt design. Whisky Alpha had been delivered to Cuba, new from the production line in the Soviet Union, in 1961. Echo Foxtrot had come four years later. They were what could be spared. They were what would not be missed if the fuel gauges ran too low, if bad weather forced them down. There was no friendly landfall for them to divert to. Hammering on through the darkness hours towards the coast strip of the Central American isthmus that they would hit at the first dirt smear of dawn lit the horizon behind them . . . They were biplanes. They were each powered by a single 1000-horsepower Shvetsov 62-R nine-cylinder radial engine. There was no margin of error available to the pilots of Whisky Alpha and Echo Foxtrot. They were laden to the maximum, and beyond, because the pilots had shrugged their agreement, with men and war materials and with the cans of fuel for the flight home.

It was a late throw of defiance from a slipping regime. Back in the past, secure under the umbrella protection of Khrushchev and Brezhnev, the regime had supported the fighters of Nicaragua and El Salvador and Guatemala, Argentina and Chile and Peru, supplied them with the courage of the Party's creed and the firepower held in the island's arsenals. No longer. It was a late throw.

A bad night for flying low over water, but a bad night was protection against the radar.

In an hour they would skim the coastline of Honduras, near to Puerto Cortés, then go north over the frontier of Guatemala, then start to search for the map co-ordinates of the landing strip . . . if the fuel gauges could be believed . . .

Beside Gord, Vee was sick.

He was sick through fear and because he had drunk too much between the time that the loading had been completed and the time of take-off.

Across the fuselage from Gord, Zed sat strapped in by the webbing harness and shivered in terror.

Further down the fuselage, opposite each other, Zeppo and Harpo gasped continuously on their cigarettes, ignored the No Smoking signs above their heads. Between their legs were ammunition boxes. They lit one cigarette from the end of another and stamped the butts out on the metal floor space between the ammunition boxes. The petrol cans that the aircraft carried were stowed aft in the fuselage but too damned close, thought Gord, for the chain of cigarettes.

Eff tried to wipe the vomit off Gord's legs.

No point, give it a rest, more to come.

When the wind took the aircraft, either battering against the fuselage or buffeting into the cockpit, then the Antonov pitched, and there had been the dead moments when it had seemed they were in freefall, and the moments when it had seemed they were lifted and tossed up and then left to drop. The flight was the worst he'd known because he was alone. Bloody, going into western Iraq in the big Puma, through a sandstorm that was great for cover, but he'd had guys with him who were his own, and the pilot then hadn't been drinking, not like the jerk who was flying them now. They'd all been drinking after the loading had been completed, they'd all hit the rum mixed with not enough orange juice before the take-off. As far as Gord could see, the other pilot had drunk more. He wondered how they were doing, the other two passengers who were in Whisky Alpha, whom he hadn't met before, who had seemed better news than Zeppo and Harpo and Groucho . . . Gord had done his calculations, knew they were at the bottom of the fuel capacity for the flight, and had the sight of the fuel cans being loaded in his mind. Bloody well on the edge. He could make out the shape of Groucho from Zeppo's and Harpo's cigarettes, and he saw that Groucho held his head in his hands, as if covering his eyes in the darkness would make the battering more bearable.

Gord thought, couldn't be certain in the black interior, that Jorge was asleep.

Gord thought, couldn't be certain through the rattled stress on the spars and wings, that he had heard Jorge snore.

He had talked to the pilot before take-off, and the Cuban had American English. Gord had rather liked the droll humour of the man. He would have appreciated the humour the more now. The pilot had told a Fidel story, a good one . . . One question each for Clinton and Yeltsin and Fidel to Jesus. How will the inner-city anti-narcotics programme go? – Fine, but Clinton wouldn't see the results in his lifetime. How will the campaign for a market-led economy go? – Fine, but Yeltsin wouldn't see the results in his lifetime. Fidel asked, 'What about my campaign against inefficiency and corruption?' – Jesus said, 'It'll do fine, but you won't see the results in your lifetime, and I won't see them in my lifetime either.'

Well, the pilot had the weather report. The pilot had kept the weather report to himself. Cracking jokes about the leader was the least of the pilot's problems. Sitting in the fuselage, bouncing in the seat, feeling the harness straps bite at his shoulders, Gord understood why the pilot had been at the rum and orange, why he'd poured half a bottle down to the last drip into an old silver-plated hip flask.

Gord held tight as he could onto the pulling arms of the cart that was sandwiched between himself and Zed. It had broken clear of his grip once, half an hour back in a roller coaster rise, hammered into Harpo's knee . . . And Vee was gone from beside him, lifted clear, and was falling into the cart's arms, and was whimpering.

'Well, my friend . . .' Jorge's calm voice above the bleat of the engine. 'What are you thinking?'

'Time I made an excuse and left . . .'

'Was it real, when you said you would quit?'

'At the time it seemed the right thing to say . . .'

They dropped. Gord clung to the cart handles. Groucho cried out in his fear.

The hiss of the question in his ear. 'Why did you come, why did you leave your home?'

The Antonov bounced and there was the surge of the engine power.

'Past caring, history . . .'

'Why?'

Gord shouted, 'Because I was asked. Because no-one else was asking me. Because you get so as you want to be asked.'

'That's a stupid answer.'

'Not the cleverest question.'

'Why?'

'I answer your question, then you answer my question.'

A chuckle. 'Agreed.'

Gord said, 'I was down in the Gulf, long-range penetration of Iraqi territory, reconnaissance stuff. The cease-fire came. It was the time the Americans were urging the Shia minority to revolt against the Sunni Moslem Baghdad regime. I was commanding a team of six and we'd ended up close to a town called Karbala. We were working with the people there, trying to get them organized, how to defend themselves. The cease-fire had left too much of the Iraqi armour intact. They'd lost their bloody nerve, the politicians, called the stop too early. Christ, and they needed help, the Shia people in Karbala. We were doing what we could for them, and we were ordered out. I had a bloody colonel yelling down the radio at me. I should have told him to go fuck himself . . . We walked out. I obeyed orders. No, I don't know what we would have achieved if we had stayed longer, but I know that after we'd gone and the tanks came, the Shias in Karbala were minced. Our bloody politicians had led these people on, then bottled out. We had a responsibility for them . . . Answer, like a bloody fool I was looking again for a small guy to stand beside . . . Question, what's the end line here?'

The engine missed. Shit. The moment's silence. Shit. The engine caught again. The sweat streaming on his forehead.

They climbed again and there was the beat of rain on the porthole window behind Gord's head.

'Thank you.'

'It was a crap answer.'

'An idiot question . . . Your answer. The end line is to win.'

Gord talking fast. 'Right, right, how far? We hit a village? We shoot up a barracks? We let them know we're around? What, a week, then out?'

'To win, Mr Brown, we must go to Guatemala City. We are going to turn them out of the Palacio Nacional. That is what I mean by winning . . .'

'And it was a crap question.'

There was just him and Jorge who slapped at his shoulder in amusement, and there was Eff and Vee and Zed, and there was Harpo and Zeppo and Groucho, and there were two men aboard Whisky Alpha . . . Why not?

'We are going to win.'

From: Fort William police HQ, Lochaber District.

To: Strathclyde police HQ, Glasgow.

Ref: A/0800/79y/4.

Attention: Special Branch.

Local report that 3 (three) native Indian Guatemalans, giving Havana/Cuba residence, visited Loch Ailort area last week to seek out Gordon Benjamin BROWN, No Permanent Address.

He understood to be former Special Air Service commissioned officer, no further detail, currently working as fish farm labourer.

Believed BROWN propositioned to provide military help for proposed invasion of Guatemala (exclaimer). No offence committed in our force area. You may wish to up follow.

End.

Gord had gone forward.

It was smooth flying now. Between them, Eff and Vee and Zed could mind the cart.

He stood, but bowed and hunched, at the back of the cockpit area and braced himself against the backs of the pilot's and navigator's seats.

They didn't seem to mind him being there. Perhaps they recognized a military man. Perhaps they were both just so damned thankful to be out of the storm belt. The navigator had the flight chart spread on his knee, and sometimes his finger pointed to a position, the crossing of the Honduran coast, the crossing of the Guatemalan frontier. They had flown west of Puerto Cortés, then south of the Guatemalan city of Puerto Barrios. He could see the land mass beneath them, dark with the first sheen of grey settling on their horizon. Dawn coming and fast. There was broken cloud above them. They had lost the protection of the darkness and the bad weather. Twice the pilot pointed to the fuel gauge where the needle had settled at the top of the red-coloured segment. Gord understood that they had to make the wide detour of Belize airspace, because there was modern radar at Belize, and a squadron of Harrier jets on the runway to come up on interception course if they aroused suspicion. They were clear of the threat of the Harriers now because they were over Guatemala.

He would have admitted it, couldn't have hidden it, the excitement consumed him. It was the excitement that stretched

72

him and pumped the adrenaline, but private and not shared . . .
The landing point was identified on the chart for him. They
were low over the water of the Lago de Izabal, perhaps a hundred feet, they would climb immediately on crossing the far
shore, over high ground and a National Park, they would cross
the road strip that was the principal route from Cobán to the
Belize border, and then ahead was only the swamp jungle wilderness, and the airstrip.

The excitement bulged in him, as it always did when he flew
forward to combat. It was why he had come, in truth, to find
again the excitement . . . Over the park, a carpet of triple canopy
trees, the navigator pointed again to the position of the landing
strip and gestured with his hands. Fifteen minutes to the destination. The needle was lower in the red section at the extremity of
the fuel gauge. No talking in the cockpit. The light was coming up
around them. Gord leaned forward to search the skies, under the
cloud fragments, for the second aircraft. He could not see Whisky
Alpha. He tapped the pilot's shoulder, he pointed port and starboard, he gestured – where was Whisky Alpha? Just the shrug of
the pilot. They were in radio silence, how the hell would the pilot
know, dumb query. A shimmer of sunlight ahead of them. He
stared down at the ground, flat and endless to a misted horizon.
The first sunlight caught the rich green of the jungle ceiling. They
were across the road. The jungle was virgin. An empty quarter of
desolation, no mark of man's hand. No cut trails, no smoke spirals, no habitation clearances. An army could have been hidden
here, below Echo Foxtrot, lost and never found.

And the landing strip was ahead of them.

He heard the pilot swear.

So damned short . . . A runway for a light aircraft . . . There
was a ribbon cut of lighter green in the darker spread of jungle . . .

An alarm ringing in the cockpit.

The needle was stationary at the bottom of the red section of
the fuel gauge.

They came in a half-circle to the north end of the runway.
Gord thought it brilliant flying, brilliant navigating. He

wondered how it was that a cockpit crew who could fly so well should have ended up on a crap mission with a drying fuel tank, and he remembered the Fidel story – the shit jobs for the livewires, just as he had always known it, the shit jobs for the men who would go home in 'ignominy' – and there was a slow smile on his face, and the bloody alarm was clamouring.

A half-turn and they were going in.

No recce, no gentle circling to spy the strip. Been past it once and seen nothing of obstacles, craters. No fuel to mess with.

Coming down onto the uncut grass, might have been a foot high, might have been a yard high. Coming down.

They hit.

The shudder of touch-down tore at his arm tendons. Gord was braced. The bounce. Down. The change of the engine pitch, reverse thrust. Swerving, charging, slowing, rushing to the tree line ahead. Slewing, stopping. The tree line edging closer. Stopped. Gord felt the numbness, and his hand rested on the pilot's shoulder and squeezed his admiration. He heard the applause from behind. All of them clapping their hands. God, and they'd the bloody right to clap. The pilot had his helmet off, and he was tearing away the silk face scarf that he wore like an old Grand Prix driver, and he had the hip flask to his mouth and the rum dribbling from his lips before the navigator snatched it from him.

Gord dropped down from the side door of the Antonov.

The warm dawn air was around him, and the butterflies scattered from the grass that reached to his knees.

There was a small wood-built hut at the end of the runway, in the trees, a dozen yards from where Echo Foxtrot had stopped.

The scramble started. Lifting out the ammunition crates. Passing down the canvas sacks that held the assault rifles. There was a low droning sound from the distance, below the tree level, beyond their vision. Forming a chain to get the petrol cans out of the fuselage. Throwing down the medical box, and the cardboard cartons that held the food, Meals Ready to Eat. Manoeuvring out of the doorway the flame thrower's cart and

74

the tubes. The droning of Whisky Alpha's engine closing. The scramble to get the small pile of ammunition and weapons and medicines and food clear of the runway and into the hut, and to push the cart to the door of the hut, and to get the petrol cans to the edge of the runway. They had started to push Echo Foxtrot to the runway's side, all of them straining together, when the engine sound of Whisky Alpha, the growing roar, was stifled. Just a cough, and gone.

Gord saw the aircraft. She was low above the trees, rolling as if the pilot was losing his power.

All of them quiet, all of them watching the silent struggle of Whisky Alpha to reach the landing strip.

The main impact point, after the tops of trees had sheared away the wings, was fifty yards short of the safety of the runway.

There was an explosion. Of course there was a fucking explosion. There was fire. Of course there was fucking fire.

Whisky Alpha crashed with two passengers, and most of the machine guns and most of the belt-fed ammunition, and the rocket launchers and the grenade projectiles, and with most of the AK-47s and half of the ammunition, and the reserve petrol for the flight home.

Gord watched the flames scorching amongst the trees.

They started to run the length of the runway.

The dawn reaching brightly across the skyline of the capital city of the Republic of Guatemala.

Not an old city. A city without history. The first capital of Guatemala, founded by the Spanish settlers of the Conquest under the direction of Pedro de Alvarado, lies under a carpet of rock and mud thrown down onto its crude buildings by the earthquake of 1541. The country around that capital city that was to comprise the modern Guatemala had been wrested from a civilization of sophistication and achievement by just 120 horsemen and 300 footsoldiers. A second capital was built at Antigua on a site beneath the twin volcano mountains of Fuego and Agua, and was ruined by a flowing lava sea. The third capital was placed in La Ermita valley in the last century, at an altitude of 5000 feet where a Spanish-descended elite could be safe from the cholera and disease they had carried from Europe and which decimated their despised workforce of ethnic Mayan Indians.

Around the environs of the capital city is a countryside of rare beauty, a land of mountains and valleys, of lakes and tumbling streams, of great forest and fertile fields. But a dark side rules. Beyond the beauty, shrouded in that darkness, is today's capital city of Guatemala.

Since the building of those capital cities, the life of the Indian majority has guttered near to extinction.

In the darkness hours, the principal streets of the city are given over to the slow cruising cars of the police, and to the thieves and muggers and pimps who prey on the stupidity of tourists who have not read and heeded the warnings. Wide pavements are emptied by the fall of the sun.

In daylight hours, the big *avenidas*, and the *calles* that cross them in a grid system, choke with the pollution of snarling motor vehicles. The big Mercedes power by to drop men at the offices of import-export companies, and their women at the smart shops and the hotel restaurants imported from North America. The beggars are out in the daylight, and the hawkers, and the hustlers.

Dawn is the finest hour of Guatemala City's day, when the clear light ripples on empty streets. The criminals have gone, the beggars have not arrived. Only at dawn is there a peace in Guatemala City.

As the crow flies, 105 miles from the capital, across mountains and foothills and swamp jungle, an aircraft had landed and an aircraft had crashed, and the city knew nothing of it.

The city woke with the dawn.

A Fireman dressed as quietly as he was able in the airless room that he shared with his wife and his small daughter, in the house that he shared with his mother and father and his sister. He left the family asleep as he went to work on his bicycle . . .

An American Archaeologist, a lecturer on a year's sabbatical leave from the University of Minnesota, dressed urgently because he must be at the airport by seven to hitch the lift back to the site in the Petén . . .

An Academic, a doctor of mathematics, searched his wardrobe to find a clean white shirt to wear the next day with his charcoal suit, and when he was dressed for the university (older and drabber clothes) he went in his stockinged feet from the bedroom, and had not kissed his wife because she would have told him, as she had screamed the night before and as she would again that evening, that it was idiocy for him to expose his safety by attending his student's funeral.

A Street Boy, thirteen years old, woke on his pavement pitch near the Ritz Continental hotel, and began rhythmically to sharpen his four-inch-blade flick-knife on the concrete kerb. He had no need to dress as all the clothes that he owned were worn against the night's cold . . .

A Priest of the Catholic faith dressed in the cell room he had been given for the night at the national seminary, and packed his bag, and worried that he would be late for the bus that would take him back to Nebaj . . .

A Civil Patroller, from the country away from the city, dressed outside the hung sacking that was the door of the shanty house, swaying and falling from the alcohol of his brother's wedding party, and knew that he would have to run if he were to be in time for the bus going north to the Ixcán . . .

An elderly Canadian, three weeks after his arrival from Kingston in the province of Ontario, dressed methodically in a pension room, and planned another day of searching for the grave of a murdered grandson . . .

The capital city of Guatemala stirred, in ignorance that 105 miles away, across mountains and foothills and swamp jungle, an aircraft had landed and an aircraft had crashed.

Gord understood. Nobody translated for him. He would have been an idiot if he had not understood.

Zeppo wanted out.

It was not quite fifteen minutes since they had landed, and not quite eleven minutes since they had watched the crash. They had been close to the explosion site, and close was a risk because of the ammunition and the flailing tracer rounds. They had crawled on their stomachs as near as they had dared. The plane was gone, the crew and their colleagues were gone, the cargo was gone.

Zeppo wanted out.

In Gord's view, if Zeppo had climbed onto Echo Foxtrot, refuelled and revving power, then Harpo would have followed him, and Groucho might just have tried to ride a wing to get clear.

Zeppo wanted out and he stood in front of Jorge and he had blustered and shouted and waved his arms. Gord had kept back, and he hadn't asked Vee to translate for him. Gord had nothing to contribute. The reality was sharp enough for him, and was a high column of smoke going to cloud that might carry rain later in the day, and was the still occasional detonation of ammunition. The intervention that had mattered had been that of the pilot. He had come from his cockpit, left his propeller turning, and said maybe two dozen words. Zeppo was still shouting at Jorge and Jorge was in front of him and with his hands easily on his hips, and when Zeppo was blown out, when the tears were in his eyes, then Jorge had talked to him.

Gord turned his back on them.

He started to carry the discarded empty petrol cans from below the wings of the aircraft and took them, four at a time, to the jungle edge and threw them as far as he was able so that they crashed from sight.

He was walking away towards the tree line when the Antonov started its run. He didn't turn to watch the acceleration through the beaten grass. He walked back up to the tree line and savagely hurled the cans as far as he was able. When he returned for the last load, the aircraft lifted off, sudden like a startled bird, and scraped the tree tops. Gord bent to pick up the final four cans.

The wings dipped each way, starboard and port, a salute. It was gone away over the tree line.

Just an emptiness around them. Just the call of birds and the grate of insects. The sun was lifting fast.

Zeppo was sitting on the grass and his head was pulled down onto his chest and Harpo knelt beside him and seemed to whisper comfort to him.

The first day, the sun not yet up, and he wondered if they were already beaten. He stiffened, straightened his back. He could have screamed into the growing light and the tree wall around him. Gord walked towards the hut at the end of the airstrip, and Jorge went with him.

'Why didn't you let them go?'

'Wasn't my decision. He was light on fuel anyway, wouldn't take the extra weight.'

'Everything that we said we needed, it was the minimum.'

Jorge said, 'He wanted to go and he is important to me. He is an engineer. You think I want to start out without an engineer . . . ? I said he could go. I said that everyone could go but that I would stay. I said that even if I was just one man, with just one rifle and just one bullet, I would stay.'

'I hear you.'

They reached the hut. The ammunition and the weapons were piled outside the open door, and the cart for the flame thrower. Jorge took Gord's arm and led him into the dark of the hut. He saw the food on the floor and the disturbed bedding.

He stepped outside. He took a rifle from the pile, and a magazine, and he broke out an ammunition box and started to load the magazine, and his eyes raked the green shades of the tree line.

She woke in the small room.

Her room was at the back of the Peace House.

Alex Pitt woke because the German boy had stumbled down the corridor for the lavatory.

She shook her head, tossed her hair. The taste of the alcohol was in her mouth, and the smell of it was on her body. It was not often that the volunteers threw their own party, no outsiders. The Swede had wrecked the party. The one with the glasses and the sunburn and the face pimples. The Swede had been clumsy, slurred, with the mix of *aguardiente* from the sugar cane and Gallo beer. She hadn't slapped him, or punched him, but she had pushed him hard away when he had groped his hand under her blouse. He'd fallen, he'd cut his head, he'd needed two stitches. End of party.

The German boy had disappeared down the back corridor with the American girl. The American boy was with the Spanish girl. It would only have been her and the Swedish boy who had slept alone. And Alex Pitt would bloody well decide, herself, who she took to bed . . .

A disaster.

They would all have rated the disaster as her fault.

She dressed fast.

She dressed in her best T-shirt and skirt. It was the blue T-shirt and the full flower-patterned skirt that was in the photograph she had sent last month in her letter to her mother and father. She had few enough clothes and would wear her best T-shirt and best skirt again for the funeral the following day.

It would be a bad week at the Peace House. The American boy and the German boy would side with the Swede, who would wear his scar like a reproach to her. The American girl and the Spanish girl would not understand why, after a party, she had not done what everyone did – go to bed with who was available. Before she was dressed in her best T-shirt and best skirt, she had already decided that she was better away for the week, that she would take the Land Rover and head for the mountain foothills. The far foothills of the Cuchumatanes range were where she was happiest, her and her dog.

She would go straight from the funeral.

Alex Pitt was in her second year as a volunteer of Peace Brigades International. She funded herself. She wrote to her father when she needed money, for the Land Rover. She accepted no expenses from the headquarters in Toronto. The work for which she had volunteered, and in which she believed quite passionately, was non-violent protection of the weak and abused in a vile society. The volunteers targeted those at risk from the Civil Patrols and the Death Squads, put themselves alongside those in greatest danger. A man who complained, a woman who protested, and whose life was therefore at hazard, would be accompanied by a volunteer. Her presence was her force, because she carried no weapon. By her presence, body to body with a man or woman in danger, she could hope to deter the violence of the army or the Civil Patrols or the Death Squads. Those who commanded the army and the Civil Patrols and the Death Squads would be loath to bring down on their heads the wrath of a foreign government if a volunteer were beaten, knifed or caught in a killing burst of automatic gunfire. It was a frail shield that she walked behind. It was a bluff, and Alex Pitt knew it. Each of them in the team were frequent visitors at their embassy. It would be known by those who tracked her and her colleagues, in the station wagons with the smoked windows, that the embassies both cursed them as interfering blow-ins and admired them for their dedication. Not enough hours in the day, not enough days in the week for the volunteers to stand beside the many who were at risk.

In the kitchen, alone, amongst the emptied bottles of *aguardiente* and Gallo beer, amongst the plates that had not been cleared, she ate her breakfast.

She heard the motion of the bed in the German boy's room.

The hardest thing for her, in her world of non-retaliation and non-violence, was to accept that the men of the Death Squads enjoyed immunity.

They had found the track that a wild boar had made. The track meandered between the wide tree trunks and avoided the thickest of the nets of clinging vine. The sun was climbing but the denseness of the upper canopy filtered out the light and they moved in a shadow world. The heat stuck to them. No wind penetrated from the skies that were hidden from them. It was good going as long as they had the track made by the wild boar, but at the first river that ran north to south the boar had veered away along the bank. They could wade the river which was low at the approaching end of the dry season, the depth of water was not much above Gord's thighs, and not much above the waists of Eff and Vee and Zed. They had been moving for two hours when they reached the river, and the crossing took them more than half an hour and the cart was murder, and then there was a rest of fifteen minutes before they loaded up again. There had been no need to talk it through. The rota that they worked was obvious. When they left the river it was necessary for a path to be found. It was not possible to cut a path, because a cut path would be too easily visible to the men of a follow-up military search.

Gord and Jorge took it in turns to twist and crawl forward and to ease back the hanging vines and to bend away the clinging scrub, make a way for the cart. There was a chance of a follow-up military search because they had left behind them a burned-out Antonov and a hut from which squatter Indians had fled. Gord and Jorge alternated the lead, and the role of the backmarker on their short crocodile column.

There was a road, a narrow red strip on the map, west-south-west on the compass, that was twelve miles from the landing strip. The road was the first target.

'Shoot.'

The Country Attaché leaned back in his chair, swept them with his cheroot smoke.

'There's a cattle *finca* in deep Petén. South of Sayaxché, it's near to the Pasión river . . .' The Intelligence Analyst stood by the map, pointed. '. . . The Brits had a radar trace this morning in Belize, thought it was two aircraft coming across from Honduran airspace, contour-flying, into Guatemala. That area up there is littered with strips. We've a CI at the Santa Amelia *finca*, he heard aircraft, didn't see them. Said it was a landing run. Might have been two runs. There's another strip about five miles south and east . . .'

'Worth taking a look.' The Country Attaché eased his chair straight.

The Chemist said, 'It's shit awful country up there, would be a good place for them.'

'Should go up there, stooge around a bit, get to know it better.'

The Treasurer said, 'We pay that creep at Santa Amelia too much, way too much. Be glad to check the credentials. If a plane's not been in, then he's off the roll.'

'Yeah? Too many reckon us a meal ticket ... Can you get us up there, Tom?'

Tom said, 'No problem. It's about a hundred there. I've got a 250-mile capacity, can always put down on the way home ...'

The Intelligence Analyst would fly, and the Treasurer, and the major on liaison from SouthCom. Two bad nights in the apartment allocated him in the embassy compound because he had thought he'd screwed, knew he'd screwed up, at the American Club.

'And, I'm going to ask Arturo to ride with you ...'

There was a smile on the Country Attaché's face, driven snow.

'I won't be inviting him to bring a battalion along, just himself, we get to see that way how he shapes ...'

And the Country Attaché was clearing his desk and pleading a meeting with the Customs Attaché, dismissing them.

They were outside in the corridor.

The Country Attaché locked his door. He called after them as they filed back into the open-plan office where they worked from.

'Oh, Tom ... a moment if you don't mind ... What happened, I've forgotten it. Believe me, by Christ, I'll remember it if you step off line again. Have a good day.'

Tom Schultz would drive out to the military wing of the airport, and he would spend the rest of the day and half of the evening working on the Huey bird. He would be working late. He had already made the excuses, worked himself clear of the invitation. A barbecue in the yard behind the Chemist's home. The little women and the little kids that camp-followed the DEA men, and it had been the intention that the slightly built serious girl from the commercial section would come to be paired off with the single guy new in town. He'd met her once, been introduced, and he'd reckoned she seemed bright company . . . Perhaps the girl from the commercial section hadn't wanted to be sidelined to a flier with the right half of his face burned off and scraped away. The invitation had just been let slip, and it was what he was familiar with. They could eat the Texas steaks and drink the Budweiser tins and chuck the softball round, and he would work at the Huey bird into the night. He would check each last rivet, fuel feed pipe, control switch, foot pedal, navigation light, filter . . . Too right . . . All of the rest of them in the open-plan office would have known he had been called back, warned.

They covered two miles that first day, and a half of that had been on the wild boar's track.

Gord took the first sentry watch.

He sat hunched with his knees against his chest and with the rifle on his lap. They were clean gone, the rest of them, asleep. The light hadn't slipped, and they were gone. He wondered what it was like, Guatemala City, at the Palacio Nacional. Wondering, and trying to stay awake because it was his sentry watch.

If it had been a mistake then it was too bloody late to be worrying about it.

He heard the noise of their dead sleeping and tried to swat the mosquitoes from his face.

# 5

Gord had organized them.

They had made the camp for the night in deep jungle, and it was only his wristwatch that could tell him that the sun would now be climbing beyond the canopy of the triple layers of the trees. At one place, ahead of them, between the trunks of the trees and through the vine trellis, he could see a single light shard cutting down where a tree had died. That was ahead of them. Where they had made the camp there was a green-washed gloom. He had been woken when the creatures of the jungle had responded to the first show of the sun, and with it had come the cacophony of noise. He had been driven from his sleep by the call of the birds and the screech of the parrots and the chatter cry of the monkeys. The mosquitoes played at his wrists and his neck and his face, coming noisily to attack him from the droning mass that was always inches beyond the reach of his flailing hand. Around him was the smell of rotting vegetation. He had taken control, natural to him, and wanted to believe that he alone had the authority and would be heard.

He had his own supplies that would last him for one month, his own tablets and pills and ointments, not for sharing. If he shared them they would last for three days . . . They had not been suggestions, they had been orders . . .

Jorge was left to pore over the map, to plot the route forward. Gord had given his lecture and had Groucho translate it on for Zeppo and Harpo, and had Vee interpret it for Eff and Zed. The lecture was on personal hygiene, and personal security.

Jorge had the map spread out over the jungle floor and manoeuvred the compass between the crossing ant columns.

He had lectured on the principal danger of mosquitoes, of malaria and dengue fever, and of the worm laid under the skin by the biting mosquitoes. The three Indians had been sent to forage around the camp, disappeared into the jungle, for wild garlic. They were bubbling, Eff and Vee and Zed, because after the exile years they could scent the country that was their own. Gord thought it was as infectious as the damn mosquitoes, their enthusiasm.

He could see the sweat running on the body of Zeppo. His shirt was stained down to the stomach bulge with the sweat damp. He breathed hard. The job of Zeppo was to clear up the camp. He was to stow the sleeping bags, load each pack, clear the ground of every piece of litter, and, last before they moved out, Zeppo had been told to scatter dead leaves, small wood twigs over the camp site. At the edge of the clearing Harpo swatted at the insect flight and leaned on the short-handled collapsible entrenching tool. The digging of the hole had already exhausted him, the big man who was flab and who tried to wipe away with his sleeve the sweat streams on the wide baldness of his scalp. The work for Harpo was to dig the hole for the litter to be buried in, and then to dig another hole, deeper, for the latrine. Their eyes met, Gord's and Harpo's, over the width of the clearing, Gord challenging him and Harpo caving and hating.

The task for Groucho was to make ready the meal, and to draw up a ration list, and to find water from tree pockets. Smaller and slighter than Zeppo and Harpo and grinning often so that the steel on his teeth showed, and suffering less.

If he didn't push Zeppo and Harpo and Groucho, then they would walk over him.

They were eight.

They had nine AK-47 rifles, there were sixty rounds of 7.62mm ammunition for each rifle. They had three Makarov pistols, eighteen rounds for each pistol. They had twelve pounds of military explosive and fifteen detonators. They had two RPG-7 rocket launchers and nine warheads. They had one machine gun and 800 rounds of belt-fed ammunition . . . Bloody brilliant. The noise of the explosions of munitions detonating in the fire of Whisky Alpha mocked him. It was bloody pathetic . . . They had the TPO-50 flame thrower with each of the three canisters loaded and at pressure.

There was the scrape of a match.

Gord looked up.

Harpo had the cigarette in his mouth and his hands cupped to protect the flame.

Gord called quietly, 'I told you, no cigarettes.'

Harpo stared back at him. The hands moved to the cigarette. A small smoke wisp.

Gord said, 'Put it out.'

Harpo held the spade loosely and dragged hard on the cigarette. The smoke played in front of Harpo's face.

Gord pushed himself up. He crossed the clearing. The hand of Harpo tightened on the stock of the spade. Fast, sudden, Gord had the collar of Harpo's shirt in his right fist and he had snatched the cigarette away with his left hand. Gord stamped on the cigarette and then he shook the bulk of Harpo's body, like he was a difficult dog.

'I have told you that you don't smoke cigarettes. If I tell you then you don't . . .' Gord didn't stop for Groucho's translation. '. . . You don't smoke because down here the smell of tobacco will hang for a week.'

He let the collar of Harpo slump free. He swung away from him.

When the Indians returned Gord told them all to peel the garlic bulbs and to chew them. He tried to make a joke of it, that they'd all stink, but that the garlic would keep away the mosquitoes. He supervised the loading up after they had breakfasted on Groucho's cold mess of Meals Ready to Eat, Moscow style, and after they had all squatted over the latrine pit.

Jorge leading, and the Indians carrying more weight than was fair, and Harpo loathing him and Zeppo despising him and Groucho avoiding him, they moved out of the clearing. Gord allowed them to get clear then checked the ground and the filled holes and cursed when he saw that the squashed cigarette butt was still visible in the stamped dirt. It was Groucho who disappointed him, not the fat bastard and not the bald bastard, but it had been Groucho who had come to the hotel room and pleaded, little smarm talk Groucho . . . He spent time on the site before he was satisfied.

He followed them, drawn closer to them by the slow squeal of the wheels of the flame thrower's cart.

FROM: Strathclyde police HQ, Glasgow.
To: Special Branch, Metropolitan Police, London.
REF: A/0200/79y/4/blj.
ATTENTION: Aliens Section.

See attached ex Fort William. Further to Gordon Benjamin BROWN – He is ICI male, 5´10, prop build, hair colour light brown (style short), tanned complexion, eye colour grey blue, only DM is 1/2 inch scar lower chin.
   No interest here.
   Where is Guatemala, query. Do we care, query.
   Have fun.
   End.

The pilot lay on the wet towel on the beach sand. The water of the rising tide played amongst his toes. He slept away the exhaustion of the flight from his home base to the jungle strip in Guatemala, and back. He slept in the warming sun because he had taken to the limit his resources of strength, exhausted them in bringing home Echo Foxtrot. He had nursed her back. He had flown wave top at reduced speed to conserve fuel. Out in the depths of the Cayman Trench were the seats of the Antonov Colt that had been wrested out by the navigator, and the lavatory unit that had been wrenched clear with a tool kit jemmy, and the overhead racks that had been taken down with a screwdriver. He had brought Echo Foxtrot home as bare shell.

He had spent the late afternoon and the early evening with the maintenance men of the ground crew and the first part of the night with the wife of the pilot of Whisky Alpha and the last of the night with the family of the lost navigator.

The pilot was alone on the beach beyond the base perimeter wire. The point on the beach was close to the SAM missile battery, always manned, always facing towards the Florida land mass beyond the horizon. The men on the missile battery had watched him come in the late afternoon, barely clearing the fence, barely reaching the tarmac of the runway. It was spoken of, all around the base, where he had been, what he had achieved.

He slept. He dreamed while the sea trickled at his ankles. In his mind was the face and the body and the grip of the Englishman who had ridden in the cockpit the last miles before the touch-down in the Petén.

He had told his base commander, 'It was madness. They had nothing. They have gone to be killed . . .'

From: Aliens Sect., SB, Met Pol, London.
To: Security Service, Gordon St, London.
Ref: A/1100/79y/4/bli/ark(3).
Attention: Central America Desk.

See attached ex Fort William and ex Strathclyde. Flash inquiry indicates BROWN, Gordon Benjamin, UK passport C796217, DOI 03.5.76, ex Heathrow for Madrid.

Three Guatemalan citizens travelling on Cuban documents on same flight.

Illegal to stage revolution in Guatemala, query. Know location of Guatemala, query. Affirmative, your baby, query.

End.

He had assumed it would be their attempt to dominate him from the start of a relationship.

Colonel Arturo was dominated, willingly, by no man.

He had made a show.

He wore his best field uniform, the camouflage combat tunic and trousers that he would have worn for the Army Day parade on the Campo de Marte, the uniform of the Kaibiles, with the flash on the upper arms of the tunic of the bayonet and the fire. He wore his maroon beret. His boots for jungle marching were highly polished. The webbing harness over his shoulders and around his waist was pristine. There was a holstered pistol on the webbing and a water bottle and spare ammunition magazines for the Israeli-made Uzi machine gun that was slung on a strap to his hip. He sat stiffly, erect, in the forward passenger seat of the open jeep, and he waited.

Colonel Arturo had come to the corner of the military wing of La Aurora a full twenty minutes before the flier had arrived. Take-off was scheduled for 0800, the time given him in the casual, he thought patronizing, telephone call from the Country Attaché. He had seen the flier's surprise that he was already there and waiting, awkwardness that had merged to embarrassment. It was as he had planned it. He had nodded crisply to the flier, offered no other greeting, permitted the man to begin his pre-flight checks. He had noted the deep scar left by the plastic surgeons on the face of the flier. He made his point, he sat in the jeep with his escort of Kaibil troops around him.

They came at seven minutes after the given take-off time.

The big station wagon speeding across the runway, as if they believed the runway were their property, and the brakes screaming, and them spilling out.

He remembered faces, had always been good with faces. There was the one who went under the title of Intelligence Analyst, quiet and superior. The one who was called the Treasurer, spectacles and austere, like the bank man who had his account in Florida. The one who was the Liaison Officer down from Southern Command, who seemed to believe that an American infantry officer was a favoured creature. The flier went to them, pointed to his watch.

He let them come to him.

They were dressed in old fatigues. Their caps were DEA, set clumsily. The Treasurer and the Intelligence Analyst had not shaved. They carried Colt carbines. He thought that they took enjoyment from playing at soldiers, dressing up as military men. He heard the grovelled apologies. Something about the traffic coming south out of the city. He thought that they hated to apologize to anyone, and in particular to a Guatemalan officer.

Colonel Arturo smiled with sweetness. 'Well, if you are ready, gentlemen . . . ?'

He walked to the helicopter. He knew the Huey UH-1H. The air force of Guatemala had five of the UH-1H machines, difficult to maintain now after the ban on all military supplies imposed by the Washington liberals for so-called human rights violations, just shit. They banned the supplies for old Guatemalan Hueys, and rippled enough muscle to *demand* the right to station their own helicopters and DEA personnel on the sovereign territory of Guatemala. He felt the small surge to his anger . . . They came behind him. At the hatch of the helicopter he asked to see the flight plan. He asked to be told the schedule.

He made the last point. He checked his pistol and his Uzi, confirmed they were unloaded and then looked into the faces of the flier and the Intelligence Analyst and the Treasurer and the Liaison, challenged them.

'I'm sorry, it is a rule of the Guatemalan armed forces that firearms must always be checked before they are taken onto a helicopter or fixed wing. I am sorry if that is not the procedure of the Americans . . .'

They cleared their weapons. He would not be dominated.

FROM: Security Service, London.
To: Ministry of Defence, Intelligence, London.
REF: BREN/Rm129B/CentAm/932.
ATTENTION: Personnel.


See attached. Backgrounder required soonest on BROWN, Gordon Benjamin.
    Brennard G.
    End.

They were away from the part of the graveyard where the tall stones stood shoulder to shoulder in parade, the crosses and Virgins of remembrance. The burial plot for the disappeared son of a street salesman was rough ground at the far edge of the graveyard, where waist-high weeds had been cleared. Alex shaded her eyes. The moisture was in the armpit of her best T-shirt, and streams of perspiration ran to the small of her back and were held at the tightness of the waist of the skirt. Before she had come to Guatemala she had only attended the funerals of her grandparents; her knowledge of funerals was just about all from Guatemala. The priest talked fast. Only a small attendance. If the student had died in a road accident, if illness had taken him, then the whole street in which he had lived would have come for the funeral. He had died after being seized, tortured, by the Death Squads, and few had the courage to be there. She thought the priest gabbled the service; only the strongest call of duty had beaten his fear of consequences.

The man beside her, tired, middle-aged, smelled of sweat. She was in the third row back from the graveside and the first earth had been thrown to rattle down onto the box of cheap wood. The man beside her wore a white shirt and a good tie, and a suit that showed the creases of life in a wardrobe, and he mopped at his high forehead with his handkerchief. The father of the disappeared student was supported by his wife and his daughter. Alex thought the strength of the mother was magnificent, humbling. The man beside her, several times, swore under his breath, and his face was screwed in sharp anger. The wife and the daughter of the disappeared led the father from the graveside, and the priest was hurrying away.

The gravediggers ladled the earth into the pit with long-handled spades.

'How did you know him?'

'I taught him, I taught him the seditious subject of *mathematics*. I also told him that he was stupid to go to demonstrations, naïve to think that because a civilian sits in the Palacio Nacional anything is different in Guatemala. He was only a boy who held banners and ran from the police when they fired the gas, and shouted. He was no threat to them ... You are from the Peace Brigades, yes? You are the people who preach the non-violence? I tell you, the non-violence is rubbish. Nothing will change in Guatemala without violence. They will have to be burned out, the generals and the colonels and the men of the Death Squads ... My wife this morning will be crying in fear in our house because I have made the slight and insignificant gesture of going to my student's funeral. My dear young lady with the fine intentions, it would be difficult for you to understand the fear in which we live.'

Alex said simply, 'There is no-one to burn them out.'

He made a reply. She did not hear his words. A helicopter went low overhead. It seemed to tilt in its flight as if to give the crew and passengers a better view of a dispersing crowd in a city graveyard. She followed the flight of the helicopter, watched it soar and head away for the north.

It was what she believed, there was no alternative to the turned cheek.

He was gone from her side.

She walked back to the Land Rover.

She saw the set teeth of her dog.

There was a plain envelope tucked under one of the wind-screen wipers. She snatched it, crumpled it, threw it onto the floor in front of the passenger seat.

Down the road was the car with the smoked-glass windows and the idling engine.

FROM: Security Service, London.
TO: Secret Intelligence Service, London.
REF: BREN/Rm129B/CentAm/934.
ATTENTION: Central America Desk.

See attached. Require soonest assessment of stability of current Guatemala regime. What possibility insurrection?

What opposition group could BROWN, Gordon Benjamin, be recruited to? What Cuban involvement?

Brennard G.

End.

The helicopter crossed above them. Vee was further ahead and Zed was further behind, but the rest of them were gathered close and squatting and sitting and flopped, rest halt, near to the wide root base of a ceiba tree. The butterflies were around them, but there were fewer mosquitoes, the bastards would be back by the end of the afternoon and Gord had seen Zeppo scratch at his neck and ankles ... He had not spoken through the morning, at any of the rest halts, to Zeppo nor to Harpo. He had watched and he had learned. Jorge spoke to them, cudgelled them and encouraged them, and won grudged response. Jorge had the way with them ... The helicopter, he thought, would have been at an altitude of little more than a thousand feet but the tree canopy could have muffled the beat of the rotors, it might have been higher. The noise of the engine grew. All of their eyes, useless, were turned to the wigwam frame of the stacked rifles. The noise of an engine was a threat, recognized by all of them. Groucho's tongue slipped to his lips, nervously moistening them. Zeppo was peering up into the leaf ceiling of the trees. The helicopter was directly over them. Harpo clenched, unclenched, his fists. The power of the engine beat down through the canopy. Eff had giggled and made a play with his hands of shooting upwards. Jorge grinned, a flash of teeth. The helicopter was moving away. Their world was the jungle and the tightness of trees and vegetation and vines, and it was the world of the mosquito swarms, and it was the world of the bright fluttering butterflies. And outside their world was the fighting ...

Gord pushed himself up.

He said it grimly, 'Time we were moving.'

He stood and wriggled the straps of his pack over his shoulders. He could watch and he could learn. Jorge pulled Zeppo up and laughed, and then Jorge lifted up Harpo's pack and helped him to take the weight of it. He saw the way that Groucho gazed on Jorge, rank admiration. Gord felt almost a jealousy. Bloody Jorge, pretty boy, doing the rounds of hearts and minds, winning friends and influencing people, while all the won friends and influenced people detested the pompous bully that was Gordon Benjamin Brown. His turn for the pretty boy's attention.

'All right, Gord?'

'Fine . . .'

'You are a bit afraid?' said quiet, private.

'I am not afraid,' Gord hissed.

Jorge said, 'Then you are alone, and lucky, we are all afraid of the helicopter. Perhaps it was with tourists, or with oil men, or with a rancher, or perhaps it was a military helicopter. We don't know, so we are all afraid – all but you. You should be a very happy man. Gord, that you are not afraid . . .'

He was squashed. Gord's creed of leadership dictated that the front runner must never show weakness nor demonstrate hesitation. The young man fragmented the concrete of the creed. Gord thought the more of him. It was the humanity that had captured him, but then he knew sweet damn all about humanity.

'We have to make ground,' Gord said.

He could no longer hear the helicopter, only the creaking cart wheels of the flame thrower.

FROM: BREN, Rm129B.
To: HOBBES, Hispanic Affairs Desk. Rm93A.

Meeting, please, at your convenience.
Thanks,
Brennard G.
End.

They ran courses on most projections at Quantico, the Virginia training base. But they hadn't allocated lecture time on how to confuse the ass off a ranking Guatemalan field officer. The guy smirked, like the plan was baby games, like they'd telegraphed him the identity of their Confidential Informant.

A fast walk round the buildings of the *finca*, and the cattle stockades, and the fodder barns and the tractor sheds, and then the Intelligence Analyst and the Treasurer had disappeared, and the *caporal*, the work overseer who had been walking with them and hanging behind the manager, he'd gone as well. What Tom saw was the smart satisfaction smile of the colonel. They'd taken tea in the manager's office, and sandwiches, and just about finished the meal when the Intelligence Analyst and the Treasurer had shown again.

'There's another strip, south-east, I'd like to see that, Tom . . .'

'No problem.'

Tom shrugged his agreement to the Intelligence Analyst. It was done like he was being asked a favour, to take them to the next strip. But he was just the ferry man. He was the flier and he provided the lifts, and his bird was the workhorse. He could see the frustration of the Intelligence Analyst, fidgeting, smoking, and not willing to believe the Confidential Informant, the *caporal*, until the second strip had been checked out.

Tom had had his supper in the embassy dining hall the previous night with the Treasurer. The Treasurer had said this was the most fucking corrupt country he'd served in, worse than Peru, made the Brazilians seem like altar kids. The Treasurer had said that he hadn't yet met a Guatemalan that he trusted. The Treasurer sat now boot-faced, like it was dollars going down the deep drain.

They'd all taken their weapons when Tom Schultz had parked the bird, and they all checked them before they boarded again.

He took her up carefully.

The colonel was beside him, but the guys behind were quiet. It was shaping into a bad day . . . They didn't look in the DEA, the recruiters, for men and women who thought they were on crusade when they were off narcotics-hunting. Crusaders were unstable and would have been weeded out in the Total Background checks. They had their commitment, and bad days were not welcome . . . He flew low. There was cloud gathering with a poor ceiling. He stayed under the cloud the few miles to the strip that was south-east of the *finca*.

It was clear from the air.

It was like a kid had used a brown crayon marker on the green of the landing strip. There were the two sets of brown tramlines. He saw the run of the landing wheels and the run of the lift-off wheels . . . The colonel banged his arm and the bird bucked because the blow shook his hand on the cyclic control stick . . . Asshole . . . Mad, he turned . . . Shitface . . . The colonel was pointing down. Tom saw it.

Beyond the end of the strip was a black gouged hole in the tree line.

He was at the hover. He was shouting. He was gesturing for the guys behind. He could feel their weight craning forward against his shoulders.

Tom brought her down. First touch of the skids and the colonel was unbuckled, jumping and running.

He shut the engine. The Treasurer was left to watch the Huey.

He tramped through the long grass and the butterflies played in flight near him and he went with the Intelligence Analyst and the Liaison the rest of the length of the strip. They walked between the two lengths of wheel tracks where an aircraft had landed and where it had been on a take-off run. It had been a heavy aircraft but with good Short Take-Off and Landing capability. It had to have been good STOL because of the length of the strip. By the edge of the strip they found where grass had been flattened by trampling boots. They went into the trees.

Before they were through the trees, Tom could smell the bodies. He had smelled the burned flesh, the scarred flesh, in the Gulf, but that wasn't what he was remembering now. His father had taken him to a pig roast once, and an idiot had made a mistake with an unmarked canister and poured gasoline onto the carcass rather than cooking oil. It was that smell. He had his handkerchief to his nose. They came into the blackened cleared space. Near to the fuselage, close to the port side where the wing stumps had been sheared off, was the shallow grave. He reckoned it had been dug only a foot and a half deep, probably in panic, probably without ceremony. There were heaps of earth and dead scorched grass beside the grave and he thought that animals had dug at it. The Intelligence Analyst gagged, was fighting to hold his vomit. He walked round the wreck of the aircraft. The upper and lower starboard wings had been taken off, severed, the same as on the port side. He muttered something, to himself, that was almost a prayer. A pilot trying to hold his lady up in the air over the last line of the tops, and failing. The same prayer that he had yelled once, when the power was going in the bird, when the fire was spreading.

Away from the fuselage, at the extreme of the cleared area, the colonel watched over three squatting men. The colonel covered the men with his machine gun. The men were Indians. On the acclimatization course, out in the California sunshine at San Diego, he had learned about the Guatemalan Indians. Like it was a uniform they wore check shirts and jeans and had wide straw hats. He saw that the hand of one of them, maybe the youngest, was taken off at the wrist.

He went to the fuselage, he squinted to peer into the darkness and he slipped his glasses up onto the crown of his head.

The colonel called from behind him, 'One of them tried to handle the cargo, lost his hand for it.'

Seconds ticking. Acclimatizing. Seeing more. The Intelligence Analyst was close, trying to share. Tom pointed to the skeleton shapes of the machine guns, and to the outlines of the rocket launchers. He pointed to the peppered holes in the fuselage, where bullets had exploded. He pointed to the rifles that had been in canvas bags of which only the straps remained.

He stepped back.

Tom said, 'It was an Antonov, An-2, we call it Colt. It was stacked with war material. One aircraft made it in, and the other was short. I wouldn't have thought it's narcotics-related, looks to be insurgency stuff . . .'

He looked across at the colonel. The colonel knew the same answers.

The Liaison queried, 'Who's bringing that sort of shit in?'

'Ask him.'

The colonel gave no response to the Liaison. With his boot the colonel drove the Indians to their feet. He made them walk ahead of him back to the helicopter. It had been a place of death and none of them, not Tom nor the Intelligence Analyst nor the Liaison, had the stomach for the familiarization swan-round that had been planned. At the helicopter the Liaison bandaged the wound of the youngest Indian. Tom thought that the colonel didn't seem to care whether the wound was sanitized and covered with a field dressing.

They were all subdued, all had had the guts taken out of them, and the smell of the flesh seemed to cling to their fatigues.

The colonel took the rear seats in the bird, and he was talking hard at the Indians, using a dialect that hadn't been taught at San Diego, and he was winning nothing. The Liaison took the seat left side of Tom, and the Intelligence Analyst and the Treasurer were in the seats between Tom and the colonel . . .

The starter whined, the rotors began lazily to turn, the turbine roared, power growing, nose lifting . . . He had been told when he had come to Guatemala City that the guerrilla war was finished, gone. That was all the chat in the embassy dining room from the Liaison and from the spooks and from the Defence Attaché's staff. They all said that the fighting was history, that the guerrillas were fucked. Heh, then someone hadn't been told.

He could fly the Huey in his sleep.

The concentration was second nature. His mind flitted. Inside the flying helmet he was alone, cut off. Heh, some poor bastards down there had been waiting for a war material shipment, and perhaps had lifted something off the successful flight, and perhaps had wept and kicked and screamed at seeing a load go down . . .

There was the motion behind him.

There was a shoulder belting into his back.

For Christ's sake . . .

Tom turned, strained on his harness to see behind him.

Heh, cut the fucking . . .

He saw the colonel. The colonel stared straight back towards Tom. The two older Indians were cowered back in their seats away from the colonel. The seat next to the open hatch was empty, the harness straps hung loose. He heaved the cyclic stick over, banked the bird.

It was done fast enough. Tom saw the spreadeagled body, falling and drifting towards the green of the tree carpet.

Throwing the voice switch. 'What the fucking hell happened?'

The Treasurer in his ear, booming. 'He fell, Arturo says he fell.'

'But . . .'

'It's what Arturo says. He fell.'

He took the bird back to Guatemala City.

'I think that to take it any further is simply to waste our time.'

He was Gary Brennard, fast-stream graduate intake into Five, and he liked to be known as Bren. Since his return from Belfast he had risen at speed in the Security Service ranks, and he could thank the new witch's broom that swept hard from the top-floor office for that. Wilkins retired, Carthew and Foster invited to look elsewhere for employment, Charles and Archie and Bill jumping before they were pushed, many others that he hadn't known cleared out to shape the leaner Five. A new style that required fresh personnel was the message from the Director General.

He had the paper laid out on Hobbes' desk. The messages from Fort William and from Glasgow and from Metropolitan Police (Special Branch) were displayed, and the replies from MOD Intelligence (Personnel) and SIS (Central America Desk).

'Your opinion?'

'Just another of these covert jerks with a chip on his shoulder the size of an omnibus. *Mr* Brown was drummed out of Special Forces after going native in the Gulf. There was something about a medal commendation down there but that was wisely withdrawn. He was only a captain, one more of them who believed he was God's gift to soldiering. Done two tours in Northern Ireland, and my experience is that the Province gives Hereford people a hugely inflated sense of their importance. A decided question mark over a shooting on his first tour, observation on an arms cache, but he slipped through the inquiry net, as they always do, that crowd. Served in Germany before reunification. Been an instructor, you know, all of that running up mountains for the salvation of the soul. It is the usual career pattern before he went down to the Gulf and made a total fool of himself. Unmarried. Seems to me to be rather an inadequate personality . . . Anyway, a Guatemalan connection is just ludicrous. The conflict is finished there, has been for at least three years. The opposition to the legal government has been whipped. Safe to assume he's ripping off some peasants, giving them crap and lining his pocket. Forget it.'

'Your recommendation?'

Bren took out his Parker biro, his present to himself after this last promotion to the recently created Central America Desk. Over each sheet of paper laid out in front of Hobbes he wrote in bold fist, No Further Action. 'Just thought I'd check with you.'

Hobbes smiled. 'And be so kind to initial it, there's a good fellow.'

He did that. Bren wrote his initials on each sheet of paper that would now be consigned to Library under No Further Action. He knew the type that was BROWN, Gordon Benjamin, and reckoned them stale piss.

Gord was at the back of the group, against the trees that ringed the clearing.

A grim day finishing.

It was, in truth, the start of the mission, and he knew it as they all knew it, but he hung back.

For the last time Jorge lectured Eff and Vee and Zed, and Zeppo and Harpo and Groucho were close with him and with the Indians, all of them huddled together. Three hours after the helicopter had crossed back over them. He had hoped there would not be a helicopter or a fixed wing, not so soon after the landing, not before the fast jungle growth had the chance to grow and twine over the Antonov wreckage. He didn't understand the soft talk of Jorge, nor the blunt interjections of Harpo, but he saw the way that Groucho slapped Eff's back as if he were a child for encouraging. Zeppo grinned at the three Indians, winked at them, and held Zed's hand as if to strengthen him. It was the beginning of the mission.

The first village, the first settlement they could find, and their task was to slip inside a village or a settlement and avoid the Civil Patrollers and spread the secret word that Rodolfo Jorge, son of Ramírez of Acul, was again in Guatemala and looking for men. It was the beginning of the mission. Without men coming voluntarily to join them, they were dead.

He snatched at a mosquito. The clap of his hand was fast enough. He saw the blood smear on his palm.

It would be dusk soon above the tree canopy.

The Indians were gone.

They went in silence.

Within seconds their footfall was lost.

Gord sat hunched on the edge of the clearing. It was Zeppo for the first sentry watch, and Harpo to follow him, and then Harpo to wake Gord. He had time for drifting thoughts. Zeppo was back down the trail they had made in the approach to the clearing. There were the murmur voices of Harpo and Groucho and Jorge. They were home.

He sat beside the flame thrower and his fingers touched at the cart and the tubes and the pipes and wires that were linked. A light rain had started, a steady beat far above, and the drips falling sporadically on his head and his neck and his shoulders and his knees. Drifting thoughts that tried to identify a place as his home . . . if there had been a home then he would not have been hunched and quiet on the ant trails of the Petén jungle. Had to be a home . . . Home had been a suburb street and a semi-detached house that was both pebbledash and mock Tudor where his father came back to when the courts weren't sitting and when the detectives no longer wanted to drink . . . Home had been at the Lines in Hereford where he had a room and a mess for eating and socializing, and a firing range, and a shower house for after the long runs on the Brecons . . . Home had been the flat of a girl in London's Battersea, near the river, where he had once been given floor space, where there was an answerphone that he had learned to talk with, where a last letter from him had been sent and then returned as Not Known At This Address . . . Home had been the bar of a hotel on a sea loch near to the mountain of Sidhean Mor where the eagles flew . . .

There was no home.

Around him was what he possessed. His clothes and his boots, his pack and what it held, the AK-47 rifle and three magazines loaded, and the flame thrower slung on the cart. His fingers ran on the lines of the cart on the metal frame. He was not ready for sleep. He thought that none of them would sleep well that night, because Eff and Vee and Zed had gone and it was the start of the mission. He could find his way, without sight, around his pack and he took the plastic soap box from near the bottom, recognized it by touch. He threaded a needle with the strong cotton that he kept in the soap box. He was sewing together the worst of the thorn rips in the sleeves of his jungle shirt.

Jorge sat beside him. 'You don't wish to sleep?'

Gord said roughly, 'If I leave the tears in the shirt then the mosquitoes have more scope to chew me.'

'It is a big time for us. You know that, Gord?'

'I know that.'

'I considered going myself, but I don't have the language for the Petén.'

'It'll come, your time.'

'I don't know what is the power of my name, and my father's name.'

'You have to wait, we all have to wait . . . Was there a manual?'

'What?'

Gord asked it like he was shamed. 'Was there a manual for the flame thrower?'

The chuckle, the laughter, Jorge's mirth. 'You demand it, you *require* it, and you don't know how it does . . .'

'I don't bloody know how it works.'

'I love you, Mr Brown – So correct. So severe. So logical. You are the professional man. The professional man demands, *requires* a flame thrower. We find a flame thrower. We take the flame thrower into the middle of the Petén jungle. All the time it takes two men to move the flame thrower – and you do not know how it works.'

'It's not necessary to tell the bloody world . . .'

'It is necessary to be told you are human. God bless you, Mr Brown. You ask the engineer, when he finishes the watch . . .'

Gord heard again the chuckle. He had ripped the cigarette from Zeppo's mouth. He would sidle to Zeppo. He would cringe. He would *request* help.

'Yes.'

'Have you killed, Gord?'

'Yes.'

'Because you were ordered to?'

'Yes.'

'I cannot order you. Would you kill for me, for us?'

'Yes.'

'Why?'

He looked into the clear sallow skin below the light beard fluff of Jorge's face, and into the depth and boldness of his eyes. He saw the humility. The spell wove around him, but damned if he'd tell him . . .

'Because where I have put myself it will be my life or their lives, and for me my life is worth killing for.'

He heard Zeppo come back and growl down at Harpo, and he heard Harpo shuffle away and swear when the thorns caught his clothes. He smacked at the mosquitoes. The rainwater dribbled down his face. He wanted to sleep before his turn on the watch.

# 6

A wall of whitewashed concrete surrounded the villa. The wall and the sheet-metal gates were too high for a pedestrian on the broken street pavement to see anything of the building other than the angle of the tiled roof. All of the villas in the street on the west side of the capital city had their privacy ensured by the height of the walls and the gates. Few cars, few visitors came to the villa in the hours of daylight. To the right of the villa lived an agrarian consultant, employed by the sugar growers on the Pacific seashore. To the left was the home of a construction-materials supplier who specialized in contracts for the building of the Development Poles of the New Model villages in the interior. Behind the villa, shielded by the wall and evergreen trees, was the residence of a retired officer of the Guatemalan navy. None of them, not the consultant nor the supplier nor the retired officer, would have admitted to knowing anything of the occupants of the villa.

Behind the gates, a gardener splashed water from a hose haphazardly over the colour of the geranium beds. On the porch patio, a man lounged on a chair and read the day's edition of *La Prensa Libre* and gazed at the photographs of the girls of elite society. Inside the front hall, a man had thrown back the floor mats and used a rush broom to sweep the dirt towards the front door and listened to Latin rock on Radio Conga, 99.7FM.

The gardener and the man sitting and the man who swept the floor all heard the scream.

The scream was muffled, carried from the basement of the villa and through the closed door at the bottom of the basement steps and through the closed door at the top of the steps and

105

down the corridor that led to the kitchen and into the hallway. Colonel Arturo sweated, not because he felt guilt at the crying scream, but because the closed doors and the lack of ventilation built the heat in the basement. There was a body close to his feet where he leaned against the wall, a mess of rag clothes that were stained and limbs that lay awkwardly. There was breath still in the body, spurting and occasional. He watched the work of the young man whom he knew as Benedicto. It was the fourth time in that session that Benedicto had hooded the second Indian who lay full length on the floor. They had still not learned what they needed to know. Each time the hood was removed from the head of the Indian the question was asked, and each time they faced the dumb silence, and when they pulled back the hair to lift the head and cover it again with the hood then there was the scream.

There had been three, one injured. The one who was injured was now a lost cadaver in the tree canopy of the forest of the foot-hills between the Cuchumatanes mountains and the Petén jungle.

There had been two, but the one who now lay against the wall was beyond further questioning.

The remaining creature was of *importance* to Colonel Arturo. He had the report from the troops lifted in the previous after-noon to the site of a crashed aircraft. The wings of the aircraft, severed and clear of the fire, had been examined. Recent paint-work had been scraped off but still there had been no insignia marks overpainted. It was important to Colonel Arturo to have the testimony of the Indians who had witnessed the landing then gone to scavenge the aircraft's wreckage. He had assumed that the sight of a man spiralling down from the helicopter would have encouraged the survivors to talk of what they had seen, but he was incorrect in his assessment. They called the hood the *capucha*. The wrists of the Indian who lay in the centre of the basement floor were bound behind his back. His ankles were trussed. When the hood of latex rubber was over the head of the Indian then the young man, Benedicto, tightened a length of string around the neck of the hood and reduced the air supply, and he stamped onto the back of the Indian to make his lungs heave for oxygen that was not available. When the young man, Benedicto, believed that the Indian was losing consciousness then he loosened the string at the neck of the hood and drew it clear and turned the Indian's head and splashed water from a bucket onto the Indian's face. When the Indian had recovered, when he could breathe again, then the *capucha* was used the next time. If Colonel Arturo were to know who had landed, what they had taken from the aircraft that had successfully touched down, then the Indian on the floor and with his mouth bubbling in the water pools from the bucket must live.

A dribble seeped from between the lips of the Indian beside the wall.

There was a meeting that he was late for.

'You understand the importance . . . ?'

'Of course.'

'The information is . . .'

A careless smile from the young man called Benedicto. 'You will have what you need to know, my promise.'

The hood was off. The water had been splashed onto the coarse pallor of the Indian's face. The young man knelt in the water and whispered the question into the ear of the Indian. Colonel Arturo went out through the basement door and closed it after him. He climbed the steps and closed after him the door in the corridor that led to the kitchen. He heard the scream as he passed the man who swept the hall floor, and he heard the scream again as he stepped out into the sunlight of the porch patio where a guard swung his chair upright and stood in respect, and he heard the scream the last time as he walked across the tarmac to his car and stepped over the hose used by a gardener for his watering.

There had been two days in which he could have gone to Zeppo, but Zeppo had found the honeycomb in a tree. The big man with the gut hanging across the trouser support of his belt had found the honeycomb in the crook of a tree.

Gord could have told him. Gord should have told him.

. . . Zeppo had lain two days in the blanket that was his bedding, wrapped around with a groundsheet, with the rain lightly dripping on him while his stomach bellowed in diarrhoea. He had lain for the two days, unmoving and moaning, except for the times when he found the strength to dive for the trees round the clearing where Groucho had dug the deep pit only for Zeppo's use.

Gord could have told him that a honeycomb was the certain way to the runs and the cramps, should have told him.

Two days after he had come clean to Jorge that he did not know how to operate the TPO-50 flame thrower, after two days of sitting, brooding in the camp, Gord took three precious pills from his store.

He crossed the clearing.

He left his own side of the clearing, his stores packed neat and precise in his backpack that rested against the wheel of the cart, for the side where Zeppo and Harpo and Groucho had parked themselves. He had thought that Jorge would apply the ointment, work the reconciliation, and Jorge had turned his face from the problem, as if it was something men should be big enough to sort for themselves. Jorge was gone from the camp, had taken food for a day, had gone ahead.

They watched him cross the clearing. Zeppo was sitting up, Harpo was crouched beside him, Groucho was opening a tin of Meals Ready to Eat.

There was the growl rumble of Zeppo's stomach.

The ants moved in column across Zeppo's legs, scurrying on the groundsheet that blocked their appointed route. He hadn't seen the monkeys that were above them but could hear them tossing in the high branches. Bright lawn-green flies swarmed around the stinking hulk of Zeppo. He brought the pills because they were marooned while the diarrhoea was with Zeppo, and in the morning they would have to move forward and they could not travel with a passenger and they could not leave a man behind and alone. He could have, and should have, told Zeppo not to eat the honeycomb. They watched him.

He squatted on his haunches beside Zeppo. He saw the paleness and tiredness of the man. He put the three pills, treble dose, on Zeppo's tongue and he washed them down with water from his own water bottle . . . They should, none of them, have come. They were all, Zeppo and Harpo and Groucho, right for a coffee shop in Havana, for a hotel bar. They were none of them, Zeppo and Harpo and Groucho, right for a march in jungle conditions. He muttered something about one of the pills stopping a river in its tracks, and three of them blocking a waterfall.

'You are an engineer. I am a soldier. I don't know about compressed pressures, valves, ignition firing. I know that the flame thrower is an exceptional weapon that will take out defended positions, more important is that it makes fear. I know the circumstances in which to use it, how to get best value from it, but I don't know how it works . . . What I want is your help . . .'

Zeppo swallowed and smiled.

'Listen, *please*, I have come here to try to help . . .'

Harpo sneered, cold.

'Listen, *please*, if we're not together then we fail . . .'

Zeppo closed his eyes, as if he was tired and wanted to rest.

'Listen, *please*, you people are the most stupid bastards I have ever tried to work with. You're out of condition, you are over-weight. You are pig stubborn . . .'

Harpo spat into the ground.

'See if I care. I don't care. I can walk away . . .'

Groucho caught at his sleeve. 'When you have given us the proof. Then . . .'

He turned. He walked back across the clearing. He kicked the wheel of the cart of the flame thrower.

An hour later Jorge came back to the camp clearing. Jorge said that a mile ahead was the road and that on the road was a block. Jorge said that he had counted seven troops manning it.

'Did you or did you not . . . ?'

It was the third time of asking. Tom hadn't known him long enough to be certain of it, but he did not reckon that the

Country Attaché liked to ask a question, wait for an answer, a third time. It should have been done the first evening and while it was hot but the first evening the Country Attaché had been gone, down to Bogotá. Bogotá was where, Tom had learned, the Country Attaché spent damn near as much time as in Guatemala City. It was where the cocaine came from, where the packages were made, where the aircraft took off, where there was the best intelligence of flights staging through his own patch.

'Was he pushed or did he fall? Did you or did you not see him pushed?'

'I strapped him in,' the Intelligence Analyst said, awkward. 'I fixed the buckle on him.'

Tom needn't have been there. He had been flying the bird. Tom need not have been in the Country Attaché's office. It was his kindness, his gesture, to the Intelligence Analyst that he had come. The Country Attaché had had a bad trip up from Bogotá, a delayed take-off and then turbulence that was fierce over the Salvador coastline. His temper said he'd been shaken, cocktail style.

'The buckles can be opened by a dumb kid, that's the way they make them. The last time I ask the damn question – did you see Arturo push him out?'

'It's the oldest interrogation ploy in the game,' the Intelligence Analyst said. 'When you have a multiple of prisoners you pitch one out of the helicopter to beef up the talk of the rest . . . He had one hand severed. He was buckled in good and tight, and he went flyabout.'

'You didn't see him pushed.'

'Right, shit, correct. I did not see him pushed . . .'

It had gone the way that Tom had thought it would go. He would have taken good odds that Arturo had played the helicopter game, what the vets in his old flying team said was standard practice in the bad, black Vietnam days. He would have bet on it and not been able to prove it. The Intelligence Analyst's head hung. Tom thought him an honourable man and a caring man, and shot to hell. It was not about 'human rights', not about campus jargon. It was about goddamn *decency*. He thought that it was about middle America, white-front-fence America, tax-paying America, flag-respecting America, trying to do the decent thing, and put down like he was a college kid with a plac-ard, and that was just not right.

Tom said, 'I'd like to add . . .'

The Country Attaché's anger blazed. 'You correct me, you tell me I'm wrong. When you're flying a helicopter then you look forward, you are not studying your passengers stowed behind you. You know sweet fuck on this, Schultz, better for all of us if you remember that . . . I am not going to the Ambassador to make fire over a matter not proved. Guys, this is a tough place, a shit country. Colonel Arturo is our liaison, and stays that way because I cannot raise hell without facts. Thank you for your time, guys, and learn to work with the asshole.'

Tom followed the Intelligence Analyst out of the Country Attaché's office.

He went to his desk. He had the lists in front of him. No more thought of coca compounds, nor of precursor chemicals, nor of the bank accounts of the narco-traffickers in the Caymans and Miami.

Big work ahead of him, high grade work.

The government's inspectors were in next week to check the inventory of DEA station, Guatemala City. As he had seen in St Louis, a government inspector dissatisfied with the inventory could break a station chief, like he was dried wood. He was on the engine spares list, held in the lock-up area out at La Aurora. A government inspector was more important than knowing whether a kid had been pushed, or fallen, from the open hatch of a Huey bird, no argument.

He was deep in his inventory lists.

The Treasurer had told him that it was hassle for all of them if one slipped up. The Treasurer wanted to know each last paperclip that was not accounted for so that the cover excuse could be manufactured. Apparently, two years back, the DEA team's oldest jeep, bad steering and worse brakes, had gone over the edge of a hundred-foot ravine off a rain-damaged track up in Totonicapán district. Tom guessed that jeep would have been loaded down with paperclips and everything else that could not be accounted for in the inventory. It was the way of government service . . .

'You take it personal?' The Intelligence Analyst stood behind him.

Tom said softly, 'It's just a job . . .'

'It can be hell and it can be great.'

'The bastard pushed him.'

'Sunny Guatemala, Tom, where life comes on a discount. They say that for twenty-five dollars you can get a man killed here. It's that sort of place . . . Listen to me, and this isn't meant unkind, it wasn't necessary of you to have gotten involved, it wasn't clever. You're best staying with the flying.'

'If you'll excuse me, I've a heap of paper.'


The rain had cleared. The jungle steamed in dampness. It had been a short and overwhelming thunderstorm, vivid sheet lightning.

Harpo was better than Gord had rated him.

They had taken a position on a great rock mass and they had crawled forward under the vine and ivy covering of the rock, and they looked down from the edge of the cliff onto the road. The road was beaten stone and ran straight as far as they could see, right to left, and there were water pools in the potholes. The block on the road was not immediately in front of the rock mass but about seventy-five yards right of it. The rock mass gave them the best vantage point and the height to cover the block and to see what approached from either north or south. Harpo was better than Gord had rated him because he had moved quietly, steadily, on their approach to the road, crawling the last hundred yards. It was good work for a man of his age and his size, and Gord acknowledged the quality. They lay on their stomachs and the network of vine and ivy filtered the sun that fell on them. They were through the tree line and they relied on the vine and ivy for concealment.

The ground either side of the road, twenty yards back from the beaten stone, had been bulldozer-cleared. It was standard in counter-insurgency warfare to hack back foliage from beside a military route. He thought the soldiers, seven of them, had been dropped by lorry, had been abandoned on the road for several days' stay because they had pitched tents on the cleared ground and they had no wheeled transport. The soldiers rested in the sunshine. Their confidence was on show. No sentries were out down the road, neither to the north nor the south, nor back against the tree line. The transistor played loud Latin music. Through an open tent flap, Gord saw the communications radio, and an aerial had been draped from the roof of the tent. Three of the soldiers, as they ambled on the road, carried Israeli Galil rifles. There was a light machine gun with a bipod mount, there was a small mortar, and more rifles lay haphazardly on the ground near the tents. They had laid a chain of spikes across the road.

From the high rock Gord heard the engine before the soldiers. Butterflies hovered close to his face, parrots called in the tree line behind him.

He studied the place for the potential of a killing ground. It was Gord's way, his training. He had known a killing ground in the South Armagh district of Northern Ireland, and in the interior of Iraq, and he had tried to help the Shia of Karbala choose the best ground for killing.

He thought it was the engine of a bus. Coming from the south, it roused the camp. The lethargy was slung off the soldiers. A soldier lay behind the light machine gun. Two of the soldiers took a theatrical position in the centre of the road, posturing authority. Gord saw the bus.

The bus was ancient, multi-coloured, and a haze of fumes followed it. When it was a hundred yards from the spiked chain on the road, when the soldiers in the road were waving their authority at the driver for him to slow and stop, one of the troopers was gestured by the soldier who wore a corporal's stripes back to the largest of the tents. The bus halted in the centre of the road. A soldier shouted through the driver's window. The passengers, men and women and children, spilled from the door of the bus down onto the road. The passengers were all Indians. Gord saw the jumble of straw hats and bright blouses and skirts, and he could hear the crying of children. The passengers were lined up at the side of the road. A man, civilian clothes, had been brought from the largest tent. He was hooded but Gord could see, just, the eye slits in the hood. There were two soldiers inside the bus to search it. The hooded man was escorted by the corporal along the length of the line of passengers and near to the end of the line he stopped and he pointed, and Gord saw that the man who was recognized crumpled the moment before the soldiers dragged him clear of the line. He thought it was routine. The bus was searched, the passengers were screened. The bus was loaded again. The hooded figure was taken back to the tent. The spiked chain was pulled back and the bus drove away slowly, coughing a cloud of diesel. The man who had been marked out was kicked as he knelt beside the road, then taken across the cleared ground to the edge of the trees. Gord had no need to watch. He heard the cocking of the weapons. The man who had been marked was shot not more than forty paces from the rock mass where Gord lay with Harpo.

In the evening, as the dusk gathered on the clearing, it was talked through.

Gord said, 'We should bypass the block. Once we start shooting then we are running. We fire the first shot, and that is the beginning of the charge. It is not the right time.'

Harpo said, 'The people will not rise until they hear of us. Each time they hear of our strike then more will come.'

Jorge said, 'Where we find them, we kill them. We light the fire.'

He was the outsider, the intruder. 'So be it.'

On the ground of the clearing Gord scratched with a stick and made a plan of the roadblock and the tents and the position of the communications radio and the siting of the machine gun.

In the morning the play-acting would end.

He lay on the ground and he wept.

First time that he had sobbed tears since the rabbit that was his pet had been taken and eaten by Mrs McFarlane's cat.

The Archaeologist dragged himself away from the bodies and into the long grass and howled at the jungle round him, shouted his anguish. He was twenty-nine years old. It was the first time he had sobbed tears since the cat had come over the fence and into the yard of the prim home in Garden City outside Ames, the town on the Chicago and North Western rail line that cut the state of Iowa east to west. He had been eleven years old when he had last sobbed tears.

The place was not like Tikal. There were no guides and no souvenir shops and no hamburger bars and no tourists round the temple pyramid. The place was where he had been most happy in all of his life. It was the place of the hidden civilization of the Mayan Indian dynasties that had lain lost, unmapped and unexplored, for a millennium. Trees rising to the light of the sun had towered over the pyramid construction, hiding it from aerial photography, protecting it from the abuse of the New World. He had found the place.

The Archaeologist was on a year of sabbatical leave from the University of Minnesota.

Sixty miles south-west of Flores which was the central city of the Petén region, near to the village of Chinajá, in a fly-blown coffee shop, an old Indian who had no teeth had told the Archaeologist of the place in the jungle depth.

It was his own place. It had been his own place until that morning.

With two Indians, good and solid men with the strength of oxen, he had made the camp late in the previous year. He had lived native, eating what his workers ate, dressing as they did and leaving his American-tagged clothes in his rucksack, learned their language. The power of modern government had bypassed this empty quarter under the high tree canopy. It had been his first visit back to Guatemala City since he had found the pyramid site and he had posted to his department at the University of Minnesota the records of seven months of archaeological detection, and he had returned. He was not to know who or what had broken the secrecy of his hidden life: a marked map left in the sleaze hotel in the Guatemala City backstreet; the driver of the Mitsubishi jeep who had brought him down country from Flores and dropped him at a roadside kilometre marker; the Indians who worked with him and who had returned to their villages while he was gone to the city.

They had come in the dawn to his place. They had worn army uniforms. He had seen them, out of the corner of his eye, as they had approached the flattened ground where he slept alongside his Indian workers. Raised rifles, the long bursts of firing. Two bodies straddling his. He had spread his fingers, so carefully and such slow movements, into the wet warmth of their running blood and smeared his own chest, his own face. He had lain as dead. They had used crowbars and pickaxes to hack the stela writings from the face walls inside the cave entry of the pyramid. They had grunted, laughed, struggled to heave the slabs with the hieroglyphs away ... Not daring to move. Cursing the flies that played at his nostrils. Smelling the death against him ... Everything that could be carried was taken. Everything that he had so lovingly collated was taken. It had been hammered into him by his professor back at the Minnesota campus that he should maintain secrecy on all virgin sites because the dealers in New York paid fat fees for undamaged stelae, no detail of ownership and acquisition required by the clandestine collectors who hid artefacts in secret cellars behind electronic beams. Money talked loud in the world of the private collectors. The Archaeologist despised, more than any persons in the world, the ageing collectors hobbling down cellar steps to view what they should not have owned.

Long after they had gone, he lay motionless in the grass in front of the pyramid.

His father taught school in Ames, and the first weekend in every month his mother did the flowers for church. In his youth and his adulthood he had never struck a fellow human, and he would have hoped that he had never wished hurt to a living person. He had never played football voluntarily, nor baseball, nor hockey. He had no weight to his body, no muscle on his shoulder. No fool and no idiot, he could recognize the deep change that caught at his psychology. It was as if decency had died in him with the murder of the Indians, as if compassion had been extirpated from him with the stealing of the stelae. Just the span of a full day before, he would not have believed it was possible for him to lose decency and compassion. He wanted to strike and to hurt . . .

He wanted to kill . . . He felt no shame in it.

It was the voices that woke Gord. Half up from his sleeping bag and angrily scattering the mosquito net off his face and ready to hiss at them for quiet. He saw them in Jorge's flashlight. Eff and Vee and Zed were back. The light moved on and there were four men diffidently standing behind them.

It had begun . . .

He turned away from them to regain his sleep.

It had begun, the charge, and in the dawn there would be the first action.

He had no knowledge of them and no hatred of them. Gord watched the young soldiers whose death he had planned.

He tried to think only of the plan.

Zeppo had argued. The pills had constipated his gut. Zeppo had wanted to be forward, and been refused, and had argued that the plan was crap. Eff and Zed and the village recruits they had brought, unknowns, were at the back. Gord had Jorge close to him on the rock mass and Harpo north of the block and Groucho south. They were not to fire until he fired. It was the way he had lectured them. If any of them fired before he fired then he would break that bastard's neck himself.

They would have wives and mothers and sweethearts. Over the V sight and the needle sight of the machine gun he could follow the soldiers. Two were wrestling in fun in the middle of the road. They were all conscripts, forced men, except for the corporal. Gord had not seen the corporal, and the flap of the tent with the communications radio was not yet opened.

They had done him no harm.

One was on the edge of the tree line, squatting in cover.

They had done him no hurt.

The two who had killed the passenger from the bus were hunched over a low fire and heating a tin.

They had done him no wrong.

The informer, without the hood with the slits, sat in the road, round-shouldered and head down and threw small stones at the spikes of the chain. They were all for killing. One carried back a bucket of water from the dribbling stream on the far side of the road. The call of the birds, in delight at the rising of the sun, was around Gord.

There was the rush of breath in the throat of Jorge beside Gord.

The flap of the tent with the communications radio broke loose, was thrown back.

The corporal stepped into the light and was zipping his fly and coughing on his cigarette.

The start of the charge. Gord had the weight of the machine gun tight on his shoulder. The beginning. He edged the barrel right to left and it covered the corporal and the communications radio. He squeezed on the trigger, waited for the explosion in his ears. Squeezed tighter . . .

A toucan thrashed in the upper foliage for panic flight.

A monkey family screamed and jumped in unison to make distance.

Only the butterflies near to him showed no concern.

The sounds of the firing cascaded at the Archaeologist's ears. He was drawn forward. He should have turned, run, like the toucan, and the monkey family. All night he had been on his stomach, sport for the mosquitoes, and at the first light he had started to move again in the direction where he thought the road cut the jungle. He would have known where the road lay if he had not blundered away from the pyramid site in the dusk. It was a compulsion that carried him forward, to the tree line at the edge of the cleared strip alongside the width of the road.

He saw the bodies. Bullet ricochets puffed dust from the road stones and sang, and one of the bodies jerked then collapsed.

Across the road from the Archaeologist was a cliff face of reddish-brown rock. There was a sharp shout. The shout was in the English language. 'Stop firing.' There was another burst on automatic, longer. He saw the bodies of the soldiers and he saw that two more soldiers stood, bolt upright, in the road with their hands raised. 'I said to stop firing.' A man stood on the top of the rock. He was dressed in filthy and torn camouflage trousers and a tunic of green-brown pattern that did not match the trousers. There was a strip of khaki cloth knotted as a bandanna around his forehead. The man carried a machine gun at his hip level, like it was a toy thing. If he had not heard his shout then the Archaeologist would have thought the man to be American, but he had heard the accent that he knew to be English. Another man, younger and Latin, armed with a rifle, had come to the Englishman's shoulder and seemed to cuff it as if that were a gesture of congratulation.

There were others moving onto the road, one was old and fat and bald and grinning, and one was old and short and hesitant, and there was an Indian running towards the two soldiers with their hands raised.

The Archaeologist looked, in staggered disbelief.

Gord was at the side of the road.

It was for Jorge to lead.

He watched the young man. He had checked the tents, empty. There was no threat now on the road. Jorge had his fingers in his mouth and whistled, a shriek, into the jungle. There were the bodies of the corporal with the cigarette crushed in his fingers, and of the informer, and of four of the soldiers. He saw Groucho cover the conscripts who had surrendered with his rifle held dramatically at his shoulder, and he saw Zeppo swagger towards the prisoners and kick the legs from under the nearest of the two so that he fell onto the road. Jorge moved briskly, what Gord would have wanted of him, and hurried to collect the soldiers' weapons and Vee was with him and sweeping up the weight of the light machine gun and the mortar tube and then stowing the mortar shells into the webbing of his belt and then swathing his body in the ammunition belts from the machine gun. The light was growing, and the heat. The road to the north shimmered and the road to the south bent away at an angle. Gord strained for the sound of an approaching vehicle. It was the time of the charge . . . Jorge went to the prisoners. They were both now flat on their faces. Gord was far enough away from the prisoners to be detached from the pleading in their faces, but he saw it. He knew what had to be done and he felt a coldness. Jorge came to Gord. Jorge said that they could not cope with prisoners, but the prisoners were only village boys, that they could not be trusted but they were little more than children, that they could not be abandoned . . . Gord knew what had to be done . . . Harpo shot the first prisoner, and Groucho shot the other. It had been Jorge's decision and it was the right decision and Gord hoped that Jorge took no pleasure from it.

It was Jorge's whistle that had brought forward those who had not fought. Zeppo led them across the cleared strip and onto the road, and Eff pushed and Zed pulled the cart, and the recruits were burdened down by all of the packs that had been left behind, and they had the weapons and the food and the transistor radio from the roadblock. They left the bodies to the fly swarms and to the ants. They pushed into the jungle beyond the rock mass.

Not a hundred yards gone and already Gord, back-marker, was cursing for more speed ahead.

\* \* \*

120

Four hours after the road through the Petén, going north to Sayaxché, had been made a killing ground, the relief lorry from the garrison base at Chinajá reached the place. The fresh soldiers, as young as their conscript colleagues who lay in the light rain that was now falling, pattering on their uniforms, raked the jungle at the edge of the cleared strip with frightened gunfire. They loaded the bodies and the shredded tents and the smashed radio set over the tail of their lorry. They drove away at speed, their fear chasing them, north to Sayaxché.

He was not satisfied with the pace of the march. He could not blame Jorge because Jorge did not have the fitness for leading at forced pace, and he did not have the training. Gord lectured them at the fifth rest halt.

He would lead.

He would cut the rest time from fifteen to ten minutes in each hour.

'They will be confused because they will have thought this a safe area, but they are trained military and it will take them only a few hours, certainly by tomorrow, to get men into the area. They may try to throw a cordon round this sector, difficult but they will try, and they will set the cordon at a distance beyond what they estimate is our possible progress. We have to be beyond that cordon. We have to have moved faster, gone further, than they will think possible. Any man who slows the pace endangers not only himself but all of us. It was what you chose when you wanted to attack the block. We don't go back now and we don't lie up. It is too late for going back . . .'

Vee whispered the translation to the new recruits. They were scrawny men but they could cope with the pace he wanted and they held the weapons that had been given them as if they were gold plate, and one of them had Zeppo's backpack slung on its big straps so that it rose low on his haunches. He thought Harpo was going to speak . . .

'No debate. You can argue when you are in Guatemala City. We will march an extra hour tonight, until it is too late to see ahead. There will be no talking on the march. Movement and distance are critical. Load up . . .'

He felt a desperate tiredness in his legs and an ache in his lungs and the flies played round them and there was no time now to send any of the Indians out to search for garlic roots. He stood sharply upright. He had to set the example. He had not wanted to take it away from Jorge because Jorge was the leader, and Jorge looked up at him and nodded his agreement.

A snap of breaking wood behind him.

His hand went fast down to the ground to where the rifle was, beside the machine gun. They were on an animal trail, perhaps a pig's track. He used signs. The flat of his hand held out, no movement. The finger across the lips, no word.

It was a weed of a man.

There was no height on him, no weight to him.

The moment he would have seen the rifles aimed at him . . .

'Don't . . . no, help me . . . don't shoot me,' he blurted.

It was English, American-spoken. Gord said, 'In the name of God, what . . . ?'

'Followed you . . . tried to kill me . . . would have. I saw what you did. I saw it at the roadblock . . . Where are you going?'

'Who needs to know?'

'They stole the stelae . . . I saw you kill the soldiers. I want your help . . . Where are you going?'

Gord grinned. 'I'm told we're going to the Palacio Nacional, Guatemala City. It's what I'm told.'

'Why?'

'I'm told it's for a revolution.'

'Count me . . .'

'Stop babbling . . .' The grin was gone from Gord. Playtime was over-extended. 'If you are smart, lose yourself. You saw nothing, you heard nothing, you know nothing. Go and hitch yourself a ride, get yourself to Guatemala City, buy a ticket out. Forget, Mr Stranger, what you saw and heard.'

'Please . . .'

Gord said, cold, 'Go home and write a letter to your local

paper, and tell the readers that Guatemala is an unhappy place. Leave it at that.'

'For what they did, I want revenge.'

Gord said, 'I am losing time, I have one thing to tell you . . .'

The man blazed back at him, '*Revenge*.'

'I am trying to say it so that an imbecile will comprehend. Death warrant, got me? Bad news, got me? High probability of pain and tears, got me? So, do me the favour of turning round and getting lost soonest.'

The panted answer, defiant. 'I want to help you to kill them.'

He stood his ground. He had not backed off. It was Gord who buckled.

'Can you shoot?'

It was ridiculous. He saw the torn clothes of the man. It was grotesque. The man had no strength, and the glasses on his face were cracked in the right lens and the left arm was twisted so that the frame hung askew down his nose. It was pathetic. His sneaker shoes were shredded. There was blood dried on his face, smeared.

'I am an archaeologist from the University of Minnesota. I have never fired a gun in my life . . .'

'If you screw us I will break your back, that is not probability but certainty.'

Gord led.

There would be three minutes' less rest time at the next halt.

'You are a shit woman, you know that?'

'There is no requirement, captain, for abuse,' Alex said quietly.

'You are a shit woman who comes here to interfere.'

'I am accompanying the lady. The interference is the obstruction shown to her.'

'You are a shit obstinate woman. You have no business in Playa Grande, no business in Guatemala.'

She was dogged. 'The lady seeks the information that your government says should be freely available. The lady seeks the information . . .'

'You are a shit woman, because you have an education and you come here amongst these simple people and you confuse them. You bring trouble here.'

'She seeks the information, captain, as to the location of her husband's grave . . .'

The captain carried in his two hands, held it across his thighs, a short and polished stave of ceiba wood. He held it tight and flexed his fingers round it and the whites of his knuckles showed. He had called her obstinate. The captain was correct in his judgement of Alex Pitt.

'You should be off the base area within five minutes, out of Playa Grande within thirty minutes. Shit woman, understand me, Playa Grande could be a dangerous place . . .'

'There is no need to add crude threats to insults, captain. I am merely seeking your co-operation in locating the grave of this woman's husband. It is a justifiable request . . .'

'Hear me, five minutes.'

She stood her ground. The captain glowered at her. There were armed men behind him. The widow tugged at her wrist. The widow wanted to be gone. The husband of the woman had been disappeared for four years. She had heard the story: men had come after dark to the house of wood and tin sheets and taken her husband and driven away with him, disappeared him. He would have been killed a day later, or a week later, or a month later. She was familiar with the case history: the man had had the courage to protest that land he farmed had been appropriated for the spread of a cattle *finca*, had complained to the owner of the *finca*. She felt the bone fingers stabbing in her flesh. She thought there was no more that she could do. She turned. Their loathing of her speared into her back. She tried to walk straight, as if they should not have the satisfaction of intimidating her. She stepped down from the verandah of the command centre of the military base at Playa Grande. She walked across the parade ground, past the soldiers, and past the armoured cars with their machine guns loaded, and past the sentry's sandbagged wall. She should never show fear. She held the widow's hand and felt the fright tremble of the small fist. She walked past the coiled barbed wire of the perimeter fence. The dog in the Land Rover roared for her, bounced at the back window. The widow broke Alex's grip and scurried, elfin small, to other women who waited outside the camp gate. They were close to each other, the bright-dressed women, talking and gesturing. She tried to stay composed. Her safety was bluff. If she thought all the time of her safety then she might as well take the next flight out to Miami, turn her back on Guatemala and this widow, and the other widows. She poured water from a plastic bottle into the dog's bowl and let it drink and fondled its neck. The widow came back to her.

'It was not the right day to come . . .'

'Any day, any different?'

It was the third time that Alex had accompanied the widow to the army base in the attempt to find the unmarked grave of the disappeared. The first time the captain had laughed at the request for information. The second time he had first kept them waiting five hours, then coolly given a statement that the killings were the work of the communist subversives. She hoped she had hidden it, her fear.

'Not the right day. There has been a battle. There are many soldiers killed. The battle was in the Petén jungle. Many killed, it is why they were angry, Miss 'Lex. Not the good day.'

She put the water bottle away. She quietened the dog. She helped the widow into the passenger seat of the Land Rover and started the drive back up the wet dirt road to the village.

She talked. 'It is absolutely idiotic of the guerrillas to go on killing soldiers. It is totally stupid. It makes life so much harder for people like you, your family, your friends. When soldiers are killed by the guerrillas then it is you and your family and the rest of a village that suffer. Guerrilla violence only creates army violence . . .'

The widow seemed not to hear her.

'They say, Miss 'Lex, that many soldiers were killed.'

'Solves nothing,' Alex said sharply, impatient.

'It is what the women talked of.'

*     *     *

125

'It's Schultz, right? Tom Schultz? You got a moment?'

Tom swung in his chair. He was nearly through. He had a headache from the coffee. Ahead of him the Country Attaché's office was dark through the frosted glass at the top of the door, and the other desks in the DEA's work area were empty. They would have gone back to their little women and their little kids. There was no little woman in the life of Tom Schultz, and no little kids, and not much chance of it while he carried a scar from his ear to his jawbone of reddened skin, the best a field surgeon could do . . . He gestured for the man to sit. He was two Huey bird skids short . . . Now, how the hell did a flier, his predecessor, lose two skids in a pranged touch-down and replace them and forget to note it? Last week in the dining room the Chemist had pointed out Kramer, from the Agency.

'Be my guest.'

He thought Kramer might have been a college man. Looked more like a classics scholar, maybe mathematics/physics, than a field man of the Agency. Dead pale skin, and eyes magnified by pebble spectacles.

'I hear you were up in Petén district. I hear you found a crashed aircraft. Be grateful if you'd talk me through, tell me what you saw.'

'There's an Intelligence Analyst, there's a Treasurer and a Chemist and a Liaison. Wouldn't you do better there?'

'Heh, come off your high horse. They don't give me the time of day. Please, just talk me through what you saw.'

Tom did. Kramer had a pocket recorder on the desk, didn't interrupt. The Antonov, the fire, the evidence of the cargo, the tracks of the second aircraft, the prisoners . . .

'. . . There were the prisoners. I'd have thought when Arturo sat them down to tea and cakes they'd have told him what they'd seen.'

Kramer sniggered, high-pitched, like that was stupid. He switched off the recorder.

'Thanks, I appreciate it.'

'Why the interest?'

The shrug. 'Just, there was an action up there today. Nothing has even farted in that area for a year and a half, and a plane comes in, and some government troops get pretty efficiently put alongside their Lord and Maker . . . and, of course, when I file then it shows them at Langley that I'm a busy little boy . . . It was well done, so I hear, a professional attack. Good night.'

# 7

His opinion was not asked for. Tom Schultz was the punch-ball. The Country Attaché had told him that the Ambassador gave good parties and had the habit of inviting along, just the once, each junior grade federal employee assigned to Guatemala City. They came to him, where he stood by the bulletproof window, and lectured him, and moved on.

A cattle rancher with twenty-four square miles of grazing land in the distant Franja Transversal del Norte.

'. . . I think you Americans have seen the light, and it's not before time. The old days, you were forever telling us how we should live. You've put that out of your system. The "America First" policy is so much more appropriate, look after yourselves and let us look after ourselves. We are a democratic country that has seen off the threat of a communist insurrection, and we had no help from Washington. That is the justification for us to stand together as equals, the United States of America and Guatemala. Mutual respect achieves so much more in results. What I am saying is that I believe your administration in Washington should continue to leave us alone, get off our backs. I tell you who I would like you to meet, my future son-in-law, in the army, an excellent young man, a real patriot . . .'

The Ambassador's wife was radiant in an off-the-shoulder dress.

'. . . You've no family here, Mr Schultz? A pity. Such a lovely country for wives and for children. Herbie and I, we've been all over, but I tell him that this is the most beautiful country we've ever been privileged to be stationed in. You should get up to

Lake Atitlán, so restful, such tranquillity. And such friendliness from the people . . .'

The evangelist preacher was from Louisiana and wore polished cowboy boots and a wide buckled belt and 150-dollar jeans.

'. . . You won't have been here long enough to realize it, but this is grand country for missionary work. The Catholics have had the free run at the Indians for five hundred years and they've taught them subversion and dissent. They've had their time, and we've a government here that is wise enough to realize that the evangelist movement is what this country needs. We're teaching the Indians the *true* word of the Bible, not this liberal nonsense that's peddled by the Catholic Church. What the Indians need is God, not Catholic politics. I tell you, Mr Schultz, it's a fine government here. All this talk of human rights violations is based on the lies of the Jesuits and the liberals back home. They're very dear people, the Indians, all they want is a roof over their heads and enough maize for the cooking of tortillas, this talk of *freedom* is just communist crap that bewilders them. My church is the Bethel Temple, my call is "Jesus Loves You", we're up at Chichicastenango and you should call by one Sunday morning and you'll find what a grand little country this is . . .'

The general in uniform had a chest of medal ribbons and introduced himself as i/c G-4 (Logistics).

'. . . It's the strength of this country, Mr Schultz, that we saw off a communist-inspired revolution without having to beg for American help. You can go to any country in Central or Latin America and they will tell you that we have the finest trained and motivated armed forces, we are the best. We won the argument on the battlefield and we won it in the political arena. We broke the guerrillas militarily, and we dumped that shit – you excuse me – about the "freedom struggle" in history's trash can. I note that we now have the support of the United States because at last your government has shown the wisdom of recognizing its true friends in this region. Let me ask you, what would have happened if the communists had won in Guatemala? No, I will tell you, there would have been another Cuba here. I believe you liaise with Mario Arturo, an excellent officer, a most dedicated man . . .'

The businessman's suit looked to be from New York, expensive, and he mixed the champagne with orange juice from the waiter's jug.

'. . . I like Americans. I have some very good friends in the steering committee of AmCham, that is the American Chamber of Commerce. You should know, when it was *difficult* for us here, when we faced an unprincipled policy of isolation from Washington, it was the American Chamber of Commerce that was steadfast in their support of us. They understood that all of the liberal talk about trades unions and workers' rights was just destroying this country. We pay generous wages in Guatemala, we have good conditions of employment. People who have never been to Guatemala will tell you that our Indians are exploited and live in poverty. What does the Indian want? He wants work and a roof over his head and food in his belly. Do you know Florida, Mr Schultz? I take my family twice each year to Florida, in the spring we stay at the Sheraton Key Largo and in the autumn we are at the Hyatt Regency Grand Cypress . . .'

None of them, not the cattle rancher nor the Ambassador's wife nor the evangelist preacher nor the general nor the businessman, had asked about his scar. They hadn't made a big thing of it, and neither had they made light of it. All had damn well looked at it, scalpelled it with their eyes. He felt like he should have cracked two glasses together, made the salon quiet. 'Hear me out. I was busted out of the sky by a shoulder-held SAM, lost an Apache and I lost a weapons man. Bad shit landing, bad fire. It's not the big-shot way, getting blown down, it's fucking failure . . . And what burns the failure is the scar and you bastards looking away from it.'

It was raining when Tom Schultz left and he had to run to the back of the parking lot behind the residence, past the lines of limousines and waiting chauffeurs and clustered bodyguards.

\* \* \*

130

The first night after the action, when they had made camp in the confusion of darkness, Gord had recognized the new confidence in the group.

There had been thunderclaps above them and sometimes the nearness of the sheet lightning had thrown pale light onto the small clearing they had made for the bivouac. Gord had sat away from the group, that was his fashion, and had heard the excited whispering of Harpo and Groucho as they told Zeppo what they had achieved. And he thought Jorge had strutted for the first time, as if a conceit ate at him. The Archaeologist wanted to talk with him, and was ignored by Gord, too tired and too much running in his mind; he would have said that the Archaeologist had walked well under the load that had been given him, and he had made a mental note to get boots for him when they hit the civilization trail, but he couldn't bother himself to talk with the man.

The next morning, moving off after the camp site had been cleared and the latrine pit filled in and the rubbish buried, Gord had seen that the performance on the march was reduced. He had taken the role of routemaster. He alternated between leading with Eff and Vee and Zed, slashing alongside them when there was no trail and when there was no possibility of crawling under low growth, and taking the back-marker where he could push and chivvy at Zeppo and Harpo and Groucho.

He believed their loathing of him was building.

Zeppo sitting down when they were stopped ahead and when the column had moved again he had stayed sitting, massaging the weight of his stomach, stroking it as if it were a cat's back, and complained to Gord that it was time for the rest halt, and it was four minutes and twenty-eight seconds short of the schedule for the next rest halt. He dragged Zeppo up, propelled him forward.

'. . . We never needed you. Better you had not come . . .'

The middle of the morning, and Harpo in mid-march unslinging his pack and bitching at the opened sores on his shoulders and calling for the new recruit Indians to carry his pack for him, smearing with a muddied cloth across the hairless width of his scalp, and the shouting match had developed because Gord would not tolerate it and Eff and Vee and Zed and the new recruits were already laden beyond their fair share and had the cart of the flame thrower.

'. . . You think you know everything. You know nothing. We are better without you . . .'

The early part of the afternoon, and Groucho stopping and contorting his face, supported by the sympathizing Archaeologist, and whining at the cramps in his stomach, and Gord had thought him genuine and made a play of coldness because there was no alternative to pressing on, and snapped at the Archaeologist to mind his own business and load, and punched Groucho in the small of the back to get him again going forward.

'. . . You push too hard and you will break us, and what is then achieved? We showed in the action we could fight . . .'

It would burst, he knew that.

They stumbled ahead in the suffused green shadow light, and the rain was more regular.

Always, as they moved, there was the creaking action of wheels on the axles of the cart.

Each time that they stopped, slumped down for water, Gord would go to Jorge and ask him for the map and he would spend the ten minutes studying it and checking with his compass, and each time his finger would trace the phantom route from the lime colour of the jungle to the primrose of the ground rising from 450 feet above sea level to the ochre of the foothills that started at 900 feet above the shoreline of the Caribbean, and on towards the browns and mauves of the Cuchumatanes where the peaks were 9000 feet and upwards. It was his Grail, to reach the cool uplands, to leave behind him the stinking fetid clinging bloody mess that was the Petén jungle.

They had done twelve miles in two days and Gord rated that as a miracle.

And it would be worse the next day. As they made the evening's camp, Jorge was huddled with Eff and Vee and Zed.

Before the groundsheets had been spread, before the mosquitoes had found them, before Groucho had searched in his emptying ration sack, before the latrine hole had been dug, the three Indians moved out.

A rendezvous had been set. They would be gone for twenty-four hours. They had moved out to forage for recruits.

The rain ran on their heads and their shoulders and gathered in their laps, fell heavy from the upper leaves. They were together in a small circle as they ate the gruel meal of dehydrated powder mixed with rainwater. It was not possible that Jorge did not realize the tension volcano growing but he set himself apart from it. Jorge talked quietly of his father, of the legend. A soft voice, touching the mystic, and they heard him in quiet.

Gord let it ride until the meal was finished. He could not see their faces . . .

He whipped them.

'Right, that was just fine, and that was an indulgence, and out of indulgence comes complacency. If any of you believe that anything that has been achieved so far is meaningful, then you are totally *wrong*. We are nowhere and have achieved nothing. We have the first of the rains, and the wet season, I reckon, is our best chance. The wet season gives us two advantages. We are going for high ground, and the rains and low cloud will reduce the hours fixed-wing aircraft and helicopters can operate. We need them grounded by weather, most particularly when we leave jungle conditions. On the high ground, in bad weather, the roads will foul up, wash away, they will have problems moving armoured vehicles . . . We are on a charge. We always have to be further forward than they believe it possible for us. That is the basis of the military operation . . .'

He heard Harpo's snort of derision.

'. . . And there is my personal position. I can turn round now. I can leave you here, *now*. I can walk across the Petén and I can cross into Belize. In Belize I will get from my own army a good bath and a hell of a good meal and as many cans of beer as I can drink. I can get a flight back to Britain any day I want it. If I do not hear it from each and every one of you that I am wanted, that I will be heard, then I am *gone*. I want to hear it . . .'

The Archaeologist muttered, nervous, 'Not my place, but it's a hell of a way to run a revolution . . .'

A silence. The mosquitoes droned in flight around him.

Jorge said, 'You are wanted.'

The coughing shriek of a wild turkey.

Zeppo said, sour, 'You should stay.'

The stampede flight of a pheasant.

Harpo said, grudged, 'We can work together.'

The dripping rain spattered a drumbeat.

Groucho said, hesitant, 'We are as one man.'

Six guerrillas joined them in the morning. They were skeletal thin, their clothes were rags and they wolfed the food that Groucho gave them.

Gord took the lead, set the pace faster.


He read the digest of the interrogator's report.

The vantage point had been from behind trees, their vision had been incomplete.

Colonel Arturo scanned the single sheet of typed-up paper.

The first plane had landed, two wings on each side. There had been eight men who had come from the plane. They had unloaded boxes. There were guns in the boxes. There had been three Indians amongst the men, and three more who were old and *Ladino*, and one who was young and also *Ladino*. There had been one last man, one who had worked the fastest to get the boxes from the plane. The last man was European white. The subject under interrogation had known that he was European white because he had once worked on an oil drill under a German engineer, near Sayaxché. The subject under interrogation could tell the difference between a European white and *Ladino* stock. A second plane had crashed on attempting to land.

The fist of Colonel Arturo was clenched on the sheet of paper. He wondered how the man he had seen, splashed down, regaining consciousness, questioned, hooded again with the *capucha*, breathing broken, had come to make so factual and chronological a statement.

He telephoned an office in the G-2 behind the Palacio Nacional.

No, he was told, it was not possible to question further the subject of interrogation.

He tried to call the office of the Chief of Staff, gone to a restaurant party for his wife's birthday. He called the office of the Director of Intelligence, gone to the Army Club to play tennis. He called the HQ of Army Command, Petén region, and was told the brigadier was not available.

He swivelled in his chair. His chin rested on his locked fingers. He stared up at the wall map that displayed the chinagraphed symbols denoting the location of the country's armed forces. He had placed on the map an orange-headed pin at a spot southeast of the Santa Amelia *finca*, and a second orange-headed pin on the Sayaxché to Chinajá road.

The excitement had worn.

The Archaeologist struggled to hold the pace that was set. The Englishman was merciless to him. When he slipped back, when the Indians who manhandled the weight of the cart with the tubes came past him, when the old *Ladinos* elbowed him aside, when he was at the back of the column, then he felt the shove of the Englishman's hand or the weight of the boot into the seat of his trousers. He would have thought that he was in good condition, and he was wrong.

Impulse had taken him into the jungle to follow the group and he had tracked them for six hours while he had dragged for the courage to close on them. The impulse was long gone. His breath sagged, the muscles in his shins and thighs ached pain, his arms and body were scratched raw. With each step that he took, weighed down by the rifles and mortar shells that he carried, so the decision of the impulse became more binding. There was no going back ... The straps of three rifles cut into the flesh of his shoulder and the burden of the mortar shells bowed him. As the moment of impulse drifted more distant, and the sense of excitement thinned, the Archaeologist found himself drawn more closely to the silence of the Englishman who bullied the column forward.

At each rest halt he slumped down beside the Englishman.

At each stop he sat close to the Englishman, a dog at a master's feet, like when he'd been young and his parents had owned the cross Labrador and spaniel bitch and the dog had sat the winter evenings against him. He would settle beside the Englishman and watch him at his work, checking his backpack straps, cleaning his weapon, poring over the frayed map, boots off and socks off and massaging his feet.

He spattered the questions.

'I'm really interested, Gord, why you're here . . .'

'. . . Is it politics brought you, Gord, would you be a liberal . . . ?'

'. . . Eight men killed back on the road, does that bother you, Gord . . . ?'

'. . . Your family back home, do they know you're in Guatemala? What do they think . . . ?'

'. . . A revolution and going all the way to the centre of Guatemala City, real or just joke talk . . . ?'

'. . . Gord, this is an army country. Can you win? Is winning something that can actually happen . . . ?'

'. . . Is it that you saw something that was wrong and wanted to change the wrong . . . ?'

Never an answer. Sometimes a slow smile, sometimes the slap at a fly in irritation, sometimes a quiet curse of annoyance. He had a girlfriend, a good but on-hold relationship, in the psychology faculty on the campus at Minnesota. They used to talk through her study work . . . and he could not read the man, and he didn't think his girlfriend could have done better. He'd hack it, too right . . . in time he'd break the silence wall . . .

On the last march session of the day, as they pitched ahead in the falling light, they came to the cleared space.

\*     \*     \*

Groucho told Gord that it was a place of the Communities of Resistance. Scattered through the space were small huts of rough-cut wood walls and with wide leaves stacked as roofing. Not a person to be seen, not an animal, not a chicken, and the quiet hanging in the dusk, and the rain falling heavier through the canopy.

Groucho told Gord it was a camp for a community which had fled the army and made new homes in the secrecy of the jungle. Jorge had gone forward, only Zed with him. With hand motions, back at the edge of the tree line, Gord gestured for the others in the column to fan out. They were all wary. Jorge had left his weapon in Zeppo's hands and walked unarmed to the centre of the clearing. There was a half-kicked-out fire smouldering in front of a hut. There were worn paths. There were filled buckets of water near Jorge. There were children's clothes strung from a vine line and still dripping from their washing. There were a dozen huts that Gord could see, maybe more that were masked from him, there were corral fences of cut thorn to hold animals, there was no sound and no movement.

If the planes found the place, Groucho told Gord, it would be napalm bombed, if the soldiers found it they would level it and herd the community back to the new secure villages.

Gord motioned for the others to stay back. He held the machine gun across his hip. He moved lightly on his feet towards Jorge. A few minutes and the darkness would have enveloped the place, and they had walked well the last part of that day, and they needed their food and their sleep. He felt almost a sense of anger that they had happened across the place and now the food and the sleep would be delayed.

'Jorge, we don't have time. We should move through. We should keep on going. We should . . .'

He was falling.

He was going down. The earth rushed at him.

There was the shrill screaming around him.

Panic movement, tipping and tumbling. The screams piercing at him.

The machine gun was wrenched from his hands as the rim of the hole cracked against his elbows.

The pigs were in flight, scrambling from the pit and scratching at his body, jumping from the hole, and his face was filled with the wing feather beat of the chickens. He heard the laughter echo around the cleared space. When had he last heard laughter? The loud laughter of Zeppo and Harpo, and the giggle of Groucho, and the squeaked chuckling of the Indians. He blazed in his fury. His fury was his humiliation. The laughter pealed in his ears, louder and gayer. He was shouting for quiet. It was the breaking of discipline, it was the loss of control. The pigs had fled, the chickens had flown. He pulled the pencil torch from his tunic pocket. He bent below the snapped mass of branches that had been covered by an inch of earth to hide the tunnel hole. He shone the torch into the recess at the bottom of the hole. He saw the child that clutched, as if it were a nursery toy, the piglet not older than a week. He saw the wide eyes of more children. He swung the torch. A crouched man held a knife. A woman drew a swaddled baby closer to her bosom. Gord turned the torch again. He shone it into the fullness of his face and he smiled into their fear. He offered his hand to the man with the knife. He jacked himself up out of the hole and he reached down to help out the man who held the knife.

There were calls in a language he did not recognize, and there were sharp whistles that aped the jungle birds.

The clearing in the last light was filled with men and women and children emerging from the tunnels, and animals that had been hidden in pits, and chickens sprouting from the ground.

Groucho came to Gord and he still grinned, and he carefully wiped the earth filth from Gord's trousers.

The Archaeologist was at Gord's side. 'Because of these people, and people like them, is that why you came?'

The captain at the garrison camp at Playa Grande sat in his office and dully turned the pages of a newspaper and thought of his girl who was in Guatemala City, and awaited a response to the signal he had sent to the offices of the G-2. The signal requested orders as to what should be his response to the activities of a shit woman of Peace Brigades International. The captain knew in which village Alex Pitt stayed that night.

The major of G-2 murmured, 'If nothing were seen . . .'

'On the open road,' Benedicto prompted.

'If it were at a place without witnesses . . .'

'Alone on the open road.'

'If it were in an area with evidence of subversive attacks . . .'

'Foreigners are warned that the villages around Playa Grande should not be visited.'

The major of G-2 scratched gently at the hairs in the lobe of his ear. 'If it were possible to interrogate, to trace the lines of contact, to search deeper into the network of involvement . . .'

A chilling and hollow laugh. 'A person taken into custody, interrogated, is a witness.'

'If . . .'

Gord had said to the Archaeologist, quietly, would he be so kind as to leave him alone.

He sat on the edge of the cleared area and his back was to the jungle and the machine gun was across his lap, and the cart was behind him with its angles gouging at his shoulders.

There was a fire of leaping tongues in the centre of the cleared area, heaped high with wood. A pig had been killed, its throat cut with a knife after capture in a stampede chase. Meat slices were cooked over the fire, skewered on long sticks. They had drunk the fermented maize brew. Gord thought it was the atmosphere that Jorge would have wanted. There was a marimba frame that was played, the beaten tubes making a throbbing and compulsive music, not like anything he had heard.

He sat alone and he watched.

They were gathered in the sweep of a half-moon and they faced into the fire. Mixed amongst them, scattered with the women and men and children, were the guerrillas who had

139

joined, and Eff and Vee and Zed, and the peasant villagers they had brought to join the march.

Jorge stood on the far side of the fire so that the flames seemed to leap around him and his face was lit, and the camouflage of his tunic was highlighted, and his hands in their gestures with the rifle threw bouncing shadows onto the low walls of the homes behind him. It was done in an Indian dialect and Gord understood not a word. But it was the stage for Jorge. It was the first bravura performance, and the young man seemed to Gord to have thrown off the exhaustion that was common to all of them. He held his audience in spellbound silence. He was able to speak with a soft resonance that carried from the brightness of the fire's side and across the half-glow of the middle ground and right to the darkness edge in which Gord sat.

Gord watched Jorge play the recruiting sergeant, and he felt no pride that he had himself glanced across the men of this hidden community and judged them on their fitness and on their muscle and estimated what they could carry and how they would fight. At the end Jorge spoke of the future, kneeling close to the jumping flames, speaking with the conviction of a missionary father. Gord felt the sense of sadness because he could not know where any of them who joined would be led, and he felt no pride because there was the certainty of forced marches and battles and more forced marches and more killing fights on the road ahead to Guatemala City. There was the final peroration, Jorge on his feet again and standing tall and with his back straightened and his voice rising at the end in the call for their help. It was well done . . .

The morning would show the truth of how well done. In the morning they would know how many of the men with the shoulders and the muscles and the quality to learn how to fight would join their march. On the map, Guatemala City and the Palacio Nacional were eighty-two miles away, direct line.

There was the clatter of applause.

There was the throb of the music, and the jugs of the fermented maize passed faster round the half-moon and the fire was piled higher and the wet wood crackled as with gunfire.

The children danced.

The children held hands. Gord thought he saw the one who had clutched the piglet in the hole. They lived in the mud and they lived in the wasteland of the jungle, and their mothers had dressed them in their best clothes, scrubbed shirts and washed dresses. The children held hands and they moved to the marimba music in a snaking and joined line. They wove close to the fire and were lit, and away from the fire and were in shadow. The line, once, twisted away from the fire and passed in front of Gord and the children's small feet, bare and muddied, skipped over his legs. Dancing feet and dancing eyes and dancing smiles, and one boy reached out a hand to try to pull Gord to his feet, and he freed the child's grip, and he locked his hands onto the barrel and stock of the machine gun. He watched the line of dancing children, silhouetted by the fire, meander away from him.

Groucho was beside him.

'Pretty, beautiful – they are the future.'

'If you say so.'

'It is what we fight for, the future of the pretty and beautiful children.'

'Emotion doesn't help you.'

'If you have nothing to believe in, Gord, can you fight and win?'

He stared down at the darkened barrel of the machine gun, and the fire's light caught for a moment on the line of the belt of ammunition.

Groucho asked, 'May I tell you a poem, Gord?'

'I never had much time for poetry.'

He recited.

> 'I,
> a man struggling
> in the middle of the century
> tell you: at the end
> of this century

> the children
> will be happy,
> they will laugh again,
> be born again in gardens.'

They were just words. Words were empty. There had been children playing in the streets of Karbala, and there had been children standing in those streets and crying as they had driven away in the Land Rover for the desert waste, and there would have been children cowering in the cellars when the armour of the Republican Guard had smashed back into the holy city of the Shias.

> 'From
> my bitter darkness
> I go beyond
> my own hard times
> and I see
> at the end of the line
> happy children!
> only happy!
> they appear
> they rise
> like a sun of butterflies
> after the tropical cloud burst.'

He thought of the butterflies they had seen that day, and there were some that he had swatted at in his impatience as they fluttered into the sweat of his face. The gold and ochre and amber and scarlet of the wings he had lashed at . . .

The fire was dying. The party was ending.

Groucho said, 'The poem was written by Otto René Castillo. He was captured by the troops of the government in 1967. I was twenty-five years old then, with my doctorate, and I was in love with the books of my study. He was captured and he was tortured and he was burned alive by the troops of the government.

It was when I had read the poem that I left my books and went to the mountains and found the father of Rodolfo Jorge Ramírez. It was for the children.'

'I hear you,' Gord said.

And Groucho was gone from beside him. He cradled the machine gun. He watched the children in the growing darkness and the chain of their hands had been broken and the butterflies in light played at his mind.

The Fireman gazed down onto the bodies.

The bodies were in a ditch and the way they had fallen had made a dam for the water and a pool had formed to the right side of them.

The Fireman and the men on his team were given the order. They splashed down into the ditch. They dragged out the upper body first and laid it without reverence on the earth of the roadside. The rain fell continuously. The rainy season had started early in Guatemala City, more rain that day than the day before, more rain that week than the week before. The first body was unmarked, no bruises and no cuts on the face, only the ligature line at the neck. It was near to a year since the Fireman had seen the death signature of the string that was fastened around the *capucha*. He scrambled down with another man into the ditch again. There were slugs in the sockets where the eyes of the second body had been. He could recognize the signs. The first had died too early, and the second had resisted interrogation too long. He imagined a knife moving closer to the eyebrow, eyelid, eyeball. Perhaps, one eyebrow, eyelid, eyeball taken out and then the confession to the interrogator. Perhaps only after the second eyebrow, eyelid, eyeball had been knifed had the confession come . . . He lifted the body clear.

There were others who carried the two bodies to the back hatch of the fire engine.

He was given a cigarette by a policeman. The policeman was talkative, rambling because of what he had seen.

The policeman told him the story that was told, what he had heard from a friend who had a brother whose wife worked as a waitress in the officers' dining hall of the *estado mayor*. The waitress at the High Command officers' dining hall had told her husband who had told his brother who had told his friend that she had heard the colonels and brigadiers discussing an aircraft landing in the Petén, and an action on the road between Sayaxché and Chinajá in which many soldiers had died. It was the story that the policeman with the cigarettes offered to the Fireman.

When the bodies had been left at the morgue, when his duty was complete, the Fireman went home. In the room where he slept with his wife and his daughter, in the house that he shared with his mother and father and sister, he packed a small bag. The Fireman told his wife what he had heard. He kissed his wife in the privacy of the bedroom. He left her numbed and holding their baby. He walked to the Zona 4 bus terminal and bought a one-way ticket.

Because nine men joined them, they started late and there had been the drawn-out farewells, and the arguments, and women had hung on to their sons, and children had clung to their fathers. They had nine recruits because of Jorge and the speech that he had made against the fire flames in the night . . . They needed the men and they needed the speed, and the two were unmeshed cogs in the charge that he demanded.

His guts were loose from the coarseness of the drink and the richness of the cooked fresh pork meat. It was a humiliation to Gord that he had to stop once after the march had started and dig his small hole and squat over it.

He chivvied and he kicked and he persuaded.

In the fourth rest halt of the morning he was called forward.

Zed, ahead, had reached the road and seen the men.

The map showed Gord and Jorge that the road ran from Playa Grande to San Benito and then on to Chinajá.

Zed led Gord and Groucho away from the rest halt and to the road.

Where they reached the road there was a sharp left bend. Like the Sayaxché to Chinajá road the sides had been cleared. There was no vantage point. They lay on their stomachs on the wet grass and the rain ran from the leaves above and onto them. Gord could hear the voices of the men and he could see the upper bodywork of the grey-blue painted station wagon. They talked like waiting men, lowered tones as if all the time they listened, small laughter as if all the time they were keyed for the work ahead. The vehicle was pointed back up the road, where the map told Gord Playa Grande lay. There were four men and the rain streamed down onto them and they wore no hats and their shirts were plastered to their bodies and their jeans were dark blue from damp. Two carried Uzi machine pistols and one held a rifle across his chest, readied, and the fourth had what Gord recognized as a Colt revolver placed loose in his waist belt. Gord pressed his hand down through the grass and into the earth below and he ground his hand at the earth until the mud stuck to the palm and he wiped the smear of mud across his face and across his hands, and he did the same for Groucho, and he wriggled two, three yards further forward. He motioned for Zed to stay back. He was concerned . . . if the men were to stay long where they waited beside their vehicle then he must return to the column and lead them on a detour, and lose the time that was so precious to him. He wanted to be laid up outside Playa Grande by the evening because that was the village and the garrison that had been chosen. He lay quite still, which was his training, and once he fastened his fist into the shoulder of Groucho's tunic as the man fidgeted.

He would know the sound anywhere. A man who had been in the British army would never forget the engine whine of a Land Rover.

The men on the road were alerted. They moved sharply. He guessed they were soldiers, perhaps paramilitary police. He thought they knew their work. Two had taken position behind the tail door of the vehicle and one was crouched in the cover of the forward wheel, and the fourth man, with the Colt in his waist, sauntered to the middle of the puddled road. It came round the corner. The Land Rover was swerving to avoid the potholes and coming slowly because of the tightness of the bend and the man with the Colt revolver blocked its path and waved it casually down. The shout rose in Gord's throat and was stifled, and the weight of his hand pressed down onto Groucho's shoulder and demanded his silence. The Land Rover stopped. He could see the broad smile on the man's face and his relaxed arm hid the butt of the revolver. The man opened the door of the Land Rover. There was the explosion of movement. The man in cover at the front wheel of the vehicle throwing open his own door. The two men behind the vehicle sprinting forward. Gord saw the flash of the young woman's hair and he heard her shout. She was dragged from her seat. A man on each arm and running her to the station wagon, and the cacophony of barking from the depth of the Land Rover, and her door kicked shut behind her. He saw the trapped dog leaping and clawing at the window of the Land Rover. So fast, Gord had the palm of his hand over the muzzle of Groucho's Kalashnikov. They would not shoot. His other hand loosened on his own weapon. They would not intervene. His decision was made. He watched. The engine of the station wagon was gunned. The young woman, blonde hair, shouted at the skies and the tree line and the bend in the road. A garbled cry for help. He heard the mess of the words, English, incoherent, *English*. She was thrown into the back of the station wagon and there were two of the men piling in after her, and the station wagon accelerated past the Land Rover and raked it with a long burst of firing on automatic.

The station wagon disappeared at the corner.

The engine sound was fainter. The dog roared in the closed interior of the Land Rover. He took his hand from over the muzzle of Groucho's rifle. He saw the bitter anger on Groucho's creased face.

'You let it happen.'

'It wasn't the place . . .'

'You let the Death Squad take her.'

146

'You don't question me . . .'

'She was English, your own.'

'It's not important . . .'

'Do you not have a soul?'

Gord said, grim, 'It would have screwed us . . .'

He went forward. He sat on the road beside the driver's door of the Land Rover. He spoke quietly to Groucho, told him what to do, and Groucho climbed across the bonnet of the Land Rover and reached to open the driver's door and then lay on the bonnet. The dog came out fast and it circled Gord and its bark hammered at his ears. He crooned to the dog, as he had when he had first met the Rottweiler that had guarded the fish farm when it was run by the manager who had been replaced by big Rocky. The barking died. The dog came to him. He had no fear of the dog. He held his hand out to the dog's nostrils and felt the hot breath on the skin of his knuckles. The dog whimpered. He held the dog in his arms and tried to soothe its fear with the gentleness of his voice. He sat in the road and the dog seemed to cry to him and he told Groucho to clear the Land Rover. There was a handbag and a crumpled envelope on the floor with a page of a letter in it, and there was a half-sack of American-produced dog food and a tin bowl. There was a brightly coloured camper's rucksack and when Groucho rummaged in it he found blouses and T-shirts and two pairs of jeans and spare boots and a woman's change of underclothes. He ordered Groucho to leave the clothes and the rucksack in the Land Rover.

Thirty minutes later the column crossed the road.

The dog was beside him. Gord was at the back, cursing them for slowing to gawp at the abandoned Land Rover, pushing them on towards Playa Grande.

# 8

They had no trust for him. Colonel Arturo sensed their suspicion.

'You accept the information I offer you, or you do not . . .'

He stowed the map, neatly creased, back into his briefcase. He shared, in common with most of the senior Guatemalan officer corps, a fervent dislike of Americans.

'. . . You take advantage of the information, act decisively, or you do not . . .'

He could have listed with the stubbed fingers of his hand the occasions in his life when that dislike had erupted. His father, with a young family to rear, sacked by the American manager of a United Fruit Company banana plantation, accused of theft from petty cash . . . At the Escuela Politecnica, the officers' training college at San Juan Sacatepéquez, an American Ranger sergeant, one of the last before they were withdrawn, had humiliated him in front of a class of peers because he had failed to put together, blindfolded, the working parts of a rifle . . . In the mountains, north of Huehuetenango, in a bad firefight, the American-supplied helicopters had been unable to fly with close support rockets because the supply of spare parts had been banned . . . At the Kaibil base of his battalion, in Quetzaltenango district, the visit of a 'fact-finding' group from the American Congress, and the persistent and disbelieving questioning on the lies of human rights abuses . . . In the airport at Miami, flying in with his wife and daughter, subjected to rudeness and delay by the American immigration officials . . . At the parade of Army Day, sitting at the back of the VIP stand, the civilian-suited officers of the American military group from the embassy laughing and sniggering through the march past, yawning and talking through the address of the Chief of Staff . . . He had no love for Americans, and Colonel Arturo thought they recognized his feelings.

He believed now that he had confused them.

They were around him in a half circle. There were two chairs taken to the right side of the Country Attaché's desk, the one he had learned was the Chemist and the one who was the Treasurer. To the left side of the Country Attaché, forehead furrowed, was the Liaison from SouthCom in Panama and beyond him was the Airwing agent. They seemed to weigh what he said, and were unable to make the balance.

The confidence brimmed in Colonel Arturo. 'I do not understand your hesitation. The Chief of Staff himself gave me the most explicit instruction, I was to offer my help to you for twenty-four hours in every day. I do not understand why you hold back, gentlemen . . . I offer you information that can only have the result of diminishing in some slight way the flood of cocaine upon which your country seems so dependent. I offer you an operation of total discretion. I would only be the guide. You would search the *finca*. You would destroy the laboratory. You would make any arrests that were justified. If you are not interested then you should say so . . .'

The Country Attaché shrugged, like he was boxed.

'It's worth a try . . .'

Colonel Arturo clapped his hands. It was the intention of those who had appointed him that he should worm his way into the confidences of the Drug Enforcement Administration agents serving in Guatemala. So difficult for G-2 to learn the workings of the DEA's distrustful and secretive Intelligence Analyst. Small favours, small gifts. The gentle prising open of a door, overheard conversations and dropped words. Beyond the DEA, through that door, were the men of the Central Intelligence Agency and beyond them were the men of the Military Attaché's office. The smile wreathed him.

'Excellent . . . I hope we have success . . .'

He offered them the location of a deserted *finca* in the extreme south-eastern corner of the Franja Transversal del Norte. The co-ordinates placed the *finca* halfway between the village of Playa Grande and the town of Cobán. He offered them, in their distrust, intelligence information of a laboratory used for the transforming of the raw stirred coca paste into crushed cocaine powder. It was his intention to own them.

The flier hesitated. 'The weather's not great.'

'I am sure that an American military aviator can cope with the meteorological conditions of Guatemala . . .'

'Take-off at seven?'

Colonel Arturo's laughter rang in the Country Attaché's office. 'If you wish to be as late as that . . .'

The dog was always close to him and the pace Gord set was cruel.

He had no charity that day.

Gord Brown had been taught well how to force a march forward. He had done it himself on the Brecon mountains of Wales when he had been tested on the induction course, and he had been on the same mountains to watch over recruits striving for selection to the regiment. As then, he heard the fatigued moaning of men pushed to the limit of pain. On the course for induction and selection there had been men who had dropped back, preferred the lorry ride return to base camp and the fast journey to the barracks for the shower and change of clothes and the railway warrant ticket away to the units they had tried to leave. The dropouts would have blisters for a week, stretched muscles for a month, and the sense of failure for a lifetime, but they had been given the choice to fall out. No choice for Zeppo and Harpo and Groucho who were bent under the load weight of their backpacks, and no choice for the Archaeologist who tramped in the torn sneakers and who sometimes cried in pain, and no choice for Jorge who gritted his teeth and flared his lips and refused to complain, and no choice for the villagers and the one-time guerrillas and the men and youths from the jungle camp. There was no choice; a man who fell back was a lost man. He played a game with them. Gord told them of the inevitable military reaction. There would be cordons behind them, and search areas, there would be roadblocks, and there would be the interrogators of the intelligence units and there would be the torture cellars . . . It was the game that fuelled the fear and pushed them on.

Playa Grande, where there was a garrison, was ahead.

He pushed and pulled the pace of the march because he had seen the face of the young woman in terror. He shoved and he dragged them forward because he had heard the cry for help. It was his agony. No dream, no nightmare, because the proof was the dog at his knee. The face and the cry belted his mind, and the anger tore at him.

He had seen Groucho talk to Zeppo, a panting whisper at a rest halt, and he had seen Groucho with Harpo, and Groucho with Jorge.

Gord was allowed to force them and slash them with abuse when they slowed. He was not challenged.

At the mid-afternoon rest halt, double the length of the hourly breaks, while most flopped, while Groucho busied to produce food, he rifled the handbag. The dog was pressed against his body. The half-sack of meal and the dog's steel bowl were strapped into the top of his backpack. The jaws of the dog were beside his hands as they searched the handbag. He thought that the dog bonded to him because he had the handbag . . . There was a plastic ID card of Peace Brigades International, and he read the name of Alexandra Clementine Pitt . . . There was a passport with a photograph that showed a grudging stare of rebellion in the face of a teenage girl who wore a school tie. From the date of birth he saw she was twenty-six years old and the passport had been issued when she was seventeen, and he imagined a private school's trip to France, and there was the visa stamp for entry to La Aurora, Guatemala, that was dated back to the previous August . . . There was a ring of keys . . . There was a letter from home.

It was an intrusion.

He read the letter.

Gord had no business with the letter.

Good headed paper, a village address outside Taunton in Somerset. Below the address were the names of Hugh Pitt, LLB, and Jennifer Pitt, JP, and his eyes darted to the bottom of the reverse side . . . 'Stay safe, Daddy sends his love. Of course I do. Very proud of you. Kisses, Mummy' . . . Gord read the letter that had been written by a local Justice of the Peace, married to a country solicitor. The fucking mission was never permitted to take second place to crap emotion, shit sentiment. It was what he had learned in the fucking regiment. The mission was priority. He read about who had come to dinner, where they had been for drinks after church, the health of the man who cut their lawns, the daffodils in bloom on the drive, the convalescence of an aunt. Groucho came to him with the food bucket, foul mashed gruel, and caught him in the letter. He swept the letter back into its envelope, deep into the handbag, with the keys and the passport and the ID, and zipped the top of the bag shut. When he ate, struggling to swallow the food, the dog had its front paws on either side of the bag.

Gord saw that Zeppo watched him. Zeppo was licking round the rim of his bowl.

There had been another girl, so long before, working in danger, and in her London flat there had been left, carelessly, letters from a mother who had written the mundane routine of life as if that were a protection against the reality . . .

'Move it. Hurry your bloody selves. For Christ's sake, snap together. Get loaded.'

They went forward. The cart wheels of the flame thrower, pushed and pulled and dragged by Vee and Zed, were ahead of him, squealing and complaining. They were learning from him. All had watched him and now copied him. They worked round obstacles, rather than tried to crash them, they twisted and ducked to avoid the clutches of the hanging vines, they no longer dragged the thorn scrub off them but tried to unpick the barbs, they searched more keenly for animal tracks. Going better and going faster . . .

There were daffodils alongside a tarmacadam driveway that led to the home of a young woman whose terror he had seen and whose cry for help he had heard.

Zeppo was ahead of him and waiting for him and the sweat sheen glistened on his body . . .

. . . The sweat poured from his face and it ran on his cheeks and his nose and his lips and his chin.

That morning, the first time, he had hunted for a length of string, and the string was now around his waist and holding his trousers at his hips. It was as if his gut had shrivelled.

And he could hold the pace that was set.

He let the Englishman come level with him.

'Walk with me.'

'If you say so.'

'I was told . . .'

'Yes.'

'. . . I was told that you could have shot the pigs of the Death Squad.'

'Yes.'

'. . . I was told they took a woman.'

'Yes.'

'They took an Englishwoman.'

'Yes.'

'I was told that you did not shoot because that would have endangered our march.'

'Yes.'

They could go now only in single file. He was ahead of the Englishman. He stopped when the Englishman stopped and bent and freed the dog's shoulder hair from the thorn tangle.

'What you did was for us.'

'Yes.'

'And now you feel only the pain of it.'

'Yes.'

'That is your commitment to us.'

'Yes.'

They hustled forward.

Zeppo talked.

'. . . I was an engineer and I lived in Guatemala City. I was married. We were blessed with a son. We lived humbly because everything that we had was spent on the education of our son. We sent our son to the Colegio Americano, because we wanted the best for him, half of the teachers were from the United States. From the Colegio Americano we enrolled our son at the University of Francisco Marroquin. At the University of Fran-ciso Marroquin there was none of the radicalism of the San Carlos campus. It was a place of study . . . My son was with the brightest and most privileged young people of the country. He took a degree in social sciences, with honours. He could have worked for the Civil Service . . . We had made great sacrifices for his education. I cannot tell you why, but he went, two weeks after his graduation, and we never saw him, nor heard of him again while he lived. It was six months after he left us that the *judiciales* came to our house. It is twelve years ago now, and I remember it like it was this dawn. The Security Police came into our house after breaking down our door with hammers. We were made to sit in our night clothes, watched by guns, while our home was searched. He had joined the guerrilla movement. He had become one of the *compañeros* of the Ejército Guerrillero de los Pobres. The officer of the *judiciales* told us that he was the commander of a unit, and he was captured. It was only later that I heard how my son had died. The small unit that he com-manded had made their base in the high forest near to Cotzal which is in the Ixil triangle. He was held at Cotzal and his fin-gers were amputated, and they flayed some of the skin on his body and then he was tied to a tree near to the gate of the sol-diers' camp. He was tied to the tree for five days and four nights and the flies and the mosquitoes and the insects crawled in the

154

blood of his wounds and on the flesh where his skin had been stripped. Later, I was told in Cotzal by a woman that after my son was dead an officer had urinated in his mouth. He was my son . . . I had never, before, supported the movement of revolution. I had no politics. I worked as an engineer in the factory of the Marlboro cigarette company. Politics were not a part of my life. We are not responsible for our children, we cannot choose the way they care to follow, but he was my son . . . It was the death of the mind of my wife. I heard in Cotzal of the father of Rodolfo Jorge Ramírez. I crossed the mountains and I came to the village of Acul and I told the father of Rodolfo Jorge Ramírez that I would fight alongside him until I died . . . Just words, because together we went into exile. I am fifty-eight years old. I am blessed to have the chance to honour the promise I made to the father of Rodolfo Jorge Ramírez. He was a fine boy . . .'

Gord thought he saw tears run in the sweat streams on the engineer's cheeks.


'. . . He was a fine boy. He made the ultimate sacrifice of his life because he believed that the armed struggle was justified.'

'Yes.'

'We should stop earlier tonight. I will need the time while there is still daylight to look at the flame thrower. I will help you to fire the flame thrower.'

'Yes.'

The Englishman held out his hand to him, and he ignored it.

The passion was in his voice. 'I tolerate you because you are useful, and because I want to see them burn.'


Too easy to weep . . .

She had been in darkness since they had taken her. Over her head for the bumping ride in the station wagon had been a sack that stank of damp maize cobs. She had heard the shouts when the station wagon had finally stopped, military shouts. She thought they had brought her to the garrison camp at Playa Grande. Off the tail of the station wagon and left to fall into the mud puddles. Dragged to her feet, her arms pinioned behind her back, pushed forward. Hands clutching at her to hurry her and fingers tugging at the lightness of her T-shirt and once groping at the waist of her jeans. Running and stumbling, tripping on a step. Along the length of a corridor that echoed from the scrape of their boots. Pitched down concrete steps, and her knees scraped and her lower lip split. They had taken off her hood and shone torchlight into her face so that she was dazzled, and untied the pinions binding her wrists. Tasting her blood as the door slammed. Still the darkness around her. She understood. Nothing was an accident in this country. Everything was activated by orders from a higher echelon. An order for her to be arrested, an order for her to be detained, an order for an interrogator to travel from Guatemala City, an order for her to disappear, an order for a grave to be dug in the night hours. She understood. She had seen the bodies.

Too easy to cry . . .

Just before they broke the hold of the jungle.

Alone in his thoughts . . .

Gord was back-marker. The dog growled.

His thoughts had been jumbled between the young woman and the flax-blonde hair and the scream in fear for help, and the action they would fight in the morning. The dog growled and turned to face back down the trail they had used, and Gord followed the eyeline of the dog as it stood its ground, but its tail was wrapped down between its haunches and close to its lower belly.

They were followed.

He crouched low so that his chest was against the dog's shoulder and the weight of the machine gun was across his bent knee. He ruffled the collar of the dog to calm it. He waited . . . The sounds behind him of the advance of the march died. The hackles of the dog were up . . . He saw the cat. There was the low growl of the dog, frightened, and there was the hissed spit of the jaguar cat. Its ears were flattened back and the far tip of its tail switched. The jaguar came on. Gord thought they trespassed on its route. It was an old cat, male, and it had no fear of them, only annoyance that its preserve was invaded. It came to a dozen paces from them. The muscle ripple ran in its shoulders. He thought that the dog was the reason that the cat stalked them on the trail. It had stopped. He saw the amber gold of the eyes. He could smell the foul breath of the cat. It was as long as the dog, and as tall. If it had sprung, Gord was calculating, then he would have used the barrel of the machine gun to ward off its weight. He saw the pride of the beast, and the arrogance, and he saw the slashing teeth of the beast. God, and it was magnificent . . .

And it was gone.

It was gone, gliding, into the cover of the undergrowth beside the trail.

The tremble had taken him and he hurried forward to rejoin the column of march and the dog shivered beside him.

They broke the hold of the jungle.

For the last hour of the march they moved fast. They skirted the maize fields where the harvest had been taken and the ground had been dug for new planting. They saw smoke columns ahead of them. Clear of the protection of the jungle the rain fell harder on them and the smoke merged fast into the sprawl of the low cloud. Once they froze, all of them, and the dog stood motionless amongst the trees, as women went by on a track carrying under black umbrellas their bundles of wet cut wood. They could see the red tiles of more substantial buildings and the tin roofs of the shacks. Where Jorge called the halt it was possible to identify, between trees, the limp fluttering of the red and white and blue flag of Guatemala.

It was good for them, the rain.

They could see down into the village of Playa Grande. The rain would blur the vision of the sentries that were posted around the garrison's camp and it would keep men and women and children in their homes. On the road into the village they saw a military truck pass and they saw a work party returning with shouldered spades and pickaxes.

They ate what Groucho gave them.

They were quiet while they ate.

No need to tell any man that in the morning he must fight for his life and for the life of his enemy. Gord left his own canteen of Meals Ready to Eat for the rain to fall in while he rummaged in his backpack for the half-sack of dog food and the metal bowl.

In the last light, Gord tied the dog to the wheel of the cart, and he moved out with Jorge and Zed. There was a spread of light around the gate of the garrison camp to guide them forward. They had covered, as the crow would have flown, forty-eight miles from the landing strip where the Antonov had put down, and it was just the beginning . . . The guerrillas worked to clean their weapons, and he heard Groucho and the Archaeologist arguing history, and the villagers had taken the perimeter watch, and the *campesinos* cleared the debris of the meal for burying in a pit and then would dig the latrine hole, and Zeppo was kneeling beside the cart, with the dog's body against him, and taking the screwdrivers that Harpo passed him.

As they moved away, left the faint noises behind them, Gord could hear the gentle whistling of Zeppo, perhaps a hymn and perhaps an anthem, busy at his work.

Jorge whispered, 'We will light a fire here, Gord, and the fire will be seen the length and the breadth of Guatemala . . .'

The image locked in his mind, himself and a sergeant and a gaggle of troopers from the regiment, perhaps in the dunes of the Gulf, perhaps in the hedgerows of Armagh County, perhaps beside a darkened road on exercise in Germany . . . He, the officer, muttering about seeing fires and lighting fires, and the sergeant belching derision and the troopers giggling ridicule. The blood ran warm in him. It did not seem wrong from the youth of Jorge. No derision, no ridicule . . .

Just the beginning.

Sometimes running low, sometimes crawling in the slithering mud, they went towards the lights at the gate of the garrison camp.

\*    \*    \*

Nothing, of course, to be found in the pages of *La Prensa Libre* or *El Grafico*, but they practised self-censorship for survival and so were worthless to him. Nothing, of course, broadcast on Radio Conga 99.7FM nor on Radio Fiesta 98.1FM but their news bulletins only carried military stories authorized by the High Command. It was rumour and he wished to believe it.

The Academic sat in the vastness of his office in the mathematics block of the University of San Carlos, and on his desk, beside the computer console, lay a single sheet of photocopied paper. The lights burned dully in the office and beyond the window were the hurrying shadows of the last of the students leaving the campus. The Academic had been offered the rumour by a junior lecturer, specializing in mathematics and theoretical physics, who had been his student a decade before. He had read the sheet of paper many times, and the ash from his continuous cigarettes flaked on the message. The junior lecturer had been told the rumour by his girlfriend whose sister was married to a doctor whose brother worked on the staff of the Petén Military Zone Commander. He wished desperately to believe the rumour. The Academic could recall it, the last time that a young man had sat with three other students in tutorial on the worn easy chairs across the room from the desk, and he had congratulated him on his work, praised him, and he had gone to his burial. The officer on the staff of the Petén Military Zone Commander had told his brother who had told his wife who had told her sister who had told her boyfriend of an action on the Chinajá to Sayaxché road in which many soldiers had been killed. He *believed* the rumour, and he believed also the further rumour that follow-up operations were severely hampered by adverse weather. He believed the rumour, wanted to, because of the sheet of paper on his desk.

'... We alert you. Your movements are being strictly monitored by the commandos of our heroic front, and they have strict orders to end your life. We want your head. We are only a few hours away from the great demonstration to our beloved people that our front fulfils justice and makes it prevail against terrorism. Our weapons are already over your body ...'

There was his own photograph, taken at the previous year's graduation day ceremony, sellotaped to the bottom of the sheet of paper. The sheet of paper had been on the floor, pushed under the door, when he had returned to his office from his last class of the day. He *believed* the rumour . . . He tore the sheet of paper into small pieces, dropped them in his ashtray, and he stubbed out the last of his cigarettes. In the spidery hand of a man more familiar with the computer console, he wrote a note for the junior lecturer offering him the permanent use of his library and his research work, and he finished with the flourish of an apology for any inconvenience caused. He locked his office for the last time. He walked across the campus and politely asked a doorman to open up for him the padlock on the door of the law faculty. He was considering, as he walked along an empty corridor, what clothes he would take, and how to tell his wife that she should take the train in the morning to Puerto Barrios and then the bus to the Honduran border. He chided himself that he was not more logical. A sad smile. First he must tell his wife to go to their branch of the Banco Guatemala in Zona 13. The walls of the law faculty were slogan-daubed. He had come to read the poem of Otto René Castillo, *subversivo*. He read the poem that was painted on the wall to help himself to find the courage . . .

> 'One day
> the apolitical
> intellectuals
> of my country
> will be interrogated
> by the simple
> man
> of our people.
> They will be asked
> about what they did
> when
> their nation was slowly

extinguished,
like a sweet and gentle fire,
small and alone . . .
. . . apolitical intellectuals
of my sweet land,
you will not be able to answer.
A vulture of silence will devour
your entrails.
Your own misery
will gnaw at your soul.
And you will be silent,
ashamed of yourselves.'

He thanked the doorman, gave him two quetzals, and heard the door of the law faculty slammed shut and padlocked behind him. Before the Academic drove away he looked a last time, and wistfully, back at the darkened buildings of the San Carlos University. He had believed the rumour.

The light shone into her face.

'Good evening, Miss Pitt. I am sorry if you were asleep. I apologize if I awakened you. It was the problem of the weather. I was able to fly only as far as Cobán. Dreadful conditions. I tell you, in truth, I feared for my life. Then by road, not possible without four-wheel drive. You know, it has taken me sixteen hours from Guatemala City . . . In order that we should not misunderstand each other, Miss Pitt, may I explain a few small matters. The men who took you, Miss Pitt, state quite categorically that there were no witnesses. You were travelling in an area close to the Mexican border which is one of the last areas where the EGP guerrilla group operates. You were, Miss Pitt, a victim of those guerrillas, probably taken for their sexual gratification. That is how the minister will explain it to your ambassador, and they will take a glass of sherry and they will express their mutual surprise that you had shown such folly in driving alone in an area of difficulty . . .'

There were tears in her eyes from the light. The voice of an unseen young man, caressing her.

'. . . Further matters to be explained, Miss Pitt. You came to Guatemala, to *interfere*. We are a proud people and we do not permit outsiders to tell us how we should govern our lives. I said that we should have a conversation, I sincerely hope that is possible. In your ignorance, Miss Pitt, you will have contacted a lunatic minority who seek the overthrow of the state. You will have been flattered by their attention, they will have been gratified by your interest. I want to talk about them, Miss Pitt. There are many organizations which offer a front of respectability but are, in truth, no more than runners and couriers for the subversive campaign waged with brutality against the people of Guatemala. I want the names of those you have met, I want the dates and the times of your meetings, I want the addresses of the safe houses that were used . . .'

She blinked back at the light. She ground her fingernails into the flesh of her waist, tried to turn her mind from the smooth softness of the voice.

'. . . There would be doctors who treat subversives when they have been wounded, there would be trades unionists who call the strikes with lies and false promises that hinder the economic development of Guatemala, there would be lawyers who advise on how our constitution can be manipulated, there would be women who claim their men were killed by government forces when we know they were the victims of the subversives. I want the names, Miss Pitt, of all those you have met who perjure themselves and defame our country. I hope for a pleasant conversation, Miss Pitt . . .'

The fear welled in her. The light burned at her.

She had seen the wounds on the bodies, and the blood.

It was the flying that Tom Schultz had been trained for.

The weather was what the veteran instructors at the Army Primary Helicopter School talked about in the dining area, made jokes of. At the Primary School at Fort Wolters in Texas, and later at the Advanced School at Fort Rucker in Alabama, the old men liked to frighten the recruits with bad weather stories.

Right from the time of the first whine of the starter motor and the thrash of the transmission through the turn of the big rotors it had been dumb weather to be up in. And if it had not been that Colonel Arturo was his passenger then Tom would have aborted the flight, done it there on the apron at La Aurora, and the Intelligence Analyst wouldn't have complained, nor the Chemist. It would have been sensible, *prudent*, to have aborted the flight, and he had the squat little bastard to thank for their being up and belted in the storm winds. He was trained for this flying; the flying was freedom, challenge, the beauty in his life and the passion, the only goddamn glory that he knew.

The roads went in the valleys, and he had to stay in the valleys because the goddamn mountains were hazed in the rain cloud. He went a hundred feet above the road from Guatemala City and out north to Salamá and they were low enough over the town for him to see the Indians ant-like on the scaffolding covering the facade of the old church. From Salamá to Cobán, and lower because the cloud was thicker where the metal road finished. He hovered a full minute at sixty feet above the plaza of Cobán and his rotors were below the height level of the cathedral's towers. A shit bad twelve miles from Cobán, hugging ground like it was combat flying, over the coffee fields, with the wind growing and the wipers spearing the rain off the glass. Picking up the valley of the Chixoy river and diving on it and flattening out over the flood water.

He'd get the squat bastard there.

And not a squeak out of the squat bastard, not anything, and they'd been chucked by the winds and there had been driven rain through the window hatches and the closed side doors.

He put the bird down.

He hadn't flown such bad weather since he had come out of the army. In three years of DEA they hadn't let him close to a government-owned helicopter, and he'd had to buy his own flying time at the club outside St Louis. The guy who owned the club would have needed bypass surgery if Tom Schultz had taken up the bird in this shape of weather.

The strip was sited halfway between what the map called the Ixcán region and the village of Playa Grande.

He put down.

It was a crap landing for a right seat qualified pilot, army talk for a quality flier, pranging the skids.

He looked across, left seat, and the Chemist had crossed himself and not been ashamed. He looked back, and the Intelligence Analyst reached forward to hug him. He saw into the squat bastard's face and there was a small grin, no fear. They were all combat-geared. They ran from the Huey bird towards the low wooden complex of buildings. The rain drenched them. He reckoned Arturo was older than any of them, and faster than any of them. He was behind Arturo, and his legs ached from the pressure of the kicking pedals and his fists on the Colt carbine seemed bruised from holding the weight of the flying stick. It was as if Arturo knew where to go, which door to belt down . . . Too goddamn easy for the squat bastard.

Arturo led them inside. They hugged the walls ready to fire. They checked each building.

There was the laboratory building, and the tanks. There was the store house that held the chemicals. There was the living building with beds and a kitchen. There was the communications building.

The escape had been frantic. Beds unmade, blankets rumpled. Food on the table. He had made one pass only before landing, suicide to come in without checking an LZ. It stank of set-up . . . Tom thought that Colonel Arturo made marionettes of them, but it was too good to sneer at . . . The squat bastard was sat in a chair, the Uzi on his lap, and watching them as they itemized what they had found. In the laboratory tanks were forty-nine kilos of coca paste. In the store were the supplies of sulphuric acid and aqueous potassium permanganate and ammonium hydroxide, along with the jars of ether and hydrochloric acid. In the communications room was an HF radio, warm. In the living area were two rifles and a grenade launcher and a pearl-handled pistol.

'Good, yes?'

The Intelligence Analyst was writing his inventory. 'It's useful.'

'It is what we can achieve when we work *together*.'

Tom said, 'I tell you, guys, I don't want to be hanging about here.'

The rain hammered on the roof of the building, streamed the dirt off the windows.

Colonel Arturo called to him. 'You should not be impatient, Mr Schultz. Is it every day you intercept forty-nine kilos of coca paste on its way to your fine country . . . ?'

They were on the start line.

They were synchronized to go at noon.

It had been as second nature to Gord to make the dispositions, organize them. *Request* was forgotten. *Require* was the present.

They were in the line of fields beyond the furthest shack houses of the village of Playa Grande. He was crouched down. He watched the speeding second hand of his wristwatch. Zeppo was away to the right with the guerrillas and the mortars. Harpo was to the left with the jungle people and the machine gun. Groucho was between Gord and Harpo and with the villagers and the rocket launcher. Jorge was between Gord and Zeppo and with Eff and Zed.

All through the morning he had gone through the plan with each group, and last he had spoken to Eff and Zed and smacked his fist into the palm of his hand for emphasis and told them their responsibility was the safety of Rodolfo Jorge Ramírez.

Always the excitement, always the fear, waiting for the second hand of a watch to hit the moment . . . and always the style of a fighting man to hide the excitement and the fear . . .

One minute to noon. They were 200 yards from the gate of the garrison camp. A long morning it had been, watching the camp from dawn, going over the plan until it could be recited by them all, checking the weapons, memorizing what Zeppo had told him, remembering the route used on the reconnaissance. A shit long morning because all of them had wanted to go at first light, and he had insisted that noon was the time of maximum relaxation in any garrison camp.

Watching the second hand, controlling the excitement and the fear.

On his feet, and grabbing the cart handle, and running.

Gord led the scramble out of the rain ditch, dragging the cart after him, and onto the track and through the scattering chickens and past the screaming pigs. The Archaeologist was sprinting to catch him and whistling pain when his shredded sneaker caught a stone flint. Vee was beside him and snatching at the cart's handlebar. The warmth of the rain ran on Gord's face and on his arms and his hands slipped on the cart's handle and if Vee had not steadied him then he would have pitched over. Slithering for the foot grip on the smoothed mud of the track between the shack homes and seeing the gape of the faces in the doorways and the children running from ahead of them to hide. The cart leaped, bumped, careered in front of them, and the wheels screeched. Halfway, and the swerve to the right track through more mazes of wood slat walls and tin roofs and the smell of cooking and women screaming and drunk men lurching away from them. All the time there was the rattle clatter of the wheels smacking against stones. He heard the first mortar bomb explode. Turning, the short spasm second, to grip the arm of the Archaeologist who was fading, ripping him forward. The second mortar blasted in his ears. There was the chatter burst of the machine gun, then the impact crack of the rocket launcher's grenade. Swinging left and slipping and stamping a foothold. The gate was in front of them.

They were running for the gate.

He thought he heard, at his shoulder, the Archaeologist cry for God.

He saw to his right that Zeppo would be hard behind him to the gate.

The bar of the gate was up. A sentry had fallen on his sand-bags, chest down onto his machine gun, and the sentry in the poncho cloak who would have controlled traffic at the gate was writhing in the roadway. Gord ran onto the parade area. In front of him was the principal concrete building with the raised steps. He could see bullets spatter the walls of the building. It was what Zeppo had told him.

Through the night, through the dawn, through the morning, Zeppo talking to him and showing him. He wrenched the cart to a halt. On the ground behind the cart. Taking short seconds to familiarize again with the ignition trigger and the firing lever. He aimed at the door of the building, he pulled the cart so that the clusters of nozzles on the tubes faced the door of the building. His fist dragged the firing lever back. A dribble at first, a choking spurt, then a cascade of black smelling oil leaping in front of him and across the parade ground space and onto the steps of the building, and through the door.

He saw the surprise and confusion of the officer, framed in the doorway, scrabbling for the pistol in his belt holster, as the oil film caught him, covered his legs and then his torso and then his face part hidden by the wraparound sunglasses.

Cold, as it was just an exercise, as if he was on a firing range, Gord squeezed on the ignition trigger.

Fire following the oil.

An orange-and-red fire scrambling towards the doorway of the building. It seemed to move slowly but that was a deception. The officer was caught. The fire took him. The fire brushed the officer aside as if it had a weight that clipped him, and the fire cascaded into the heart of the building. He felt the dragging pull on his shoulder and ignored it. He marvelled at the power of the fire he had thrown at the building. What he heard, first, was the screaming. It was the screaming from the building that broke the wall of silence around him. Vee was punching him, pointing frantically to the single-storey wooden building to the left. Gord saw the men spilling from the building, some armed, some defenceless, running in panic.

Catching them, holding them, drenching them, and then the fire running after the oil film.

The terror screaming, the agony crying.

It was Gord Brown's work. His work was the fire climbing into smoke above the roof of the main building, and the fire flicking the windows and doorway of the accommodation block, and the fire draping rolling and heaving men. His work . . .

She heard the mortars explode, muffled, and the rocket's grenades. He had gone. She heard the chatter crack of the machine gun. Alex Pitt heard the noise of the battle and lay on her stomach in the darkness and the wet of the cell.

She lay rigid in her pain. To move was to feel the hurt of what he had done to her in the blackness of the cell. Always the soft sweet voice, and the kicking and the punching.

She had told him nothing. It would have been her victory if he had shown impatience, but only the cloying drip of the voice to tell her that he had time and would be back, and that the later pain would be worse. She had not given him the names.

She could not see it, but the smoke was seeping into the cell, spreading and climbing, piercing the space under the door, gathering in her mouth and nose and throat.

He had told the flier, Schultz, that at Playa Grande the tanks could be topped with aviation fuel.

The flier had said that, with the weather, they should have filled tanks for the flight back. The flier had said that it was a shit day to be short of fuel.

Behind them, at the strip, were the spilled precursor chemicals for the process between paste and powder, and the broken radio communications system. In the helicopter, sealed in bags so that the fumes were contained, between the legs of the Chemist, were forty-nine kilos of coca paste. Tied together and knotted to the seat supports below the Intelligence Analyst were the weapons they had found. Colonel Arturo had taken the left front seat. He thought the grudged appreciation had won him the right to wear the flying helmet with the built-in earphones and the attached microphone.

They were low above the tree tops.

It was the smoke that Arturo saw first. Dark and piling, it rose from the ground and flattened in collision against the cloud ceiling.

He had never been stationed at Playa Grande, but he had been there for a night, using it as a jump point, during the campaign of Determination '88. Playa Grande, from what he remembered, was a command building, two dormitory sleeping huts for the conscripts, a separate block for the regular army officers and NCOs, a dug-out armoury, and fuel storage beside the helicopter LZ. Forty conscripts, five NCOs and two officers, from what he remembered of the garrison.

'Take her in.'

'What do you reckon . . . ?'

'How the fuck should I know?'

'What do you want . . . ?'

'Get us close.'

'My ship, my responsibility . . .'

He had hold of the flier's arm. They bucked in the air. He gripped the flier's arm and pointed ahead, an order.

'Close on the camp.'

They came in fast. He thought the flier was combat-experienced. A sharp approach, and then a sudden banking twist that threw him sideways and his weight was held by the shoulder harness. The garrison camp was laid out a hundred feet below him. He saw it all. The flame thrower belched ahead of him and caught one of the two conscripts' living huts, a great caterpillar of rushing fire. He had the Uzi machine pistol on the webbing belt held across his lap and the helicopter travelled too fast, and his balance was destroyed, and he could not have opened the window flap to shoot down. He saw into the face, for a moment, of the man lying behind the flame thrower's cart. He saw the machine gunner and the tracer arc that ended against the walls of the NCOs' and officers' block where he had slept the one night before the jump-off in Determination '88. The fire flashes of shooting. Blackened men lying on the open space of the parade area and their bodies convulsed. Tracer rising at them, hunting them. Calm in his ear . . .

'Receiving fire. We are receiving fire.'

The calm of a combat flier. They were over the edge of the perimeter wire. Ahead of them, Arturo saw the man. The man was caught in the wire, and struggling. The man flailed his arms at the helicopter. It might have been a sledgehammer that smacked the lower fuselage of the helicopter. The bird jolted . . .

'Taking hits. We are taking hits.'

Seeing the face of the man caught in the coiled razor wire. Recognizing the face and not placing it. Seeing the villa in the suburb of Guatemala City . . . a gardener hosing the flowers, and a guard reading a paper, and a tiled floor swept . . . seeing the face, pleading, of the interrogator from the basement of the villa.

'Put her down . . .'

'No fucking way.'

'Pick him up.' Shouted into the microphone, yelled at the helmet of the flier.

The calm of the voice in his ear. 'Forget it, colonel.'

They were gone beyond the perimeter wire. The struggling man in the wire was lost from the side window vision. He strained to see behind him. When he turned, the flier was pointing to the cockpit dials.

The flier's finger rapped the fuel dial, and the needle was plunging.

The firing had stopped.

Gord stood in the centre of the parade area.

He was numbed, and he held his hands tight on the handle arm of the cart and tried to control the shake of his arms.

To his left, sat on the ground with their hands over their heads, were the prisoners. In front of him, framed against the licking fire of the command building, some charred and some grotesque from shrapnel and bullet wounds, were the bodies. To his right, some lying and some sitting and some standing, were the wounded and a soldier with a red cross on a white arm band moved amongst them. And standing and staring was an indulgence. So tired . . .

'Jorge, I need the armoury broken open. I need to know every weapon that is available to us. I need to know the ammunition for each weapon.'

He had dismissed him like a boy, and Gord bit on his tongue, but it was done. He saw the anger flare in Jorge but, like a boy, he went as he was ordered.

Zeppo walked to him. Zeppo asked him if he wanted to be shown how to refuel the cart's tanks.

'Do it yourself,' snapped Gord.

Harpo came to him. Harpo grinned and there were cordite stains on the height of his forehead and he carried the machine gun loosely on his shoulder, and Harpo said that he had hit the helicopter, definite.

'At that height you couldn't have missed it,' whipped Gord.

The Archaeologist reached him, red-eyed. A villager was dead. A guerrilla had been hit in the knee cap. A man from the jungle camp was wounded in the pelvis, bad.

'What did you expect?' cracked Gord.

The rain sluiced on his face. The rain ran on his cheeks and his nose and his lips . . . The only chance was to make the charge . . . The door of the armoury broke under the weight of the sledgehammer blows. It was as if he alone understood what was their only chance.

'Jorge, leave that, leave it . . . Get into the village. Do your talking bit. We want men . . . Jorge, we move in an hour.'

He saw Groucho. Groucho skirted the fire of the command building, came from its rear. Funny little bastard. Groucho punched the air, like he'd scored the goal that mattered, like he was a kid. Funny little bastard . . . She was behind him. Zed had a hold of her and supported her. Her face was smoke dark. Groucho led her closer to Gord. She had a split lip, and a closed eye. He felt the weakness in his knees and his weight was taken by the handle of the cart. They were all watching him. They knew what had been his *priority*. He saw the blonde gold of her hair against the mist. The rain beat down. It was the one chance . . .

'Jorge, we must have men from the village. One hour and we are gone. I want the weapons brought from the armoury. I want any food we can find. I want any radio set. I want medical supplies, bandages. One hour and we move. Get the prisoners back up where we were, get them to carry down our packs. Get . . .'

He saw the wounds on her face.

He asked it of Vee. Would Vee, please, be so kind, a favour to him, run like shit back through the village, back across the fields, back to the tree line, back to the dog. Would Vee bring the dog to Miss Alex Pitt, please.

'One hour, and we move . . .'

# 9

The impact, shaking up his spine and wrenching his shoulders against the restraining harness, left him shambling and awkward as he tramped round the bird. Tom passed the Intelligence Analyst who sat with the rain puddles already round his haunches and who seemed to whimper little cries. The Chemist was lying full length, mud-covered, as if the ground was heaven's bosom. Would have been worse for them because they would only have heard the alarms singing, and the drop before the rotors steadied them would have put their guts into their throats and they wouldn't have seen the field that he aimed for.

He had feathered the bird onto a cut maize field. Part luck and part skill, he had put down at the higher end of the field that was a small oasis in trees. The lower end would have been wetter, and he had come down hard, and without engine power, and if he had been at the lower end of the field then his skids would have sunk.

If he had had the time, and he hadn't, then he might just have been proud of the landing.

They might have cleared the garrison camp by a mile. Tom didn't reckon it was more than that.

It was the first evaluation that was critical, because the first evaluation was about fire. All the way down, the macroseconds of memory, he had tried to shut the fire fear from his mind. The memory was of a gunship Apache bird, the shudder hit of a shoulder-launched missile, control going and the stick not responding, the fire spreading from the tanks behind the cockpit seat, and the ground rushing to meet him. It was the memory. The fire spreading after landing impact and the heat growing on the harness buckle, and dragging through the window because the door was jammed, and the jagged Plexiglas slashing the side of his face as he had thrown himself clear. It was the memory of the consuming shame of being shot down behind the lines of the enemy, and it was the memory of the blood coming from the wound that ran from his right ear to the line of his jaw . . .

He circled the bird warily.

No fire, no smoke.

Tom went closer to the hull.

All the Huey birds made available to the DEA were dredged from the army's supplies of obsolete ships. The machine-gun mounts, port and starboard, had been stripped off, and the rocket pods. The armour had been left. On the armour of the hull, underneath the skids, Tom saw the smudges on the high-grade steel where the machine-gun bullets had struck and been deflected. It would have been a one-chance shot. The last of the fuel was dripping down, technicolour in the rain streams. One shit chance, might have been when he had made the evasive banking manoeuvre. One goddamn shit chance. The technicolour trail led up behind the passenger hatch to the fuel tank filler . . . if he had not banked . . . it was a see-through plastic tube, and it was neatly severed.

He climbed back inside the passenger hatch. He picked up two rifles.

'Heh, don't you think you'd do better mounting some sort of perimeter watch . . . ?'

He threw a rifle at the Intelligence Analyst, where he sat, and the second rifle towards the Chemist, where he lay. He threw the rifles hard into the field's mud. He watched them struggle to retrieve the weapons. He started to rout in the maintenance box that was set behind the rear passenger seats. He wanted cutters for the fuel tube, to tidy it, he wanted . . .

He was at the hatch. They were moving drunk slow.

'Heh, where's Arturo . . . ?'

\*　\*　\*

Demanding and pushing and bullying, Gord had the weapons out from the armoury. He had the food supplies stacked, he had the medical equipment stowed. He checked his watch. He had said it would be an hour and he would take no delay on the schedule he had made. The fires burned well from the wooden sleeping buildings. He felt the flatness that was always with him after the rushing elation of combat, as it had been in the Gulf and as it had been in Ireland, always the emptiness afterwards. In the radio room, amongst the burned and broken equipment, slumped over it, had been the blackened body of a technician. It was enough for Gord. He drove himself to beat the emptiness with demanding and pushing and bullying.

Fifteen minutes before the withdrawal time, and Groucho was showing him the list, carefully made, of the food supplies and the medical equipment.

'Fine, get it loaded up . . .' Gord hustling away.

Ten minutes to the end of his given hour and Zeppo was coming back across the parade area and a trail of men, villagers and jungle people and guerrillas, behind him pushed the cart and a wheelbarrow. Zeppo told him, proud, that the tanks were full, and showed him in the wheelbarrow the oxygen cylinder and the spare jerry cans of fuel and the plastic holders of motor oil. Zeppo was telling him that the cylinder would compress the mixture of fuel and oil for the tubes of the flame thrower.

'Great . . .' Gord walking away.

Five minutes before the move out and Harpo was at his side and reciting the inventory of rifles and machine guns, loose ammunition and belt ammunition, and mortars and sub-machine guns, and what it would weigh and how many men would be needed to carry the extra weight.

'I want it all, down to the last bullet . . .' Gord striding away.

The Archaeologist sat amongst the piled heap of the back-packs and tightened the laces on new and shined army boots.

'It's not my business, sir, but may I tell you that if you continue to try to push men then, and I'll be very sorry if it happens, all they'll want is to see you fall flat on your pretty face. No offence.'

Gord went by him.

It was three minutes to the hour when Gord heard the singing. They were coming up the hill from the village. It was like a marching song. There were the children in front and at the side of the column of men. The children darted and ducked and ran and skipped ahead of and beside the column. *Butterflies* . . . As if it were a carnival for the children . . . And around the men were Eff and Vee and Zed who worried at the edges of the column. He counted thirty-one men. Behind the column, behind the butterflies, he saw Jorge. The young man walked with Alex Pitt, and the dog was beside her. He could not hear what she said, but her fingers jerked into Jorge's chest as if to reinforce the ferocity of her argument. Behind the column, behind the butterflies, behind Jorge and Alex Pitt, a crowd of women trailed. There were weapons to be gathered, handed down by Harpo. There were the big cardboard cartons of food and medical supplies, allocated by Groucho. There were the metal boxes of ammunition to be loaded onto shoulders. Gord was jockeying them, chivvying them, calling for speed and his watch hands had already slipped away from the hour that he had allowed, and the temper was rising in him. She stood by the gate with the women and her eyes seemed to follow him and accuse him.

They left the camp behind them, and they left the prisoners sitting in the parade area with the wounded. Amongst the army wounded were their own.

They were across the first field beyond the camp perimeter when she caught him. The forward men of the march were near to the tree line. She ran, she slipped in the loose ploughed mud of the field, she pushed herself up and ran again. She caught him and the rain streaked the hair across her face.

She shouted at him. 'For God's sake, do you know what you are doing?'

'I know exactly what I am trying to do.'

'Those men you've hijacked, they're innocents . . .'

He kept on moving for the tree line.

'. . . You're taking them to their deaths . . .'

She had washed the smoke grime from her face.

'. . . Have you thought it through, what'll happen to the people left behind in Playa Grande . . . ?'

Her upper lip was split and swollen.

'. . . It's not just the lives of the men you're taking, it's the lives of those you leave abandoned behind you . . .'

She twisted her head as she spat the words at him because her left eye was closed in bruising and useless to her.

'. . . God, you bloody men, and your bloody war games. You're English, right? You're a bloody mercenary, right? You're making money out of these simple people's misery. God, you and your kind make me sick . . .'

There was a cigarette burn in the middle of her cheek.

'. . . Everything we're trying to achieve here, you've undone . . .'

They were at the tree line. The column ahead of him was disappearing, pushing aside the dank foliage that swallowed each man and the cart and the wheelbarrow.

'. . . Don't expect thanks from me. I know I was dead, but I know bloody well that it was just luck, pure bloody luck, that you got me out. Doesn't make right what you're doing. And when you've destroyed these people you'll have forgotten what they looked like, where they lived, what their bloody names were. You'll get no thanks grovelled from me, not while you're juggling people's lives. Are you too stupid to have thought out the consequences . . . ?'

Gord said quietly, 'There are things I have forgotten, and that is stupid of me.'

Her voice was raised. 'And a bit bloody late for the hand wringing . . .'

'It makes you ugly when you're angry, Miss Pitt, so *shut up*, please.'

He saw that her breath gagged. Fast movements. The machine gun down. The backpack slung off. He unfastened the top flap of the backpack. He took out the sack of dog food and the tin bowl.

'Stupid of me . . .'

He pushed lower into the backpack. He lifted out her handbag, solemnly gave it to her.

'. . . Stupid of me to have forgotten them. Look after yourself, Miss Pitt.'

He heaved the backpack up, and he shouldered the machine gun. He turned away from her. The lie was in his mind. He had told her that she was ugly when she was angry. She looked just bloody brilliant when she was angry.

He was gone into the trees.

He had freed the interrogator from the razor wire.

He had picked the wire barbs from the ripped clothing where the young man had panic struggled.

He had heard the clear commands in English and he watched the column move out from the garrison camp.

He had gone to the centre of the parade area to drink the sight dry.

Arturo looked around him. He would have considered himself, and it was the way that he was ranked by his superiors, an expert in counter-insurgency warfare. He knew the enemy that the armed forces of Guatemala had fought over the last decade. The enemy was capable of blowing a bridge, toppling an electricity pylon, murdering a *finca* supervisor, ambushing a small patrol. The enemy had never before overrun a defended military position and destroyed it. It was because of the Englishman . . .

After he had freed the interrogator he had crawled closer. He had seen the rat vermin in rags ransack the armoury and the food store and carry clear the boxes of medical supplies, and seen the way they ran when the Englishman barked. He had seen the older men, *Ladinos*, who had played at command with big voices, now slink to the Englishman's orders. He had seen a young American, heard his voice, known from the way he carried his rifle that he was no soldier, and seen the way he stayed close to the Englishman as if proximity were safety. He had seen the boy leader bring the line of men from the village, calling his

178

encouragement to them, and bow to the Englishman's command call. Always it was the Englishman . . .

He could recall, and his memory was always sharp, eight years before, in the officers' mess bar at the High Command, he had met two officers, one from the marines and one from artillery, from Argentina, and over whisky they had told of the battle in the Malvinas when they had fought the English paratroopers. A battlefield called Goose Green, and the drink had flowed. A thousand and a half men, dug into defensive positions, and beaten by a force a quarter of the size. One had called them 'barbarians', the other had called them 'ruffians', both had called them 'superb'.

Colonel Arturo looked around him. Some survivors slowly dug the graves of the dead, some tried to make a tarpaulin shelter that would withstand the wind and shelter the wounded, some wandered aimlessly in shock. He was told by the NCO that it was thought an emergency radio transmission had been made between the time of the co-ordinated attack by rocket, mortar, machine gun, and the moment that the flame thrower had hit the command building. Time for him to wait, until a relief force arrived at Playa Grande, and time for him to ponder on the Englishman. It was clear in the mind of Colonel Mario Joaquín Enrique Arturo that the life of the Englishman was the pivot point of the rebellion.

It was the death of the Englishman that was required.

Pushing them forward, whipping them on the climb.

Gord accepted no stragglers.

Reaching towards the uplands that were hidden by the rain mist.

Gord showed no pity.

Driving the column on, urging them like stubborn cattle to take to the water tracks that sluiced their boots and shins.

Gord cursed them when they slipped and toppled the load from the wheelbarrow.

Scrambling for distance because he had been told that a radio message might have been sent . . .

Harpo was beside him. '... What you understand of us, I don't know. What is your commitment to us, I don't know. I will tell you of myself ... Can you imagine the life of the political exile? It is the existence of the coffee shop and the passing around of the newspapers that are weeks old and the whispering of rumours that most likely have no fact. No money. The exile is the prisoner of the regime that is host. Each year our position in their scale of importance declines. Each year we must move to worse accommodation because the money is not increased and the inflation drives us out. The room I rented, one room, there were rats in the winter when they came up to the first floor to escape the rain ... You can get to love even rats when you are in exile and alone. Two highlights of each day as an exile. To meet in the morning at the coffee shop and pass the old newspapers and to wonder if anyone back where you came from remembers your face and your life. To sit in the evening in the wet season in a single room and talk to the rats ... We had all softened. We all *talked* about going back. If he had not died, if the boy, Jorge, had not taken the challenge given him then we would have gone on, year after year, feebler and weaker, dreamed, waited for death. I am prepared to walk with you, take the crap from you, so that I do not have again to be in exile.'

'What will happen to those left behind?'

'They are the betrayed. When was it different? We used to be told that we were the victims of fascist oppression and that the flag of red with the sickle and the hammer flew above us for our salvation. We imagined that the great men of the Politburo met each week and considered only the ways to aid the fight of the oppressed in Guatemala. Is that ridiculous to you? In the apartment of the father of Rodolfo Jorge Ramírez there was on the wall a photograph of Leonid Brezhnev. We thought he *cared* about us. We were betrayed. In the Kremlin of Moscow there would not be a single man to care what happened to the people of Guatemala. It is a bad feeling, Mr Gord Brown, to know that you have been betrayed ...'

'What will happen to them ... ?'

*    *    *

'We should find what the hell's moving.' The Intelligence Analyst shivered in a back passenger seat, and covered the tree line with his carbine rifle.

'Doesn't sound like a great idea to me.' The Chemist lounged in the left pilot seat.

Tom said, 'Count me out, because this is where I'm staying.'

The light was going under the low cloud. Maybe in the morning it would be right to find what the hell was moving, maybe in the morning that would seem a great idea. Not with the light going. The radio wasn't broken, just that it was useless where they were, on the ground, with the mountain wall of the Cuchumatanes blocking the possibility of a signal to the basement communications system at the embassy.

'You saw that flame thrower, shit, that was a mean thing.'

'That was serious business.'

Tom said, 'I don't think it was meant to be fun and games up there . . .'

At dusk, headlights spearing the gloom, the relief convoy reached Playa Grande. A lumbering armoured car snouted through the village and towards the garrison camp leading two lorries carrying the infantry.

The brief and unrepeated radio message had been received at Barrillas to the west, but there was no road between Barrillas and Playa Grande. The content, garbled, of the radio communication had been passed to area headquarters south at Santa Cruz del Quiché, then relayed to army headquarters in Guatemala City. From Guatemala City the message had been sent to Cobán, east.

There was a poor road between Cobán and Playa Grande, and worse in torrential rain, and twice the convoy had unloaded the troops while the vehicles edged past a rockslide, the wheels knife-edge close to the precipice. It had been an emergency call, confused and incomplete. The officer commanding the convoy did not know what he would find. The armoured car nosed into the deserted street. No lights, no cooking fires, no smoke piling from roof gaps.

The headlights of the armoured car caught the figure standing in the gateway of the garrison camp. He wore mud-smeared combat fatigues with the rank of a colonel on his shoulder flaps and with the Kaibil insignia on the upper arms of the tunic. A young civilian in torn clothes sat at his feet.

The troops of the convoy were led by the colonel through the gloom of the camp. They were shown the graves, and the wounded, and the fire-ruined buildings, and the broken swinging door of the armoury into which the rain drifted. Using the lights of the armoured car and the two lorries to guide them, the troops fanned out to search the village of Playa Grande.

'What will happen to them . . . ?'

It had been open ground, thick with rock but thin with trees, for the first hour of darkness. He had driven the march harder and further than on any day since they had landed in the Petén jungle.

'Some will have fled from the village,' Harpo told him.

They had found the cover of trees for the night, and he had allowed a fire to be lit. The fire was slow burning but was comfort and he had permitted cigarettes to be smoked.

'Those who won't leave?'

They lay like the dead around him.

'It was what they learned from the Americans. It is called the "psychosis of terror". What you have to believe, Mr Brown, they are intelligent men in the Guatemalan army. There will be some who will not have left Playa Grande, the old and the sick and the stupid, and they will be killed. They will use the "psychosis of terror" to counter the rumour of our presence. They will try to make the young men too frightened to join us, so they will butcher the old and the sick and the stupid.'

He thought of the girl, Alexandra Clementine Pitt, whom he had walked away from, and the children who had fluttered as butterflies around the marching men, and the women who had trailed behind them.

'It seemed important to me to know. Thank you.'

*   *   *

At first they had seen, from the upper ground behind the church of Playa Grande, the roving headlights of the armoured car and the lorries. Later, they lost sight of the headlights because the brightness of the fires swamped them. After they could no longer see the village and the fires, they could hear the shooting. In the darkness, amongst the trees, it was not possible for them to go fast enough to lose, quickly, the sound of the shooting. There were children shouting, crying that they were lost. There were women weeping because their men had gone forward in the marching column from the garrison camp. There were the piercing whistles, each different in pitch and beat, as men tried to herd together their families. Alex carried a girl child who fought and kicked her and screamed for her mother. The rain fell on them and the sounds of gunfire were intermittent, and when the shooting and the village were behind them there was a glow of fire resting against the cloud base. They were driven through the night by their fear. And the bloody man hadn't seemed to listen to her. The bloody man and his kind had brought the catastrophe down upon these people. The bloody man was responsible for this flotsam of people blundering and stumbling through the trees, falling on raw rock, fleeing the fire glow and the distant shooting.

It was later, when they could go no further, when the fire had died, when the shooting had ceased, when they were rain-soaked and flopped, when the dog nestled against her and the girl child slept, that the thought smashed her.

She had the dog beside her and alert to each sound near her, and she had the dog's food in a sack that was knotted at the neck with string and tied to her waist, and the dog's tin was in the sack, and she had her handbag.

She had not thanked the bloody man, filthy and unshaven and smelling and husbanding the death cart, for the life of her dog. She had not thanked the bloody man, organizing and ordering and cursing, for the gift of her handbag. She had not thanked the bloody man, hard eyes and cold mouth and fighting chin, for her life.

The bloody man . . .

\* \* \*

He had changed buses at Santa Cruz del Quiché, and the second bus had dropped him after dark in the plaza at Nebaj. The Fireman had walked through the night, going north on the mud dirt road. It was the weight of the big boots that had finally killed his progress. He sat at the side of the road and the wide brim of his hat kept the rain from his face. The Fireman had no doubt that it was the right place to wait because now that the dawn had come he could see further ahead on the road, and back behind him, that small groups of men had gathered, and some had brought machetes, and he had seen a pick-axe, and more had the long-handled forks for turning cut grass, and two had old bolt-action rifles.

He had driven his car, the old Fiat, up through Chichicastenango and on through Santa Cruz del Quiché. Peering through the rain-washed windscreen he had crossed the high ground to Nebaj. And on from Nebaj, straining for the potholes and subsidence slips, until he reached Chajul. He had left the car at Chajul, paid a man too well to keep it safe and in a shed behind the church of the Christ of Golgotha. Past midnight when he had banged on the post office door until the sleep-ridden face had come, and with the help of more money, he had been told where a pack pony might be hired, and a guide.

He was bruised and chafed now. It had been a release, a sacred release, when the first light had come and he had paid off the guide and watched him trail away, leading the horse.

Sore and aching, the Academic sat at the side of the road, just as he had seen other men sitting and waiting. He nibbled a small piece of cheese. He had no idea how long he would have to wait, an hour or a day or a week. There was more cheese in the pocket of his raincoat. The cloud was barely a hundred feet above the road track but the mist had cleared enough for him to see the man who sat thirty paces from him. He could recognize the boots that the man wore. He pushed himself up and went to share his cheese with the Fireman.

\*     \*     \*

And with the dawn a brigadier from Cobán had reached Playa Grande and brought with him a company of troops.

He had been told of a silence wall behind which the villagers of Playa Grande had sheltered, those who had not already fled. He had been shown the bodies of those who had not broken the silence wall. He met the young officer from G-2 who had failed at the silence wall. The brigadier had pronounced decisively that the raiding party responsible for the attack on the garrison camp would now be fleeing for the Mexican border. The border was five miles, direct, to the north. There was a road from Playa Grande towards the border and then twisting to run parallel to it. The brigadier gave orders for the border to be sealed.

It was a logical decision.

A block on the border and more troops fanned out to drive towards them. Guns and beaters, the way it was when they hunted the jaguar cat. Logical . . .

Colonel Arturo led the men, who slithered on the field's mud, weighted by the jerry cans, one on each shoulder, each holding five gallons of aviation fuel. The young officer, Benedicto, had hung back behind him. Arturo gestured to the flier, saw him jump down and go to the fuel point. The flier steadied each can as they poured the fuel. There were 150 gallons to be loaded. The flier looked at him, puzzled, and he grinned back. The young officer, Benedicto, sloped towards the helicopter.

'Shall we go, gentlemen?' Arturo clapped his hands.

'How did you know . . . ?'

'That you wanted fuel? Because I have eyes and when we came down you were without fuel.'

'How did you know I would have fixed the problem?'

'Because you are an American. I understand that even if an American cannot run on water at least he can repair a damaged helicopter. Am I right?'

'I fixed it.'

'What I expected, of an American.'

They sized each other up. He gazed into the face of the flier, challenged him, broke the eye hold. The flier looked past him and towards the young officer, Benedicto.

'Who's he?'

'A colleague.'

'I'm not a taxi run.'

'And I am not a gasoline pump attendant. Can we fly, *please*?'

The flier shrugged. It was about small victories.

'The weather's shit.'

'You are an American combat pilot . . .'

He navigated. They lifted off into the grey cloud mass. They had a mountain cliff ahead of them that climbed to more than 10,000 feet, they had an engine capacity to get them an altitude ceiling of 9,900 feet. They could not climb it and clear it. They flew with the grey-white blanket around them, they were hit by the wind eddies slipping at them through side valleys. Arturo strained to see ahead, through the slash of the wipers, and he could see nothing, and the cloud barrier seemed to close in on him and pressure against him. The worst flight of his life. He scribbled the calculations on the pad on his knee, rocking hand, clumsy figures, speed and compass direction and height. Twice, once over the Reserva Natural Cerro Bisís and once over the road from Uspantán to San Cristóbal Verapaz, he had screamed. The land mass looming at the cockpit glass. Grey cloud to broken cloud to the flash of trees to the rock formation filling the cockpit screen. The scream because there wasn't the time to be quiet-spoken. The scream and the wrenching turn and tilt of the Huey bird. The sweat water gathered in the fold of his gut against his waist belt, and the shake of his hands so that he could not hold the pencil for the navigation calculations. He thought the calm of the flier was exceptional. Half an hour out from La Aurora the flier radioed their arrival schedule, matter of fact, no particular deal. He could think about it afterwards, when they were clear of the Sierra de Chuacús, and on the plateau running for Guatemala City, that the evasive turn was already in place each time he had screamed to warn of the rushing rock face. They broke the cloud when they were above the airport tarmac. He tore up the sheets of paper he had used for direction, altitude and speed, and pocketed them. They bucked in the wind as they came down. He felt the hit of the skids.

He sat limp.

Into his headset . . . 'Personally I'd prefer a crap and a shave and a shower, but being Guatemalan you'd probably prefer to sit there all day . . .'

He took off his helmet. He could hear the gentle crying of the young officer, Benedicto, behind him. He thought the flier was a genius, and told him.

'Flier, you are an ugly shit. You are an awkward, obstinate, poor-mannered, mutilated shit. You are also the finest flier that I ever rode with. Understand me, I go short in giving out compliments . . . You are the best.'

He thought that, for a carved fraction of a moment, the brooding face of the flier cracked in pleasure.

He scrambled for the waiting staff car.


It was the decision of the High Command, gathered in the dark wood-panelled office of the minister, to endorse the orders given in the field by the brigadier from Cobán. Older men, and stouter, and peering through the spectacles they now needed, and gazing without approval at the filthy uniform of Colonel Arturo, and hearing him out and dismissing him.

Drinks were poured. The maps were studied. Bold chalk lines were drawn. The subversives would be driven north from Playa Grande towards the waiting blocking forces. A soft metal nail caught between the anvil and the hammer.

He was escorted down the corridor by a major, Operations. The mud from his boots, dried now, scattered on the corridor's floor.

'What if they have gone south?'

'Really, colonel, what for? If they go south they can only meet bigger garrisons, more heavily armed defences, greater obstacles. To go south for them would be suicide. No, colonel, they will have hit and they will have run north for the border. I think, colonel, what you need is sleep . . .'

\*       \*       \*

'How did they know?'

The Archaeologist had run to catch Jorge at the front of the march. They had come through the trees and climbed the loose rock to the road track. The squeal of the cart wheels was behind him, and the scrape of the barrow's wheel was ahead of him. They had been less than a mile on the road track and there had been four men, quite separate, who had stood as the head of the column had passed and then, quietly and without explanation, had joined it. Two more men stood now, and the Archaeologist saw the heavy boots and rough clothes of the one, and the dark but cared-for trousers and shoes and rain-coat of the other.

'How did they know?'

A broad smile from Jorge was his answer, and at the back of the march, again, was the shout in English for speed.

The new boots had rubbed the blisters raw on the Archaeologist's heel and on the upper skin of his toes. The march pace was harder than it had been the previous days, and the shouted voice at the back was merciless.

They were away from the shadow facade of the church that had no roof. They were clear of the few buildings that had survived a long-ago battle. They had come to the old graveyard, had trampled the undergrowth flat, and they listened.

Gord was at the back, and a little apart. Just Vee with him. He looked over the dimmed heads and shoulders of the villagers and in front of them a single small torch beam shone into the face of Rodolfo Jorge Ramírez. Vee told him that Jorge spoke the language of the triangle, and tongue of the Ixil Indians. Above them, on the higher ground, damped in the rain cloud, Gord could see the occasional swinging lights over the tin roofing of the new village, and higher still were the brighter lights on the perimeter fence of the army's compound. Vee told Gord that Jorge stood at the head of his mother's grave.

The rain fell. The wind beat the force of the rain onto their faces.

The voice of Vee was soft in his ear, and beyond was the voice of Jorge that was rich and penetrating in the night, and between the voices were the coughing of throats and the mutter of words and the fidgeting of bodies and the quietening of children.

Gord listened rapt.

He needed the men.

Without the men . . .

'. . . You knew my mother, special to me, but suffering as your mothers suffered. You knew my father. My father tried to lead you to freedom beyond the reach of the guns and tanks and aircraft of the army. My father failed. He did not die as your fathers died, in the fire of the church. He died lonely in exile with the dream of returning unfulfilled. *I* have returned. I have come back to Acul, to my village and to your village, to break for all time the hold of the army over your lives. You are the majority and you are not heard, and it will not be the same again. March with me . . .'

In the torchlight Gord saw the excitement flush the face of Rodolfo Jorge Ramírez.

'. . . We came to the Petén. Did you hear that we fought a battle in the Petén? Did you hear that the soldiers crumbled from our attack? Did you hear that?'

Gord heard the clucking of agreement, waves on a pebble shore.

'. . . We came to Playa Grande. That is a big garrison camp, a huge camp, many soldiers. We destroyed the camp, we broke the will of the soldiers. We burned the camp, as the soldiers once burned the church of our village where our fathers and your brothers and your husbands had been put. Did you hear that we fought at Playa Grande? Did you hear that they screamed for a mercy they had never shown to your fathers, brothers, husbands? Did you?'

The response was gale-whipped water on a loch's shore.

'. . . We go from here to Guatemala City. We go to the office of the President. We go to his office and we tell him of the new Guatemala that we want, and he will listen. If you have heard of the big battle in the Petén, and the victory that was ours at Playa

189

Grande, he will have heard also. He will listen . . . Come with me, my friends. I want you with me when I walk across the plaza, up the high steps, through the great door of the Palacio Nacional. I want you with me, all of you, when I speak our demands in the office of the President. Will you come . . . ?'

The murmur of talk, fast, excited, the blow of the gale amongst forest pines.

'I trust you. I am here for the night. For all the night I am at the grave of my mother. I am here with those who fought in the great battle in the Petén, and who fought at Playa Grande. You can go to the soldiers in their camp, any of you who have forgotten what the soldiers did to your fathers and brothers and husbands. Any of you can inform on me . . . I am a part of you and I trust you. Are there any amongst you who would wish to go to the camp of the soldiers and inform them, be their ears and be their eyes, that Rodolfo Jorge Ramírez is at the grave of his mother? Are there . . . ?'

No movement, only a stilled silence as when the gale died across the slope of Sidhean Mor.

'I have with me a man that you should love. You should call him Gaspar. All of us from the triangle know the story of Gaspar. He is of us. They see him and they stamp on him, but he is not there. They throw him in the water and they push him down with sticks, but he is on the other side of the river. Gaspar is with me. He has come from far away, but he is with me now. The army will lose and Gaspar will survive. Gaspar has brought the fire with him . . .'

The torch beam jerked in Jorge's hand, away from his face and across the rows of sitting and squatting villagers. It caught the body and then the head. Gord blinked in the light.

'Gaspar is with us, he is our spirit, he is our identity, he marches with us and he brings fire . . .'

And the light was off him.

An awful sadness.

He thought of the young woman, what the young woman had said.

\*     \*     \*

The message was brought from Operations. It was read quietly and passed from hand to hand by the officers deep in their after-dinner chairs. They nursed their last drinks of the evening and curled cigar smoke to the ceiling, and read the report from Playa Grande. There had been no contact. The hammer had beaten on the anvil, a metal nail had not been crushed.

The Street Boy stirred. The boot ground at his ribs. He was awake. There was no flesh to cover the ribs. He was blinded by the light that beamed down at him. His body was pinioned by the boot. He felt the panic. The wallet was under the small of his back. He should have thrown the wallet, taken only the money and the traveller's cheques. He had gained the wallet, the shove and the push, the hand darting for the inner pocket of the jacket, from the German tourist leaving with his wife from the Piccadilly on 6 Avenida and 11 Calle. He usually worked Zona 1 in the late evenings because it was there he found the best pickings. They might beat him and they might shoot him. The policeman's boot hacked again at his skinny body. He was thirteen years old and for three years he had worked the restaurants around Zona 1 of Guatemala City. He had kept the wallet because it was embossed in old heavy leather and he had thought he might get as good a price for the wallet itself as for the AmEx card and the Diners Card and the Visa Card. He cowered away from the light and the wallet bit in his back and his hand was underneath him and clasped the handle of the knife. He had been dreaming, when the boot had woken him, of the two ambitions that sustained him. The ambitions were that he should one day ride in the aeroplane that brought the tourists with their wallets to Guatemala City, and that he should one day own a gold-faced watch such as the tourists wore. He knew how to take the wallets, shove and push and jabbing fingers, he did not know yet how to take a watch with a gold face . . . His friends had been beaten, and when he had stayed at the children's home, the Casa Alianza, he had been taken in a washed shirt and with flowers in his hand to the cemetery for the burying of his cousin, shot by the police. The blade on his knife was four inches long, double-edged. He was ordered to stand. The torch was off his face. He squinted to see. The policeman held the truncheon ready to strike him and there was the wide smile on the policeman's fattened face. A second policeman leaned relaxed against the patrol car. He came up fast, and he slashed and heard the scream, and he stabbed and heard the groan. He ran . . . There were three shots before he reached the corner of the street, but high and wide. The Street Boy ran . . . They had all heard the word. The word had slipped amongst the thieves and pickpockets and pimps and muggers before they had dispersed for the work of the evening, before he had gone to wait in the shadow near the entrance to the Piccadilly on 6 Avenida and 11 Calle. He ran . . . He thought that when he found them they would give him a machine gun to shoot policemen.

'This talk I'm hearing, is it true . . . ?'

He had unlocked his door, he had staggered back to the bed. Tom Schultz sat on the bed and cursed the pain in his head. He sat on the bed in his pyjamas and across the room from him was the litre bottle, damaged, of Glenlivet malt, twelve years old.

Kramer had started to pace the tight room, and the small cigar was in his mouth.

'I want to know if it's true.'

There was a note beside the damaged bottle. 'Motto of the Kaibiles: IF I ADVANCE, FOLLOW ME. IF I DELAY, HURRY ME. IF I RETREAT, KILL ME – but we cannot FLY! Respectful good wishes, in admiration, Mario Arturo.' The damage was that he had drunk a near half of the bottle.

'What's true?'

Kramer lit the cigar. 'My friend says that there is an Englishman at the heart of a rebellion. The good colonel says that an Englishman, young enough, Special Forces type, is running their show. The good man says the fat cats at *estado mayor* have yet to wake up. You saw him . . .'

The pain beat in his head. 'I saw a guy.'

He had drunk the whisky to drive himself to a torpor sleep, because that was the only sleep that could shut out, kill, the nightmare of a falling helicopter, ground impact, spreading fire, and the panic rush to break clear of the heat. It was the nightmare that had been hidden from the psychologists of the DEA. Without the whisky the nightmare would have burned him . . .

'English?'

Anger. 'I was flying a bird. I was taking hits. I wasn't asking a guy a hundred feet below for his fucking passport . . .'

'Could he have been English?'

'Christ, I wasn't hanging out of the hatch and gawping – he was Caucasian. Listen. He was in control. He had the flame thrower. The flame thrower would have been their top weapon. They'd done the hurt with the flame thrower. I'd never seen before what a flame thrower did . . .'

Kramer was the caged animal, tracing a track across the thin carpet. 'And he could have been English?'

'Did you wake me just to ask . . . ?'

'I woke you to see if you would confirm that an Englishman is running a rebellion, because if he is, don't doubt it, the wires are going to start singing.'

'What the hell would he be here for?'

'Be coming to Guatemala City, wouldn't he? Wouldn't be shoot and scoot. Would be coming the whole way, trying to . . .'

'And that's not a lot to do with me.'

'Good night.'

The cigar smoke hung under his ceiling. He opened the window. The rain slashed into his room.

Still dark when they started out. Still the beat of the rain as the column went forward.

He knew that Jorge had sat the whole night at the head of his mother's grave.

He needed a week. It must rain for a week. On the folded and frayed map they were sixty-one land miles from the outer edge of Guatemala City. He needed the cloud cover and the rain for the days and nights of a week.

# 10

The rumour slithered in the high country of the Cuchumatanes mountains, a snake on its belly.

The rumour was heard in the villages of the Ixil triangle, the communities that were bounded by the towns of Nebaj and Cotzal and Chajul, and it was heard further north up the mud and stone track that reached to Sotzil and Ilom and Sajsivan. The rumour was carried by men who had gone through the night along trails that were streams of rainwater. The rumour was carried to the village and to the Pole Developments that were under the watch of the army and to the loggers in the forest and to the road repair gangs that huddled in huts and waited for the weather to change. The rumour would reach a village house and then fan out in secrecy, taken by whisper, avoiding the homes of those who collaborated. Before the dawn, in the villages of the triangle, men gathered together in the homes of the elders. Vee was in a village, and Zed in another, and Eff gathered around him a road gang. Soldiers slept, the men of the Civil Patrols manned their blocks in ignorance. The message that had been carried from the village of Acul demanded that men who would join the march should move out before first light.

The rumour spoke of *fire*.

A growing column on the move.

The column headed south and west, going slow, towards the garrison town of Nebaj.

'I am a professor of mathematics,' the Academic told Gord. 'I deal with a world that is logical, quite predictable. There is no

room in the world of my study for the possible or the proba-
ble . . . Will we get to Guatemala City?'

'If I have the weather.'

'I was a fireman in the city.' Broken English quietly spoken,
and the sloshing in mud of the heavy boots. 'I have no knowledge of the army. Can we win?'

'If the weather stays with us.'

They were masked by the low mist, climbing and then sliding
in chaos into the steepness of the valleys. Harder for Gord
because the numbers were increasing and the control that he
demanded was slipping, and the breaks for rest were down now
to five minutes in each hour. They stayed in the tree lines, away
from the roads and tracks. Each time the march stopped, each
time the rain fell sheer on his face and his shoulders, each time
he peered into the blanket of the mist, he heaved a great sigh of
relief. While the rain fell then the mud roads would slip and the
heavy transport of the army would be blocked. While the mist
cloaked them then the fixed-wing bombers of the army with
high explosive and napalm and the helicopters with rockets and
machine guns could not fly to find them. Driving the march
forward . . .

A flash signal. Sent in code. Given PRIORITY designation.

Kramer alternated between his sandwich and his cigar and his
Coca Cola. He watched the signal go, rolling on transmission. He
grinned, a little wickedness, because he anticipated the bluster
and the argument that his signal would achieve, and the hastily
gathered meetings, and the summoning up of Guatemala detail,
and the scratching of appointments. The signal was beamed from
the roof aerials of the embassy to the Agency's regional headquarters in Panama City, then relayed to the antennae farm
serving Langley beyond the beltway of Washington, DC.

Good and choice . . .

The Archaeologist saw it all. It happened within his earshot, not
twenty yards ahead of him.

They were more than two hundred men and the column stretched ahead into the trees so that he could not see Jorge who was the front-marker and it coiled away behind him so that when he turned he could not see the back-marker.

The cart wheels were playing in his mind, angering him. All the time that he pushed, shoved, dragged the awkwardness of the cart, the noise of the wheels scraped in him. They were on a track that might have been used by farm workers going to distant fields from a village, narrow and hardly beaten down now that the maize harvest had been cut and collected. He thought that the wheels of the cart owned a personal bloody-mindedness, difficult to shift over each raised stone or protruding root.

Gord came past him again, chivvying at the column, and he took a turn at the weight of the cart and there was his brusque smile, and he was going forward again. They came round the corner of the trail and the nozzles and tubes of the cart smacked into the back of Gord's legs. Going to apologize, and the cry again . . . The apology stayed in the Archaeologist's throat.

It was a bundle of rags.

It was in the middle of the trail. The big man was over the rag bundle and his boot scythed at it, kicked it. It was the big man, the bald head, who had shot the prisoner back on the Sayaxché to Chinajá road. It was the big man who had directed the machine-gun fire that had cut down the gate sentries at Playa Grande. The big man with the stubble beard kicked with ferocity and the bundle shrieked. The Archaeologist saw what Gord would have seen. He saw the face amongst the rags, frightened and defiant, and he saw the silver light flash of the knife blade . . .

'What's your problem?' Gord's gravel voice.

'He's scum.'

'What's your problem with that kid?'

The big man kicked again, fast, and the knife's slash was too slow to cut the leg. 'He's a thief.'

'What's with a thief?'

'I don't want scum . . .'

The big man had the rag bundle boy pinioned now on the ground and the barrel of his rifle pressed against the chest of the child.

'Leave him.'

The march was stopped. A circle of men gathered around Gord Brown and the big man and the rag bundle child. The Archaeologist saw the nerve flicker in the eyes of the big man.

Bombast. 'We don't want thieving scum, we don't want this . . .' He went to kick the rag bundle where it was pinioned by the rifle. It was the show of the big man's independence of Gord Brown. The boot swung. Gord going so quickly, a blur of movement, and the catching of the big man off balance, and the toppling of him. So fast. The big man on his back, and Gord walking away from him, like he had no more interest, and the child scampering after him. The march starting again . . . The Archaeologist saw the wallet that lay beside the pressed ground where the rag bundle child had been pinioned. It was a tourist's wallet. It was the kind of large wallet that his father would have owned back in Garden City. It was a wallet for credit cards and cash and traveller's cheques. Each volunteer who came to join the march was searched before he was allowed to go forward.

Did it matter that the kid thieved tourists' wallets?

The Archaeologist tugged at the cart wheels to get them moving again.

The Archaeologist stumbled on, striving to match the new urgency. Ahead of him the big man walked sullenly alone, and further ahead of him Gord Brown marched under the weight of the backpack and the machine gun and the swathes of ammunition with the Street Boy dogging his heels. Gord needed a week of rain and ground-level cloud. It was the first day of Gord's week. They were manhandling the cart across the torrent of a small river. The wheels cleared the underwater rocks, then were stuck again. Gord was on the far side of the river bank, and he seemed to clutch at the collar of the Street Boy and throw him easily into the torrent's heart and the Street Boy ducked in the water and then surfaced and had a hold of the cart and was dragging it with them. The Archaeologist saw the excitement of the Street Boy, and the sharp pleasure grin of Gord Brown, and he saw the bitter anger stare of the big man. He wondered if they could hold together for a week . . .

By the end of the day they looked down onto the town of Nebaj.

The government's inspectors were in. They had taken the far end of the open-plan area of the office space, and they had required a wall safe to be cleared and then they had made it their own with a changed digit code on the lock. Three desks were available to them, and they worked there with their laptops and their calculators and the files they had demanded. They were at the desks within two hours of the Houston flight smacking the tarmac at La Aurora. They accepted nothing, made their own coffee, hiked down to the dining area for their own open sandwiches, had booked into a hotel on their way from the airport to the embassy. A woman led the inspectorate team in a navy two-piece that would have been smart if it hadn't creased in the cramped airline seat, and there were two men who crawled to her. The work of the DEA, Guatemala City, was on hold. It was the way when government inspectors called in at a field station. They could be called forward at any time, Tom or the Intelligence Analyst or the Chemist or the Treasurer . . . Hell, and why not, Tom Schultz thought, because there was no way that a war against drugs importation into the United States great and beloved of America should take priority over the crime of lost paperclips. He'd slept well, and the bottle of Glenlivet malt was dead in the rubbish can of his room, and by sleeping well he had sidetracked the nightmare of a downed bird falling with fire. They were squashed into customs territory, pushed off their own ground. He shared a table with the Liaison major who smoked sweet tobacco in his briar.

He turned sheets of paper, a blur to him, because he thought of a man he had seen, a hundred feet below a banking Huey, a man crouched at a cart that carried a flame thrower . . . He picked at the scar.

'You should leave it . . . Sorry, what the hell's it to do with me?'

'Not a lot.'

The major bored on. 'Was that in the Gulf, Desert Storm, I heard you were there?'

'Right.'

'I heard you were downed . . .'

'Right, too.'

'Where was it?'

He pushed the paper away, wished the major would wrap. 'Over a shit piece of sand.'

'I'd have given an arm to be there. I was at Bragg right through it, hell of a disappointment. Behind our lines or their lines?'

'Their lines.'

'You must have been in some state, that hole in you . . . Christ, you feel bad when you miss something like that. Don't suppose you could walk out. Rescued . . . ?'

'Right again.'

'That must be quite a thing. I mean, to be rescued from behind their lines. Special Forces, those guys are real heroes. Quite a thing to owe your life to a man, group of men. Get up each morning, crap and wash and dress, and know that some place there's a guy who's the reason you're still with us. Do you get to see him?'

Flatly said, 'No.'

'But you write . . . ?'

'No.'

'Heh, if I owed my life to a man I reckon I'd want to know how he was going.'

Tom said quietly, 'I don't see him, I don't write to him. I don't like to *owe* any man anything. You don't rate when you're downed. It's not exactly the accolade of success. It's not just bad luck, you know, it's because of a *mistake*. The mistake cost a life and a machine, and I don't care to be reminded of it. So, I don't go visiting and I don't sit writing chat letters . . . Subject matter closed.'

\*    \*    \*

Three meetings scratched.

'What the fuck do the Brits think they're playing with . . . ?'

Guatemala printouts called up from the computers.

'Isn't that place an island of stability . . . ?'

A gathering of an assistant under secretary and a grade 3 staffer with responsibility for Central America and two at grade 5 who specialized in the affairs of that country.

'Imagine the chaos if that place went down . . .'

Coffee on the table, and the grade 3 staffer breaking rules and smoking, fourth cigarette, and the large map spread wide.

'The British have no right to be interfering . . .' the older grade 5 man said.

'Intolerable, the end game could be a disaster for the region . . .' the younger grade 5 woman said.

'Playing the goddamn end of empire game again, like the tune's stuck on the needle, like they're still in goddamn vinyl . . .' the grade 3 staffer said.

'Let them know they're off field. Don't take crap from them. Who is this jerk? How does he get rubbed? Kick their asses in London . . .' the Assistant Under Secretary said.

The signal was drafted.

When the dusk came, when the hammering rain shone against the light of the high perimeter lamps, the boy was moving closer to the sentry on his raised platform. The boy played with stones, piling them, moving on and finding more, making new piles. A tin roof over the platform gave some shelter to the sentry, but there were no sides.

The town of Nebaj was 6000 feet above sea level, and the figures would have meant nothing to the sentry who had not learned to read nor to write, but he understood the cold and the loneliness that was sentry duty on a platform above the perimeter wire round the Nebaj army camp. All of the duty of sentries had been told by their sergeant to be watchful. There had been a battle, he had heard, at Playa Grande, but that was two, three days' walk away, or many hours in the bus. He could see only to the rim of the light thrown by the high lamps, and caught in the light, moving casually nearer to him, was the boy, and each time he stopped so the boy found his amusement with the stones, making the small piles. Beside the platform, which was sited to guard it, was a gate. The gate was higher than the razor fence, a wooden frame with barbed wire slung across it. The gate was an entry point to the back of the camp, set between the coils of the perimeter razor wire. The sentry stamped his feet, shivered. His boots bucked the plank platform and rocked his machine gun that rested on a bipod with a belt loaded and readied for use. The sentry heard the new sound, strange. It was beyond the rain wall and the darkness wall and the cloud wall into which he peered. The boy was calling to him, soft but excited. The boy was away from the stones that he had piled and was close to the front spindle legs on which the platform stood. Beyond the rain and the cloud and the darkness was the squealing sound, not that of a young pig but that of metal on metal. It was what the boy had seemed to pick from the ground in front of the platform. What the boy held up shone brightly. It seemed to the sentry to be a ring. He crouched on his platform. The boy was reaching up to him and offering him the ring. His arm was out. The sentry's fingers touched the bone hand of the boy. There was the squealing sound of the wheels, brought by the wind. He looked up, sharp. He saw the shadow movement where the light and dark merged. And the hand had hold of his wrist and pitched him forward, off the platform. The sentry hit the ground and the blade of the knife flashed in his face.

They were in four groups.

Golf and Oscar and Roger and Delta, Jorge's thin joke . . . Golf was the flame-thrower cart and the mortars. Oscar was the machine gun and the rockets for the main gate of the camp. Roger was for the police barracks in the town. Delta was for the plaza in front of the church and the market.

Gord led Golf. Harpo led Oscar. Zeppo led Roger. Jorge led Delta.

The scream of the cart's wheels going over the cleared ground, Gord and the Fireman and the Academic dragging it. Belting forward in the stampede, and Gord saw the stone piles as he had wanted them. Groucho, with guerrillas and men from Playa Grande and Acul village, waved by Gord to the stones and setting the mortars. What he had told the Street Boy who was scum and a thief, and brilliant, was to line the stones as he played so that one line directed a flight path for the mortar bombs to the administrative block, and another to the biggest dormitory building of the camp. Charging on past Groucho and rushing the wired gate.

They were halfway across the flooded football pitch, the cart's wheels gouging the track, and the Archaeologist panting behind with the wheelbarrow, and the mortars were in the air.

The first mortar explosion, short of the command building, was the signal. The machine-gun fire of Oscar group at the main gate . . . the muffled shooting of Roger group and Delta group away in the streets of Nebaj. Tracer in the air. He was in the shadow of the latrine building. It was as he had argued it through. It was the way he had told them that it would be.

He could hear the shouting over the explosions and the shooting. The officers trying to gain control in confusion. He waited and he watched. He was fifty yards from the command building and seventy yards from the near corner of the dormitory building where the officers, in cover, were rallying frightened men. He wrenched the lever. The jet flew. Compressed petrol and oil arching forward. Gord pressed the ignition trigger.

The fire swarmed forward.

The fire caught at men who had been eating or resting, men who had been dreaming or washing their kit, men who had been reading or preparing to walk out into the town on the evening after market. Gord saw the fire catch at men, hold them, and he heard the screams of men who had been caught and held by the oil in the fuel. Moving now . . .

Running with the cart for the protection of the wall where the garrison's vehicles were parked. Stopping. Dragging forward the cart and squirting the black snake forward and then the fire leaping after it and finding the walls and windows and doors of the command building. He saw the silhouette of a man who tried to close steel shutters to a window and who was beaten back by the stream of flame. He hosed the command building . . . Running with the cart and throwing himself down in open ground and aiming the nozzle ahead and towards the low concrete structure without windows that would be the armoury. There was a gaggle of men, shouting in hysteria, at the door of the armoury, and one trying to insert the key into the padlock, and the race for them to open the door before the fire reached them. A lost race . . . Going with the cart, needing to hug shadows, searching for darkness. There was the shrill laughter of the Street Boy beside him. There was the whisper of the Academic's prayer. There was the wheezed gasp of the Archaeologist's oath.

Gord ran for a new firing position.

The two lorries were returning troops, on rotation, from Chajul to Nebaj.

Had it not been for the weather, for the state of the road, the lorries would have been back in the garrison camp four hours before. There had been earth slips, rock falls, there had been a forty-foot-high conifer tree down across the road. The lorries had been crossing the plaza when the first mortar shell had hit the camp.

The Priest saw it.

He was a man of middle years and long experience of the triangle. Apart from nineteen months in Italy, studying in Perugia, and seven months in the Belgian theological centre at Louvain, he had spent the last thirteen years of his life in Nebaj. He had come to Nebaj to assist a Spanish Jesuit, shot dead on his bicycle on the road outside the town that led to the waterfall. He had worked with a German priest, fled from death threats. He had been his bishop's man in the town until the bishop had closed the parish, too dangerous for the church to work. He had given last rites to thirteen women shot by the army in front of the church steps. To those who worshipped in his church he was a man not known to permit fear. He had taken that evening a cooked meal from the nuns at the Sisters of Charity orphanage, and shared laughter with them, and later it had been his intention to go again to the garrison camp to continue his protest at the health of coffee *finca* workers, who, it was his belief, had been systematically poisoned by the insecticides sprayed from aircraft. He had a file in his lodgings behind the church of the death threats that he received, and he liked to show the file to foreign visitors, bishops from Europe and aid workers and television crews. The Priest came from one of the cobbled narrow streets near the plaza.

The gunfire whipped the plaza. Market night, and the trading done, and the money gathered, and the drink started. Men and women and children scattering in panic. The rabble army ducking and firing, weaving and firing. The soldiers in cover beside the high wheels of their lorries.

They ran for the church doors. They abandoned their stalls and their drink, they dropped their food. The marimba music died. The fear rush for the doors of the church.

Where the Priest watched from, the corner of the plaza, an officer crawled up the steps of the church and, arm raised to get better distance, threw two grenades through the open door.

He had seen it, the grenades rolled into the church door, and the soldiers had fled. They were cut off from the camp, they scattered into the town.


The sheet had been ripped and tied to a broomstick. The sheet waved through the window at the end of the command building.

Gord called Groucho to him. The men were to stop firing, they were to stay down and not to show themselves. 'Tell them that we recognize the flag of surrender. Surrender is unconditional. They are to come out unarmed and with their hands up. They are to come to the football pitch and they are to sit down. They will not be harmed . . . Tell them that.'

It was a dribble at first, and then a spurt. A river of men walked through the rain towards the football pitch, and there were others who were helped and some who were carried.

The senior officer was a tall man with dishevelled hair and he wore a silk dressing gown that was open to his body and the singlet and underpants, and his boots were unlaced. Perhaps he had been about to take a shower when the first mortar bomb had exploded, or perhaps he had been changing before his dinner. The senior officer, alone, ignored the stream of men who went under the cover of the rifle and machine-gun barrels to the football pitch, and walked to the shadow darkness where Gord crouched beside Groucho. The senior officer stood in front of them. His shape was thrown forward across them by the flame light. A neatly trimmed moustache, and half-glasses that were askew. Gord thought the man had dignity.

Groucho's hesitant question, and the senior officer replied, curt, 'Yes, I speak English.'

Gord pushed himself upright. 'The surrender is unconditional, do you understand, sir?'

'My men refuse to fight . . . you are a mercenary?'

'I asked you, sir, if you understood?'

'My men refuse to face the fire . . . you are an agent of your government?'

'Do you understand, sir, the terms of surrender?'

The senior officer stared at him. He would have seen the hollowed eyes of tiredness and the caved cheeks of exhaustion, and the stubble on the cheeks and the black oil smears.

'I understand them.'

More shooting from the town, a long burst of automatic fire. Gord snapped the orders at Groucho. Men were to guard the prisoners, to escort the medical orderlies, to break into the armoury, to gather together food supplies.

They walked down from the camp and past the guardhouse at the gate. They went through the old streets where the windows were shuttered, the doors closed, they went through the old streets where the *Ladinos* lived. The Fireman and the Academic pulled the cart that carried the flame thrower and the wheels squealed over the cobbles and the wheelbarrow was pushed behind them by the Street Boy, and the Archaeologist was beside him.

The crowd pressed around him. He heard the murmur of a name. Women in bright-coloured blouses, girls in brilliant-red skirts, men with hope alive in their faces, pushing against him, touching his clothes and his body. The name was Gaspar, and the murmur had become a shout. He saw Jorge, beyond the crowd, near the swinging body of an officer, who stared down at him from the church steps. He shouted to Jorge that he should make his speech, draw in his recruits. The crowd grew around him, groping to feel him, calling the name of Gaspar. He saw Zeppo, swaying helpless in the crush, carried along, and could not read his face. He shouted to Zeppo that he should make his way, fastest, to the camp, help with the sorting of supplies. He told Groucho that he wanted to move by midnight, that Groucho should escort the prisoners from the hotel and the senior officer back to the camp. He was Gaspar, he was the spirit of the legend. The blood ran in him. The tiredness and the exhaustion were gone from him. Men reached to grasp his hand, women lifted their small children so they could gaze into his face. He stood near to a wall and the sound of the name beat in his ear. In an entry behind him the Fireman was helped by the Academic to refill the tubes of the flame thrower. There was the smell, acrid, of the thick oil and the hiss, sharp, of the air cylinder. The name was a ferment around him. A button was pulled from his tunic, as if it were a token, and fell to the ground, and men and women and children scrabbled for the prize . . .

The Archaeologist tugged at his sleeve, pushed back an old man without teeth. Foul breath and the whined call of 'Gaspar'.

'You have to sleep, Gord.'

'We don't have the time to sleep.'

'You can't do it all yourself.'

'When I don't, no-one else does.'

'That's arrogance, Gord . . .'

\*      \*      \*

He had a full head of hair, almost white now.

He wore a well-cut toothbrush of a moustache.

Percy Martins was finely built for his years. He could easily have carried for himself the grip bag and the tackle box and the sleeve for the rods. One of the old guard from front desk trailed Martins along the corridor, bearing his burden.

A day's fishing, midweek, was not unusual now for him.

Two young men, their jackets already discarded in their offices, ducked their heads to him, and right that they should show some bloody respect. A young woman, carrying a wrapped sandwich and a closed polystyrene coffee beaker, glowered at him, would have been of the new intake that was provincial and force-fed with education, but stepped out of his way.

He clumped into his outer office, past the bat who was now his secretary, not for long . . . unlocked the door of his small room and smiled sweetly as the man stacked his bag and his box and his rods in the corner.

His secretary brought through the signal, passed on by North American Desk.

. . . Bloody people in Washington. Bloody Americans.

Too much shit taken from the Americans, too much rolling over like a whipped cur, tail across the privates . . .

He reached for his telephone, dialled the internal number of North American Desk.

'. . . You're level with me. Five had a name, right? We helped Five, right? No Further Action, right? Thank you . . .'

Percy Martins would have considered himself armourplated if it came to inter-departmental argument. He was one of the few remaining of the former men of the Secret Intelligence Service. He had survived, comfortably, the weeding-out process of the new Director General. He had, now, no specific designation, no stated responsibility. He occupied an office that was flanked by Personnel (Records) and Expenditure (In House), on the fourth floor of the new building by Vauxhall Bridge; if he craned from his window, pressed his nose against the glass that could not be opened, he could just see the river. Bits and pieces

208

came his way, things no-one else could pigeonhole, but not too many.

There had been so many who had been cleared out with the move. A scandal. Too many for the formality of even the briefest leaving parties. An utter scandal. Good men, more than twenty years' service in, and let go on a Friday afternoon with a brown envelope on internal delivery issuing them with fifty pounds of vouchers for the Army and Navy store. Not even a clock, not any more, not even a sherry decanter. Not for 'Sniper' Martins, oh, no, not yet . . . The young men and women, with their *good* degrees, eyed him in the corridors with suspicion and yet with envy because his achievement was still talked of, grudgingly. A marksman in the Beqa'a valley of the Lebanon, controlled by Percy Martins. The shooting of a Palestinian assassin, organized by Percy Martins. The presence in a former Prime Minister's attic loft of a high-powered rifle, de-activated by Royal Ordnance, presented by Percy Martins. More than any of these Johnny wimps of today would achieve, a killing in the Beqa'a . . . The in-tray caught his eye, what the secretary bat had left there. He riffled the sheets of paper. There was his four-page digest, unrequested and written from his own initiative, on the need for closer monitoring of the nuclear warhead stockpile held in the Ukraine, his suggestion for a field agent to be put in; scrawled across the top sheet was 'Better Left to Satellite Photography', and then the spider initials of the head of Europe (East/Former USSR) Desk. Intolerable . . . Three stapled pages submitted to Near East (Iran) Desk, detailing the need to aid and arm and control from the sovereign base in Cyprus the Iranian dissidents operating inside mullah-land; 'Thanks for your interest, will come back to you if relevant'. Disgraceful . . . Accounts wished to see him, personally; his expenses. Bloody cheek . . . The Deputy Director General regretted a full diary prevented the fixing of a meeting; a hands-on and meaningful future. Bastard . . . His position was secure, so *they* attempted death by a thousand cuts. Not his intention to make it easy for them.

He walked out to his secretary. He chewed on a peppermint, spoke through it. 'Over at Five there's a creep called Hobbes, I want to see him, soonest . . .'

'I have just had, Brennard, one of the most opinionated, self-satisfied, under-achieving creatures from Six in this office, not just lecturing me but pissing down at me from on high. I didn't like it. Why am I covered in this piss . . . ? Because you, in your wisdom, wrote "No Further Action" on the matter of Brown, Gordon Benjamin. Brown, Gordon Benjamin, I think you called him "a total fool", is currently leading a rebellion in Guatemala that could, if successful, destabilize the region. Ten out of nine for judgement, eh . . . and we just have a series of platitudes to tell us about him.'

'What do we want . . . ?'

'Not what we want, the Americans want this *total fool* dead in his tracks. We probably wouldn't mind helping them . . . Trouble is that Brown, Gordon Benjamin, is our man and we know nothing of him. Am I getting there?'

'What should I do, Mr Hobbes?'

'I remember that before promotion out of the nursery, you used to run to Mother.'

'That's not fair.'

'Very little is. Get Parker on it.'

It was down by the bridge outside Nebaj that the front of the column met the flotsam refugees from Playa Grande. They came off a track that idled beside the river and Gord saw them as they stumbled and trudged clear of the trees. Children and women and older men, they meant little to him because he was still giving out the orders. Sometimes the orders had been given through Jorge, and sometimes when he could not find Jorge then he cracked those orders himself and left Groucho to translate for him. The orders covered the organization of the march, and who would go faster and scout ahead, and where in the column the machine guns should be carried, and where the food should be, and where the mortars, and where the medical supplies.

He snapped the orders, because he had already been over-ruled by Harpo. Gord had said that women and children from Nebaj should not accompany the men recruited by Jorge's speech from the church steps. Women and children from Nebaj would accompany the men, Harpo had said, because otherwise the men would not march. They were a winding column at the bridge, a flickering of torch lights in the dark-ness of early morning. He had not slept. He was moving forward, hurrying to gain the head of the column, when he saw the debris people of Playa Grande. He was surrounded by what had become his personal guard of the Fireman and the Academic and the Archaeologist and the Street Boy. When he had talked with Jorge, to choose the route of the march, Jorge had stayed silent and it had been Gord's stabbing finger that had decided on the climb into the 9000 foot-high Cuchuma-tanes; he was too tired to care that he humbled the leader. He was moving forward, and always there was the obsession drive for speed. The rain was carried into his face by the wind that blustered between the trees by the bridge. His uniform was clinging to his body and he had no warmth left in his arms and chest and legs. The cart was dragged behind him, and the wheelbarrow was pushed behind the cart. He saw her . . . She was at the back of the group. A torch beam found her face then lost it, then found her again. A shrunken man leaned on her right arm, her left arm supported against her shoulder a sleep-ing child. The dog would have smelled him. The dog bounded forward. The dog's tongue licked the grimness from his face. She came to him, and she let go of the man and she reached forward and with strength she dragged the dog back from him, as if the dog should not show affection to him.

'So you took Nebaj?'

'Yes.'

'And how many did you kill?'

'I don't know.'

'Because you took Playa Grande, the village is now destroyed. Is that what you wanted for Nebaj?'

'I needed Nebaj.'

'Oh, "*I*" . . .' she mimicked him. 'Yes, "*I*" burned Nebaj, wonderful. "*I*" killed the conscript soldiers. "*I*" didn't care what happened to those left behind when my precious back was turned . . .'

Gord said softly, 'What happened to you?'

Her voice rose. 'Is that important? Is it bloody important that we were hunted by that army? Roadblocks, you know about blocks? It is hardly important that we have run, hidden, been in terror, run again, eaten bloody roots, berries . . . We buried a child, the child died of bloody hypothermia. We dug a grave with our hands, with our fingers. I wouldn't expect a bloody hero to find that important . . .'

'You should join the march.'

'Of course . . . Yes, *sir*. Right, bloody *sir*. Reporting for women's work . . . Look after the casualties, no medicines. Patch up the wounded, no bandages. Minister to the bloody ego of the men. Why not, *sir*?'

'You will please yourself.'

'Don't you understand, you bloody stupid pig-headed conceited man . . . Stop, before it is too late.'

'It is too late.'

He was moving forward, away from her, and the wheels clanked in their ritual behind him.

She shouted, 'Before you destroy everything.'

He muttered into the wind, into the rain. 'We have to go on.'


The sentry at the gate saluted Colonel Arturo. His staff stood for him as he bustled into his office.

The telephone was ringing on his desk before he had discarded his drenched coat. He listened to what he was told. He was told the place and the name and he was told of the fire.

The cold shudder took him. He offered no explanation to the hovering staff. At the wall map he took a further plastic orange-headed pin and he placed the pin into the map. Easy for him to see the line that ran through the pins from the airstrip to the Sayaxché-Chinajá road to Playa Grande to Nebaj in the Ixil triangle. He dragged his coat back from the hook behind his door. He ran through the rain to his car. He drove fast towards his home. The place was Nebaj. The name was Rodolfo Jorge Ramírez. The fire was a flame thrower.

A wheel turned . . .

He seemed not to see the trees of the avenues bent in the wind, nor the rain sluicing on his windscreen, nor the huddled street traders, nor the porters sprinting with bags from taxis outside the big hotels, nor the boutiques, nor the restaurants, nor the sodden life of a great city that was his home.

. . . A wheel turned in his mind.

He remembered a fading photograph, much creased, of a man standing with his wife and his small boy child. He had carried the photograph with him into the battle. He had taken the photograph so that if he captured the whore Ramírez then he would know him. The wheel turned because the whore's child had come back . . . He remembered the men who were driven by the barrels of rifles towards the church. He could scent the fire from a burning church of charred timber frames, and smell the scorched flesh. The wheel turned because a flame thrower had destroyed Playa Grande and Nebaj . . . How many other wheels to turn in a country pocked with unmarked graves . . . ? The route of the plastic orange-headed pins on his wall map led to Guatemala City, no doubts. And his mind showed him the flame thrower and the rabble horde, and the flame thrower and the rabble horde rushed together on the wide tree-lined avenue that was his home.

He told his wife that Nebaj had fallen, that the triangle was beyond control, that she should pack suitcases that night, and in the morning she should fly with their daughter to St Petersburg in Florida.

There would be many others, that morning, officers and administrators and interrogators and politicians, who heard the news from Nebaj and the word that was fire, who felt a fear that vengeance was carried closer.

'You are intelligent?' The Archaeologist walked beside her.

'If you say so.' Alex bridled.

'You are a college graduate?'

'Could have been, didn't bother with it, I let it go . . .'

She knew, Alex Pitt had been told, that he was a professional academic, that he had a post at the University of Minnesota. He wondered why she seemed to sneer at him, take the opportunity to rubbish what was important to him. He sought to throttle his rising distaste of her.

'But you are intelligent, if not educated intelligent . . . ?'

'It's your privilege to have your opinion.'

'You have the potential of intelligence, and I apologize for my rudeness, but you behave like a stupid bitch.'

'Then back your apology by walking somewhere else.'

He saw the flush high on her cheeks. He bored in at her. It was what he thought necessary to say. 'What you should know as an intelligent person, what you should have realized, is that without Gord this thing has no chance and no hope and no possibility. If you didn't want to be in the real and the big and the bad world, then you should have gone somewhere else, taken in Greenpeace, or . . .'

She said quietly, and he thought she was chastened, 'Whales and dolphins didn't seem as important as people.'

'You could have worked in a village in Somalia, fed the starving, nice and clear cut . . .'

She tossed her head, threw back the blondeness of her hair. 'And moaned when the camera crews came visiting, played the heroine. Plenty queuing up to get into that act. I get your message. It seemed, it seemed *decently* anonymous here. It seemed the right place to be. Contrary to what you think, I do actually believe that non-violence wins . . .'

'Not in this country.'

'I believe in non-violence, and I would have thought you

214

would. And I believe this march will cause only a degree of suffering that is quite out of proportion to what it will achieve . . .'

'Then you should have quit.'

She stopped. She turned. She blocked him. She stood in front of him. She cursed him. The passion flew. 'I can't, you can't, none of us can quit. He started it, he's going on with it. He trapped us.'

The Archaeologist softened. 'He is the only hope. Without him it goes down the drain. He has so many problems, Alex, without your nagging, drip-dripping away at him. What I'm saying is, please, don't add to it . . . Oh, and you should know, Gord thinks you are a hell of a fine woman.'

She snorted. She lengthened her stride. He grinned.

He heard the light knock at his door. He swung his chair. She was standing in the doorway.

'Please come in, Miss Parker.'

It was more than seven months since Bren had last seen her, and that had been when he was hurrying along a corridor in the annexe and she was queuing at a coffee machine. Nothing said, just a thin smile from both of them. Nothing much to be said because he had only been in her bed when she was devastated by stress. She seemed aged from the young woman he had worked with in Ireland, a little of the red-gold lustre gone from her hair, and more weight at her hips, the colour gone from her face now that she was office-chained. Of course it was awkward, him on a promotion ladder and her on the plateau. She had come home, from what he'd heard, because tinted hair in a different style and glasses and a new operational location had still left her in danger. He had not been with another woman since he had left her, at the informer's house, with death in the air.

He passed her the file.

He couldn't lie to her. 'I'm not the flavour of the day. We had a sniff at the guy and I marked it "No Further Action". We need to know much more about him.'

She read the name on the file. 'What do you need to know?'

'Background, personality, military history, motivation psychology.'

'What for?'

'To ship across the water to Langley . . .'

'Why?'

'They can pass it down to Guatemala City, their field station – the detail is all in the file. Might help them to do the business with him.'

'Does it matter to us?'

'He's our citizen and he's rampaging in their back yard. Yes, it's important . . .'

'What's the business?'

'The better the profile they have of him the better the chance they have of stopping him . . .'

She seemed to rock for a moment, only a moment, and then her composure was regained.

'. . . of stopping him and killing him,' Bren said.

# 11

They climbed. They were above the tree line now. They wound forward in the mist of the rain.

Gord was at the back of the column. He tried to make a break between the fighting men and the women with their children, and the temper rose in him.

'Would I like England?'

It was necessary to separate the fighting men from the women with the children, and he failed. He could not split them apart, make them tidy. He tried to force the pace from the back, to move the fighting men on at speed so that they were distanced from the struggle of the women with their children to hold the link, and it was late in the morning when he gave up, admitted the defeat.

Gord ignored the Street Boy.

There was a mess of bodies around him, but closest to him was the group that would not leave him. There was the Archaeologist who limped with the rub of the new boots. There was the Academic who still wore the old raincoat and who struggled with the weight of the cart. There was the Fireman whose heavy boots slithered on the wet rock and who levered the wheels over the harsher and more difficult ground. There was the Street Boy, half disappeared now in the enveloping anorak that he had stripped from a dead soldier, who drove the wheelbarrow forward.

'Tell me, Mr Gord, what I would find in England.'

Gord's England. The train coming back from his mother's, scratching to remember the last newspaper he had read. The new unemployment figures. The new misery of houses clawed back by the banks. The new terror of the debt cycle. The new fear of walking an unlit alley. The new dread of a pensioner behind a barricaded door. The new society losing its nerve. The new police in their body armour, and the new pubs with their closing-time fights and broken glasses, and the new . . .

Gord sucked for breath. 'It's a great place. Yes, perhaps, one day you'll get there. Yes, it's a good place.'

'You will take me?'

'Shut up, will you, do me a favour . . .'

He could not see the front of the column, where Jorge was, because the front was lost in the low cloud, and if he turned to look back then there was just the body mass of men with rifles and ammunition boxes and food baskets, and the women with their children and the bags and cases they had brought. They would not leave him.

It was their trust in him.

'How long till we are in Guatemala City, Mr Gord?'

'I told you to be quiet.'

'How long?'

The deep breath and he could not fill his lungs. 'If the rain holds, in five days.'

'You mean it, Mr Gord, five days and we will be in the Palacio Nacional? Five days . . .'

Gord swiped at him, missed. 'Shut your mouth . . .'

It was the second day of Gord's week.

The rain held, stinging them. The cloud was thicker, swamping them.

He was trained for the desert sandscape in the Gulf, and he knew about jungle, and he was good in the rising hills of the province of Northern Ireland. The mountain was fresh to him. No experience of the emptiness of the lungs that could not be filled with the thin air. Searching for breath, not finding it, and the leaden weight of his legs, and the nausea rising in him . . . He thought it must have been an eagle. The bird came, near to him, in front of him, a shadow from the mist, and swooped into clarity with the falling calm of total control, then saw the column of men and women and children and thrashed the wide wing span to be clear of them. They were in the bird's place. He thought it must be an eagle, its territory invaded, because it was as large as the birds that nested high on Sidhean Mor, and there was the cry of the bird that was a protest against intrusion. It was gone, lost in the cloud mist . . .

The Street Boy called, 'Mr Gord, we could have shot it.'

He swung at the boy. This time he caught him.

What hurt Gord, wounded him, was that the Ixil Indian people of the triangle seemed to think nothing of the mountain altitude of the Cuchumatanes. They pressed on around him. They were quiet except for rare explosions of laughter. They slogged forward and at times there was only a dozen yards of visibility. What was he leading them to, in the cloud blanket settled on the mountain?

He could not show weakness.

They followed him.

The wheels of the cart ground behind him, slogging and trudging and stumbling forward.

Where Tom Schultz worked, he could see the line of stationary lorries.

He was bent inside the cockpit of the Huey bird.

The inspectors still swarmed in the embassy office but, big deal, permission had been given for Tom Schultz, Airwing DEA, to head off out to La Aurora. There was always maintenance time to be spent on the bird and he reckoned that he was well clear of the paperclip team; their target for the rest of the day would be the Treasurer and the hassle over Confidential Informant payments. Big hassle, always was, and would take an Einstein to match the payments to value and progress . . . he was well clear.

His bird was parked facing out of the opened door of the hangar that was allocated to DEA.

Their own birds were in a dismal line at the edge of the apron and the column of lorries was pulled up behind the line. He had seen the arguments. Pilots, not even changed into fatigues, and shouting and gesticulating at the officers who had come in jeeps at the head of the lorry convoy, refusing to fly.

With the argument at its fiercest, while the rain fell and bounced and glanced on the apron sheen, at least a company of the troops had been ordered down from the shelter of the lorries. They had gone, quick order marching, past the grounded birds, and they had shouted a kind of song, like it was a battle cry.

'A Kaibil is a killing machine . . .'

Mean-looking bastards. He could read it.

'A Kaibil is a man . . .'

The attempt to put some *spine* into the pilots.

'A Kaibil controls the situation . . .'

Heh, guys, don't take that shit . . . And the pilots of the parked birds were not taking shit, and were running back to the dry of their operations room, and their armchairs, and their lunch.

The troops of the Kaibil battalion returned expressionless to their lorries and their officers cursed and paced. They were mean-looking bastards, and they had the kit. They had machine guns and mortars and recoilless rifles amongst their feet on the floor of the lorries, and the NCOs wore at their belts the machetes that were carried in polished leather sheaths. Now, that would be a fight, when the guy they said was an English-man and who had the flame thrower came into close-quarters combat with these mean-looking bastards. The fight that would settle it . . .

He had his head down. He reckoned there was a problem with the aft navigation light, intermittent cut-out . . .

'You are the American?'

He looked up. The officer wore the insignia, sewn to his shoulder flaps, of a captain. It was a hard face. It was the face of a young man who would have risen from his cot at five, or four, and who would have prepared himself to be in a firefight by the middle of the morning. Tom nodded.

'You are the American pilot who was at Playa Grande?'

'That's me.'

'And you could fly in this weather?'

'Well, wait a minute, I could . . .'

The captain interrupted him. 'They are toy boys, our pilots. They say it is too dangerous to fly.'

'I don't think you should reckon it is easy up there.'

The accusation. 'You could fly.'

Tom said, 'It seemed important to be out of there, but it wasn't a good place to be . . . Why don't you just roll the trucks?'

Pain on the captain's face. 'We want to go . . . Where to go? We do not know where they are . . . They were in Nebaj, you heard that?'

'No.'

'They took the garrison town of Nebaj, with the fire . . .'

'Heh, Jesus . . . Heh, that's a good-sized town . . .' Trying to remember the map, trying to place distances from the names that he knew from the map. A hell of a distance, on foot. Right, Nebaj was a good-sized town, with a good-sized garrison . . . 'You've a situation going serious.'

The captain said, 'We need the helicopters to find them. If the helicopters don't fly then we cannot find them, cannot block them. What is the point of deploying on the road, and they will bypass us . . . How long is the weather due to last?'

He wanted the good news. Tom dashed him. 'Could be two, three days. Could be a week. It's sort of vague . . . Could they get to Guatemala City, if they have the weather?'

Tom looked into the young face.

The captain said simply, 'Fire spreads. Fire has a reason of its own. Fire *impresses* the peasants. It is a rabble out there, but the fire has brought it together. If we cannot find them, block them, then they can destroy this country. It is not a country that is perfect, but is the United States of America perfect? It is our country and the Kaibiles will die for their country . . . I apologize for taking your time.'

He ducked his head, in respect, and walked away.

Tom bent again and looked to retrieve the wiring for the aft navigation light.

His fingers were clumsy and his mind distanced. He saw the man over whom his helicopter had banked, and he saw the flame thrower. He scratched at the scar tissue on his face, at the irritation, and tried to work with the wires.

Ahead of him, where he could see them, the troops sheltered in the cover of the lorries, and the pilots stayed away.

He was rolling, as if he was drunk. Pain in his legs and the ache in his chest. Forty minutes to the next rest halt. The weight of the machine gun dragged at his arms and the straps of the backpack slashed at his shoulder flesh. Great driving pants for air and once the Street Boy had reached to help him and he had thrust the hand away, and once the Academic had sought to take the machine-gun burden and he had shrugged him off.

Always the rain and the mist of the cloud . . .

'Is the hero suffering?'

'Do me the favour, Miss Pitt, of walking somewhere else.'

'We're used to altitude. I'm here a week every month, in the mountains . . .'

'Somewhere else, Miss Pitt.'

'Is the hero too tired to talk?'

Gord snarled, 'Do I want a conversation? No. Do I want a happy exchange of life histories? No. I want to get to the top of this heap of stone, and I want to get down the other side of it. Do I want to hear about your useless degree at Warwick, Reading, Sussex? No. Do I want to hear that you were brokering for some Jap bank, and were bored? No. Do I want to hear that you've a nice little job waiting back in brokering when you've had enough of dripping compassion? No . . . Be so good as to walk somewhere else.'

'You're every man I ever knew, just stuffed up with stereotyping.'

He looked away from her, from the mocking. The Academic rolled his eyes. The Fireman was laughing and the Street Boy giggling. The Archaeologist beamed. He wanted to sleep. Anywhere, at the side of the track, he could have slept. The water ran in a river on the track.

'Please yourself, talk if you have to.'

'It's only because you looked after my dog . . .'

She walked well. The child slept on her shoulder. The old man leaned on her arm. He thought the child would have weighed at least a half of his backpack, and she had the sack of dog food still tied at her waist. The way she walked was brilliant. It was where he had first met the one woman he had cared for, walking in rain and wind at the limit of endurance. The one woman had been sent to them in Hereford, all the crack and all the snide, just a woman to be shown that the Brecons in wind and rain and at forced march speed were no place for her. That woman had kept with them, dug for the stamina, not failed. That woman had had a flat in Battersea and an answer machine. Good talk with the answer machine. He'd gone to the Gulf, she'd gone away. Just the memory of her flat, a long weekend in a sanitized two rooms that told nothing of her, and the silence of the answer machine afterwards when he had called. A last letter, sent from the post box beside the bar on the loch, returned as Not Known At This Address. Only the long weekend to remember a woman who could have walked the Cuchumatanes as she had walked the Brecons.

'It doesn't matter . . .'

'Talk if you have to.'

Alex said, quiet, 'I thought you'd want to know.'

'Talk.'

'. . . I didn't take my first-year exams at college. My father used to have to spit to use the word, "dropout". I went on the road. I suppose you know what that means, do you? It wasn't really political, not a protest, but it seemed the right sort of thing. Quite exciting actually, looking for a place to park up with the caravan. You have to find a place where the ownership of the land is vague, or it's common ground, that way the police can't get the eviction order. I was three years on the road. I used to talk to my mother, at first, on the phone, when I knew my father would be at work. Got out of the habit of ringing . . . On the road you get to meet some pretty dreadful people, so aggressive, the new rich were the worst and the new rich in the Thames Valley were hideous, like all they wanted was fields that were empty, no-go zones. Sometimes we were only three or four vehicles and a dozen of us, sometimes we were a big group. One of the big groups was in Wales and those smug awful television people were there, and I was in a shot that was broadcast, and then I was summonsed by the police for a defective rear light, it was just harassment. The rear light was broken. Trouble was that the case was in the papers because I was able to prove that it was a plod's truncheon that had broken the light. My father saw the television and he saw the court report. He put a private detective on me, to find me. They just turned up one afternoon, my father and mother, in their BMW. It was quite an event actually, them coming in a big car. I think I'd had enough anyway. I loaded up their boot, I sat in the back with my dog, and I gave the crowd a good wave, and I went home. All right, I'm a bit ashamed. I wounded my father, but what really upset me was that my auntie was ill, poorly, and I should have visited her, I didn't know. We had a formal family gathering, pretty grim. They were all lined up, telling me that I was a privileged person and that I should do something with my life. I could do anything I wanted, and they'd back me, just so long as it was *positive*. So . . . I went to the Peace Movement. I had a choice. I could go to Sri Lanka or to Guatemala. I chose, for my sins, Guatemala. My father paid the air fare, my mother sends an allowance, my uncle gave me the money for the Land Rover. I suppose, Mr Hero, that fits the slot you'd given me – poor little rich girl on the loose. I tell you what, Mr Hero, if you ever accuse me again of dripping compassion then I'll slap your bloody face . . .'

Gord trudged on.

'. . . Well, you wanted to know . . .'

He dragged his feet forward, each pace harder than the last.

'. . . That's who I am . . .'

224

Struggling to breathe, fighting for the air in his lungs.

'. . . Are you all right?'

They were on the wilderness, wrapped in cloud, smacked by the rain.

In the middle of the afternoon the Priest had reached the tail of the column. He had learned the language of the Ixil people.

Where would he find the one they called Gaspar, the spirit with the fire?

He was directed ahead. Hurrying past the women and the children. Striving to catch the armed men.

Where would he find the one they called Gaspar, the leader?

Finding the strength from his commitment. Going past the wheelbarrow and the cart.

Where would he find the one they called Gaspar . . . ?

On a ridge, on the summit line of the Cuchumatanes the council of war. The little group was huddled down and rain-soaked and wind-whipped. There was a man who had once been obesely overweight and it was as if the fat had flaked from his body and left the caves on his face and the sunk corridors at his throat. There was a man with a bald head that shone from the rain. There was a man of slight build who was placing stones at the edges of the map that was covered in a small plastic sheet. There was a man who seemed still to cling to youth and whose finger was pressed against the map surface and who talked urgently. There was a man who sat with his back to the Priest's crabbed approach through the wind, and the big pack was slung on his shoulders and his upper body was wrapped in a harness of belt ammunition and whose hand rested on the stock of a machine gun.

'I am the priest from Nebaj . . . If the majority just stand and watch then there can be no change. I ask for a rifle . . . Which is the leader . . . ?'

The man who seemed to cling to youth, his hand came up from the map, was stretching in greeting.

'. . . The one they call Gaspar?'

The Priest saw the anger blaze on the faces of the bald man and the once fat man and the slight man, and he did not understand.

'. . . I'm talking to you, Miss, because he's been bad-mouthed too much. I've your guarantee that you've no harm meant for him, for Mr Brown. I've that guarantee, copper solid, right? He should have had the medal. There were bastards back on their arses who never heard a shot fired, had air-conditioned rooms, three bags bloody full, sir, and they had medals, they trooped up to the bloody Palace – excuse me, Miss . . . We were on the long-range recce job, where we were out west of Baghdad. We had to scout through for what was going to be the northern push. It was bloody awful – excuse me, Miss – country because there wasn't no cover. We had a good Land Rover, plenty of fuel, but we couldn't use the thing in the day, had to lie up all day, try and find a dip in the dunes. The message came through on the set. There was a Yank shot down. He was a helicopter Yank. Well, it was their show, wasn't it? They pulled the bloody – excuse me, Miss – strings. We knew we were in trouble if we went to get him because it was daylight movement. Mr Brown said we'd go for it. Mr Brown said there was no way he was leaving anybody – even a Yank, he said – out there for being captured. It was a kind of race. The 'Raqs had wheels out to get to the helicopter, and we were going shit and bust – excuse me, Miss – for it. We beat the 'Raqs to it, not by more than half a mile. They had two lorries, must have had twenty men. Couldn't miss what we were heading for, bloody great heap – excuse me, Miss – of smoke, and the other side of the smoke was the dust of their lorries. The Yanks had helicopters every day, bumming over the sand. We heard afterwards it was just chance that they hadn't anything in the air that could have made it faster than us. It was an Apache job, gunship job. The weapons guy was dead and the pilot wasn't good. He'd cut his face up pretty bad getting out and he was in shock, couldn't help himself. We were taking machine-gun fire all the way in to him. I don't suppose you know much about shooting, Miss, but we couldn't get a decent line on those lorries while we were belting, we were like ducks in a fairground. Mr Brown did the driving on the Land Rover. He didn't back off, Miss . . . We were going to get that pilot or we were going to buy it. Me, it would have to have been my best mate for me to have driven into that shit – excuse me, Miss – to get the Yank. That was when I was hit, just as we were grabbing him. We got him on board and we beat the hell out of it. Mr Brown had a hip flask with him, used to say it was his father's and his father was a right piss-artist. Hell of a big hip flask. He used to fill it each day. I tell you, Miss, we were all half cut by the time we'd lost those lorries of 'Raqs . . . Good job we didn't find the filth out there. Sorry, Miss, my joke . . . You see, Miss, we knew what happened to prisoners if those bastards had them. No way that Mr Brown was going to let them have that Yank. They sent a casevac ship in that night, lifted out the Yank and me. I haven't seen Mr Brown since. I just heard that he was shat on. I should have written to him but I didn't get round to it. Something in his head and he doesn't let go, all the way to the wire. Don't suppose you know where he is now, Miss . . . ?'

Later, after tea and biscuits, the invalid lance corporal limped on his stick to the front gate of the terraced house in east London, and he shook Cathy Parker's hand.

'You've been very kind, Francis.'

'Call me Eff, Miss, that's what Mr Brown called me . . . He's the sort of man, Miss, you'd follow to hell.'

The Civil Patroller knew little of life outside his village. The village was astride the Sacapulas to Uspantán road. The two towns were eighteen miles apart and the Civil Patroller's village was almost exactly halfway between them. The Civil Patroller sought only to survive. Survival was the yardstick by which he judged every act of his life.

Once, a foreign aid worker had come to the village, and the teacher had told the foreign aid worker, in the hearing of many men who had gathered around the stranger, of the life of the villagers under military rule. The teacher had said, 'You lift your head and they break it. You open your mouth and they shut it. You take a step forward and they kill you.' The teacher had indeed lifted his head and opened his mouth and taken the step forward, and he was dead in a dried ditch by the morning. The Civil Patroller had never, from that day, lifted his head nor opened his mouth nor taken the step forward. He sought to survive.

He would go twice a year with his brother and his cousin, and their wives, to Sacapulas to collect salt. He would go to Uspantán twice a year with his brother and his cousin, and their wives, to sell the *huipiles* blouses that the women had made and the panama hats of woven straw that the men had made, and they would coincide the journey to Uspantán with the fiestas when they would eat meat, chicken, and buy thread for making more *huipiles*.

All the men in the small village on the Sacapulas to Uspantán road were members of the Civil Patrol. They went out into the night, one week in four, and set up roadblocks. Sometimes, if there was an officer from the regular army with them, or an NCO, they would be awake and alert. Sometimes, if they were not supervised, they could make a shelter of palm fronds beside the road and sleep the night away.

It had been a difficult day for this Civil Patroller, an agony of a day. He needed the tree. There was no escape from the need of the tree as firewood. A beautiful tree, and he had prayed to the tree for its forgiveness. He had prayed alone through the morning for the forgiveness of the tree and then after the middle of the day, in the rain, he had started to hack at the tree's life with his axe. He had hacked with ferocity at the tree's trunk, just as he had seen the soldiers hack, with their machete blades, at the screaming body of his father.

The Civil Patroller sought only to survive.

He was issued with the old bolt-action rifle. He had the dried tortillas in his pocket and five rounds of ammunition. The patrol would not be accompanied by an officer or a regular NCO.

They were told where they should go, what track they should watch. He neither lifted his head nor opened his mouth nor stepped forward.

Where he stood, the old rifle on his shoulder, listening to the officer, was only a few paces from where his father had been hacked to death by the machetes. It was said by his brother and his cousin, whispered, that there was rebellion. Gaspar had risen, come with fire, many soldiers had died. It was said by his brother and his cousin, muttered so that the words were beyond the hearing of informers, that the soldiers had been burned by Gaspar's fire.

The wind tugged the clothes he wore, the rain dripped from the wide brim of his hat, and the Civil Patroller hoped that the beautiful tree had heard his prayer for forgiveness.

There were a thousand to feed.

It should have been Groucho's work, but Groucho was half on his knees.

It should have been Zeppo's work, or Harpo's, or the Archaeologist could have helped and so could the Academic.

But it came down to Gord.

They had to be fed.

There were tins of food and condensed milk, taken from Nebaj barracks. There were tortillas, stale and hard, that had been carried from Playa Grande. Not possible to make a fire, not in the gale wind and the rain.

Groucho lay on the ground and Gord kicked him. Where were the tin-openers, who carried the bread, why had he not thought through the problem of food? Gord kicked him in frustration and Groucho just rolled away, disappeared.

They were down on the south side of the long ridge of the Cuchumatanes. The force of the weather hit them. The darkness was around them, pinpointed by torches and the flares of flame that men sheltered with their bodies. The darkness had come before they had reached the lower tree line. They had to be fed, a thousand souls, in the open. They would have to sleep in the open . . . Alex helped him, and the Street Boy. Christ, and he missed Eff and Vee and Zed, gone ahead . . . The Priest came to him, and helped. It was an hour after darkness that he found the tin-openers, and it was two hours after darkness before he had the lines in place, seven of them, waiting for food, and taking it away into the black night. They were wonderful, and he thought their patience was magnificent. He loved these people. Each man and each woman and each child, standing in the line, taking what they were given, bobbing their heads in gratitude, disappearing. No complaint from any man or woman or child that the food distribution was screwed up.

The Priest had them singing, as they waited in their lines, and away in the night was a guitar.

Hungry, himself . . .

Tired, himself . . .

Short-fused, himself . . . The lines were in place. The food was being given. The lights winked in the mist darkness. He made his way down, towards the head of the column, away from the singing and the guitar.

Gord found them in a shallow cave. His torch caught their faces. Jorge was at the back of the cave and there was a rain-damp blanket draped over his head and his shoulders as a tent. Harpo held the tin and the moment the torch was on them was as Zeppo gouged with his fingers into the tin. Groucho hissed at him, might have been a cat defending territory, couldn't speak because his mouth was filled. He smelled it, long days since the taste had been in his throat and the smell on his clothes. Harpo was looking up at the torch beam, challenging him, holding up the tin for Gord to take his share.

Gord said, 'Well, they're only fucking Indians, aren't they . . . ?'

Jorge's head was down, shielded by the blanket, staring at his knees.

' . . . Quite right, let the *Indians* sort themselves out. Top buggers first, eh . . . ?'

Harpo gazed back at him and did not flinch.

'. . . Filling your guts with salmon. A good tin of salmon liberated from the officers' mess at Nebaj, not put in the pool, not put in the pot, kept for the big bastards, right . . . ?'

Zeppo's defiance, feeding from his fingers, then pulling the tin back from Harpo for more.

'. . . Back there, they're half dead for lack of food – only Indians – they're not sitting down, not in shelter, waiting to be fed – only Indians. Right . . . ?'

Groucho cringed from him, swallowing.

'. . . You're not fit to lead, but then they're only Indians, eh?'

Harpo said, 'When I lived in Guatemala City we employed a maid. It was the one *luxury* we allowed ourselves. We employed the maid to do the work that was dirty. The maid lived in a shed at the back of the house, in the yard, because we did not have a big enough house for her to have a room inside. The maid knew her place. She did not expect to join the debate in the family when there was a matter to be decided. She was content with her position.'

'I am not your fucking maid.'

He heard Harpo's dry laugh. He stepped between Harpo and Zeppo, and Groucho wriggled fast away from his boots, and he settled beside Jorge.

'Can we have the map? Can we plan tomorrow?'

Jorge shrugged, as if it was not important, lethargically pulled the map from the wide pocket of his trousers.

Gord jabbed at the map. 'Where we are, good? Early start in the morning, moving at six. Straight across the Sacapulas – Uspantán road, no stopping for a bath and coffee . . . Need someone local to get us across the Negro river, all the bridges will be defended, and I don't want to fight again just for a bridge. I want them not knowing where the hell we are . . . Then, straight south . . . I want to get into that high ground by night, no roads and no villages. Great, and the day after it will be Santa Cruz del Quiché, right? Departmental capital, right? Is that straight, Jorge?'

He cuffed the wet blanket over Jorge's shoulder, encouragement.

'They tell me we have gone far enough.'

'What?' Like he had not heard the voice muffled in the blanket depths.

'They say we cannot go further.'

The silence hung on them. Jorge's head was bowed. He thought that Jorge was beaten by the bastards. He shone his torch into their faces.

Deliberate, quiet. 'Who says we have gone far enough? Who says we can go no further?'

Groucho said, 'You have pushed us too hard, beyond the limit of what is possible for us . . .'

'You should take a bus down to the airport and present yourself at the ticket counter, cash, one way to Havana.'

Harpo said, 'We are exhausted and sick and ill. We should go back to the triangle.'

'Where they can surround you, mince you, as they did before.'

Zeppo said, 'We should stand our ground here. We should tell them that we demand political negotiation, a cease-fire in exchange for dialogue.'

'They will laugh at you, and know that you are beaten.'

Groucho shouted, 'Can you not understand, we have no strength left . . .'

Harpo spat, 'You have pushed us too hard, broken us . . .'

Zeppo cried, 'It is one thing to fight, another to go in a place fit only for goats . . .'

'There are a thousand people behind you. They are not in a cave. They are not eating salmon. They are marching to Guatemala City. They will tell you about *strength*, and about *negotiation* and about *retreat*. Go and ask them, and tell them that you are not feeling well, and want to run away, and want to talk. Only fucking Indians, of course. Perhaps they don't have opinions. We can get to Guatemala City, I promise you, if . . .'

'If.' Zeppo rolled the word.

'. . . if the weather holds for us . . . Why have we not met a blocking force? Because the weather helps us, they do not know where we are. Why must we force the march? Because

232

they do not believe we are capable of crossing this ground at this speed.'

'We should consolidate,' Harpo said.

'Coward's talk.'

'We should negotiate,' Zeppo said.

'Failure's talk.'

'We should quit while we have the strength,' Groucho said.

Gord had hold of Jorge's shoulders. He shook the young man. He shook him as a cat shakes a rat, cruel.

'What do you say?'

Hands off Jorge's shoulders. His fists grasped Jorge's beard. He pulled Jorge's head up. Cavern eyes staring up at him. Slow words.

'In the morning . . . I decide in the morning . . . the morning will be time . . .'

'Oh, no, no way . . .' Gord dragged Jorge to his feet. 'With me now. You come back with me now, and you tell a thousand fucking Indians, and a few others, that you've had enough. You tell them, men from Nebaj and Acul and Playa Grande, that you're chucking it. You tell them that you're going for retreat or negotiation. You tell them they can go back to where the army's waiting for them, at Playa Grande or Acul or Nebaj, or whatever bloody hole they came out of . . .'

'Thank you,' Jorge said hoarsely.

Gord growled, 'For nothing.'

They went together back up the mountain slope.

'I apologize.'

'You don't have to apologize to me, Jorge.'

'I apologize because I have abused you, Gord, and because I have failed those who follow me. Because it will not happen again I can, in sincerity, apologize.'

Never explain and never *apologize*, what they taught the officer entrants at Sandhurst Academy, what they spelled out on the regiment's induction course. The anger ran from him. He wondered what they would make of Rodolfo Jorge Ramírez, the instructors at the academy who knew it all, and the officers at

Hereford who had seen it all. Leadership material or wet shit? Well, Gord Brown, if he were asked, could tell them that Rodolfo Jorge Ramírez could lead several hundreds of men on a journey of madness into the mouth of bad hell.

After Gord had dropped down, drained, he watched Jorge's light move amongst the huddled, sitting men. He heard the low voice, calm. He heard the chuckled laughter. He saw the figure shrouded by the blanket slip forward, then settle again. His stomach groaned for food, too tired to go and look for it. He lay on his side on hard rock and the rain beat on him. He was asleep before the singing had died.

Chaos swirling in the terminal.

The morning light not yet on the avenue in front of his home, Colonel Arturo had started out for the airport.

Holding the tickets in his hand, queuing and kicking forward the bags each time the counter neared. His wife and daughter behind him, and dressed as if it was Disneyland they were headed for and vacation.

There had been a general ahead of him in the queue, and there were two brigadiers behind him. He had seen a general in the adjacent queue, and a senator, and an official he knew to be senior in the secretariat of the Foreign Ministry.

The shouting, the shoving, the whining was around him.

He reached the head of the queue. He slapped the two suit-cases on the scales. He dropped the tickets onto the desk. The young man on check-in looked at him with contempt, moved with studied insolence, glanced in his own time at the tickets. The flight was full. The list was closed. The Arturo ladies had been off-loaded. The tickets should be changed for the follow-ing morning. All other flights today were full. He started to shout . . . He was Colonel Mario Arturo . . . He was a colonel in the Kaibiles . . . He had friends on the General Staff . . . The check-in clerk was bored. The face of the clerk showed he had heard it before, that morning, many times, showed that he had heard of influence and power and position. All around, the clipped accents of privilege, money whispered of a rabble swarming towards the capital city and the army in confusion.

He knew the answer.

No more shouting, no more posturing importance.

His voice softened. His hand was at his wallet. He paid the *mordida*. The bribe he offered was, first time, one hundred American dollars, pocketed by the check-in clerk. The tickets still lay on the desk. A second hundred-dollar note. A third . . . The check-in clerk tore at the ticket pages, hammered with his stamp, reached with the baggage tags for the handles of the suitcases. The tickets and the two boarding cards were passed back across the desk. The check-in clerk looked past him for the next passenger.

He watched his wife and daughter through the passport examination.

He stayed at the airport until the aircraft took off, rising into the low cloud off the shine of the tarmac.

He strode, bullocking his way out of the terminal building, away from the fetid stench of defeat.

# 12

The dream left him.

Gord woke.

The dream was of rotted flesh and the wheelbarrows of decayed bodies and shovels that scraped up the flesh and the bodies. The dream was of the fire that hissed, sparkled, as the flesh and bodies of the salmon were swung by the shovels onto the pyre. The flesh and bodies of the salmon fish hit the petrol-driven fire and he saw the carcasses of children. The fish were dead children. The dead children were butterflies. The butterflies tried to rise from the climb of the flames and were caught, and their wings were withered. The bright colours of butterflies' wings crumpling in the fire heat, and there was the shriek of children and the spit of the fish flesh. The bodies of butterflies fell back into the fire heat . . .

He woke.

He started up.

The light of the day, grey-white under the cloud, pricked at his eyes. Should have been dark, should have been night. Should have been the blackness around him, and the phlegm cough of men roused from sleep. He lay beside the track and there was a lip of rock a yard high into which he was huddled, and which took the weight of the falling rain. He looked back up the mountain slope, the way they had come, and he saw the trail beaten by feet, and its emptiness . . . Christ . . . He swung his head. He could see down the same slope, and there was the same emptiness before the track merged into the short misted horizon. The sag in his stomach . . . Christ . . . Gord bloody Brown, whip master and taskmaster, sleeping on past the time of the loading up and the moving out. A terrible stillness in the silence. Gord bloody Brown, sharp tongue and hard tongue, lying down on the job . . . Christ . . . They were sitting above the lip of the rock.

The cart and the wheelbarrow were with them.

They were waiting on him.

There was the Archaeologist, eyes closed as if he remembered distant music. There was the Academic, brow furrowed as if he took a calculation in his mind and worried it. There was the Fireman, lips pursed in concern as if he cared. There was the Street Boy, gazing on the open blade of his knife as if he remembered the slashing blow against a sentry's throat. The silence clung in the air. There was the emptiness of the mountain slope ahead of him and behind him.

Gord started to push himself up. The load of the backpack crippled his effort, and there was the weight of the machine gun across his waist, and there was the binding of the ammunition belts across his chest. He pushed, he writhed, and he fell back. It was a haze in his memory, dropping to the side of the track in the darkness, not having the will to shrug out of the constraint harness of the backpack, falling in sleep as Jorge had moved away further from him . . .

'You bastards.'

The Archaeologist said, 'You had to sleep.'

The Academic said, 'Without rest you kill yourself.'

The Fireman said, 'If you lose your strength then none of us have strength.'

The Street Boy said, 'You snore like a pig, you know that, like a big mother pig.'

He was on his feet. The taste of the night was in his mouth, and the ache was in his legs, and the pain held in his lungs. He used the stock of the machine gun to hold himself upright. Gord looked down the track, where the beat of the feet had been. His clothes dripped water. He squinted his eyes to clear the fire of the dream and the blank grey-white of the cloud base.

'How long?'

'Two hours since the men moved off,' the Archaeologist said.

He started to move, but they were faster. They were around him. He should eat. Had to make up ground. He must eat. Had to recapture lost time. He would eat. Had to hurry . . . They were around him and blocking him. It was a conspiracy. He struggled and heaved with his shoulders and could not break the hold of the Archaeologist and the Academic. He thrashed with his legs and the Street Boy kicked him smartly on the bones of his shins. The Fireman fed him, like he was a child, like he was a sick patient. While they held him, and while the Street Boy dared him to try to take a step forward, the Fireman forced the dry wedges of tortilla down his throat. Gord submitted. A lump of tortilla at a time. Swallowed, gagged, belched, swallowed . . . The food fell to the pit of his stomach. He knew the boy would kick him again if he struggled again.

He felt their love.

'You should not have allowed me.'

He saw in his mind the great column loading up, taking on their shoulders the mortars and the bombs and the machine guns and the ammunition and the launchers and the rockets.

'The men knew you had to sleep,' the Archaeologist said.

He saw in his mind the men sliding in darkness down the mountain slope under the burden of what they carried.

'The men believe in you,' the Academic said.

'It was Alex who said you snored like a big mother pig,' the Street Boy said.

Gord wiped his mouth. He was freed.

'Do it again and I'll break your bloody backs . . .'

He thought that he felt their love and the blood ran again in him.

He led. They were the children. They careered down the mountain track. The wheels of the cart and the wheels of the barrow bucked and jumped on the rock stones. Going fast. They were the children who yelled and shouted. They were the butterflies dancing. A sort of joy with them all, as if hunger were forgotten, as if fatigue were gone. All liberated, and charging down the rough track where the column had gone before them.

The mist was around them and the rain splashed at their faces and ran from their clothes. A wildness in them all, and a madness. Twice the cart turned right over, and once the wheelbarrow toppled to lose the petrol cans and the air cylinder . . . it was the third day of Gord's week.

He was the survivor, and he alone stood his ground.

The rifle with the five rounds of ammunition in the magazine was on the ground by his feet.

The Civil Patroller raised his worn and calloused hands until they were straight above his head.

The echo of the rifle shots beat in his ears.

The others at the roadblock had run. It was very clear to him, everything that had happened. He had been coming from the bush scrub at the side of the track that led away to the cloud-hidden mountain ridge. There had still been grass stems in his hands, from what he had used to wipe between his buttocks. He had seen the first men coming fast down the fall of the slope. Tightening the rope that held his trousers at the waist, scraping the last grass from his hands on the thighs of his trousers, whistling the warning to the others who still slept in the shelter of the high trees. He had seen a mirage of men, bearded and filthy, coming like hunting dogs towards him. Out of the mist, hazed in the rain stream, and he had shouted. And endless march of men emerging from the invisibility of the cloud, and he had shouted and then frozen. The swarm powering closer and no gap behind them in the ripple of advancing men. Five other men on the roadblock, and the sleep still in their minds, and running. The volley of shots, past him to the right and by him to the left. The crack of the gunfire around him.

He stood so still, and he held the trembling in his legs. He wondered if he would be shot himself, and whether it would hurt to be shot, and he wondered if it were a punishment for the killing of the tree that was beautiful.

He heard a voice. He thought it was the voice of the spirit that his brother and his cousin had told him of. The spirit was given the name of Gaspar. He saw a man who was fairer than the *Ladinos* around him and who carried a heavy machine gun and was swathed in ammunition belts and there was a cart pulled on wheels behind him, and a barrow. He thought that the voice of the spirit, Gaspar, had saved him from the rifles at the head of the column.

As far as he could see, behind the voice of the spirit, the mountain moved with men advancing from the cloud.

The questions were barked at him.

Of course he would join. Of course he would guide them.

He was permitted to lower his arms.

He could look now behind him. He could see the bodies of the men from his village on the Sacapulas to Uspantán road. He had known each of the men all the days of his life. He had worked the fields of maize with them, and gone down on the lorries with them to work in the sugar *fincas*, drunk himself insensible with them on *atol* at the fiestas, seen the killing of his father by the army with them, danced with them . . .

Of course the Civil Patroller would join the march, guide it, and survive.


'You are paralysed. It is an impertinence for me to say so, but it is necessary to say it.'

It was a liberty that Mario Arturo took. There was the fourth cigarette of the day in the general's fingers and the room smelled of stale whisky. The rain beat steadily on the windows.

'An impertinence, yes.'

'We have to be proactive. It is too late to be reactive. We have to go in there, get them. If we are defensive, hull down, we will lose. It is as if we show them fear.'

'A grave impertinence.'

The general had taught him at the Escuela Politecnica. The general had commanded him at brigade level in the Firmness '83 campaign, and in the harrying operations against the sub- versives of National Stability '85. The general had stood by Mario Arturo nine years before when he had written the seven-page paper, 'Belize: Implications of Intervention', in which he had predicted humiliation and defeat should the Guatemalan armed forces be ordered to invade Belize territory and confront British troops and British strike aircraft; not a popular paper; a paper said by some staff officers to be an insult to the army; a paper said by many unit commanders to be defeatist. The general had protected him.

'If we don't act we will lose . . .'

All through the previous day Colonel Arturo had abandoned his desk and tramped the corridors and sidled into anterooms and wheedled with staff officers for access. He had been rejected. Ignored by generals and distanced from brigadiers and held at arm's length by the colonels who scurried from meeting to meeting, from the conference room of the *estado mayor* to the war operations room of the Mariscal Zavala garrison camp. Ignored, distanced, held back, minutes into hours, hours into a day, he had been deflected. He was dressed now in his best uniform. He wore his medals for service and gallantry. He had been at the *estado mayor* from 7 a.m., and he had bearded this general of logistics, in command of G-4, as the staff car had pulled up. He had forced his way past an ADC, he had flicked with his swagger stick at the outstretched hand of a military policeman. He had won the access.

'. . . If we lose and we are still here then we will be swinging from lampposts. If we lose and we are gone then we will be washing dishes in hotels in Miami. If . . .'

He broke off. The telephone rang, was answered by the young adjutant. The adjutant listened, and his fist tightened to white on the receiver, and he bit at his lip. The general would be hanging, and high, the general was known in the area towards the southwest strip of the Mexican frontier as the Butcher of Jacaltenango. The adjutant put down the telephone carefully, and spoke in the general's ear. There was the bleak smile on the general's face, and the irritated tugging at his moustache.

'If you are not decisive, if you do not go for the throat of this rabble, if you do not crush them, *now* . . .'

The hand of the general waved for him to be silent. He saw the old veins on the claw of a mottled hand.

A quiet voice, the passion exhausted. 'I have asked the artillery to be brought forward from Escuintla, 75mm and 105mm, but I am told that too many men are under training for it to be an effective response force. I have asked for mechanized infantry to be driven in from Huehuetenango, M-113s and V-150s, and I am told that the personnel carriers are undergoing the annual maintenance programme. I have asked for the light tanks from the garrison battalion at Jalapa, M-41A3s, but I am told the road is washed out. My dear friend, we are a political army and we are in the hands of politicized officers, and politicized officers are content to wait until they see the fall of the coins. It is the time for the excuses of *pragmatists* . . . What do you want?'

No hesitation. Colonel Arturo stood forward on his toes. He felt his power.

'I want command of the Kaibil battalion.'

'He is my nephew.'

'Full command.'

'He is married to the daughter of the cousin of the minister.'

'Full support.'

'The officer you would replace has the connection to break you.'

'Full command, full support. Let him try.'

'You ask much . . .'

'Or you will hang from a lamppost in front of the Palacio Nacional, or you will end your days washing dishes in a hotel's kitchen.'

He saw the hostility of the adjutant. He wondered who was the uncle of the adjutant, who was the father-in-law of the adjutant. He owed nothing to any man. He had no *finca* in the Franja Transversal del Norte where the military commanders had scuttled for free land. He had no link to a construction company that built for the ministry. He had no villa on the shore of Lake Atitlán, no share of a hotel, no investment in car parks, no arrangement with the army's bank. He knew none of the foreign businessmen of the American Chamber of Commerce, none of the Japanese car importers, none of the Taiwanese contractors. He was owned by no man.

He was told when he should report back, the next day, at what time in the evening.

'If you fail then there would be nowhere you could hide . . .'

'I want the command of the Kaibil battalion.'

Off the high ground, back amongst the tall forest trees of ceiba and pine, coming through paths that were bright with the *tamborilla* blossom beaten down by the rain from the trees. They skirted a village, they bypassed cleared ground. The breath was back in Gord's lungs. The wilderness of the mountain was behind him. They were across the Sacapulas to Uspantán road, and there was the growing roar ahead. He had not counted, there had been no formality because the drive of the march's speed had again been raised, but he had reckoned there to be a hundred men waiting at the roadside for them. There had been villagers with axes and with forks for turning the hay crop and with sledgehammers, there had been Civil Patrollers with their veteran bolt-action rifles, there had been tattered guerrillas who seemed to blink in the light of open ground, and a policeman in a soaked uniform, and more women and more children, and all running to catch the end of the straggled column. Gord could hold the speed of the march, just . . . Short of the Sacapulas to Uspantán road he had broken from the column, gone to the shelter of the bushes and opened the buckle of his belt and peeled his combat trousers down. He had squatted. The first time in two days, and the food that had been forced on him had blown through his gut. Not much of the paper left, and he did not have strength to dig the latrine hole that he had preached for in the Petén. He had dragged his trousers back up and looked down and seen the white parasite worms . . . He could hold the speed of the march now, just, because the Street Boy carried the weight of the machine gun.

The roar was in his ears.

It might have been the sickness, and it might have been the tiredness, or the effect of the parasite worms in his stomach, or the altitude.

He walked forward, towards the roar ahead, and his feet tramped as an automaton's. The thought of his father, and what his father had said once, drunk, about making footsteps on life's path. Heh, old man – heh, TeeJay – bloody great footsteps here. It squirmed in him, the opportunities missed between a son and a drunk. The old man, TeeJay, gone, dead, and the epitaph was a slurred reminder that a son should make footprints. Heh, TeeJay, if you're watching, pray God you're watching, these are hellish big footprints. All lost, the opportunities. TeeJay Brown had cut the passing-out parade at Sandhurst because a crown court case had run an extra day. TeeJay Brown had cut the short leave when he had called home after being accepted into the regiment because a detective from the Porn Squad was retiring and throwing a thrash. TeeJay Brown had cut the Sunday lunch when he'd travelled down to the suburbs after his first Irish tour because Features had demanded a rewrite. He wondered if there were any left of the old scribblers, who still told jokes about TeeJay Brown, recognized the footprints. He thought of his father, in what he thought was a sort of delirium, and in his mind were red-eyed detectives in church and scribblers who were snivelling. Too much missed . . .

They came to the Rio Negro.

The tree line of big pines reached to the rim of the gorge.

Fifty, sixty feet below them, the swelled river crashed and spumed and burst over the boulders.

There was a bridge seven miles, on the map, upstream and a bridge could be held by a dozen men, and would be held. There was a bridge, on the map, nine miles downstream . . . The high pines lowered above him and the cloud caught at the top branches, and below him the spray hung over the crashing power of the river. He sank to the ground. He did not know the answer.

\*　　\*　　\*

Jorge looked for him.

It was the reflex.

Always he looked for Gord. Gord, with the solution. Gord, with the idea.

Hunched down. His little group around him. On the ground and his eyes closed and his head bowed.

For Jorge to decide . . .

It was after he had eaten his breakfast, two eggs scrambled and orange juice and good coffee, that the Canadian found what had been done to the tyres of the Shogun four-wheel drive. It was a good jeep, the best that he had been able to hire on his three visits to Guatemala. He didn't rage and he didn't swear and he didn't weep, because it was his third visit to Guatemala and he had learned, hard, that anger and cursing and crying won him nothing. The four tyres had been slashed, and the spare. They had not been punctured so that they could be repaired, they were in ribbons as if wide-blade knives had been used on them, and there was no place in Chichicastenango where a man could buy five new tyres for a Shogun four-wheel drive. It would have been the kid's birthday . . . it would have been the end of the road . . . it would have been the day they dug in the cemetery. They should all have been waiting beside the jeep for him to finish his breakfast, the men who were to dig, and the coroner from Santa Cruz del Quiché, and the attorney from Guatemala City. It was his third journey to the country, it was the trip on which he had at last believed he had identified the grave of the kid. So the kid was stupid, so the kid had messed a potential career, so the kid had bummed in Central America, but the kid was his grandson. The kid was his grandson, and a fool and a messer and a bum had the right to something better than death in a police station and burial in a clandestine grave. There had been no-one waiting beside the Shogun four-wheel drive when he had come from eating his breakfast in the small dining area of the Posada Santa Marta, but the plainclothes men of the Treasury Police were across the road, lounging in the rain, watching him. It was the goddamn fear . . . He knew about the fear in goddamn Guatemala . . . The men that he had hired to dig, and for whom he had bought corn liquor the night before, would have seen the slashed tyres and gone home. The coroner that he had worked a month with for the paperwork of exhumation, and bribed well, would have seen the tyres and driven away down the rain-soaked road to Santa Cruz del Quiché. The lawyer he had now known with meetings and correspondence for three years, and who had had in the last week a live bullet round in his post box, would have turned his car for a return to the capital. No chance from the hotel of an international call, difficult enough with shouting to raise Guatemala City, no chance of getting Kingston, Ontario. And a poor call it would have made, better that his wife was left in her ignorance . . . There was a room in the bungalow that was behind the Irish pub in Kingston, set back from the marina frontage, and the room was as it had been when the kid had gone. The room had the fluffy bears and the aircraft model kits and the hockey photographs and the school textbooks, and his wife would probably have been in there that morning and said the prayer that she always said when she sat on the kid's bed . . . No, he hadn't known where Guatemala was when he had first gone down to the travel agent to book a ticket, three years back. Yes, he knew about Guatemala now. His son, the kid's father, his son said that the living had to live. Not his son's business because his son was divorced, and an engineer on a bulk carrier, and had long before failed to make a home for the kid, passed the role of parent to the grandparents of the kid. His son said that the kid was dead and that throwing money after finding a grave was waste. He was in his seventy-first year, and he had a mortgage now on the bungalow, first time in eleven years, and the mortgage had paid for a private detective and the lawyers and the correspondence and three trips down to Guatemala. The mortgage money had tracked the journey of the kid, his grandson, through the Mexican border post and into Guatemala at the La Mesilla frontier check. The mortgage money had found the Indian woman who remembered the kid in San Rafael Petzal, smoking, and found the storekeeper who remembered the kid at San Cristóbal Totonicapán, drunk, and found the priest who remembered the kid with the beggars outside the church at Nahualá, destitute. And big money, what the bastard would have earned in a year, for the policeman who remembered the kid running from the soldiers at Chichicastenango, stoned and drunk and destitute. There was a police station at Chichicastenango, where the kid would have been killed. The killings were plenty that year, and there was a cemetery, grass-covered, unmarked, on the road out to Santa Cruz del Quiché, where the kid would have been buried. He would have driven that morning out to the cemetery, with the gravediggers and the coroner and the attorney, if the tyres of the Shogun four-wheel drive had not been slashed . . . It was the girl who washed the glasses in the bar, pretty little Indian girl and no shoes on her feet, out of sight of the plainclothes policemen across the street, who told him of the rumour, of the spirit who had brought the fire.

'Where are they?' The fist of the general, driven by his anger, smacked the desk.

'We do not have a precise position.'

'What is precise? Is "*precise*" that you do not know?'

He had been at school with the G-2 officer. He played bridge with the officer. His wife rode with the wife of the officer.

'It is the weather . . .'

'So you do not know where is a rabble crowd of illiterates, vagabonds, peasants . . . ?'

The G-2 officer flushed. 'You have to understand the circumstances. There are difficulties of transport, there are problems of communication. It is impossible to have reliable people where you need them. There are reports, only reports, of an incident near to the Sacapulas to Uspantán road, reports of the killing of some Civil Patrollers – there were tracks. Maybe them, maybe fewer men . . . around the whole Ixil triangle area . . . it is alive with peasants on the move . . . if it is them then they will find the Rio Negro across their path. There are bridges and they are defended. The river is in spate.'

'What do you tell me?'

'If they wish to come south, towards Santa Cruz del Quiché, and we are full battalion strength there, then they must force a bridge, they must identify their position.'

The general eyed the G-2 officer. He could goad men, drive them. His staff officers, hovering behind him, clung at his words. He had goaded men forward, driven them, in the days of the bad casualties of Victory '82. 'They cannot cross the Rio Negro other than by bridge where they will be identified, you promise me?'

The silence. The staff officers in the room considered the price of a promise. It was said, not proven, that once the general had, himself, shot dead with his pistol a platoon commander accused of abandoning a road junction to the Ejército Guerrillero de los Pobres, shot him first in the testicles then in the head.

The silence, then the deep-drawn breath of the G-2 officer. 'They cannot cross other than by bridge, and the bridges are guarded . . .'

Axes and machetes had cut down the great pines.

Two ant swarms of men, swinging the axes, hacking with the machetes, had brought low the two great pine trunks that had a century before taken root at the rim of the gorge above the rambling torrent river.

Each man, swinging his axe and hacking with his machete until the spark had gone from his strength, had reeled away, and another had taken up the attack.

A whining commune of prayer as the resin bled the life from the great pines, a cry for forgiveness as each blow had struck home. It had been Jorge's decision. She could see the way he had sauntered among the men, new confidence, urging them and whispering encouragement to frantic effort.

The great pines had groaned, cracked, cried. They had fallen, slow at first, then rushing, down together across the width of the gorge, scattering the men from the path of their collapse. A tangle of men had run then to the pine trunks and slashed at the front branches as they had advanced above the roar of the water course.

The bridge was made.

The charge started.

A man fell. His scream was lost in the spume spray. Another man fell and went spreadeagled down to the white water, but the swarm rushed and clung and slipped and made good their grip.

She would go at the end when the women and the children crossed. Alex Pitt watched as the man mass wriggled on the bridge of the great pines, cutting from sight the branches and the foliage, a maggot motion going forward. Another man fell, spiralled down to the washed rocks, and the gap that he left was closed.

She saw that Gord now stood alone because the men who were always around him had gone across with the cart and the wheelbarrow. The swarm slackened.

He was going forward. Slow and tired drunk strides towards the rim. She could have shouted and she would not have been heard. Because so many had crossed the flow was sparser. She could have shouted the warning that he was to wait, that he could go across with the women and the children. She looked to the far side. The Academic was there, and the Archaeologist, good men and she liked to talk with them. The Fireman stood with the Street Boy in front of him, resting his hand as a father would on the mischief boy's shoulder. The Civil Patroller was with them, the one whose friends had been shot down and who showed no hurt. She could have shouted the warning that would not have been heard. The fat man, the *Ladino*, agile despite the weight on him, the bully man, was halfway across. Gord going next, rocking on the branches and foliage, swaying as if he were a scarecrow in the wind. The bald man, the *Ladino*, bright head held high, shoulders back and confident and sure, stepped onto the bridge.

The fat man going tortoise slow and the bald man going crab quick.

Halfway across.

Gord was sandwiched between the fat *Ladino* and the bald *Ladino*.

She knew the hatred. The Archaeologist had told her of the spat fights in the core of the group around the young leader.

Gord looking up, and seeing the fat man. The hesitancy seemed to cloud Gord. Caught in the wind, lashed by the rain, a leg slipping into the pine frond mass that was treacherous. She wondered how deep was the hatred. She heard nothing over the thunder fall of the river, but she could see the mouth movement of the fat man who turned towards Gord and blocked his way. She had seen three men fall. He seemed to sneer and taunt. His foot had slipped and she saw that Gord used a big effort to drag his foot back up and he pulled at a branch and the branch broke clear in his hand. He dropped. He was astride the bridge mass. He would be looking down, down onto the tumble pace of the river, down onto the smoothed rocks, down onto the driven current.

There was the cry of a name.

The name cry grew to match the thunder noise of the river.

She heard the cry. 'Gaspar . . . Gaspar . . . Gaspar . . .'

A thousand voices, more, willing him to cross.

'Gaspar . . . Gaspar . . . Gaspar . . .'

The fat man was over, walking away onto the rim and not looking back.

Gord crawled forward.

'Gaspar . . . Gaspar . . . Gaspar . . .'

The name cry carried him over, and died, and she was left with only the thunder noise of the river.

The bald man was across.

She hitched the child higher on her shoulder. She went towards the bridge. Ahead of her, over the gorge, the column was already on the move. New pace and new urgency, the march headed away into the cloud mist of the great pines.

She knew it, she had cared.

\*     \*     \*

'He is married to the daughter of my cousin.'

The general said, 'I want Arturo to have command of the Kaibil battalion.'

'It is an insult to the son-in-law of my cousin,' the minister said.

'I tell you two things . . . G-2 promises me that the Ramírez rabble is now blocked behind the Rio Negro, they must find a bridge and force it, they must search for that bridge, when they attack it we have located them . . . When they are located, I need the Kaibil battalion to be waiting for them . . . Arturo has the stomach for the work . . .'

'How long do I have, to weigh the insult to the son-in-law of my cousin?'

The general saw that the civilian minister wavered. 'You have until tomorrow because you have the time that the Rio Negro has brought us . . . Understand me, I am not interested in the sensibilities of the son-in-law of your cousin. If you do not appreciate, minister, the consequences of failure to use that time bought us, then you should go to La Aurora and try to buy a ticket for a flight out . . . I must have Arturo.'

'. . . It was disgusting what was done to him. If you're trying to put it right, like you say, then it's a bit bloody late. Okay, okay, I know where you want to pick it up. It was a big risk getting to the Yankee birdman and we took a casualty, had to fly them both out on a casevac in the evening. We got the hell out after that because the 'Raqs were alerted. We had another rendezvous with a bird that topped us with fuel and ammo and more grub, and brought us in a new radio because ours was blinking. It was a pretty lonely old world when the resupply bird left us . . . Our job was to report back rather than do demolition. We weren't supposed to be identified, just to stooge around in the area where the north thrust was going to come in and report back on ground defences, artillery positions, tank movements. Wasn't the death-or-glory stuff . . . You won't want a bloody encyclopaedia of the war. The thrust came in. The 'Raqs didn't stand

251

and contest it. They were running and shitting, shitting and running. We were ahead of the push, and we got down to Karbala. Place was in uproar. I don't know whether you know about Karbala, ma'am, but it's big in the Shia religion. The 'Raq army was in full retreat, fast as they could bloody go. All the radios, BBC, Voice of America, Saudi radio, they were all telling the Shia guys that it was time to get off their arses and do the business. Uncle Saddam was a goner, that's what the radios were telling them in Karbala . . . Then there was the ceasefire. The big politicals and the big generals, they let Uncle Saddam off the hook. Mr Brown, he was real mad, shouting and cursing and bollocking, because we got the message quick enough that the 'Raq armour was still intact, and was coming back into Karbala. They were good people there, Mr Brown became a sort of hero in that town, suppose it was because we were the only liberation troops they saw. We knew what they had to expect. They'd shown us the security police cells. You ever seen meat hooks set in the ceiling, ma'am? You ever seen an execution shed, ma'am? You ever seen a torture room? They'd kind of burned their boats because they'd strung up any of Uncle Saddam's filth they could get their hands on. It was going to be bad for them, when the tanks came back in . . . Sold down the river. They thought, from what the radio said, that the Yankees were coming, or the Brits, or the French, coming all the way to Karbala . . . Mr Brown did what he could for them. About three days he had to train an army. They only had rifles. They hadn't anti-tank, they hadn't recoilless, they hadn't mines. Mr Brown tried to show them how to block the streets, how to make Molotovs, where the armour was unprotected. They believed in him. He worked twenty hours a day for three days, and all through those fucking tanks were getting closer . . . I'm not saying that if we'd stayed, five of us, that it would have made a twopence damn of difference. What was such a bastard was that they trusted us, and they believed all those fucking lies from the radio. We had tanks, guns just a few miles up the road and Mr Brown was on the radio the last night before the 'Raq armour hit Karbala. He started sort of level, pretty cool, didn't last. He was bloody yelling by the end . . . We were ordered out. What they actually told him, it would be the equivalent of desertion if we didn't come out. It was a direct order, and you can't buck a direct order. I suppose the bastards thought he'd gone native. At the forward barricades, all through that last night, we could hear the 'Raq armour warming up. We knew they'd come at dawn. He didn't talk a lot that night, but he was round all the barricades and he was trying to give them some heart . . . We knew what was going to happen to them . . . He said we should leave the Land Rover behind. We kept our rifles, that was all, we left them our machine guns, all the belts for them, all the grenades. We smashed up the radio and we walked out on them. What hurt, they all said they understood, some fucking chance. We walked out of Karbala about an hour before the first attack came into the other side of the town . . . He was very bitter, he took it personal like it was his fault . . .'

The one-time trooper in the regiment walked Cathy Parker to the gate of the building site. He left behind him the pile of bricks to be laid. Civilian life had come hard to him.

'I'm really grateful, Vernon, for your help, your time.'

'It's Vee, that's what he told me my name was . . . I had the gut rot and a lift out on a Frenchy bird, only one place going. They came on after. I tell you the last thing he said to me. Mr Brown said that he'd never walk out again, not if any other poor little beggar shouted to him for help.'


'I'll have one more . . .'

'Heh, Tom, wrap it, man, you've had your share,' the Intelligence Analyst wheedled.

'I said I'd have one more . . .'

'No call for being sparky, Tom, but you're full,' the Treasurer slurred.

'What's up with you guys . . . ?'

'We've got the little woman at home, and more's the pity you haven't,' the Chemist grunted.

Tom shouted over the music. 'Barman, come here, runt-face. Barman, whisky double . . . I'll see you guys in the morning . . .'

'There's work in the morning, Tom.' The Intelligence Analyst tried to pull Tom up and was shaken off.

'Always fucking work in the morning . . . Piss off, guys.'

They did. They left a heap of quetzal notes on the table, their share. They left him . . . The paperclip team had gone out on the evening flight and the guys had taken to the bars. He reckoned the paperclip team had turned DEA Guatemala over, good and hard. He would hand it, Tom would, to the bossman and the Intelligence Analyst and the Chemist and the Treasurer. They had done well to keep the paperclip team at arm's length. Right down to Guatemala City they had come, right back to Washington, DC, they were going, and damn nothing to complain of. Worth celebrating, worth leaving the little women at home, worth getting pissed up on fuck-awful Guatemala City. Started on the La Quinta, place for geriatrics, on to La Zocala, all kids posing, hitting Las Vegas and the music was hammering and the whores at the tables were watching the guy who was now alone. His whisky was brought him. That, man, was a hell of a thin double. He pushed notes towards the barman, couldn't count. He drained the whisky. Shit place, no life, wanted some action, needed a little woman at home, fuck . . . Out into the rain on the street that ran behind the train station. There was a bar with a dwarf girl who scratched his thigh, ugly as a pig, two drinks and he was gone. There was a clip house with an Indian woman, fat and old as his mother would have been, who tried to hold his privates, one drink and he was gone. Needed a little woman at home, fuck . . . Needed love, like the Intelligence Analyst had love and the Chemist and the Treasurer. They pushed him out of the clip house, and they'd snatched what had been on the table, the quetzal notes. The rain ran on his face. The other guys would have been all tucked up, all nice, with their little women. Shit . . . Not a cab in sight. He started to walk. He thought he knew where the embassy was. There were bars and kids and whores around him. He was sobering. Just a guy who had wanted a drink . . . Shit . . .

Didn't happen quick, but then his mind wasn't going fast. Didn't happen so that he could see when it started.

A couple of kids following him, and another kid ahead of him, and more kids around him. Cold-faced kids.

There was the music beat of a dozen bars, and there were whores tugging at him and leering at him and thrusting at him the heavy lipstick mouths and the painted faces.

Last time drunk was the night he had come out of the army. Last time drunk was the night after the day on which he had signed the forms and handed in the kit and uniforms. Last time drunk was the night when he had scratched around for some new pilots, without little women at home, to come share the loneliness of no longer belonging. A kid had a hand in his hip pocket. He wasn't carrying the Glock automatic. His fold-over wallet was in his hip pocket. A hand going for his wallet, and a shoulder jostling him, and the faces close, and Tom Schultz was sobering.

He lashed around him, he lurched to turn. He had the wrist of the kid whose hand had been in his hip and the wallet fell.

The wallet lay in the rain on the broken pavement. The wallet was half covered in the puddle pool.

He bent for it. His fist clasped it. The first boot went in.

Tom Schultz clung to the wallet. The fists battered him and the boots belted him. He was the punchbag and the football. Pain climbing through the drink. He found the strength. It was the strength that had taken him from the Apache when the fire was spreading. He pushed himself up. He saw a knife and he saw a small club with a nail set in it. He flailed around him. He had seen it on the television, the jerks around a bull in the stadiums in Mexico, darting with knives and with spears, that sort of shit.

He spun in drunk giddiness and lashed at them.

Tom had driven them back. They were a ring around him. He caught the taunt words.

'Heh, gringo, heh, fuck *yanqui*, you're going home . . . Keep your shit out of Guatemala, gringo . . . All over for you, fuck *yanqui* . . . Coming out of the mountain, gringo, coming with fire to burn you . . .'

Spinning and losing control, and the hands closing at him, and the knife nearer.

'Heh, gringo, the fire's coming for you . . . You like the fire, bastard *yanqui*? . . . Get off our streets, get out of our place . . . You wait, gringo, till the fire comes for you and for all the fat bastards . . .'

The circle around him was tightening and the club caught at his hand and the nail slashed his fist. His mind was blurred from turning and turning and turning. He saw the boldness of the street kids and the music of Michael Jackson beat in his ears, amplified from the bars. A hand had his neck. Beyond the circle was a crowd of older men, watching, passive. A boot caught the tendon of his ankle. He started to crumple. The kids had no fear of him. Going down. If he went down . . .

There was the battering of the shots.

The gunfire crashed around him.

He was alone on the pavement.

He was on his knees.

He looked at the open window of the car and the pistol and the face of Arturo.

Deliberate action. He put the wallet back into his hip pocket. Deliberate action. He wrapped a sodden handkerchief around the cut in his hand. Deliberate action. He walked round the car and opened the door and slipped down to the passenger seat. The car pulled away.

'Do I ask . . . ?'

'No.'

'Do I ask what an esteemed pilot of the Drug Enforcement Administration is doing in the red light quarter of our capital city?'

'Thank you . . .'

'It is a short cut for me, my friend. It is the fast way between the G-2 files library and my home.'

'Thank you, I was gone.'

256

'Would you walk alone at night in south-west Los Angeles?'

'I say it again. Thank you. Can we cut the shit?'

'Turn it on its head. I am in south-west Los Angeles, I have gone for some tail, I am in trouble. The man that I call my friend drives past, the man I admire. Would I not have the right to expect him to stop, try to intervene, to hazard his own safety . . . ?'

'Close the windows, lock the doors, foot on the gas.'

Arturo grimaced. 'A friend, a man you admire, you would leave him?'

'Cut it. And don't think that I go round carrying gratitude debts to people who bail me out of holes. You want to get up my nose then you walk round and parade that I've debts owed you. I said thank you, and that's end and finish.'

'As you please . . .'

'What they said, they said the fire was coming to Guatemala City. They said the fire was coming out of the mountain and coming to Guatemala City.'

Arturo drove easily. One hand on the wheel. The rain peeled from the windscreen. Lighting a cigarette casually. 'You saw our scum. It is what is at stake. The scum believe that the rat vermin are coming. Up in the country, in the mountains, the rat vermin are moving as if in sewers, hidden from us. We have a country of tolerable sophistication, and our country will be destroyed if the rat vermin win and let loose the scum . . . It is not where I would have expected to find an esteemed pilot of the Drug Enforcement Administration . . .'

'Don't categorize me.'

'I merely expressed surprise.'

'I am not your categorized American. I wasn't brought up behind a white-painted picket fence. My mother spent more time screwing round than baking apple pie. My father spent more time selling spiv insurance than taking me fishing. I wasn't reared like it was in Disneyland. I don't care to leap to my feet just because it is God Bless America time, just because the god-damn flag is going up. I make my own way. I want to fly big birds, and this is the best way I know . . .'

They were at the embassy. The floodlights lit them in the car. Arturo leaned across him and had his handkerchief out and wiped Tom's face, where the pavement dirt had smeared it. It was a good suit that Tom wore, four hundred dollars, and it was grimed and soaked.

Outside the warmth of the car the rain beat onto the road, spattered back up. The smile was off Arturo's face.

'These conditions, is it possible to fly?'

'Thank you . . . Only if you have to.'

'But *possible* . . . ?'

He went through the gates. The car drove away. He thought the marine on the desk, best dress, looked at him like he was shit.

# 13

He had a table that the clerk had allocated him and, with only the clerk shuffling between the filing shelves on his dead leg for company, he burrowed into the yellowed material collected when the whore Ramírez had raised rebellion in the triangle. For two years the files had fattened on the whore Ramírez and the men who had collected around him, and fastened with sellotape on the wall in front of him were the photographs of a funeral in Havana. It was the first time that Arturo had been to Record Section in the basement of the G-2 annexe and he had thought he might be blocked, so he had bullocked his way in and had worn the flap of his holster open on his belt. He had been given what he wanted, poor grace but given it, and as the hours had passed so had the frequency of his visits from the clerk increased. The clerk would come with more files, flip them open, point and walk away.

He had been there since dawn.

There was a professor of history at the University of San Carlos who specialized in the period of the Conquest by Pedro de Alvarado, ruler of Guatemala from 1524 to his death in 1541 . . . There was an engineer from Guatemala City, middle-class *Ladino*, would have been a government supporter, until his son joined the rabble vermin and became a cell commander, captured, died. The engineer had gone to join the whore Ramírez . . . There was an attorney, practising in company law, in Puerto Barrios, a good living. He had had no reason to be involved in subversion, and he had appeared in court to argue the case for better wages for the dock labourers, imbecility. A death threat, an equal imbecility, and a man of obstinacy had hiked off to join the whore Ramírez . . . Others, of course, had been round the whore Ramírez, and held influence. The files charted them. The one who had been burned in the church at Acul, the one who had been hunted down and shot running near the Mexican border, the one who had been captured in the safe house in Zona 5 of Guatemala City, all of them dead now . . .

He studied the photographs. He squinted and lowered over them. A man sitting in an academic gown at a graduation ceremony, a man in shirtsleeves leaning against a heating turbine generator, a man in an evening suit posed with his wife.

Digging deeper into the old files of three men, and cross-referencing reports from G-2 and the Treasury Police and the Department of Criminal Investigation and the Mobile Military Police and the National Police Special Operations Brigade. The daughter of a professor, working in Guatemala City for an American bottling company. The brother of an engineer, driving the slow sugar train from Escuintla to Champerico on the Pacific coast. The mother of a lawyer, living out the last years of life in a villa home close to the rusted cranes of the Puerto Barrios seafront. He put the files on one side, the files on a professor and an engineer and an attorney, the files on a daughter and a brother and a mother. He had the photographs from the old files. He had the interrogation report of an Indian in the Petén, and the Indian had witnessed the landing of an aircraft. He had the photographs of mourners at a graveside.

He made the match.

War had always been dirty in Guatemala.

He had no fear of the dirtiness of war in Guatemala.

Colonel Arturo thought dirt could always be washed away.

There was a clear written notice beside the desk of the clerk that no photographs or files were to be taken away from the basement. He took what he wanted.

He drove away from the G-2 building.

He headed out towards the far side of the city. He wondered how it would be that morning for his wife and his daughter. The previous night, a poor line and little to say, they had told him that there was nothing in the papers in Florida of *problems* in Guatemala, and nothing on the radio stations and nothing on the CNN bulletins. But then there was nothing on the stations he had heard as he was dressing, eating, driving. There was a vacuum of information except for the brief announcement from the *estado mayor* that over the next week there would be widespread military exercises. Rumour bred in vacuum, and the rumour creep was there for him to see as he drove. The middle of the morning and gangs of the street boys lounging on the intersections, and the police had not dispersed them. The middle of the morning and queues already formed outside the bread shops and the meat shops and the supermarkets. The middle of the morning and a scurry of men and women making their way up the steps of churches. He could not know how deep was the cancer that fed from the rumour of fire.

He came to the Guatemala Club. Fewer cars than usual. His wife had, in the last year, twice appealed to him to get them family membership of the Guatemala Club. Groups, small and male, sitting in the bar area, watching the soaked courts and dropped nets, drinking and sombre. His daughter had sulked at him that all her friends were members of the Guatemala Club, didn't he know? It was where he had been told that he would find the lieutenant, codenamed Benedicto. He hated them. Smug. Fat. Digesting the rumours, swilling in their gin and their Scotch, playing while the fire approached. He walked through the bar, down the long corridor past the trophy cabinets and the honours boards. He pushed open the double doors onto the indoor court. A rally in progress. A dark girl, might have been attractive if she had dieted, catching a backhand lob attempt on the wood. The ball looping up. He walked beside the net. He caught the ball, one-handed, and threw it back at the girl, and he gestured for the lieutenant to follow him. No apologies. The lieutenant trailed him off the indoor court of the Guatemala Club. No explanations.

In the car, Arturo tossed the files from his attaché case onto the lieutenant's lap.

He said, 'We will fight dirty, or we will lose . . . We have to search for the weakness around the fire. There is always a point of weakness.'

They moved in pace and in silence. They had gone west of San Bartolomé Jocotenango, east of Tzujil. They had been in forest. The beat of their feet had been softened by the pine needle carpet. West of Santa Rosa Chujuyub, east of San Pedro Jocopilas. They had forded rivers that would have been a dribble before the rains had come, and they had clung to ropes and struggled against the force of the water drive. They had stampeded down the slopes into the valleys, careering and running and falling. They had fought up the valley walls, used the tracks of wild goat, and the march had been strung out. The pace was set by Jorge.

They climbed again. They stood astride the high ridge that was 8000 feet above the sea level of the Pacific and the Caribbean. Jorge had told them it would be the last time they climbed at mountain height. A man could not see a dozen yards ahead of him in the cloud fog of the ridge.

Jorge led, and around him were the men who had come from the exile life with his father.

Gord was behind.

The group with Gord formed the back-marker for the march, between the fighting men and the women with the children. As if he had handed the sword forward. As if the light were slipping from him. The group was close to him, supporting him, and he moved in the middle of them with a shambling stride. They were the men who were always with him now. There was the Archaeologist wheezing encouragement in the thinned air to the Academic. The Fireman had charge of the cart and drove it and pulled it and cursed it, and the Priest helped him. The Civil Patroller, no talk, had made the wheelbarrow his own. The Street Boy, keeping his mischief, had the weight of the machine gun on his shoulders. Always they were around him.

The column snaked away from the ridge, descending.

The group paused, took their own five minutes of rest.

The Academic stood beside Gord and he allowed Gord's arm to rest on his shoulder. He already had the weight on his shoulders of five mortar bombs and two boxes of belt machine-gun ammunition and a food basket. He looked with a reverence at the young man that he knew as Gord. When his student had been disappeared, before the body was found, he had telephoned the personal number of the American Ambassador. The telephone had been picked up by the Ambassador's wife. He could remember it, the small hours of that morning when he had telephoned in his desperation. He had had the personal telephone number of the Ambassador because once he had been invited to dinner at the residence, and he had later been asked to punch basic mathematics into the Ambassador's son through the heat of the summer vacation, so that a high school grade back in a Vermont boarding school should not be dropped . . . He had blurted the circumstances that he knew of to the Ambassador's wife and hoped, prayed, that the life of a student could be saved . . . He had been to the funeral. He did not know, would never know, whether the Ambassador had taken the message from his wife, had intervened, had been rebuffed. He had been to the funeral of a disappeared student. He thought, and the weight of Gord bent him, that the Englishman was the sole man he knew on whom he would rest his life. All through the day, through the climbs and the descents, and this last climb to the last ridge of high ground, the greater worry had nagged in his mind.

If the Englishman could not go on . . .

He would have liked Gord to have known that favourite student, who marched in demonstrations, who had been taken, tortured, killed.

They started down again.

Too steep a track for him, for any of them, to support Gord as they went down.

The man needed to rest, had given too much. There would be no rest. When they came down from the mountain slope they would hit Santa Cruz del Quiché, night attack, they would bring the fire to the garrison town that was the departmental capital.

And he had heard, Gord's last muttering, like there was a madness, that it was the fourth day of his week.

When they came down from the slope, they would be four miles from Santa Cruz del Quiché.

He vowed to himself that he would be beside Gord through the night, as he had been beside him in the battle for Nebaj. It was only if he were beside Gord that he would not feel the terror in battle.

Driving on, scrambling and sliding down the slope . . .

He shook his head, he played at astonishment.

'You've had *nothing* from London . . . ?'

The grade 3 staffer said, 'They have a man in there making havoc, and not the courtesy of an acknowledgement.'

The Assistant Under Secretary said, waspish, 'You get sweet fuck from them unless it suits. I want to know who he is, how he craps, what hand he wipes his ass with. I want to know about this jerk. I want him stopped before the damage is outside limitation. Don't ask a second time, *demand*. Action . . .'

The modern town of Santa Cruz del Quiché was built beside the former capital of the Quiché Indians, destroyed by Pedro de Alvarado in 1524.

A swollen town that day, the population of eight thousand souls was weighted by the Indian collaborators and the *Ladinos* fleeing into the safety of the garrison perimeter. The plaza in front of the church, built by the Dominicans with stone from the Quiché capital, was a crush of refugees fleeing ahead of the rumour of fire.

There were many with cause for fear because the modern town of Santa Cruz del Quiché had been, a decade before, the hunting ground for the soldiers and the torturers and the Department of Technical Investigations. The rumour said that the fire was coming, and the rumour also said that the fire was blocked beyond the Rio Negro. The bulging town waited for news that was more than rumour.

\* \* \*

'. . . We came out, Miss Parker, on an American transport chopper, a CH-47, that's a Chinook if you don't know. We were four men because one had been case-vacked, and one had stomach trouble. We'd got rid of them and we had to walk another couple of days before anyone else had the time to pick us up. We knew what had happened at Karbala when we were picked up, a pocket radio job. We knew that the 'Raq armour had gone back into the place. It would have been a knife into butter business because they had nothing to protect themselves with, not against tanks. We'd seen what the 'Raqs had done to the Shia people before, we'd been in the police barracks where they did the executions and where they did the torture. I wouldn't say any of us felt good about what we heard, but Mr Brown took it worse than the rest of us. He was very quiet that last day while we were waiting at the LZ for the chopper . . . We were picked up. They were all American on the Chinook and to them it had been a great victory. Mr Brown didn't see it their way, they really pissed him off because they were larking about in the chopper. Wasn't their fault, they were just kids, but they were right under his skin. We flew into Dhahran. You have to understand, Miss Parker, that we had been away for more than six weeks. We hadn't washed properly in six weeks, not changed our fatigues, not shaved. We must have looked like we came out of the Ark. That's just so as you understand better what happened. We put down at the Dhahran base. There was a scramble from these Americans to get off, I reckoned that some of them had been out in the sand for at least forty-eight hours and they seemed to rate that as a real survival effort. There was a brigadier general there to meet them. They paraded for him, pretty sloppy I thought, but that was the form, and he shook each one's hand. It was all happy time and the war was over and everyone was going home, and the job had been done. Well, at least, these Americans thought the job had been finished. Am I going on, Miss Parker? He hadn't said anything in the chopper. He was just brooding . . . God knows what we looked like when we walked off the Chinook. We were filthy, we smelled and we thought we had failed. He was last off. The

265

brigadier general saw us, and it would have tickled him to meet some Special Forces people. He wasn't Special Forces oh no . . . He might have been transport, or tank recovery, or the guy who puts shower units in for the base camps behind the front line. He looked the sort who hadn't made a bigger decision in the war than whether to have fried chicken or boiled chicken for his tea. He was turned out really smart, all the creases right and he had a little pistol on his hip that a woman would have put in her handbag. Mr Brown came off the Chinook and the rest of us were belting for the bus. It was Mr Brown that the brigadier general caught. Actually, Miss Parker, it was really rather funny . . .

'This was how it went . . .

'The brigadier general shouted, "Well done, soldier, you have played your part in the destruction of tyranny . . ." That sort of rubbish.

'Mr Brown looked him up, looked him down, like he was dirt. Mr Brown said, "Bullshit . . ." Straight at his face.

'Mr Brown kept on walking. The brigadier general, red like scarlet, not the sun, was bawling after him, telling him to come back, telling him to stand up straight, telling him he was a disgrace. Mr Brown never said another word, just ignored him. The brigadier general could have let it go, didn't. Mr Brown could have apologized, but he didn't. The brigadier general was running after him, and the doors of the bus closed and the guy was beating on the windows. By the time the bus was at the big building there were military police there. There was no way he was going to apologize, and no way that brigadier general wasn't going to have his pint of blood. It was all round the camp in an hour, that a Brit had told an American brigadier general he was talking bullshit . . . It didn't have to happen, Miss Parker, but my Mr Brown is a hell of a cussed sort of man . . . He could have apologized and he didn't. It's a sort of self-destruct. They broke him for that bloody cussedness . . .'

The former sergeant escorted Cathy Parker from his small office at the back of the premises of a firm that specialized in providing rural security to the owners of shooting moors and fishing rivers. They paused on the pavement of the London street.

'I'm sorry for interrupting you, Zachary, I appreciate your help.'

'Please, Zed, what he always called me . . . Has he hooked onto another group of no-hopers? You wouldn't tell me, would you? Nice to meet you, Miss Parker.'

The colonel toured the town in his jeep. His driver nudged through the narrow and crowded streets of Santa Cruz del Quiché, hooting, forcing the refugee mass to divide. He commanded a battalion-strength force of infantry, with the support of heavy mortars, recoilless, and armoured cars. He could sense the fear in the streets, and he could sense also the resentment of many of the Quiché people. The fear in the faces of the *Ladinos* and the resentment in the faces of the Indians.

He toured the town to check the siting of the mortars and the recoilless weapons, and the fields of fire given to the machine guns, and the platoon positions and section responsibilities. He could not know how his men would fight . . . The colonel could expect no reinforcements, he had been told over the radio, but then intelligence had told him that an attack was not yet imminent. Intelligence talked of the Rio Negro obstacle, and the radio talked of great trees felled across the road from Joyabaj and the road from Sacapulas and the road from Momostenango and the road from Guatemala City. He had heard that the attack, when it came, would be spearheaded by fire.

'Well, you'll just have to tell them, Mr Martins, that they'll have to wait. They may not be familiar with having to wait, but they'll bloody well have to start learning . . .'

Hobbes boiled into the telephone. He could imagine the opinionated, self-satisfied, under-achieving Percy Martins sitting in that monstrosity of a building by the Thames and jumping to a signal from the bloody Americans. And arrogant, all of them at Six, since they had moved into that monstrosity, green jelly and yellow blancmange like the sort of Sunday pudding his mother made. A monstrosity fit to house monsters of incompetence, in Hobbes' view.

'. . . We do have other things at Five to concern us, business other than the activities of one man on the other side of the world. I have a very good young lady on it . . . Yes, young lady. We employ young ladies at Five, perhaps you don't at Six. Try it. They have a pair of tits and a fanny, and they work rather well, if you didn't know . . . When she has completed her report it will be forwarded to you. So just tell your bloody Americans to get out of our hair, *please*.'

He slapped the telephone down.

It was the start of his day, bad and angry. The call would set the tone for the day. He could analyse the anger. It was a lie that he was busy. To pretend that his desk was cluttered with matters of greater importance was at best a half-truth. He was off Ireland. The new regime at Five had swept the Ireland Desk clean. He had very little to concern himself with and there was the growing worry that an idle hand might just be selected for the compulsory redundancy, the sack, the boot, that lay as a shadow across so many of them . . . Fliss had been to Guatemala. Soon after they were married, before the children came, with a girlfriend, his wife had travelled to Guatemala. She had come back with a strain of gastroenteritis that had cut her down for three weeks, and she had come back with stories told her by aid workers and priests that were foul in the telling.

He might, that evening, break his own house rule, and over supper tell his Fliss about a man who was leading a revolt in the highlands of Guatemala . . . He was a civil servant. He was a government man. He knew about holiday charts and the pension scheme and expenses chits, and covert action in government's name. He doubted, if the redundancy note came, that he could swim in the rivers of free enterprise, not massive scope there for the skills of covert action. Thank God, thank whoever smiled down on him, that he had insisted the awful 'Bren' should write, in his own fair hand, No Further Action on the report concerning Brown, Gordon Benjamin. Staring down at an empty desk, sitting in a silent room, he thought of the man who had brought revolution to Guatemala . . . lucky bastard.

A town of strangers' faces. A town of unknown men. A town of the whispered and secret word that was beyond the hearing of the *orejas*, the informers. A town where, as the darkness came from the dusk, knives were sharpened on stone, and axes were taken from the hidden places in the roofs of the shanty homes, and bottles were filled with petrol and corked with cloth. A town that breathed the mood of vengeance. A town where the son of the whore Ramírez huddled anonymous under a tent blanket amongst the refugees on the plaza. A town in waiting for a signal.

Bursts of firing and the thud of the mortars' bombs and the rich light of the machine guns' tracer, and the snake of the cart's flame.

The tiredness had gone from Gord.

Chaos in the town of Santa Cruz del Quiché. A pandemonium of screaming and stampeding people. Oscar led by Eff. Roger guided by Vee. Delta shown the way by Zed. The darkness around Gord, saving him and clinging to him, the darkness broken by the flame running from the cart in pursuit of the fuel cascade.

The dusk had settled when they had met Eff and Vee and Zed sitting patiently beside the track, and the fast briefing on the situation in the town and the layout of the defences. Their crying laughter and their hanging on Gord's neck and chuckling their excitement, and their wanting to be praised.

God alone knew how much they should have been praised . . . A town too large to have a secure perimeter of defence, a town around which the roads had been cut and blocked by fallen trees, a town into which an enemy could be guided.

She had brought the dog with her. He had not argued, the anticipation of combat surging in him. She had come with his group, and brought the damn dog.

They had infiltrated the town. They had become a part, in the fading light, of the fleeing mass reaching the town for safety. Not using the roads that led into the town from Joyabaj and Sacapulas and Momostenango and Guatemala City, but coming through houses and skirting the blocks and coming in the narrow mud lanes between the shanty homes and avoiding the check-points.

The signal had been given . . .

Oscar had isolated the villa and office complex of the military governor, kept a bullet rain on the buildings until Gord had reached them with the fire and burned the heart out of the defence. Roger had reached the old Spanish colonial facade of police headquarters, pinned down the sniping retreat of the commanders and interrogators and detectives until Gord had come with the fire and made a torch hell for them. Delta had identified two machine-gun positions, the one under the great bell in the tower of the church, and the other on the flat roof of the school block, and the two machine guns had been blasted until Gord had come with the fire to scourge them down. They went where they heard the firing in its ferocity. Dark and narrow streets, the lights shot out, shadows thrown by the fire from the flame thrower on the cart. The group was around him. The exhilaration took him. Not people, that the flame took, but *objectives*. Not men, that the flame destroyed, but *targets*. He was a man lifted by the drug of killing and the narcotic of going forward. The tongues of the fire were about him, climbing and licking in the roofs and rampaging in the old wood. The town was taken. There was the great surge towards the fence and the gatehouse of the garrison's barracks. It was the force that the flame from the cart had unleashed, rabid in hatred. The mob was around him, driving him forward, and the Academic was tugging at his arm to hold him back, and the Fireman was yelling at him. He turned. She was behind him, dragged by the leashed dog. He turned and the Fireman was screaming and pointing down at the cart as the body mass broke over them. Needing to fill the tanks. Having to replace the fuel oil under compression in two of three tanks. The mob going forward and the Academic was swept past him. The Archaeologist was pushing the cart and the Priest pulling it into an entry alley between two buildings of lichen-covered stone, the Civil Patroller behind him with the wheelbarrow.

There was a body.

Gord saw the body, and the stripes of a corporal on the tunic arm of the body. He watched the Fireman and the Archaeologist and the Street Boy and the Civil Patroller, clear of the torrent crush, hustling with the tubes and the air cylinder and the jerry cans.

The hiss of the cylinder.

The intake of her breath.

The hiss . . . The gasp . . .

The tunic arm of the body had the pistol raised and pointing at him.

The pistol wavered. Gord saw the burn scrape on the face of the body. The body was half risen and the charred chest, where the tunic shirt had dissolved, was in front of him. The pistol aimed at him.

So sudden, the tiredness. He was locked to his feet.

The pistol aim had swayed, came back to him.

The tiredness taking the life from him.

Alex jumped. She came past him and her elbow caught him and bounced him aside. She flung herself. Her hand and her strength caught at the pistol arm and the pistol jerked away and clattered on the wall and then the cobblestones of the entry. The body shrieked as her weight hit it. Gord lost sight of the face with the burn scrape. He saw her frenzy. She had the head in her hands, her fists were in the hair of the head of the body, and the dog worried at the leg of the body. She beat the head down, again and again, down onto the cobblestones, until the scream died.

She rose from the body, peeled herself off it.

She wept against the wall. There was the murmur of the Priest's prayer. The dog held the still leg of the body.

When all the tubes on the cart were filled they joined the swarm heading for the garrison's barracks.

It had been a pig day for Colonel Mario Arturo and the evening was worse.

He prodded the jeep slowly forward. The lieutenant, code-named Benedicto, was behind him and standing braced against the roll bar and clutching an Uzi.

The road had been good to Sumpango, difficult to Chimaltenango, and then the problems. There were floods on the road between Chimaltenango and Zaragoza requiring them to stop and take advice on which track to proceed over, two hours lost. There had been a landslide between Zaragoza and Tecpán Guatemala, and he he had had to go into a village and stir the men out at pistol point to come with their spades and clear a way for him, two more hours lost. After the flood and the land-slide, beyond Tecpán Guatemala, they had hit the first block on the road, a tree felled. A small convoy of lorries, four, filled with conscripts, led by an officer without balls, had been parked up short of the fallen tree, nervous. More shouting, more yelling for some action, more organizing, and the tree had been dragged aside. Two more trees across the road before Agua Escondida. More convoys held up, more jams. A pattern emerging to Arturo. Each time between Tecpán Guatemala and Agua Escondida that he found a tree down, the road blocked, there was high and forested ground above the road. Each time he had to berate an officer into deploying his men, always conscripts and fright-ened, up and through the forest above to comb it for an ambush site, and only when the hillside was pronounced clear could he kick more men and the vehicles forward to heave aside the block, four hours lost on the Tecpán to Agua Escondida road.

The light was failing into grey mist when they crawled to the Los Encuentros Junction, and there they had lost the three lorry convoys, going for Quetzaltenango and Huehuetenango. They had gone north, the Santa Cruz del Quiché road.

One more felled tree, three miles south of Chichicastenango, and it had required them to edge to a precipice slope, stones spinning down from under the wheels, as they had rounded it.

Another man might have turned back, another man might have claimed the importance of an evening meeting with the general commanding G-4 (Logistics). He had pushed on. Getting up speed through Chichicastenango, scattering the silent crowds in the dark streets, belting through the town and on towards Santa Cruz del Quiché. It was the way with him, to drive himself forward.

They were at the checkpoint.

The checkpoint was three miles south of his destination, Santa Cruz del Quiché.

He was dazzled by the stream of car and van and lorry headlights approaching him.

It was a column of flight.

And amongst the cars and vans and lorries he saw the mass of struggling people, women pushing prams with suitcases stacked, men carrying children and bundles, boys and girls dragging along a precious pig or goat. There were soldiers in the mass. Soldiers were running alongside the cars and vans and lorries, some without weapons, some still armed.

The sergeant at the checkpoint shouted. 'They came to the town, they came with the fire.'

In the lights of his jeep he watched the rampage of the approaching soldiers. 'Stop them.'

Derision on the face of the sergeant. It was flight, it was fear. The fire was behind them. The sergeant turned away. The sergeant showed that his concern, in the darkness and the rain, was to break the log jam at the checkpoint. The sergeant ignored a ranking colonel, fool and idiot.

Arturo had reached for his own Uzi. He would have fired into the running, panic-driven soldiers, but a fist behind him had belted his arm and thrown up the short barrel. The volley of the shots cracked high into the night. The soldiers were past him, split by the bonnet of the jeep, running. They would not have stopped unless he had shot them down, each last one of them would have kept running until shot. He threw the Uzi down onto the seat of the jeep and turned and the lieutenant loosed the grip on his arm. The log jam was broken. A civilian lorry broke clear. Arturo could see into the back of the lorry as it passed him, lit by the following car. Only a moment, but he saw the casualties in the back of the lorry. He saw the burned faces and the burned bodies. He shuddered.

He said quietly, 'You know what you have to do?'

Calm on the face of the lieutenant. 'I know.'

The lieutenant hitched onto his shoulders the backpack that held the radio.

Arturo said, 'To wherever you call me, I will come.'

He saw the lieutenant go. A tall but slight figure, in black, disappearing into the advancing mass of the flight.

He started the drive back to Guatemala City. He had seen the fear that was carried by the fire.

When the shooting had started, when the fire had come, the Canadian had without fuss slipped off the bed where he was resting and crawled underneath it. The bed in the first-floor room of the Posada Calle Real was in the far corner to the window of the room, and the Canadian had settled himself on the tiled floor against the wall. He rated that as the most sensible place to stay until the shooting stopped. The Canadian was in his seventy-first year and it was close to half a century since he had last heard close-quarters fighting.

When the shooting had finished in that part of the town, near to the plaza, he hitched into his windcheater, and put on the tartan cap that he always wore when it was cold or wet, and he went down the stairs of the Posada Calle Real and out onto the street. At home, back in Kingston, Ontario, when he went walking with his wife, to exercise the Labrador dog, he took a stick to ease the age in the joints of his hips. He had no stick now, and he hobbled along the streets, rolling his stride to lessen the pain.

He did not wish to be a nuisance . . .

Three visits to Guatemala and he knew enough of the language to make himself understood.

Half an hour after he had left the Posada Calle Real he found the Englishman.

He had been directed, then tugged, then pulled, towards the place where he found the Englishman. He had expected a military man, a good uniform. He had anticipated that he would meet a man surrounded by a staff and with radio communication to co-ordinate a battle. He had thought he would meet organization and control . . . The man looked as though he had come from the gutter. There was a gaping hole at the cap of his right boot and the socks were through and he could see the flesh of the toes. The trousers were ripped equally at each knee. The tunic jacket, under a quilted anorak, was blood-splashed on the chest. The man was unshaven and the rain smeared his beard and the mud dirt matted it. The man sat on a petrol can near to the gate of the garrison's barracks, there was a group around him and in the group was a young woman who stroked the shoulder of a big dog. In the circle of the group, beside the sitting man, was a cart-carried flame thrower and a wheelbarrow piled with an air cylinder and jerry cans. Hell no, not what he had anticipated . . .

'Excuse me, sir, I apologize for the interruption . . . Are you the man with the fire?'

A soft voice, wearied. 'Yes.'

'Are you the leader?'

A hesitation. 'No.'

Big breath. The short pain spasm in his hip. 'Where do I get to join?'

A slow smile, lovely to him, cracking the beard and the dirt. 'Are you quite sure . . . ?'

It was because of the pain spasm in his hip that he flared. Should have had the operation last fall, but the money for the replacement had gone with the mortgage money on the air fares. 'You've no damned right to suggest . . .'

'What's the combat experience?'

'Cameron Highlanders of Ottawa, closing the Falaise Gap, that was combat experience.'

The smile widening. 'When was that?'

'Sir, that was 21st August in 1944 . . .'

The laugh, not mocking. 'Oh, yesterday . . . Why?'

'Because, sir, my grandson came down to this Godlost country, hippie boy, dropout kid, but that wasn't cause for them to butcher him. I'm here to find a grave and give a silly kid a decent Christian burial, and I'm blocked at every turn . . . I would take it, sir, as a privilege . . .'

A shadow figure on the move. A darkened shape flitting from doorway to alley. Fire and darkness alternating in the blackness and light of the streets of Santa Cruz del Quiché. A hunter working his ground, searching.

In shame, Tom Schultz had lain on his bed through the day and through the evening and into the night. His suit, dirty and wet, four hundred dollars and his best, was in a heap near the door. He had the bruises and the pains to justify the shame. Twice the telephone had rung and he had let it go, and the ringing had needle-pierced his skull. He had shouted at the maid's knock, driven her away. They paid bastards at Quantico to sift through the recruits for those to be classified as 'Bad Attitude'. Missed one. Should have netted him then, Tom Schultz . . . He felt the shame because he had yelped to a stranger that his father sold spiv insurance and that his mother screwed round. He had been told, they always spotted the guys with 'Bad Attitude' at Quantico or on the first year's probation.

He'd not made the grade. The Intelligence Analyst had made it, and the Treasurer, and the Chemist, and the Country Attaché had made it good. Making it good, like the Country Attaché had, meant a wall filled with service plaques, and the framed prints of local newspapers cataloguing the big busts, and photographs taken with the President or the VeePee or the Director and signed.

Washed up, and he had a head to prove it, and bruises and a closed eye, and shame. He lay on his bed which was damp, stared at the ceiling. He was out of his depth. His level was the 'mid-grade trafficking' in St Louis, inter-state violations of Controlled Substance Act, Code Title 21, playing at second-grade surveillance of bums. Wrestling with the shame and losing against it . . .

She was red-eyed. She had not spoken. Twice Gord had seen the Priest go to Alex and put his hand on her arm, and each time she had shaken it clear. She followed him, a lost soul.

His name was called.

More firing ahead.

He was going forward, responding to the shout, and the cart was squealing behind him. They were running after him.

'Heh, where's . . . ?'

Seeing the faces in the light of flames, seeing the Archaeologist and the Fireman and the Street Boy and the Priest and the new man who was struggling to stay with them, seeing Alex.

Gord snarled, 'I said we were to be together, always.'

The shout ahead for him growing, the demand for the fire.

It was what he had told them, they should always be together . . . They wanted the fire to burn out a sniper, the last resistance.

'You have the Kaibil battalion . . .'

He saluted the general commanding G-4 (Logistics). They were out in a corridor of the *estado mayor*. It was past two in the morning. The corridor was awash with hurrying feet, uniformed staff officers. The general had told him that he had listened, himself, to the last communications on the radio from Santa Cruz del Quiché before the surrender and the cutting of the transmission. He felt a numbness, rare to him, because without argument he had been given the control of the elite force in the army he had served for eighteen years. It was the summit of his aspirations, had been his goal since as a twenty-year-old lieutenant, fresh from the Escuela Politecnica, he had gone to the training camp of the Kaibiles at La Polvora in the Petén. Mario Arturo turned away. The shout came after him.

'. . . If you fail I will throw you, myself, to the dogs of the garbage dump.'

He walked away from the pandemonium mad house.

He drove away from the building where lights burned on each floor. He could imagine the earlier blow in the *estado mayor*, as the generals and brigadiers and colonels had gathered under the loudspeakers slung from the ceiling of the War Room and listened to the staccato reports, which would have lost coherence as the panic had grown, of the crumbling of the perimeter defences of the garrison's barracks at Santa Cruz del Quiché, as the fire had come closer. He could imagine the dead crackle, lifeless static, and the silence of the War Room when contact had been lost. He had no fear of becoming a body on the garbage dump with the dogs pulling at him and the vultures pecking at him and the kids turning over a corpse to see if it still wore a ring . . . He drove to the American embassy, the concrete bunker behind the high railings where in the morning the queues for the visa forms would be stretching far down 7a Calle.

He had the man pitched out of bed.

Kramer blinked in the bright light of the lobby hall.

'Is it that bad, shit . . . ?'

Kramer stood in his slippers and pyjamas and he held a cold cigar end as if for comfort.

'. . . I don't know why you came to me . . .'

Kramer wore a wool dressing gown with the logo on the back of the Cincinnati Tigers wrapped tight round him for warmth.

'. . . You want SouthCom people in here? Sorry, forget it . . . You want marines in from Honduras? Sorry again, forget it.'

'I want the flier,' Arturo said.

\*   \*   \*

The last sniper had taken a position in the cemetery. He had used a high-powered rifle but had not possessed an image-intensifier sight. He had taken targets when they were silhouetted against the fires round the field of stone crosses and marble Virgins. The flame thrower had burned him out, flushed him clear from the vault beside the big stone that commemorated the nineteenth-century family of a *Ladino* merchant in the dyes of cochineal and indigo. When the sniper had run from the flame spurts the machine-gun hail had cut him down.

Gord saw him fall.

Jorge was beside him. 'Finished.'

He heard the vibrancy, excitement, of the word. Gord said bleakly, 'Finished? Of course it's not finished, it is finished at the Palacio Nacional . . . You have to do your talking piece fast. Well, don't hang about for it, man. We have to get the food, we have to get the armoury, we have to get the new men, we have to move on . . .'

Astonishment. 'Gord, do you not understand?'

'We have to move on and out from here . . .'

'Do you not understand what is happening in the town?'

'We have to keep the drive going.'

Jorge snapped, 'We are very *grateful* to the great man who always can tell us what to do. Now, I tell you, I am going to sleep. I am going to sleep in a bed. In the morning, when I have slept, then we will talk about going forward . . .'

'One block in their time, their place, and it is over. You have to maintain the speed.'

Shouting into the rain night, at Jorge's back. Turning to the group around him for support and gaining nothing from the Archaeologist and the Fireman and the Street Boy and the Civil Patroller and the Priest and the Canadian, and nothing from Alex Pitt. Raking back over the faces and it came to him, sudden, that a secret was held by them and denied to him. Slashing over the faces and demanding the explanation. They were the group, they were together, there were no secrets. They had been an hour at the cemetery before the sniper's position had been identified, before the fire had burned him from his shooting place. He demanded to know . . . They led him. The group was sombre and the secret was held, but they took him and they showed him. He knew the secret before they came to the place. The nozzle on the centre of the cart had blocked, the one whose job it was to keep the flame thrower going, working, had not been there to clear it. Delay, Gord swearing, the Archaeologist and the Fireman trying to do the work that was not theirs to do, covering the secret as Gord had cursed . . . They led him to the small sandbagged redoubt. It was close to the gate of the garrison's barracks and the redoubt had been sited to provide a field of fire across open ground to the main road running south to Chichicaste-nango. He had been a dear good man, Gord thought. He wore the same shoes as when they had found him sitting at the side of the road between Playa Grande and the climb into the Cuchumatanes mountains. He wore the same raincoat, and the same little beret lay in the glistened mud beside the blood-ied face. He did not know his name, only that he had been an Academic at the University of San Carlos in Guatemala City. It had been their secret while he had cursed them and sworn at them, and while he had belched the fire to flush out the sniper. A great sick and personal pain. He looked down onto the ragged corpse of the Academic. He thought, fleeting, that the power of the group had been broken.

He walked away from the place.

He walked out into the dark rain-sodden fucking night, out onto the open ground between the sandbagged redoubt and the road running to Chichicastenango.

She followed him and the dog was with her.

The responsibility gouged him, the death of a dear good man who had no business in a fighting column on forced march.

He sat in the mud of the ploughed field.

She knelt beside him.

The weakness trembled in him. He drove them all forward. He felt as if he preyed on them all.

She took his head in her hands, he felt her fingers on his face.

He had destroyed the belief in her, the belief that was non-violence, and she had killed a man that he might live. She had beaten the head of a man into the cobblestones that he might live.

She kissed him.

# 14

She kissed him and she pushed him away from her and down to the ploughed mud. She eased astride him, sat over him, and her hands came from holding his head that sank in the field mud, and she started to strip his upper body.

On the road, travelling, she had known the men had thought of her as the 'bicycle'.

There was a belt of machine-gun ammunition slung over his right shoulder and under his left armpit. She freed it and slung it into the darkness. She took the belt of machine-gun ammunition that was over his left shoulder and under his right armpit, worked if from his body, discarded it, and then the belt which was shorter and which had hung over both his shoulders and dropped to his waist. All the time that she had known him, since she had first seen him on the parade ground area at Playa Grande, he had been wrapped in the belts of machine-gun ammunition, and she freed him.

On the road, moving with the New Age travellers, working the Social Security system, tight-held in the community, she had been available. There had been Johnny the Music who made the sounds on the lute, carved and strung for himself, that had seemed beautiful . . .

She took the hand grenades that were buckled to the buttons on his tunic pockets, cold and wet in her palms, and tossed them away behind her. She unfastened his belt and worked to pull from him the webbing straps that held his water bottle and his food canteen and the double-bladed slashing knife and the pouch that secured the two magazines of the Kalashnikov bullets. He seemed not to move and not to respond to the pulling, tugging, dragging of her fingers. She could not see his face, but each time that she had lost a machine-gun belt or the grenades or the webbing she came lower to him and found his mouth and kissed the life into it, her life.

There had been Johnny the Music, and Deke the Pony whose tresses of hair had reached to the small of his back and who gathered them at his nape with an elastic band and who had put the farmer with the riding crop in the river . . .

She took the heavy anorak with the bloodstains from his shoulders and she ripped at the buttons of his tunic and she pushed up his vest above the nipples on his chest. She knew that she would do it all for him, because that was the way to bring back the life in him. The mud was around her and the rain was above her and the wind was against her. She soothed the palms of her hands over the length of his chest. The mud was smeared on him, an ointment. She wished that she could have seen his face but the darkness denied her, and she could only touch his face and learn the new contours of it with her lips and her tongue against the ears and the eyes and the nose and the mouth of the man to whom she tried to give the new life.

There had been Johnny the Music and Deke the Pony, and the Van Man who had built himself a home of wood and corrugated iron that was riveted to the back part of his old Land Rover pick-up, and there had been others who had come to her vehicle in the nights and others to whom she had gone, because she was *available* . . .

She took his trousers down from the wasted place that was his belly. She led his hands under the quilt of her coat and under the thickness of her sweater and under the smelling tightness of her T-shirt and onto the looseness of her breasts. Cold hands, as yet without the life, holding the hang of her breasts with a shyness. She thought that he must have the life that she could give him. And the body beneath her shivered in the spasm of wet and nakedness. She used her fingers and the nails that she bit to keep them short to return the life to the man. She was over him and dropping onto him and guiding him and kissing the rain away from his ears and his nose and his eyes and his mouth.

When her mother and her father had brought her home in the big BMW car, the same day they had taken her to the doctor. It was just a precaution, her mother had said. It was bloody necessary, her father had said. She had still been docile and she had submitted to the tests for 'anti-social disease', as her mother had described it, and 'bloody AIDS', as her father had said, and pregnancy. She had not been with a man since . . .

She loved the life back to him. With her fingers and then with her muscles she stirred the life again in him. She did not care that she had no contraceptive. She took the bareness of him into her. The life came again.

There was the warmth in her, his hands on her breasts.

There was the drive of him in her body.

There was the tongue of him in her mouth.

It was the fire that seduced her. She had not been with a man and not felt the want of a man since she had come off the road, and the fire now caught her. She was over him and punching down onto him, and the fire was in her mind, the fire that snaked and ran and caught and destroyed. There was the power of the fire in her, and the burning in her. She clung to him. She sank on him.

When it was over, too fast for her and she did not care, when she felt the slackening of the grip of the hands on her breasts, when in her mind the fire died, she rolled off him.

The rain fell on him.

The mud was cloying against him.

She hadn't loved Johnny the Music, nor Deke the Pony, nor the Van Man, nor the others . . .

What she thought, she loved Gord Brown.

She heard the hiss and spit of new wood thrown on a fire. The glow of the built fire came to her. He lay beside her and his eyes were closed and the breathing under the whiteness of his chest was steady. She thought she had given him again the life, her life. The fire glistened the wet on his body and caught the

284

mud smears on his skin. She took his hands from her breasts and she pulled back up her jeans and fastened the belt on them, and she felt again the old cold. She turned to the fire. They were sitting there, around the fire. They were thirty paces from her. The group watched over him and she could see the silhouette against the fire of the cart and the wheelbarrow. She stared back at them, defiant. They were sitting crouched round the fire, watching him as if to guard him, and her dog was with the group and she heard it moan for her.

She said softly to Gord, 'When we get to Guatemala City . . .'

The man she loved was sleeping and naked and spattered by the rain.

They stood over Tom as he dressed.

They offered him no explanation.

They had pulled the clothes he would wear from the hangers in the wardrobe and from the shelves in the chest.

He hooked himself clumsily into his combat fatigues. Enough impatience at his slowness for the Country Attaché to bend and lace the boots, and for Kramer to check the loading of the magazine in his Glock automatic pistol.

They marched him out, like he was a prisoner on close escort, and Kramer kicked the door of the room shut after them. Coming out of the long sleep and the big shame and his right eye was half closed and there were abrasions on his chin. Tom limped between them on the corridor and down the stairwell.

In the rain, the wind tugging at them, they hurried along the path between the ornamental flower gardens.

An armed marine admitted them through the front door of the residence.

The Ambassador waited for them in the residence lobby. He had the printout sheets in his hand and the speech prepared. Tom saw the squashed cigar butt in the crystal ashtray on the table beside the flower display. It was the cigar size that Kramer now lit. They had been there before him to settle business. He thought it was the big carpet job, a government official drunk, a

DEA man loose in the cat quarter, a Federal man spilling to a local that his father sold spiv insurance and his mother screwed round.

The Ambassador intoned, 'Good to see you, Schultz. Sorry about the hour but crisis rarely comes convenient . . . The place is falling apart, fast. Santa Cruz del Quiché has gone. I won't beat round it. What stands between this rabble mob and Guatemala City is the Kaibil battalion. We want the Kaibiles to win. We want this rabble mob broken, turned, and hit so as they never are able to regroup. The fact that a pitiful Congress back home denigrates the government of Guatemala at every turn precludes me from helping these people in their hour of need but, and I stress, the interests of the United States are best served by the survival of the government. Anyone thinking this rabble mob is the route to a better society has gone apeshit. I'm getting there, the success of the Kaibil battalion is critical to us. There is a new commanding officer for the battalion and he has made one request of us. He has asked for you. You are seconded to his command. Wait on, Schultz, don't go breathing hard at me, it has been cleared with State and with DEA. They want you and we're giving you to them. The quicker the killing is done the happier we shall be. Got me, Schultz . . . ?'

He rocked. 'And if I . . . ?'

The Country Attaché murmured, 'You'll be on the next bus north, up the Highway, up the Pan American, and don't be looking for a future.'

Kramer said, 'You're a servant of the American people. The American people want *stability* in this crap yard.'

The Country Attaché murmured again, 'We'll have it over these bastards here, and it'll be milked, we'll have gratitude and co-operation as long as I'm above ground.'

Kramer said, 'Just help to blow away that murderer with the flame thrower.'

'Go to work, Schultz, and go to work good.' The Ambassador stood his full height.

\* \* \*

286

'. . . I don't know what had happened to him, Cathy – you don't mind if I call you Cathy? – I don't know because he never bothered to tell me, but when he came up here he was a man with trouble on his back. He was army, wasn't he? He was something in one of those flash outfits, wasn't he? He was an officer, wasn't he? He came with trouble . . . I asked myself, what's a Para or whatever doing in this bloody place. I asked him enough times, and I never had the answer. It was like it was private trouble and not to be shared. He worked at the farm as if it was *important*. Of course it wasn't important. I work hard, he made me seem bloody lazy, Cathy. He had trouble on his back and a short-fuse temper. You shouldn't mix it with him, not when he's the temper up . . . These three gooks came for him, and they came with all the photographs of bodies and kiddies cut up, and I was arsing them, I was pretending I was him, big laugh, and when he had enough of the laugh he just told me to get myself lost. I did. Look, Cathy, I'm a hell of a lot heavier than Gord, I can look after myself. I went meek as a wee lamb. You don't cross him, not when he's the temper up . . . There were three lads crossed him. They were from Tyneside and they came up here to do the eagles' nest on Sidhean Mor. If Gord had any relaxation it was going out where it was wild, and climbing and lying up, suppose that was his training, to watch the nest, see how the eggs were. Not disturbing them, never closer than a couple of hundred yards and he'd go up in the dawn light and come back in the dusk light. I reckon those big buggers would have known he was there, bloody good eyes they've got, but he wasn't a threat to them. These three lads came for the eggs. I heard what happened from the district nurse, because one of the lads told her. They were coming up near the nest and they must have nearly walked over him. You get a good price for eagles' eggs and these lads weren't going to back off just because there's a joker up in the rocks who tells them it's better if they turn round and disappear. There were three of them and they must have rated their chances. Fair do to him, Cathy, he helped them down. He had to help them down because one of them had a dislocated

287

shoulder and one of them had a broken nose with concussion and the last had balls the size of oranges after the kicking they got. It was the only time I know of, Cathy, when the fuse blew on him . . . I am not good with words, not at explaining. I'll put it to you this way. He was like a lost man when he was here, like a man wanting to find something. Does that sound prat rubbish, Cathy? He didn't find anything, other than the times he was up Sidhean Mor with those big bugger birds, until the three gooks came for him. I reckoned he'd been running up till the time they came for him, and they showed up and he stopped running . . . The pictures they brought, Cathy, they'd have turned a hard man . . .'

The salmon farm labourer reached for his wallet and the diminishing fold of notes made from the sale of Gord Brown's wheels. She shook her head and the gold hair of Cathy Parker sheened in the low light of the hotel bar. She made her excuses, said she was driving back to London through the night. Before she left the bar she paused to gaze up at the stuffed majesty of an eagle, then ducked her head and went out into a still and clear night. Rocky walked her to the car.

'. . . I suppose he went there, yes, of course he did. I suppose he's making waves there. I said he was running, but I don't reckon after those photographs of blood and bodies and kiddies cut up that he'll want to run any more. Not unless he's won, he won't run out of there. Been good meeting you, Cathy.'


The queues were already forming outside the embassy for the opening of the visa section, the damp light was growing, and the men who would hire their services with old typewriters were setting up their pitches under high umbrellas.

The gate was edged open for Tom by a marine guard.

The jeep was parked on the kerb.

The colonel sat impassive beside his driver.

Tom slung his kitbag into the back of the jeep and climbed after it. He was jerked down onto a hard seat as the jeep powered away.

The jeep went through the grey-lit city. The colonel ignored him, studied a mass of papers that were protected from the rain by cellophane sleeves.

A barrier was raised for them.

The jeep parked outside the military hospital, and Arturo jerked his thumb for Tom to follow. They ran past two lorries in army camouflage that were being hosed down and scrubbed clean.

The ward was filled. Each bed was taken. There were mattresses laid out in the central aisle. There was a scream from a bed, and a moan from another, and a sobbing cry from a mattress. The nurses hurried on silent rubber-soled shoes, and the doctors lingered over beds and mattresses and their hanging white coats were blood-stained and showed the dark marks of charred burning. Tom hesitated by the door of the ward, beside the big heap of stinking uniforms, and Arturo from the middle of the aisle demanded with an impatient sweep of his arm that Tom follow him. The nurses and doctors were around him with the saline drips and the swabs and the syringes of morphine. He forced himself to look. He saw the dog-quiet eyes of men in shock from pain, and the trembling of the arms of men in shock from fear, and the eyes were diamonds in the blackness of a scorched face and the arms were dark stumps where the skin had bubbled in heat. The scream became a rattle and the rattle was lost and a sheet was pulled over the head of a man and the nurses pushed the bed on its wheels out through the swing door at the far end of the ward. He made himself look. Arturo covered the length of the ward, did not speak to a doctor nor to a nurse nor to a burned soldier. His boots smacked back over the length of the aisle. Tom followed him out.

He understood the fire.

He knew the wounds that the fire made and the terror that it brought.

He felt the cold of the rain and the wind as they returned to the jeep. It was about family. It was family that he searched for. He had not found the family in the DEA community working out of the Guatemala City embassy, because there he was just the ferry man who did the lifts. And he had not found the family in the military where the regimen of promotion crawling and camaraderie bonding suffocated him. Nor had he found the family at what had once been home. There had been a teacher, far back, who had been the nearest thing to family. The teacher had driven him through the grades to college, and been around to pressure him through the exams for the military. The teacher was dead, cancerous lungs. The teacher had died the month that he had travelled to Fort Wolters. He thought it was because he had never known it that he cared so much about finding family. And he wondered if he might just be finding family in a ward for burns casualties . . .

Tom grasped Arturo's shoulder. The anger bit in him. 'I didn't need to be told. I didn't need to be given a show at the theatre. My orders are to help you to hunt him down and to kill him, the man with the fire . . .'

With the first light coming the hunger gnawed in the stomach of the Civil Patroller. Through the night, watching over Gaspar the spirit and the woman who had gone to him, his gut had groaned for food. He could see the white body of Gaspar the spirit and he could see the woman sitting close to it, and they were protected well enough by the Fireman and the gringos from America and Canada and the Priest and the Street Boy from Guatemala City. He whispered that he would go to look for food. What he hoped to find, what he had dreamed of in the half-sleep through the night, were fresh-made tortillas with beans and chilli and perhaps some rice, and better if he could wash the rawness from his throat with *atol*, and not bad if he could find warm Coca Cola. The dream of the food was fanciful to him, the food that he ate on the few days a year when he went to the festivals in Uspantán and Sacapulas. The dream was of enchiladas and guacamole with mashed avocado, and *ceviche* which was marinated raw fish. He told the men in the group that he would go to look for food and he thought that each of them felt the hunger. He took the rifle with him that he had been given and started back towards the town. He did not see the shadow movement. He did not cry out as the shadow movement closed on him, took him. The thoughts of the tortillas and warm Coca Cola were shredded from his mind. He did not cry out as he felt the knife against his throat and the stale breath against his nose because he believed that to have cried out would have lessened his chance of survival.

The older ones would have known him.

The older NCOs and some of the officers at platoon or company level would have remembered Mario Arturo from Victory '82 and Firmness '83. He searched among the faces for those who had been with him in the triangle and in the Ixcán, and those who had paraded with him on the Campo de Marte on Army Day, before he had gone to lecture at the Escuela Politecnica, before he had gone to the staff at the *estado mayor*, before the shit job of liaison with the drugs hunters. They were the best, he felt the pride.

'What does a Kaibil eat? FLESH . . .'

He stood on an overturned orange box. He let the roar chant wash over him.

'What kind of flesh? HUMAN . . .'

The American was behind him. The officers of the battalion were below him. The chant was for him.

'What kind of human flesh? COMMUNIST . . .'

They were in front of him. Their boots made the hammered accompaniment to the chant.

'What does a Kaibil drink? BLOOD . . .'

The rain lashed at his face and ran on the webbing that harnessed him and dripped from the barrel of the Uzi slung from a shoulder strap.

'What kind of blood? HUMAN . . .'

He looked over the brightness of their faces and the tautness of their bodies and into the strength of their eyes.

'What kind of human blood? COMMUNIST . . .'

He hushed them and then he called them forward. There was the crush of men around the upturned orange box. He told them of Santa Cruz del Quiché and Nebaj and Playa Grande. He told them that some units of the army had surrendered and that some had run away and that some had refused to march. He told them of the fire and of oil mixed with gasoline to hold better to an arm or a body or a face, the cocktail that clung. He told them of the hospital where the burned and the maimed lay in their agony. He told them of a rabble crowd that came towards Guatemala City. He stood erect on the overturned orange box and he had no need to shout because they hung on him in silence.

'. . . It is the Kaibiles that stand between our beloved country and the dark age of disaster. This is what I promise you. We will find the rabble crowd, we will block them, when we have blocked them we will turn them, when we have turned them we will destroy them. That is my promise. We will find them and we will kill them . . .'

They cheered him, they called his name.

He stepped down.

He walked to the American.

He saw the droll smile, mocking. 'Brave words.'

'You should be ready to fly.'

'Where?'

'Where I tell you to fly, when I tell you to fly.'

'If you say so, colonel.'

He looked at the skies, into the leaden cloud mass.

'. . . Let me tell you what I was once told, by the British Military Attaché up from Panama. It was the situation in Ireland and the subversives attempted to assassinate the government of Britain, and the bomb did not work as lethally as intended. The subversives, afterwards, issued a statement. "You have to be lucky every time, we have to be lucky once." The baby whore Ramírez and the Englishman, they have to be lucky every time, we have to be lucky only *once*. We need to block them only once, fight them once, defeat them once, and they are broken.'

'In my experience, luck has to be earned . . .'

\*    \*    \*

The knife was in the small of the Civil Patroller's back, held under his coat. The tip of the knife was against his flesh, beside the strength of his spine. He had not seen the face of the man who held his arm in a vice, tight and twisted under his coat, his wrist close to where the knife pricked him. He had never been in a schoolroom, never been favoured with education. The Civil Patroller was skilled at tree felling with a long-handled axe or a double-handed saw, and at ploughing a maize field, and at slashing down the sugar crop when he was taken on the open-backed lorry to the *finca* near Puerto San José for the harvest season, and at survival. With the tip of the knife beside the life core of his spine he did not struggle. They left the town through the shanty quarter. They were two more drunks reeling together, supporting each other, after the night of chaos celebration. As the morning light rose, the Civil Patroller was taken out from Santa Cruz del Quiché and across the fields and into the trees that dripped the rainwater.

The fires were damped. The cloud mist hung on the town. Wreaths of smoke eddied in the streets and alleys. The flames of the night guttered in charred homes and burned stores.

Gord walked between the buildings that had lost their roofs and the buildings that were pocked with bullet marks and the buildings that were holed from the rocket grenades. The smell was all around him, of old fire doused by rainwater, and the destruction was around him, and the death. Behind Gord the Fireman pushed the cart and the Street Boy helped him, and the Priest manoeuvred the wheelbarrow, and the Archaeologist and the Canadian covered the doorways and windows and side alleys with their rifles. He had lost the anger.

The anger had been when he was cold from the rain, when he had dressed again in the wet clothes, when the morning hours were drifting. The anger had been when he had found Zeppo and shouted at him that there was no time to be wasted, and when he had come across Harpo and exploded because the armoury was not cleared and the recruits were not screened, and when he had discovered Groucho and learned the food was not collected. The anger was lost as he wandered the streets of Santa Cruz del Quiché.

The anger was gone and with it the peace of Alex's loving. The chill was on him.

He walked past the hardware store where the *Ladino* owner, an old man with whitened hair, had tried to protect his property of oil lamps and cooking pots and knives and plain china plates, and two looters were dead in front of the shop before the owner and his shotgun had been overwhelmed. He saw the bloodied head, the blood in the white hair, of the owner, and the shelves were already bare. There was no more to be taken.

Past the grain and seed store where a *Ladino* woman lay on her side in the doorway and moaned from the slashing cuts on her arms, and the sacks inside were cut open and emptied.

Past the corner onto the plaza in front of the church where the bodies of three policemen lay, and one had his fists frozen across his face as if he had not wished to see the last life-ending blow with the machete, and another covered his groin in death, and the last to fall had his arms outstretched as if he had appealed at the final moment for mercy.

Past the shuttered shop front where the previous afternoon liquor had been sold. A man ran from the shop and there were beer bottles in each of his pockets and he had pressed five more across his chest and he skipped the body of the shop-keeper and then turned as if in after-thought to kick the corpse. There were spirit bottles and beer bottles, broken on the pavement, consumed there when the shop had been stormed and the door broken in and the shutters ripped crazily away. The man running with the beer bottles would have been the last to find liquor in the shop.

Past the car that was overturned and burned through, the windows broken in and the petrol splashed inside and the bodies of a fleeing man and his wife and his two children petrified black.

Past the evangelical church, the Church of the Little Hill of Carmen, once clean built with pink painted boards and white painted roofing iron sheets. The walls were fire-blackened and the roof iron sheets had collapsed after buckling from the fire. The missionary preacher, six foot and two hundred pounds, had been felled at the doorway of the church he had attempted to defend with a walking stick, and the back of his leather boots and his Wrangler jeans and his check cowboy shirt were burned away by the fire's spread.

Past the lampposts from which the bodies hung. Children played under the lampposts, and the game was to jump up and spin the heels of the hanged men so that the bodies swivelled on the twisted ropes that had come from the hardware store. The bodies were of the *orejas*, the informers, and were mutilated.

Past the bodies on the street . . .

It was what he had done.

Past the drunks who slept off the looted liquor . . .

It was his work.

Past the spinning bodies and the children . . .

He was numbed. He was cold. It was the fifth day of Gord's week, and it was halfway through the fifth day and the column had not moved. He walked up the stairs of the hotel, picked his way over sleeping and snorting men. He went past the men who guarded the closed door to the first-floor room. Jorge was naked. He was naked and washed. He was sleeping. There was a baby's calm on his face. The fifth day was lost.

Gord closed the door, went back down the stairs.

He went to check again on the security of the surrendered soldiers at the garrison's barracks.

He wanted only to be back with his brother and his cousin in his village on the road between Sacapulas and Uspantán. The Civil Patroller yearned only to be home in the village where his father was buried. He wanted, yearned, to survive. Always the voice was behind him. All he saw of the man was the black cloth on an arm and a hand with neat nails and slender fingers. He sat against the base of the tree at the edge of a clearing where once maize had been grown and now the high weed grass had taken control and his arms were tied with twine around the tree. He had no thought of sacrifice . . . The voice was sickly sweet, sweet as the apple grown in the triangle, or the orange from the coast that ripened after the rain season . . . He thought only of survival. He looked at the photographs. The photographs placed on the lap of his waist showed the small man who held a single flower, and the man who mopped with a handkerchief at his forehead, and the man who shook the hand of the young leader . . . The voice was sweet gentleness, and a small bar of chocolate was given him, the paper taken from it, and the hand placing it between his teeth . . . He said that the young leader was always surrounded, that the man in the photograph who shook the young leader's hand was always with him in the centre of armed men, that the man in the photograph with the handkerchief marched in the middle of the column with the machine guns and the mortars . . . He had swallowed the chocolate and the sweet kindness of the voice prompted him on . . . The man in the photograph with the single flower, he moved from the start to the end of the marching column, was in charge of the food and had no escort of guns. The Civil Patroller, bound to the tree, talked of the man with the single flower and hoped to assure his survival.

'When I go to the Palacio Nacional should I wear a suit or should I be in military uniform . . . ?'

Gord sat on the floor of what had been the officers' mess room in the barracks. The dirt was caked on him. He looked across at Jorge, at the washed face and the scrubbed hands and the sleeked hair.

'. . . I think it is important to consider what impression I make on the foreign diplomatic corps. Castro was always in uniform, Ortega too, I think that was wrong . . .'

Jorge lounged in the easy chair, and Groucho smoked a cigar, and Harpo poured from the Scotch whisky bottle, and Zeppo drained his glass for more. Gord sat hunched on the floor and there was the weight of the belts of machine-gun ammunition on his shoulders and the tightness of the webbing harness and the pull of the grenades on his tunic.

'. . . I don't want to appear only as a fighting man, I want to represent the voice of the people. The ordinary people have been crushed by the militarization of Guatemala. We have to mark the change. I think a civilian suit. When I spoke tonight I was trying to denote that shift . . .'

A speech in torchlight. Jorge lit by the flicker of fire. Talking in the Quiché dialect. The clenched fist raised and the baying of support from across the depth and the width of the plaza.

'. . . I thought I spoke well, what the ordinary people wanted. I need your advice, all of you, a suit or uniform . . . I think I should speak with the Americans first, alone, and then address the general diplomatic corps . . . Gord, when do we get to Guatemala City?'

He did not raise his head. Gord's head was bowed. 'It is for you to decide when we resume the march.'

'Gord, you disappoint me. Gord, you have no cause to sulk. You cannot really believe we could have moved out of here last night. We go in the morning.'

Said slowly, 'Before dawn.'

Jorge smiling, 'When we are ready. Please, Gord, it spoils you when you sulk.'

Said evenly, 'If we have finished talking about *clothes*, could we now discuss the route . . . ?'

He could smell the soap on Jorge and the lotion on Harpo's and Zeppo's shaven cheeks and the talcum powder on Groucho. The map was brought out. Gord crawled across the floor. The map was tattered now and torn on the folds. They would go across country. They would avoid the town of Chichicastenango and the villages of Saquitacaj and San José Poaquil and Quimal. The contour lines showed a narrow-cut gorge west of San Martín Jilotepeque, east of Comalapa. It was twenty miles to the gorge. Gord told them they should reach the gorge before darkness the next day . . .

'Agreed.' Jorge turned away from the map.

Groucho carefully folded away the map.

Gord went out into the night. A whole day lost, the fifth day of his week, a day with the protection of the cloud and the rain. Lost . . .

# 15

'How many times do I say it, the group must be together. Where is . . . ?'

Drifting from the shanty town homes on the edge of the town. Leaving the ruin and the smoke. Tramping from the church spires that rose to meet the dropped cloud. They were going into the tree line. The marching army and its followers at last straggled clear of Santa Cruz del Quiché. Gord was near to the back of the fighting strength of the column.

Two men at the side of the track wrestled for the possession of an electric fan. Shit . . . An electric fan, and they were Quiché villagers, and there was no electricity that he had seen in the villages of the Cuchumatanes mountains, and it was so bloody cold, wet, that the need for a cooling fan draught was zero nil. Shit . . . Did they think they could carry an electric fan all the way to Guatemala City, to the Palacio Nacional, and then walk back with it to a village that had no bloody electricity? He lashed out with his fist and one man released his hold and cowered, and one man ran with the electric fan from Gord's arm reach.

The Archaeologist said, 'Perhaps he is further up the line.'

The Canadian said, 'Perhaps it doesn't matter where the hell he is.'

Gord driving the men ahead of him, pushing on. An Indian was dropping back and was weighed down by the bulk of the seed sack on his shoulder, and Gord took his knife from the sheath on his webbing and slashed the sacking and spilled the seed onto the track. Pushing on . . . Two men fighting for the right to have the whisky bottle, half drained, and lurching in their anger into each other, and missing with the swung blows, and Gord had wrung the bottle from them and thrown it crashing and spurting liquor into the rich green of the undergrowth. Pushing on . . . A man in front of him fell out of the column and bent and vomited the night's alcohol onto the wet grass. A man showed another the diamond ring he had gained in the night and held it warily so that it would not be snatched from him. He thought that if he walked with Alex then she would have deflected the anger, but she was behind him with the followers and he would not see her until the evening, until the gorge. Or he could have deflected it if he had walked with the chirping warmth of Eff and Vee and Zed, but they were ahead, gone on to scout the way to the gorge . . . The rabble army, grumbling and miserable, hung over and sated, strung out and shambling, pressed south.

The Fireman, who heaved the cart, sweated on his effort, was immediately behind Gord. They had crossed a dirt road that stretched empty either side of them into the low mist.

'They have to want it for themselves, you cannot do it all for them.'

Gord cursed. 'Christ . . . If you have no discipline . . .'

'We can get there, to Guatemala City?'

'We lost a day . . .'

'What is there for you, if we get to Guatemala City?'

Gord smiled, bitter. 'A bath and a bottle and a plane out.'

He heard the Fireman's confusion. 'You would not stay?'

'For what?'

'Is it true that you have taken no money? That is what they say . . . Would you not want to help to build the new nation?'

'I don't know much about keeping the drains clear and making the buses run on time.'

The Fireman shook his head, puzzled. 'They say that many have asked you why you are here and that you have not answered them. I am a simple man, but I know why I am here. I want to help in the making of a new Guatemala. All of my life this country has been ruled by soldiers. They can do no wrong, they can take what they wish, they can kill whom they please. The army is not trained to defend the sacred frontiers of my country, it is trained to kill its own people, to make war on its brothers and fathers and nephews and sons. I want to be the citizen of a country where it is not the task of the fireman to go out in the mornings and collect the bodies from the ditches, a country where there are no bodies left for a fireman to find. I want a country where my child is educated and my wife has health care, where I have the freedom to voice my opinion to any man without fear of the Death Squads. If that is why you have come, to help me make that country, then I thank you . . .'

Gord said, bleak, 'I just want to get you to Guatemala City.'

The Fireman dropped back. The wheels of the cart ground behind Gord. He was shouting again, driving and pushing the column faster. A day had been lost. It was the sixth day of Gord's week. When he looked up he searched the grey lead cloud blanket for breaks and holes and weaknesses. If the weather changed . . . and a day had been lost.

She was the secretary to the production manager of a bottling plant in an industrial estate that was across the tracks of the railway from the Parque Aurora, on the road to the university. It was a good position for her. The job paid well enough for her to own a seven-year-old Renault 5 car. She drove each morning from the old family home to the bottling plant and used the same route because she had no reason not to make a daily pattern. She would have thought it her own secret, dulled by the passage of years. She had been twelve years old when her father had gone. The fast phone call to her mother from her father's desk at the university, the hastily prepared bag, and his disappearance. The police had come, of course, and rifled the house, and beaten her mother, but it had been eleven years ago. His name was not mentioned in the old family home because her mother would not tolerate hearing the name of her father. She had grown to her womanhood, she had studied, she had been ignored by the authorities. And never a word from her father . . . She knew of the rebellion. The whole of the bottling plant knew of the scale of the revolt, had done since the sales manager had been turned back at a checkpoint on the Quetzaltenango road, told it was too dangerous to travel further. The lieutenant at the checkpoint had been, by chance, the nephew of the immediate neighbour of the sales manager, and the lieutenant had told his uncle's neighbour that the vermin mob loose in the Cuchumatanes was led by Rodolfo Jorge Ramírez . . . She had shivered in the closet of her secret. Nothing to read of in the newspapers, nothing to hear of in the radio bulletins, but she had trembled at the knowledge that the son of the leader her father had gone to fight with had returned to the high mountains . . . The secret had consumed her the past two days. Each of the past two days her waste basket had been filled with discarded paper littered with her typing errors . . . It happened so fast. The van with the smoked-glass side windows came past her, then swerved to block her. She braked, instinctively, as the men ran from the van towards her.

He tracked the march.

Benedicto held the high ground. He would scramble on the higher ground above the march, then creep with his binoculars to an escarpment or to a break where the big trees had been toppled by the gales, and he would study the march. He looked for the one man.

He had seen the leader, the baby whore Ramírez, at a rest halt in the march, sitting in the middle of a mass of men, seen his face once and fleeting. He had seen the one who mopped his forehead in the photograph, and the one who shook the hand of the baby whore in another photograph.

In the middle of the morning, while on the move and dragging the imbecile with him, he had seen the Englishman with the fire cart. He was not a sniper, did not have a sniper's rifle, and the sight of the Englishman might have been too fast even for a trained marksman. He tracked the march and searched for the man who held a single flower in the photograph.

He dragged the imbecile after him. He had the imbecile gagged tight across his mouth and he had the imbecile's hands tied, knotted, and a length of rope to pull him forward.

Pathetic, the imbecile, because he tried always to please . . .

There was a place where Benedicto could see twenty-five paces of the march. It was as Arturo had told it him, and as he had seen at Playa Grande. A rabble mess of men splashing in mud and sliding, slipping, and carrying rifles and machine guns, and some loaded with mortar bombs, and some with rocket launchers hoisted on their shoulders. The gurgling was beside him. A rabble mess crowding forward without shape and discipline. The guttural croak beside him. The eyes of the imbecile begged at him, pathetic . . . He saw the man. The imbecile had identified the man. The man had broken from the column and the man's hands were already ripping at his belt, and the man was pushing his way into undergrowth.

Benedicto saw the head of the man who held the single flower in the photograph.

He turned to the imbecile and his smile showed his gratitude because he did not wish to bring panic.

He slit the throat, two strokes, of the imbecile who had no further use to him.

Benedicto came down fast from the higher ground above the march.

Sirloin steak meat, twelve-ounce cuts, had been liberated from the refrigerated cupboard of the officers' kitchen in the garrison's barracks. Rich meat that had never been affordable in the old quarter of Havana. He had his trousers round his ankles. He supported himself against a tree. He was shielded from the march track by undergrowth. His bowels burst. The wind dribbled from him. The blow from the boot caught him square in the back and he was pitched over and the body was over him and the hand was across his mouth and the knife was against his throat.

'Go . . .'

He had run from the jeep with the communications equipment, across the tarmac apron, run with the scribbled co-ordinates in his hand to the Huey bird.

'You have the fix, you have the frequency. Go . . .'

Always the same with a goddamn flier. Arturo had run as fast as his short muscled legs would take him from the jeep to the helicopter, and the flier first pulled out a new stick of gum, then slowly read the paper thrust at him. They were Israelis who had installed the receiver for the beacon signal into the American's helicopter. The Israelis were the best, Arturo thought. The Israelis were the best because their help came without strings and with enthusiasm. The flier seemed again to scan the figures pencil-written on the paper, then he shrugged and he pulled a map from the pocket above his right knee. Arturo jabbed with his finger onto the map.

'East of Xecoxol, west of the river. Go . . .'

The flier put the map back in his pocket and dropped the paper wrapping and spat out the new gum. The flier took his pistol from his holster and checked the magazine. Arturo could not know whether it was dumb insolence or whether it was the routine of a flier. The flier waved him away and climbed loosely into the right-hand seat.

The rotors thrashed.

Arturo edged back. The helicopter flew.

The rain beat against his face. He watched as the helicopter merged then disappeared into the mat of the cloud.

'They have to eat, and the food has to be distributed with discipline . . .'

Gord glowered at Jorge.

'. . . It is his job to organize the food.'

Jorge shifted on his feet, embarrassed. Harpo and Zeppo were crouched down beside the track and eating their own rations. Not salmon. Christ no, if it had been salmon he would have kicked the tin out of their hands.

'I don't know where he is.'

'You should. And if you didn't know it there is bloody chaos back there because the food is not being distributed with discipline . . .'

Jorge shrugged.

'. . . Without discipline we lose time. So, when you find him, will you, *please*, let him know that his job is to get people fed, not just to piss off with a hangover, will you?'

Gord tramped back down the track. The cart and the wheel-barrow were pushed behind him. Not his bloody job to organize the food distribution at the midday rest halt. Back along the track there were cursing crowds of men scrabbling at the food boxes. If they did not have discipline . . . He was halfway back down the column, yelling for the men to form queues for the food distribution, when the helicopter came over them. Gord did not see the helicopter, only heard the thunder reverberate in the cloud cover as it swarmed over him and past him.

It was good gear that the Israeli technicians had put into his Huey bird. It was good gear because it was state-of-the-art Made in the United States of America. It was better gear than had been placed in his Apache when he was flying the Gulf. It was what they always said, the army pilots, the good gear went first to Israel. They had the pick. Fucking Israel was top of the list when it came to the good gear and what was Made in the United States of America went second to his own armed forces. How did fucking Israel pay for the good gear? They paid with what was given them, dollars Made in the United States of America.

He homed in on the growing whine in his ear of the beacon's signal. Tom could not see the ground, couldn't see the goddamn hills, nor the goddamn trees, but the beacon pulled him forward. When the beacon whine was continuous, piercing, when the good gear told him that he was directly overhead the signal, he started to flutter down. Going slow, metre by metre, searching the wrapping cloud mass for trees and rock faces.

The curtain around him broke. The good gear had brought him down through the trees into a cleared space that was a hun-dred metres across.

The skids bumped onto rock. He saw the body. There was the red slash at the throat of the body. He saw the gag in the mouth and the twine on the wrists. The box for the beacon signal, small and black-painted with a stubbed chrome aerial, was beside the body. He kept the rotors going, he was staring around fast beyond where the body lay and then he was aware of the distant scrape of the hatch door behind him. They came in fast.

There was the blurred figure dressed in black and the rope trailed behind him, and then there was the clumsy movement of the pinioned man. Tom was twisted in his seat, straining the tension of his harness, gazing into the fear of the pinioned man. The man had the European look and he had shaved recently, perhaps the day before, but the stubble was grey on his face. Fear in his eyes above the tightness of the gag on his mouth, a laundered uniform from an army barracks with the rank insignia cut off, stumbling in tiredness to lever himself through the hatch and dragged by the rope. He saw the crow's foot lines at the sides of the eyes, exhaustion. He saw the scrawny thinness of the throat, endurance. He remembered the hospital ward. It was to remember the burned soldiers that he had been taken to the hospital ward. Tom felt no pity for the enemy, stripped of potency. He remembered the flame thrower . . .

Tom lifted the Huey bird out of the clearing. He thought that the prisoner, bound and gagged and in fear, had no call on his sympathy.

Most had been fed, some had not. The march had lost an hour of daylight. Gord drove them on.

The truth was, Percy Martins enjoyed arriving at the new building before the day's first light had breached the darkness on the Thames. There was, of course, a car to bring him from the suburbs of south-west London. He felt a sense of power and a sense of belonging and a sense of importance, when he clattered his iron-tipped shoes along empty corridors. A few lights burned in the offices occupied by the night shift personnel, but before the crush came to work he was able to settle in his desk chair and dream of what had been . . . A feeble place now, Six, and losing out on Treasury funding to the new people from Five. A pitiful place where the computers dominated and field work was devastated. What he said to his wife, when he had the bloody woman sat down at her needlework and listening, was that if they had had more field work and less computer work tasked to Baghdad, if they had had Percy Martins running the show down there, then they wouldn't have been caught with their trousers round their knees when little Johnny Saddam had walked into Kuwait . . . She didn't listen well, his bloody wife.

One of the front desk men brought her to his office.

'Coffee, yes? Be a good chap, two good coffees, not that machine rubbish . . .'

He felt the front desk men respected him.

She was a fine-looking young woman, just damned tired. He thought the front desk people respected him for a drop of style, and that was in short enough supply in the new Six. A grand-looking young woman and she had driven through the night from Scotland to make the meeting. Hobbes, creepy bugger from Five, had to drive through the night from SW1, two miles maximum and was late. Sod Hobbes . . . He enjoyed working with youth.

'I'm Parker.'

'But I'm Percy, and I'm sure you have another name, or is familiarity not allowed these days at Five?'

'It's Cathy . . .'

He gave her the old-fashioned charm. He eased her into a chair. He hung up her anorak coat and saw the strong muscles bulging the short sleeves of her blouse.

'I take it, Cathy, that you have not spent an entire career at Five pushing paper round a desk . . .'

Matter-of-fact. 'Northern Ireland, handling informers. They said I was put at risk, shipped me home.'

'Field work?'

'Ditches, hedges, hides, that sort of nonsense . . .'

There was small talk about roadworks on the M6 and M40, what delays she had hit coming south, until the coffee came. Foul coffee from the machine and a grin that was pure insolence from the front desk man.

The door closed. He had clean paper in front of him and a sharpened pencil.

'Right, Cathy, let's have it. Brown, Gordon Benjamin. I have to know about him.'

He strained to hear her voice. 'To pass to Langley?'

'Correct, to pass to the Agency.'

'The better to have him killed?'

'Correct.'

'And that's what we want?'

Percy Martins eased back in his chair. Her eyes gazed back at him. Very firm eyes, he thought. God, what he would have given for a daughter such as this fine young woman, exchanged her any day of the week for the insipid little creature, his son, still studying biochemistry for a PhD, still workshy.

'Doesn't really matter what we want. It's what the Americans want that is important. We are still at the top table, only just, hanging onto the table with our fingernails. What is our best chance of staying on top table? It is to perform whatever contortions the Americans ask of us. We grovel and they throw crumbs. I don't like it but I know when I have to bob my head. We have pigmy influence in the modern world. The "Special Relationship" is a notion of self-importance dreamed up by our political masters, it counts for nothing across the water, we are not equals and we do what we are told to do. That way we get the crumbs thrown us . . . The Americans right now, the price for crumbs, want the information that will help them *kill* Brown, Gordon Benjamin, so that they can better protect that quite disgusting regime in Guatemala. That is their policy objective, and we will help them achieve it. Can we start?'

She talked. He scribbled a full note. She talked of a Land Rover operating behind the lines and deep in Iraq, of a unit commander who risked the lives of the men under his command that an American helicopter pilot should be rescued. He had never learned shorthand, he wrote fast. She talked of the Shia city of Karbala that had risen up in revolt against the regime of Baghdad and which now faced the counterstrike in response to the folly of believing the politicians of the coalition, and of the unit commander who had attempted to build a defensive perimeter for them. He did not interrupt. She talked of the radio message that had ordered the unit commander out of Karbala, and his sullen fury and his shame. The light was growing outside his closed windows, and there was the rattle of voices in the corridor as the building livened. She talked of the anger of the unit commander, and of the confrontation with an American ranking officer, 'Bullshit . . .' He laughed out loud, the belly laugh caught in his throat but he saw no expression of amusement on her face, so serious. She talked of the obstinacy of the unit commander, and his refusal to apologize, and of the complaint lodged, and the virus of the insult spreading higher in the command chain, and the sacking of the unit commander. He grunted his understanding, the pieces of the puzzle slotting. She talked of a salmon farm that was for sale and a man, alone, searching for a reason in living, yearning for involvement, wanting to belong. He flipped onto the fourth sheet of notepad. She talked of the arrival at a Scottish loch hotel of three Guatemalan Indians and the display of the photographs and of the end of the searching and wanting and yearning.

'Summarize, please.'

'I wouldn't want it to sound comic-strip . . .'

There was a slow wan smile. Her eyes blinked. He guessed it was difficult for her to be awake. A rather serious young woman.

'. . . I wouldn't want to sound facile. He's bull-in-a-china-shop material. He sets his mind and he goes for something. You can't buy him off because the going's hard. You see, it's the obstinacy, he doesn't know when to back off. He'd be going for Guatemala City and it'll take thick walls to stop him. When it gets ridiculous, when it's stacked, he'll keep going. If he believes in something then it consumes him. His tactic is the charge. Makes him into a bit of an idiot, but he's not . . .'

Percy Martins felt the cold of the morning around him. 'I think I have the picture.'

'Will that be all?'

She stood.

'You have been very helpful . . .'

He helped her into her anorak and walked her to the door.

'. . . Let us hope our American friends are truly grateful when they get down to the business of blowing him away. I think you've got me into his mind . . .'

She stared back at him. To Percy Martins she was suddenly vulnerable, a small girl. 'I should be able to get into his mind, I used to sleep with him.'

He gagged. 'I'm so sorry.'

'No call for an apology. He was with the regiment when I was first in Belfast. He was running my field security escort. I suppose he felt protective of me, and I suppose I felt dependent on him. He came and stayed at my flat in London after we'd finished there, wasn't for long. I chucked him out. My phone number, I imagine you do the same, I let the answerphone take all the calls. I never called him back and I returned his letters unopened. I expect you'd find that pretty bitchy. Where I work they reckon that emotional entanglements get in the way of the fucking job.'

'Would you like me to let you know what spills from this?'

'That would be very kind.' She laughed and the life was gone from her eyes. 'Yes, I should know whether or not I've helped to kill him . . . The fucking job always wins, doesn't it?'

Percy Martins walked her to the lift and took her down to the front hall, and signed the exit chit. He was glad Hobbes had overslept, cut the meeting. It was a fresh morning. It would be black night across the time zone in Guatemala, and he wondered what the weather was there, whether it helped Brown, Gordon Benjamin. He felt the draught of the air off the Thames as she shouldered into the swing doors.

He took the lift back to his floor. His secretary would be in within a quarter of an hour to make decent coffee, about all she was capable of, and then he would start to compose the message for Langley.

He would fight dirty. He would fight as dirtily as was required to assure he came out on top of whatever shit pile was to be contested. He would most certainly not allow a little dirt to lie between himself and the city's garbage dump. The blast of the helicopter filled the small room behind the hangar, cut out the whimpering of the bitch. The bird hit, lurched, steadied, came to rest. Colonel Arturo pressed his nose against the grime of the window's glass. The hatch door of the bird was dragged open. His view was distorted by the rain streams on the glass. He peered to see. The lieutenant dropped down. It was the strategy on which he laid his career and his life. The bitch cried out behind him and he heard the punch smack that silenced her. The lieutenant pulled the shape down. He saw the shambling figure.

The short gesture, momentary, Arturo punched the air.

Like a creature brought from the deep water of the dark sea, the man who was bound and gagged. Like a creature issued from a pit only in night cover, the man who was led by a rope towards the building. A gaunt face and hollowed eyes and a sunken throat . . . It was ridiculous. Incredible to believe that a man like this, pulled by the rope, could threaten the life of the state.

He went to the doorway and he kissed the lieutenant, codename Benedicto, on both cheeks.

The creature was pulled into the room.

The bitch was suspended by her ankles from the iron beam across the ceiling. Her floral skirt was hanging to cover her chest. The tips of the tresses of her auburn hair fell just short of the floor. The bitch moaned.

The lieutenant casually took a rifle from a soldier. He held the barrel tight in both hands. With a short jabbing swing, using

311

his strength, he hit the creature on the ankle with the shoulder butt of the rifle. The creature screamed, sank to the floor of the room.

Arturo said cheerfully, 'Welcome, my friend, welcome on your return to Guatemala City. Eleven years, I believe. You enjoyed your journey, excellent that at last you could ride after the many days of walking. A surprise, my friend . . . Perhaps after eleven years you do not recognize her, your daughter . . .'

Fifteen minutes later the Huey bird was airborne.

Percy Martins took the signal to the basement for encoding and transmission.

'Priority? Yes, I should think so. Put a first class stamp on it . . .'

Secret Intelligence Service to Central Intelligence Agency.

Little brother to big brother. Poor cousin to rich cousin. How to stop a good man and kill a good man. Of course it was bloody priority.

Gord glanced down, irritated, at his watch. It was one hour and twenty-five minutes since he had first heard the helicopter and again no sight of it. The engine noise seemed to pass high over him and then the cloud ensured that the rattle sound was gone. It was as if the security of his territory were invaded, as an animal in the rain forest would tremble when it first started at the whine of a chainsaw. They were going well now. They had a good track and the space between the trees for a man to march and hold his arms directly out from his shoulders. There was climbing and there was descent, but the track had a good rock base. He thought the time was slipping . . .

Groucho came past him.

Groucho was going fast and hobbling and putting his left-side weight on a rough-cut stick.

Gord caught Groucho's shoulder.

'Where the hell have you been?'

Groucho had tucked his head away from Gord, turned his face from him. 'I fell.'

312

'The midday feeding, it was a shambles.'

A muttered answer. 'I went to crap in the rocks and I slipped.'

The Archaeologist laughed and the Street Boy sniggered and the Fireman grinned. The Canadian took the weight of Groucho to support him, and the Priest knelt beside Groucho and pulled up the leg of his trouser and pushed down the sock. Gord saw the bruised colouring and the broken skin.

Gord said, 'I am sorry, I apologize . . . Do you want to be carried?'

'No.'

'I can get people to carry you . . .'

'I make my own way.'

They moved on. Groucho was ahead of them and distancing himself from them, stumbling and heaving his way back up towards the front of the march. He thought the man had *guts*. He rated him. Groucho was too far ahead to have heard him. Pointless to call out to him, gone too far forward. Only an hour before Alex had told him that a baby had been born on the march. Back amongst the women and the children, where Alex Pitt walked, there was now a swaddled child with less than half a day of a life lived, and a mother was carried on a litter. He would like to have told Groucho . . . it had been Groucho who had recited him the poem,

> '. . . and I see
> at the end of the line
> happy children!
> only happy!
> they appear
> they rise
> like a sun of butterflies
> after the tropical cloud burst.'

He was remembering the poem.

The Archaeologist said to Gord, 'Heh, you know what's different? You know what's changed? It's not raining . . .'

He could have been belted in the pit of his stomach. He realized it, the truth of it. The puddle on the track ahead was smooth and unbroken.

The Canadian said, 'Too right and, hell, I never noticed it, gotten like an old shirt, what you're used to. Gord, the rain's stopped . . .'

Gord surged on, tongue whipping those ahead of him forward, faster.

'I do it my way.'

Tom faced the colonel.

Arturo said, 'You tell them to stop fucking me, and to stop complaining, and to do what they are paid to do.'

'Aircrew, you'll learn, do not respond to insults, nor to flag-waving shit . . . They like to be asked whether it is possible . . .'

'Just get them in the air . . .'

Tom said, 'My way, and you keep your mouth tight shut.'

Tom led. Into the helicopter pilots' Ready Room. There were half a dozen of them in there. They wore well-cut flying suits, surplus stock Made in the United States of America, but they had their own shoulder shields sewn on, an eagle falling on prey with the hook beak readied and the talons outstretched. He walked through the film of cigarette smoke. Some shuffled the pages of magazines, ignored him. Some sipped at their coffee beakers, ignored him. He walked to the far wall and he sat himself easily on the table where the magazines were and the coffee machine. Arturo was by the door, facing him, arms folded, watching him.

'Hi, I'd like to introduce myself. I'm Schultz. I'm the resident DEA flier here, I'm from DEA's Airwing. It's the sort of shit that I attract but my government has volunteered me. For the duration of this emergency I am under Mario's command. Now, no crap, I am just another flier. I'm not super shit hot, I am another flier who managed to get himself knocked out of the air over Iraq. You got me? A guy is not super shit hot if he allows himself to get hit in an Apache by a shoulder-fired SAM-7. See this lot, see my face, that was when the 'Pache bird took the fire. I know about combat, but I'm not some Rambo nut who goes where the flak is for the hell of it. I aim to survive this tasking, I reckon to go back to flying my old bird for DEA . . . Now, have you guys taken in the new met. report? The met. report tells me that it's bad times ahead for those bastards out there. I've been up there twice today, it's not great flying but it's not crazy. I'd like to talk it through with you. I need some help, guys . . .'

A coffee beaker was drained, then flipped towards the waste bin. A magazine was closed then chucked towards the table on which he sat. A cigarette was ground out in a filled ashtray. The pilots gathered around Tom and he waved Arturo forward and the map was unfolded. His finger was over the close-set contour lines that designated a gorge that was west of San Martín Jilote-peque and east of Comalapa.

'I'd like to get some of Mario's ugly fuckers in there before tonight, and I'd appreciate some help . . .'

Because he had twice heard the helicopter and because the rain had stopped and not started again, Gord had gone to the head of the column.

He reckoned the gorge to be a little under two miles in length.

The pit of the gorge was a rushing rainwater torrent. There was a path above the torrent on the left side of the rock wall. The path was not more than a full stride in width, but better than many they had used. The path was slippery as glass from the rain and the damp held in the low clinging cloud. He knew from the map that at the far end of the gorge they would find the open plateau that would run for them right to the outer sprawl that was Guatemala City. One more argument in the dusk of the day. Zeppo and Harpo had wanted to stop at the start of the gorge, before entering the cut of the sheer rock walls. Jorge irresolute. Groucho not contributing. Gord wanting to clear the gorge before they made camp. Always, each day, each night, there was the short spat argument, wasted energy, raw nerves. Just bloody *unnecessary*. He had won. He had dragged Jorge with him. At the start of the gorge, where it narrowed, they had found a small fire's debris, made between stones, no other sign of human presence. They pressed on. The light was failing. It had been his decision, Gord's, but the delay of the argument and the shouting between him and Harpo, and the sneer of Zeppo, bloody guaranteed that the tail of the march would be struggling along the path long after the light had gone. The women would be in the darkness on the path, and the children . . . He would be gone, too bloody right he would be out, first bloody plane leaving Guatemala City, not hanging around to see what bloody suit Jorge wore, not waiting to see which bloody ambassador was first up the steps of the Palacio Nacional, *gone*. Gone with Miss Alex Pitt . . . They were near to the far end of the gorge because the cloud was thinning and the wind was up and hacking the cloud from the rock walls. There were flowers in the rocks, pretty purple . . .

There was an avalanche of gunfire ahead.

The crack of the gunfire was held inside the narrow rock walls of the gorge. .

He froze. He strained to see into the gloom of the dusk, into the depth of the mist. Tracer rounds, red fireflies blurred in the mist.

Shapes in the grey mass ahead, and the firing following them.

Gord pushed Jorge down, made him lie flat, and he hissed for Zeppo and Harpo and Groucho to drop. Not room on the track for them to get back and behind the cart. He was readied. His hands, taut, held the lever and the button of the flame thrower, and another figure down. The shapes merged again. A man dragged and a man carried. The firing died.

He recognized them.

His hands eased from the lever and the button of the flame thrower.

Zed carried Eff and dragged Vee.

They were in the gorge, they were trapped between a sheer rock wall and the tumbled power of the river below. He felt the despair.

Zed reached him, and there was blood on his chest. A small bubbled voice. 'It is blocked. It is the Kaibiles.'

She listened to the voice that probably always shouted into a telephone.

'I said I'd call you. A good meeting and I appreciate your help. Can't abide talking into these things. Your Master Hobbes had the good grace to ring and scrape, some inadequate excuse about his children fiddling with his alarm clock. Quite surprised me to know he was capable of procreation . . . Oh, yes, the latest. Brown, Gordon Benjamin, last location puts him two to three days' march from Guatemala City. I'll keep this wretched machine of yours posted on what's new . . .'

Three times she had rung through from Curzon Street to link into her answerphone at the flat. Three times she had listened to the message.

Cathy Parker went for her lunch.

He had been forward on his own.

He preferred to be alone. The leopard's crawl, then the resting, then the listening, then the probing. They were good troops, almost silent. He had been to within a dozen yards of their forward deployment.

Gord came back.

Gord said to Jorge, 'It is the Kaibil battalion and we are blocked. They have machine guns and mortars. They hold the exit. They know exactly where we are . . .'

'We should fight through them.'

'I am not sure, Jorge, that is possible.'

'We should burn through them.'

'I am not sure that is possible.'

'Then what . . . ?'

'For fuck's sake, young man, I do not have to make every decision.'

He felt like the man who stole flowers from an old lady's garden, the man who pilfered sweets from a child, the man who kicked a maimed opponent. He took the blame, took it personally, but he could not hack, spit, cough out the humility that might have, just, softened for Jorge the realization of failure. He did not care to think of the turmoil that would chew in the guts of the young man.

He edged on the path, in the darkness, past Jorge. God, and he only wanted to eat, and he only wanted to sleep. The bloody race was bloody lost . . .

*Lost.*

The Fireman loomed in front of him. The Fireman reached forward and took Gord's hands, and hugged him.

'I have to look after my family, Mr Gord. Because you are blocked it is my family that has need of me. I am ashamed, but I think you will understand the need of my family. If we cannot go forward then we are beaten. If we are beaten then it will be bad for our families. Forgive me, Mr Gord . . .'

A wraith figure, moving back down the path, gone in the darkness above the plunging water roar.

# 16

There was nowhere better.

They were on the path and the rock wall was above them and the water torrent was below them. Gord sat and Jorge crouched, and Zeppo and Harpo and Groucho stood above them. Zed hovered uncertain and close to them. There was nowhere else where it could be done. They were trapped on the path. They could not go forward to the end of the gorge, and they could not go back because the width of the path was stifled by the crush of men and equipment. In the darkness, ahead of them, were the lead elements of the Kaibil battalion. In the darkness, behind them, were two thousand men and half a thousand women . . . Gord sat and listened. He had not taken Jorge forward. He did not believe that Jorge had the skill to move at night close to the lead troops. He had told him of the trip wires that were laid, to flares and to grenades, at the exit to the gorge, and the arcs of fire of the machine guns. Gord had said that they must make the decision, their decision, and he sat and he listened.

Zeppo said, 'If we cannot go forward then we must go back. If we cannot go forward then the only way for us is to retreat. Jorge, there is no other position that is tenable.'

A distant voice, quiet. 'To retreat is to be beaten.'

Harpo said, 'If we cannot fight them here, if we cannot break through, then we must retreat to find a better place to fight them. We cannot just stand here, we must turn.'

'If we turn we are beaten.'

Groucho said, 'It was good and it was brave, Jorge, and it *failed*. They have the power and the strength now, we cannot beat the Kaibiles. It is over, Jorge, and it is lost.'

Not his argument, not Gord's. The thoughts in his mind were jagged and away from the words around him. Where was Alex, where was she on the path between the rock wall and the water crash? Where was Eff who had the head wound, and where was Vee who had the cap of his knee shot off?

Zeppo said, 'You have to be sensible, Jorge.'

Harpo said, 'You have to recognize the inevitable, Jorge.'

He stayed silent and the jagged thoughts raced. And old TeeJay had talked about making footprints ... Some bloody footprints in some bloody destruction ... And there was a baby facing the first night of its life ... Some bloody life ... Trying to run from the gin trap clutch of the responsibility, trying to shed the lead weight of being accountable ... Some bloody clutch, some bloody weight.

Zeppo said, 'Turn back, Jorge.'

Groucho said, 'Accept it, Jorge.'

Perhaps possible for ten men to have forced through. Each time that he had argued before, on what mattered, he had kicked the issue his way. Hopeless for a hundred men to have tried to force the exit to the gorge. He held his silence. No chance that a thousand men could have prised open the shut trap. He loathed to hear what they said, because it was truth.

Harpo said, 'You should not feel shame, Jorge.'

Groucho said, 'While there is still the opportunity, Jorge, turn ...'

The explosion of Jorge's agony. The great hurt cry. The man crying against the darts and the nails and the pricks of thorn.

'Where ... ?'

Gord had no comfort to give him.

'... Where ... ?'

Gord cringed. He felt the same because he did not have the strength to hold the young man, did not have the strength to share.

'... Where?'

Zeppo said, 'Anywhere is better than here.'

Harpo said, 'Back home where we came from, back to Havana.'

Groucho said, 'Where we can talk to them of mercy.'

Gord stood. He spoke briskly. 'There is business to be done. We should move in one hour. We have to be gone from here, back in the trees before dawn. Don't ask me if I like it because the answer is too bloody obvious. They have to be told. They have to know why we are turning . . .'

It was good that none of them should see his face. It was the moment the cloud broke. The curtain of the cloud was broken open and the moonlight came down onto them. It was past midnight, it was into the seventh day of Gord's week. If a day had not been lost they might now have been on the high ground and looking down onto the lights of Guatemala City . . . hindsight was shit. He felt the wetness on his face. In the moonlight he could see the bowed shape of Jorge. He did not know of anything more that should be said.

The signal was decoded at Langley, Virginia, by the big computers. From the jumbled mess of digits came the clear printed name of BROWN, GORDON BENJAMIN. The night duty officer, Central American Desk, read fast through the backgrounder supplied with the name. He encoded the signal again, the Agency's own way, for onpassing to field station, Guatemala City. He was aware that the arrival of the signal from London had been anticipated and cursed for its tardiness. He rang the grade 3 staffer, Central American Desk, woke him in his Georgetown apartment and woke his wife because he could hear her down the line snarling, and woke his brats because he could hear them down the line bawling.

'We've gotten the name of this Brit in Guatemala. We've got his biography. He's just some creep with a grievance. Didn't take Desert Storm well. Just some arrogant shit carrying a mega chip . . . I thought you'd want to know.'

They were clear of the gorge. The tail of the column edged into the tree line.

The Priest did the work that the Fireman had done, pushed the cart. Gord was ahead of him, walked in silence beside the

321

young woman. His creed, if God's work were easy then most would be busy at it. He understood the enormity of the decision to turn. His own feeling, selfish, he might just have preferred to run against the block, pushing the cart, or shooting over the open sights of a Kalashnikov. Too selfish to countenance. His religion was a church of suffering. He had often enough told his flock, the Quiché Indians of the Cuchumatanes, that there was nobility in suffering. He had often enough *not* told his flock that there was precious damn little dignity in suffering. Suffering was pain . . . He had been seventeen years old, a good student in the Zona 4 high school, when he had heard on the American radio of the meeting of the bishops at Medellín in troubled Colombia. From their deliberations had come his calling. The work was to be the *comunidades eclesiásticas de base*, the church in the country, the Bible in the village, worship with the under-privileged. It was what the boldest priests of the day called the theology of liberation. The Book of Genesis taught through the Creation the dignity of man, and the boldest priests equated the political torture of man as an abuse of such God-given dignity. To stand up, to speak out, was to invite suffering and pain. Enough suffering and enough pain for his bishop, once, to have closed the parish, complained to his archbishop that pastoral work was too dangerous to be continued . . . The parish in the Cuchumatanes had reopened. The priests had returned, and the killing had continued. The word of rumour was the word of fear, and rumour told him of the killings and the torture in his parish, and the fate of 'disappeared' men. He knew of the Death Squads and of the *capucha*, and of the clandestine cemeteries, and he thought of them each time that he rode his bicycle at night on the dirt roads of his parish.

There had been those who knew that he had joined the march. There would have been those who had cheered the young leader, Rodolfo Jorge Ramírez, in front of the church at Nebaj, who knew that he had gone with the march. They would not be hard to find, for the G-2, the Judas men in Nebaj. Because the march had turned there would be a time of suffering in the villages of the Cuchumatanes. It was the duty of the church to share in the suffering of the flock, and to share was to feel the pain.

He pushed the cart behind Gord and behind the young woman, and the light grew amongst the trees.

Kramer, roused from his sleep, gutted the signal. He read the name. BROWN, GORDON BENJAMIN. He read the biography.

He muttered happily to himself, 'Heh, Mr Brown, are you running? You should be, because your own fire is coming fast up your own ass. You try running, Mr Brown, and you're going to find there's no corner to run to . . . Crazy guy.'

They moved carefully and silently. They sprinted for each rock cover. Arturo had taken a dozen men up the gorge with him. At each bend, each wind, each twist in the gorge they sheltered and listened, and then ran forward on the narrowed path. It was beyond his comprehension. The path had been ground flat. Not a blade of grass had survived, not a fragment of the lichen growth. The path had been smoothed by the tread of so many feet. He could see the sandal prints and the barefoot prints and the shoe prints and the boot prints. They had been there in the night, and they had gone in the night. It was beyond his belief that so great a march could have turned on the width of the path and extricated itself from the block he had made. The morning sun shone on him. At the far end of the gorge, where the new light slanted down to the white spume of the river, he turned. He retraced his steps, back to the exit of the gorge and the communications system of the battalion.

Where the trees were thinned the sun came down and found them. They were strung out in the pine forest.

It was retreat and before the turning back Harpo and Zeppo and Groucho had been back down the line, on the snake path in the gorge, to talk of finding a new way forward.

Retreat.

No other bloody word for it.

Harpo and Zeppo and Groucho could talk of 'strategic with-drawal' and of 'repositioning' and of 'tactical redeployment', and the men who had followed them from the jungle and from the forest community and from Playa Grande and Nebaj and Santa Cruz del Quiché would know that they talked shit. It was retreat. He thought the helicopter would be up soon and searching for them. The Indian men would not understand 'strategic with-drawal' and 'repositioning' and 'tactical redeployment', but they would understand *retreat*. The evidence was there for Gord to see, of the understanding. Sullen-faced men around him, with the spring gone from them. Fearful-faced women around him, scurrying on the track they made. The march went fast, but in fear, not in anticipation. The evidence of understanding was in the bags that were discarded beside the path, possessions and clothes that had been brought for the entry into Guatemala City, and ammunition boxes that were unopened, and heaps of mortar bombs that were heavy to carry, and food cartons. Cases and boxes and cartons dumped beside the track to make the business of retreat easier. Gord saw the sullen faces and the fear faces.

Fighting at the first food halt.

Bitter argument over the distribution and Groucho had been kicked flat to the ground and Zeppo had fired in the air and Harpo had punched a man quiet.

Alex walked with Gord. He had helped her at the food halt and he had seen that when she fed the dog there would be enough of the meal left for two more days. She had looked at him, challenged him, as to where the dog's meal was to come from after two more days. The women and the children were no longer at the back of the march, not as when they had been going forward, could not be at the back if they were to be fol-lowed and the retreat was to be harassed. Because Gord walked with Alex he was among the women and the children.

It was the Priest who began it.

The Priest shook them, kicked the life back into them. The Priest had the guitar from off his back and he strummed the chords as he walked. The Archaeologist said that the Priest sang the song of Tecún Umán who was the Quiché hero who fought the *conquistadores* of Pedro de Alvarado, and came from the great city of Utatlán beside the modern Santa Cruz del Quiché. They were crossing a field strip. The sun beat down on them. The march was in stampede. There was the first distant drones of a helicopter. The Priest ran and he sang ahead of the squealing lurch of the cart and the creak of the wheelbarrow. The children were with him. In the sun the Priest was a moving island in the sea of the children. Only the children had the trust and did not know of retreat. The children sang with the Priest, shouted the song of Tecún Umán. The children were dancing, singing, skipping towards the tree line and the cover from the approaching helicopter. They had a beauty, to Gord, the children. He saw the laughter in their faces and a happiness. They were the future, they were what Groucho had told him, they were the dancing and singing and skipping butterflies . . . and there had been children dancing and singing and skipping in the dust-dry streets of Karbala.

He called back to the Archaeologist who dragged the cart. 'This Tecún Umán, what happened to him?'

'He fought Alvarado in hand-to-hand combat . . .'

'What happened to him?'

'You want to know?'

'I want to know.'

The Archaeologist recited, as if he had learned it parrot-fashion. He said it was from the Quiché Indian history, written down. '. . . "Launched himself into the air, for he had come transformed into an eagle, covered in plumes that grew from within himself . . . He had wings that also sprouted from his body, and he wore three crowns, one of gold, one of pearls, and one of diamonds and emeralds. Captain Tecún charged" . . .'

'What happened to him?'

'Alvarado speared Tecún Umán in the guts, killed him. Then he went and burned alive all of Tecún Umán's hotshots. Then he went and butchered all of Tecún Umán's people . . . You wanted to know.'

Gord laughed, grim. 'And that's worth a song?'

The Archaeologist said, 'It's worth a song because these people think, one day, Tecún Umán will return. They're simple people, Gord, they believe he will return, just like they believe that Gaspar the spirit cannot be killed by the army . . . Don't you understand, Gord, what you have been playing with, what trust you have taken . . . ?'

He let the Priest go ahead with the children, let them go far enough for the singing and the sound of the guitar to be swallowed by the forest.

He had the plan. He told the men with him to find wood that would burn.

They were late into the air because the equipment had failed. The equipment on the Huey bird had received only an intermittent signal, not constant. They were late because the technicians from the military aid mission of Israel had had to be flown up from Guatemala City to the forward control point. Tom had not seen it before, the beauty of Guatemala from the air. Rich sun brightening the luxury of the green forests and mountains breaking scattered cloud mass and the shine of winding rivers and the cut of mud-yellow roads. Ahead, burnished by the sunlight, were the corrugated-iron roofs of the New Model Villages in a Pole of Development. He felt the freedom . . . Arturo was beside him. He ignored the Kaibil colonel. He was his own man with the power of flight. The headset and the helmet suppressed the rotor thrash and he heard only the faint and broken signal from the transmitter on the ground to the receiver that the technicians had bolted again down onto the floor area forward of the cyclic stick and alongside the left-foot directional control pedal. He homed in on the faint signal, heard it grow casually in intensity. He flew high. Not as when he had flown the Apache, low against the level contour of the desert, but high altitude where machine-gun fire could not have reached him.

Arturo saw the smoke.

It was the flying that he lived for and that brought him happiness.

Arturo tugged at Tom's arm, pointed ahead and right.

He felt the glory of the country below him and the rain-cleaned air around him, a bastard it had been when he was grounded by the weather, and he could head further back into memory. The long, endless three years when he had worked out of the DEA office in St Louis, three years endured before he could join Airwing. The guy at the flying school who owned the Huey 1H-B, and who charged him big rates because the bird was precious to the guy, and who gave him a lecture in Safe Flying each time the bird was hired out like he was talking to a teenager about condoms and Safe Sex. Three years of shit from a guy who knew nothing of Safe Flying in the combat zone. It was what Tom Schultz lived for and the bird rolled to his touch on the cyclic stick and rocked in the headwinds . . . The signal was not strong enough. The smoke spirals came in five places from amongst the tree canopy.

Arturo's voice, excited, broke over the signal that was not strong enough, and clamoured in Tom's ear.

'I can get the Cessnas in. We have a squadron, A-37Bs, I can get them in and bomb the bastards, napalm the bastards . . .'

Tom said, 'And I'd reckon you'd be wasting your time.'

'That's too much fire for loggers . . .'

Tom shook his head. 'Forget it.'

'. . . That's not lumber people, that is them.'

'Sorry to be the wet towel.'

Tom hitched off his helmet and he gestured for Arturo to get his helmet off. Tom worked his own helmet onto Arturo's head. He let him listen. He took his own helmet back, nestled it down again over his scalp.

'We're not with the signal, not yet, the signal is ahead and out east . . . It's the oldest one in the book. Sorry if I'm teaching you egg-sucking . . . In Vietnam the 'Cong and the NVA used to heat up water and fill their food jars with it, good and hot water. We had the gear to detect body heat from the air. The B-52s would

327

come in from Guam island and blast shit out of the jungle where the heat was. The 'Cong and the NVA, they'd gone. All we did was give the monkeys a bad time. What I'm telling you, you go down there and what you'll find is a load of burned-out fires, no bodies . . . It's about domination. You'll dominate them, stress them, a hell of a sight more by following them, shadowing them, than by bombing the hell where they aren't. You with me, the domination thing . . . ?'

They hovered, they flew on. They passed the smoke spirals. They flew circles. They tracked the signal.

Gord was talking, distracted, to Jorge.

'It buys us time. They'll have a reconnaissance platoon stalking us. We can't help that. Nothing we can do about it, not in daylight where they can follow us. In darkness, yes, not in daylight. They've a helicopter up, right . . . ?'

The helicopter was there, distant, always there.

'. . . They'll have seen the smoke. They'll call up an airstrike on the smoke . . .'

He had a hundred men slashing with their machetes. A hundred men, frantic, cut branches from the lower trunks of the trees around them.

'. . . When the fixed wing go in they have to keep the reconnaissance platoon back, or they have a "friendly fire" job. We buy time back there, and we buy time here . . . I'm trying to lose them, Jorge.'

A hundred men making stakes from the branches and cutting sharp pointed ends, and running from the safety comfort of the trees and burying the stakes deep enough for the pointed ends to be just below the swaying tips of the high drying grass fronds of the clearing. And he was urging them hard and calling for the fires to be lit, and yelling at Jorge would he get the fuck out and have the march swing west.

'And in a day, two days, we will turn and fight them.'

'Yes, Jorge.'

'Fight them and beat them, go again for Guatemala City.'

'Yes . . .'

He could hear all the time, against the slashing of the machetes, the constant distant thunder of the helicopter.

He was surprised they had taken so long to fly the bombers.

He rated it as five miles ahead of the first smoke spirals. Two more white-grey columns from the burning of damped wood. With his fingers Tom gently tuned the receiver. A little to the right and less to the left. He held the signal. He pointed to the new smoke. He shook his head, grimaced. Arturo leaned against the window and was staring down onto the tree carpet and the smoke and into the green of the clearing and there were bright scarlet flowers growing through the grass.

He heard Arturo's voice, distorted. 'It is the time they must eat, they cannot keep going without food. You cannot feed that number of people on the hoof. They are feeding, and we could put in the birds. We have good ground for a landing, close-quarters fighting with the Kaibiles and they will break . . .'

'Are you looking for another lesson in egg-sucking?'

'Shit on you, Schultz . . .'

'I'll take you down . . . Don't swallow that egg, might choke you . . .'

He pushed the stick. Did it fast, violent. They dived. Arturo had his arms flailing in front of him for something to catch and steady himself. Nothing there. They dropped. Arturo's hands smeared against the side window hatch as if that might hold him. The tree canopy rushed to them, and the clearing rose to them. Good flying, great flying, hammering the Huey bird down from 3000 feet above the tree top level. He steadied. He flattened out from the drop to the hover. He was above the grass of the clearing. He edged the last few feet. Not looking at Arturo. Letting the man look for himself. He was above the grass, flattening it. Above the scarlet flowers, devastating them. The down thrust from the rotors beat the grass aside and the flowers. He held the hover. He looked down onto the stakes with the sharpened points that were erect in the downed grass and scarlet flowers.

Tom heaved back on the stick.

'It's the second oldest one . . . back to the 'Cong and the NVA . . . hope you didn't swallow it . . . You attract a helicopter force in, and when they set down they're amongst sharp poles and that's what the infantry have to jump onto, and it plays hell with the undercarriage of the birds. If you'd put your ugly bastards in there, *if*, you'd have taken casualties and you might have lost a lift, and then you're cautious, and then you don't try it the next time. It's like I said, it's about domination.'

He climbed again to the cruising altitude.

Tom chuckled.

The signal took him away to the west. The direction of the march had changed. It was a game to him, and the game made Tom Schultz comfortable.

'You have my full and warm congratulations, Mario.'

He basked. He stood by his jeep. There was a loudspeaker attachment that linked to the radio hook-up. He was surrounded by officers and NCOs. They were on the road that ran from Zaculeu to the Los Encuentros Junction, eleven miles due south from Santa Cruz del Quiché. Ahead of him, clear in the afternoon light, the blued mountain range stretched above the forest, and further and paler were the Cuchumatanes.

'They are in retreat, most definite.'

The voice of the general commanding G-4 (Logistics) boomed across the road. 'You go for the kill, Mario.'

'I take the analogy of a grape that falls from a vine. The grape falls to the ground. The flesh of the fruit rots. What is left is the seed. It is the seed that I seek. I will stamp with the full force of the Kaibil battalion on the seed, split it, break it, destroy it. The seed will never produce further fruit when the Kaibil battalion has stamped on it. Oh yes, I go for the kill . . .'

He broke the radio link. Two helicopters were in descent onto the road. The helicopter of the American was refuelled and the engine was on power. More troops spilled from the helicopters that landed. He tossed off the headset. The American was in the air. He looked into the smirking faces of his officers and his NCOs.

'They will run and there is nowhere for them to hide. They will manoeuvre and there is nowhere for them to go. They are the chicken in spasm without the head. No, I will not engage them while they still have the capacity to fight, I will not sacrifice any of you for a gesture. But, and I promise it to you, you will have no cause for impatience. It will be the Kaibiles that destroy them, the baby whore Ramírez and the Englishman with the fire, you have my promise . . .'

The helicopter of the American was a diminishing speck framed against the mountain majesty. Unseen, they were there, and tracked.

It was the drone of a sweet honey bee. They had gone west as he had instructed and the helicopter had been with them, high and hidden by the mat of the tree branches. They had gone north and he had dared to hope. They had gone north in a window of silence. The helicopter was with them again. Sometimes it was behind them, and sometimes it circled them, and sometimes there was the deeper throb of the engines as it hovered ahead of them. They went east now. Only the one bird, an albatross flying with them. The aircraft had not come and bombed behind them, as he had promised they would. A wing of helicopters had not come to land among the stakes and disgorge troops into the trap, as he had promised they would. The drone of the bird, unseen, the bee cut at the nerve of the men.

A guerrilla, one of those from near to the start, had raised his machine gun to the canopy, aimed at the hidden tormentor, blasted, showered himself in cones and needles.

A man from Playa Grande, who had fought well at the approach to the gate of the garrison's barracks at Santa Cruz del Quiché, had torn off the uniform he had worn proudly and was bent in his underpants hunting in a plastic bag for his own clothes.

A man from Nebaj who was respected, whom others fol-lowed, took what food he could carry from an abandoned sack, and shrugged at Gord, and seemed to wish him well, and slipped from the path and away between the trees.

Always the helicopter was with them. So tired. Gord carried two machine guns now, and the belt ammunition for both of them and he had the weight of his pack and the straps cut in his back. The pace of the march was hurried by the settling fear. The Archaeologist pushed the cart, and the Street Boy was alongside him with the wheelbarrow, and the Canadian limped behind and his face was screwed up in pain that he would not admit to. Jorge was waiting for him where a small stream had to be forded. Water to their waists, and a man slipped and threw down the ammunition box that he carried, lost it in the water, and crossed and left it.

Wide-eyed Jorge panting. 'We turn, yes? We have gone back enough . . .'

There was the rattle of the pitch of the helicopter's engine as the bird above them banked.

'Turn where, Jorge?'

Zeppo was there, arms folded. Harpo leaned against a tree and picked the grime from his nails. Groucho sat with his head between his knees.

'We turn, we find a new way. We go for Guatemala City.'

The march splashed out of the water, passed them.

'Have you asked them? Have you asked how many will follow you?'

Jorge had Gord held close.

'What do we do?'

His fists hung onto the wrapped belts of machine-gun ammunition and the cloth of the tunic top. Breathing hard. Pure sympathy, clean water sympathy welled in Gord.

'I don't tell you what to do.'

'It is walking again in our own blood. Going back is losing hope . . . I had memorized my speech. I could tell you what I would have said when I stood on the steps of the Palacio Nacional, and I could tell you what I would have said to the Ambassador of the United States. Do you know about arrogance, Gord? Do you know how it can destroy you? We should turn, Gord, stand and fight them . . .'

'I will take you home,' Gord said.

She had spent the night and most of the morning in a closed van that was parked where the spyholes could observe the row of lock-up garages behind the block. A wasted night and a wasted morning because the Irishman had not shown. The man with her in the van with the telescope and the camera loathed her because, in the company of a woman, he was too shy, boring slob, to use the bucket in the corner of the back of the van. When the van had been left back at the transport pool, when the man had run for the Underground and his journey home, she found a telephone box and dialled into her answerphone.

'Damn thing again . . . I'm sorry but the news is not that good . . . Open line and all that . . . They were poised for the last dash, but that's history. They were blocked and they've turned. If it was to work then it always had to be the dash. It's retreat time. More when I have it . . .'

Cathy Parker watched the litter blowing in the gutter of a London street.

The Priest had around him all those who had come from Nebaj. He had the men and the women and the children, and the guitar was on his back. The weapons of the men were neatly stacked, wigwams of rifles formed around the ammunition boxes and the mortar bombs. The Priest smiled, droll. It was not necessary for him to explain . . . Gord understood. The helicopter was still with them, tormenting in its presence, hovering, searching for carrion. He wondered if they would be rocketed or strafed or hit by the exploding napalm bombs. He shook the Priest's hand and the grip was granite hard. The people from Nebaj and the Priest moved away from the march, into the gathering darkness, away from the setting sun that threw the light shards down between the trees.

They made a different path, they went west.

Only when the darkness came, only when the march blundered in the forest in the night, did they lose the helicopter.

Gord walked with Alex, and he held her hand as he walked, and in his mind there was a prayer for the Priest.

The headlights of the big station wagon found them. Kramer went past the lorries and the armoured personnel carriers, and past the men who were sleeping at the roadside, and past the fires of the cooking stoves, and past the men who were cleaning their weapons in readiness for going forward. He detoured off the road to get by the silent helicopters. His lights found Arturo. The colonel was beside the communications vehicle and shouting into a radio. He thought he saw the flier in the shadow on the far side of the vehicle. A hell of a journey in darkness, and no escort, and each roadblock had been a cat fight of wills. Four and a half hours it had taken him, but no way that Kramer would permit the dossier biography out of his own sweet care. It was a big favour, a hell of a big favour . . . but Colonel Mario Arturo, i/c the Kaibil battalion, was a coming man, and coming goddamn faster if it was true what he had heard, that the shit column had been turned. And a big favour would be called in, some time. This year, next year, some year, Colonel Mario Arturo would be called to account by the Agency . . . Kramer bustled forward. No waiting for Arturo to come off the radio. It was Agency business, and Agency business was priority.

'Colonel, I think we have what you want. Pulled the strings damned hard, but we've got it . . .'

Arturo was off the radio. Kramer opened the briefcase that was fastened by a slender chain to his wrist. He produced the sheets of paper in a cellophane sleeve.

'. . . His name is Brown. He's the one on the flame thrower. Just a crazy guy. British. He was Special Forces down in the Gulf and would have had a medal for rescuing one of our pilots from a downed helicopter, but he freaked. He went native with some resistance group, and when he came out he insulted, bad heavy talk, one of our senior officers. Crazy obstinate. Wouldn't apologize, so Gordon Benjamin Brown went to the wall. Colonel, it's all here to help you go get him . . .'

The flier had come round the front of the communications vehicle.

Kramer passed the dossier to Arturo. Too right, he'd rein him in some good wet day. Too right, he'd have Mario Arturo pocketed.

The flier said, 'Sorry, I didn't catch it . . . What was his name?'

'Brown. Crazy bastard. Gordon Benjamin Brown.'

# 17

'Brown. Crazy bastard. Gordon Benjamin Brown.'

A downed pilot, a trigger and an explosion. An insult to a senior American officer. A going to the wall.

Three triggers, three explosions.

'I'm sorry, don't think me dumb. I'm sorry, Mario, for interrupting,' Tom said. He was close to Kramer, and it was an interruption and the frown cut the colonel's forehead, and he was gestured to be quiet. He pressed, 'Could you, please, say that name again . . . ?'

'Brown, Gordon Benjamin Brown . . .' Kramer laughed. 'You can read yourself into him, plot him and know him, colonel . . .'

There had never been a surname used. The given name had been abbreviated. Special Forces and, of course, they didn't wear their names on the combat gear. The one he had thought to be the senior NCO had used the name of 'Gord'. No exchange of names after the pick-up from beside the downed Apache bird, not time because the Iraqis were closing and the big machine gun mounted on the rollbar of the Land Rover had been hammering to suppress their advance. No exchange of *pleasantries*, just the pick-up and the body of the crew man abandoned still strapped in his cockpit seat. The officer, 'Gord', had been at the wheel of the Land Rover, and beetling it out, and one of their own guys had been hit, and it had just been a hell of a noise of gunfire. He had lain amongst the legs and the spare gear and the sandbags in the open back of the Land Rover and they'd had their hands full with their own casualty. Not a time for pleasantries and chat and introductions. They'd given him the jab and he'd been gone. They'd called him 'Gord' and that was the first trigger.

'. . . What we gather from the Brits is that he will stay with the core guys. He's not the man who'll run out on them to keep his own skin safe on his back. Me, if I were him, I'd be ditching those deadbeats and legging for the frontier on my own . . .'

Whatever it was, probably morphine, had pretty much knocked him down. And after he'd come back to the living he was the passenger and couldn't help, and the one they called 'Gord' was busy with the driving and had taken them into loose sand, gone through all the power gears on the low ratios, gone where the Iraqis in their lorries couldn't follow. What had brought him right back to the living had been the thunder in the darkness of the helicopter coming in for the casevac lift. They were more concerned, these guys, with their own man, but there had been fast handshakes before the collapsible canvas stretcher had been heaved into the hatch. Fast handshakes before the winch man on his own bird had pulled him in. He'd heard it from an orderly in the field hospital, and it was all round the Dhahran base, that a Brit Special Forces guy had bad-mouthed a ranking brigadier general and dug himself a hole in shit. It was the second trigger.

'. . . He'll be with them, that's the Brits' indication, and if he's with them he'll be at their pace. They'll get no help, not with the word going round every village, every community, that they are bad news, *failed* bad news. Their chance of making it to the Mexican border is zilch zero, not now that the weather's flipped . . .'

A general had visited him. There had been few enough casualties, few enough for each man and woman in the field hospital to get a visit from rank. How was he coming along? Good . . . Was he happy with the way he was looked after? Great . . . Did he need anything? No . . . Had he had the telephone to ring home? No one to ring . . . No, wait, sir, just one thing, he would like to thank, personally, the Special Forces officer who had saved him, brave guy. Forget it, soldier . . . Candies from home, that was OK. Letters written in child scrawl from classes in west Virginia and Arkansas, that was okay. No chance to thank, personally, the officer who had saved him. Forget it, soldier . . . And the orderly had told him afterwards, what he'd heard round the base, that the Brit Special Forces guy was on open arrest waiting on court goddamn martial and failing big to make the necessary apology. It was the third trigger.

'. . . Hope that's useful material for you, colonel . . .'

He should have written, and he was mending. He didn't have the name, and he was shipped back for convalescence. He didn't have the name and he didn't have an address, and he was mending back at the base at Fort Rucker, Alabama. He had never written and tried to find an address, never made the thanks that were deserved.

'. . . Heh, Tom, you were down in the Gulf? You didn't get to hear of this crazy mother?'

It was behind him, writing letters, finding addresses, making thanks.

'There were half a million down there. No, I didn't get to meet them all . . .'

It was easy to lie, as it had been easy not to write and search and thank.

Tom Schultz said he was going for sleep, going to sack in. There was a sleeping bag stowed in the Huey bird, and he'd have the whole of the hatch area to stretch himself. He'd try, but he doubted that he'd sleep . . .

He wanted to be back in Garden City, outside of Ames.

He wanted to be home on the campus at the University of Minnesota.

He wanted to be gone because he could no longer control the fear. The fear was new to the Archaeologist, a creeping and growing paralysis. The fear came because the heart was gone from them. Garden City, outside of Ames, was the shrinking dream. Garden City was white walls and the regimented lines of the apple orchards, and the big grain silo, and the best farmland on God's earth and it was safety, it was beyond his reach and growing further distant. The march was meandering, going west and going east and cutting back, and wading in the more casual eddies of the rivers to lose the track beaten by their feet. He thought the march was going nowhere, not going back to Garden City, outside of Ames. And the campus at Minnesota was drifting further, another dream, losing clarity. The campus was a service apartment, and a good woman that he nearly loved, and the company of colleagues that he enjoyed. The campus was home and it, too, was safety.

Now they were not going forward . . .

It was the sense of helplessness that fuelled the fear. The helicopter was with them. They had walked through the night, and they had rested up for only three hours while the dawn was coming, while the bright-plumed birds chorused the coming sun beat, and they had moved off again into deeper forest under the high canopy of big trees, and the helicopter had come and found them and circled them. The helicopter was the flame in the fear, fanned the fear and gutted it. The helicopter was the destruction of his courage and the cause of the fear. They could not fight back, and that was the helplessness. Going forward he had felt invincible, protected from incoming fire, going back and harried by the unseen helicopter above the tree canopy he was collapsing to the fear. It would be not in their time, and not in their place. It would be the ambush. It would be the curtain of bullets. It would be death as it had been for the Academic.

He did not think he could go on.

The Archaeologist did not know how he would find the strength to tell Gord. He dragged the cart, and the Street Boy was beside him with the wheelbarrow. Going nowhere, going away from the Garden City outside of Ames and the campus at Minnesota, going with the helicopter, going to death . . .

The strength of the march flaked.

The weapons were thrown down. The uniforms taken from the camps and bases and barracks were stripped off. There were some who went to Jorge before they left the march and kissed him or stood in respect in front of him or hugged him. There were some who came first to Gord. There were some who clasped Alex's hand and cried. There were some who left the march without a gesture of friendship, scuttling from the track. It was the helicopter that broke them . . . always the helicopter was with them. The women had gone with the children. No more fresh laughter in the march, no more the shouting of small shrill voices. No more the colour of the women's clothes and the dancing movement of butterflies in the dark shade of big trees.

The march struggled on towards the high ridges of the Cuchumatanes.

'I saw it once,' Arturo said into the face microphone. 'I saw it once at the docks in Puerto Barrios. I think my father had gone there for something to do with his work, and it was the holiday from school. Perhaps I was difficult with my mother, perhaps it was necessary for me to be occupied. I went with my father to Puerto Barrios. I had the time to go down to the docks to see the ships unloaded and the cranes operating. The rats were coming down the ropes of a small tramp ship. It was one of the ships that took sugar up to the Gulf of Mexico and brought back grain. The ship had come in from Galveston in Texas with the grain and it had been unloaded. Perhaps there was nothing to keep the rats, perhaps they did not like to sail back to Galveston and eat sugar all the way. The rats were coming down the ropes that tied the ship to the docks. What you always hear is that rats will leave a ship that is doomed. I used to wonder for a long time, after I had seen the rats, whether that ship ever made it back to Galveston. I mean, it is necessary to give rats a degree of intelligence. You think it possible that rats could know if a ship is going to sink? Maybe, maybe not, maybe rats just don't like sugar . . .'

They veered in the headwind that buffeted the flight of the Huey. He looked down. There was a long tree line and then the wide earth-brown scar where the logging had cleared the forest. He looked down onto the slow-moving column of people below him, and if he looked ahead and away past the American's helmet, he could see another column. Earlier, when they were first above the earth scar of cleared ground, he had seen two more columns.

'. . . It is what you said. It is about domination. We have frayed the nerves of them. We have broken their heart. It is because you are with them that they have disintegrated. Just rats, and trying now to find a place of safety in the warehouses of the docks. Even rats, simple-minded rats, uneducated rats, have the instinct to survive . . .'

All through the flight, from the time they had first locked again onto the beacon signal, the disintegration of the march had been clear to see below them. He had binoculars, German-made, $6 \times 30$, and he could see the faces of the men and women under him, and the children. He saw not a single weapon, and not a man in uniform. He watched the debris columns edging away from contact with the grape seed of the rebellion.

'. . . I think tomorrow will be right. You Americans, do you give us any sensitivity? Any intelligence? We are only *Guatemalans* . . . I could have hit them yesterday, the full force of the Kaibiles against them. The rat in the corner fights hard, but the rat that has an escape will run. I would have taken casualties if I had hit them yesterday and I would have made "martyrs" of the vermin. I can collect the escaped rats at any time I wish, with poison, with gas, with terrier dogs, with an old shotgun. I can wait a week or a month or a year to hunt out the escaped rats. That is sensitivity, yes? That is intelligence, yes . . . ?'

The flier never spoke. The flier concentrated on his controls and held the bird steady against the winds.

When he had seen the flier in the dawn, before the helmet had masked his face, he had thought he had seen a great tiredness, as if the man had not slept.

'. . . We take them tomorrow, what is left of them. We take the baby whore Ramírez, and the rabble that is with him, tomorrow, and the Englishman that came with them.'

They flew on. They banked over the perfection of the beauty of his country. The rats never looked up at the helicopter above them, walked for the road that would lead them to Santa Cruz del Quiché and Nebaj and Playa Grande and the villages of the mountains and the communities of the jungle. Such peace below him.

He called Gord back to him.

He pushed the cart alongside Gord.

The Archaeologist from Garden City outside of Ames told Gord of the old couple in the white-walled house that backed onto the apple orchards and faced the grain silos, and he told Gord about the girl on the campus at the University of Minnesota.

'I want to see those old people. We're being shepherded onto a killing ground. I want to see that girl and have a life with her. We're being pushed into a butcher's yard. It's not my usual language, Gord, we're *fucked up*. Gord, you're never going to make that frontier, and that's not just me talking. When we turned we had up of three thousand people. Christ, man, we haven't thirty . . . I don't want to be on that killing ground in that yard. I heard what you said to Jorge, and I think he's a fine and naïve young man, and you said that you were going to take him home. Gord, that was *shit*, high-grade quality. I'm going on my own, don't think I haven't thought it round, because I reckon that my best chance at ever seeing Garden City again, ever being on campus again. I admire your commitment, and I admire what you have achieved. I'm not brave and I am not a hero. Sorry, but now I put myself first and last, and I want out . . .'

All through the morning the Archaeologist had been resurrecting the courage, and the goddamn man didn't argue. He felt limp, yellow. He tore off the combat camouflage fatigues. He dragged on the blue jeans and a red shirt, and his torn old sneaker shoes.

'Good luck.'

'If I get home I will tell people . . .'

There was the fist on his sleeve, quietly laid there. A torn and bruised and calloused hand.

342

'Do something more for me.'

'Spit it . . .'

Gord going to Jorge. Gord taking the map. Gord bringing the map to him. Gord pointing. Gord taking the pocketbook from his tunic and writing on the paper that had been soaked and was now stiff dried. Gord tearing the sheet of paper from the pocketbook. Gord folding the paper methodically to the size of a postage stamp. Gord taking his hand, holding it.

'Again, good luck . . .'

He had seen on the map where the road was. He went to kiss Alex and she turned her mouth away from him, as if his lips would have the bad taste of defeat, so his mouth brushed her cheek and the lobe of her ear. He thought it was upwards of two miles to the road.

He touched the cart, gazed down at the tubes. Where the old paint was off it, the rust was getting to the cart. It was bruised, bent and scarred. The right axle might not last much further, and if the right axle went then that might just be the end of the cart. If he ever made it back to Garden City outside of Ames or to the campus at Minnesota then he would tell his parents and his girl that he had pushed the damned contrary cart halfway across Guatemala, and he would tell them that the fifth day of a man's week had been lost . . .

He walked away hard.

Alone, going towards the road, he felt a freedom from the fear. The Archaeologist never looked back.

They were going slow.

The tiredness ripped at them.

The helicopter was with them.

Gord had taken the cart. He dragged the cart and he had the two machine guns and the machine-gun ammunition, and his backpack, and he had the grenades. He did not know what was the further use for the cart but he could not bring himself to abandon it. It was as if he were fused to the flame of the cart, as if the cart were now a part of his being. He had brought the cart in and he would take the cart out. The cart was himself . . . They came to a wide dirt road and they waited and they listened, and they were all flopped down on the drying and steaming forest floor. They watched the empty length of the road and were back from the strip that had been cleared.

He felt for Jorge. Jorge was the wound in him.

Gord had heard all the fine words of Jorge at the grave of his mother and in the plaza at Nebaj and in front of the church facade at Santa Cruz del Quiché. Fine words that were nothing. The young man's endeavour had collapsed.

He lay beside Jorge and there was the throb of the helicopter behind them, above them, to break the silence.

'We'll go all night. We'll shake the bastard off us tonight. I will take you out, Jorge, I promise. It is cutting and running and quitting, but you have to get out. I don't bloody like it, nobody likes cutting and running and quitting, but it is the only gesture that is left to you. You have to deny them the *satisfaction* of capturing you, killing you. That's the only gesture that is possible to us. You can deny them that small victory, capturing you and killing you. If you want to be a trophy, a head on the wall of the ministry, then you turn and face them. You shouldn't give them the last pleasure of gloating on your head.'

The bitter murmur. 'And you save yourself . . .'

'I will get you out, you and everybody.'

They crossed the road. They ran. They chose the moment when they thought the helicopter had turned away. The cart stuck in the rain ditch beside the road, and Gord dragged it and swore and cursed and he heaved it out of the ditch and through the cut brush where the side had been cleared. He went back to help the Street Boy with the wheelbarrow, and it took the two of them to lift the wheelbarrow across the ditch, and he went back again to help the Canadian who shook off his hand, cussed, and crawled from the depth of the ditch . . . The sounds of the helicopter were more distant, going off station. They would lose the bastard, lose it because he had promised . . . They came across the road, *everybody*. Alex with her dog that stayed now shoulder to knee with her, and Zeppo who had the wounded Eff lifted on his back, and Harpo who had the arm of the limping Vee slung over his shoulder, and Zed who was in pain from the chest wound near to his left armpit, and Groucho.

The going of the helicopter, like a liberation, spurred them.

He went with Groucho. Groucho had the burden of the last RPG-7 rocket launcher, and the last mortar, and the rockets and the bombs, and he had the weight of the last of the food. They were going faster again, and strung out, and Gord was at the back of the march with Groucho.

There was the anguish on Groucho's face and the misery of his dropped head.

'It's not your fault . . .'

He tried to break the anguish.

'. . . It is nobody's fault . . .'

He tried to hack the misery.

'. . . We tried.'

The anguish and the misery were turned on Gord.

Groucho sobbed. 'You do not understand. You understand nothing. You do not understand their power. You understand nothing of their cruelty. They have made a country of terror. You do not understand the terror that makes a man turn against his friend, against his family, against his God. You understand nothing . . .'

The beacon signal was fading.

He had tapped at his watch and indicated the needle of the fuel gauge, and the colonel had nodded. They had banked away.

Tom took the new course. He navigated from the map in the plastic-fronted pocket above his knee. The rendezvous for the fuel load was marked on the map, midway between Chichicaste-nango and Santa Cruz del Quiché, a red crayon cross where the road tanker would be. Arturo was bent over his own map and was on his own radio link. Arturo's attention was taken with the staccato instructions he was giving over the radio for the move-ment of the battalion and the position reports he was receiving.

The two faces were seared in Tom's mind.

It was easy flying, a bright afternoon and horizon visibility.

There was the face of the man that he had seen beside the casevac helicopter, clean-shaven, and the droll smile and the meaningless mutter of '. . . See you some day. You never know, it's a small world. Take care.' The face of a man that was Gord . . .

He saw the lone figure on the tarmacadam road.

. . . There was the face of the man that he had seen in the middle of the parade ground at Playa Grande, from 100 feet, from the grime of the cockpit window, the face with the ragged beard of the man who lay behind the flame-thrower cart that spat the fire towards the command building. The face of the man that was Gordon Benjamin Brown.

A solitary figure, what they called ICI in DEA speak, Caucasian, white male, blue jeans and red shirt, medium height, slight build. And waving, frantically waving.

Tom nudged Arturo's elbow and pointed down, and Arturo was giving out the co-ordinates for the troop move, getting the block forces up for the morning, and because he had been interrupted, distracted, Arturo had to call the last co-ordinates again . . . The man was waving. Cheeky damn guy, waving and pointing down to the tarmac road ahead, like he was flagging a cab. The faces slipped. The faces of Gord and Gordon Benjamin Brown faded. A hell of a cheek for the guy to wave him out of the sky like he was a yellow cab and it was raining and he was late home for his dinner. He said to Arturo that it wouldn't affect the fuel, and it wouldn't delay them. He brought the bird down towards the road.

He hovered above the guy.

The guy was early, middle, thirties, and scrawny so that the red shirt billowed on him. The guy had big spectacles, twisted askew, on his face. He was looking at the guy and the thought came fast to him that this was bad country to be on the ground without protection. Either in fast and lift him, or out fast without him.

He set the Huey down on the skids.

Good guy, didn't mess him. Ran fast for the hatch and had it back and was inside and was slamming the hatch shut.

Tom powered the bird up, dragged the stick back. He took her up to cruising altitude, then turned and pointed to the head-set that was hung on the bulkhead behind him, and when the guy had it on then Tom gestured on his own headset to the microphone button. The guy looked laid out, like there was nothing left in him . . . He showed Arturo what he was doing, pressing the switches that isolated the colonel and his ground communication.

'You looked like you were anxious for a ride.'

'Grateful, I'm very grateful . . .'

'American?'

'Archaeologist, out of the University of Minnesota. It's a hell of a kindness. Are you embassy . . . ?'

'Sort of.'

'I didn't know we had advisers down here, thought that was off limits.'

'DEA. It's complicated . . . So, where you coming from?'

'An archaeological site, a dig site.'

'Where's that?'

The voice in Tom's ear. 'Up the road.'

'Where?'

'A bit up the road.'

'Whereabouts up the road?'

The pause in Tom's ear. A hesitation. 'Some miles up the road, on a dig site.'

'How long you been walking?'

'A few days.'

'Shit, man, I thought you'd been walking since morning . . . How many days?'

'Just a few days . . .'

'Don't get me wrong, but this isn't exactly vacation hiking country. What takes you walking a few days in the middle of this shit place?'

The longer pause in Tom's ear. The longer hesitation. 'I was working on this site. I was attacked. I was studying the artefacts. I log them, quite legally. I was hit by thieves. They sell big in New York . . . I was trying to get out.'

'And you have just been *walking* . . . ?'

'That's what I said.'

'From "a bit up the road" and "just for a few days"? Friend, you've a hell of a way with conversation. Where you heading?'

'I was trying to get out. I want La Aurora. Can you help me get to La Aurora?'

'Do you know what's going on in this country, "a bit up the road"?'

'I don't, no.'

'You know what's been happening, "just for a few days"?'

'I don't, no.'

Tom said, steel, 'A bit of a rebellion, just an insurrection . . . You didn't hear?'

'No.'

Tom saw below him the road tanker parked, tiny, and there were jeeps and lorries around it. He cut his microphone switch. He started the descent. He was concentrating. There were telephone wires alongside the road. He came down into the dirt swell. The rotors' draught threw mud and stones across the road, against the road tanker and the lorries. They touched down. It was a piss poor landing. It was the sort of landing that would have won him a tongue lash from an instructor of novice recruits at the Army Primary Helicopter School. He cut the engine.

He told the Archaeologist, 'Get out, get over there . . .'

He pointed away behind the lorries.

He supervised the refuelling.

Tom watched the guy. The guy was going from jeep to lorry and last to the driver of the road tanker.

Tom walked sharply from the helicopter and round the far side of the road tanker. The money was being passed. Real money, dollars Made in the United States of America. The driver took the money. Tom ducked away.

He was standing beside the helicopter.

348

The guy came to him.

'I just wanted to thank you.'

'No problem. When are you hoping to go?'

'First flight out.'

Said easily, conversation, 'How's he doing, how's Gord?'

'Who?'

Tom looked into the guy's eyes and they wavered, and they dropped. 'How's he doing, Gordon Benjamin Brown?'

'I don't know what you're . . .'

'May I tell you something . . . You are the worst fucking storyteller I ever met. You made a good decision, bunking out. Gord, he'll be cold dead tomorrow, Gordon Benjamin Brown. Friend, you made the right move. Have a good flight, and give my love to Minnesota . . .'

When the bird was fuelled, just before he lifted for the late afternoon trawl to rope in the beacon signal, he watched the road tanker drive away for Guatemala City and the military corner of La Aurora. He waved to the guy who said he was an archaeologist, to the guy running out on Gord, who had saved his life, the same Gordon Benjamin Brown who would be ambushed and killed in the morning.

'Are you never there? . . . Is it that you just leave it on even when you're there? . . . We've moved a body in from Panama where we staff . . . Seems to have his ear to the ground . . . It's desertion time, the faint-hearted are quitting in droves. The military reckon to take them tomorrow. The unit involved is called the Kaibil battalion. I'm told we should respect them, they would be expected to get a good result. It's just a small group that's left and it is likely to be rather surgical . . . Sorry about that . . .'

She sat alone on the bed of her flat. Cathy Parker drank from the neck of the bottle.

They could not have given him more help.

He had pitched up on the secure side of La Aurora, into a mêlée of military activity. The fixed-wing Cessnas were being fuelled and armed under lights. Helicopters were ferrying sticks of men and their battle weapons out into the darkness of a still and star-struck night. A sergeant took the Archaeologist from the aviation fuel depot, where the road tanker dropped him, to an officer. The driver of the road tanker had given him the name of Colonel Mario Arturo, and he had used the name effortlessly. The officer drove him to the civilian terminal. The Archaeologist could see they had won.

The military ruled and the civilian staff grovelled. The officer took him to the head of the queue for the Continental flight to Houston. He paid AmEx plastic. The way he said it, he was the friend of Colonel Mario Arturo, and the officer escorted him from the ticket desk to the passport control. He produced his passport, moulded from his hip pocket into the shape of his buttock cheek, and wet from jungle rain and now dried stiff. The state of his passport was not questioned because he had the officer with him, and he was the friend of Colonel Mario Arturo.

He went through after he had thanked the officer and shaken his hand and managed a smile of gratitude. He was saluted.

When the Continental flight landed from Houston, the Archaeologist watched it disgorge. They were coming back to their own. The women and their children swarmed from the aircraft steps and across the floodlit tarmac. He thought of the Mayan women, and their children that Gord called the 'butterflies'. The women from the plane wore their fur coats and their silk scarves and their designer suits. He thought of the Mayan women and their children who would be slogging cross-country back to their villages. The women from the plane carried their jewel boxes and their Paris bags. He thought of the Mayan women and their children going back, stoic, to their villages to await the counterstrike and retribution. The women from the plane wore thick lipstick and loud powder, and their children carried the presents bought in the shopping malls of Houston. He thought of the Mayan women and their children returning to their villages to face the vengeance that had been their fate since the spear of Alvarado was stuck in the guts of Tecún

Umán. The women from the plane and their children were met by a river flow of generals and politicians and brigadiers and civil servants and colonels and captains of industry . . . The bastards had won.

He was against the full-length window. It was seven hours after he had left the march, bunked out on Gord, and the young woman and her dog, and Jorge and his crowd, that the Continental flight was called. In his mind was the fire from the cart that was rusty and bent and bruised. His breath blurred the glass.

He said it out loud, but quiet, 'Burn them, Gord, burn them fucking hot . . .'

The Archaeologist could not help himself. He wept as he walked to the aircraft.

They did not tack right and left. They took the line of the compass. They did not swerve east and west. Straight ahead on the luminous line of the compass needle. Gord had told them what he hoped for. Like those who thrash in drowning, the energy flooded back in them. Like men and women who will flail with their arms to the exhaustion point towards a floating raft, they blundered on the path given them by the compass needle. The name of the place at the end of the path of the compass needle was Canillá. It was two full days' walk away.

Struggling when they were against the gradient, running when they were going down. Gord had the cart and Alex was with him. The dog moaned in hunger beside her, and the Street Boy wheezed as he struggled to propel the wheelbarrow. She helped him when she could. She forced back the clawing undergrowth when the prick barbs caught in his clothes and when it wrapped round the cart . . .

No anger in her voice. 'It is running out on people's trust.'

'We came and we tried . . .'

The sadness in her voice. 'It's leaving them worse than before you came.'

'We may not make it out. We have shit to go through. We have a Kaibil battalion tracking us, round us. It's not just catching a bloody number 9 bus. "Let me know, please, when it's Trafalgar bloody Square." It is a poor chance. The other way round is you and me, all of us, dragged through Santa Cruz del Quiché and Nebaj and Playa Grande, it's sadism time, slow death time. It's you and me, all of us, begging to be killed, pleading. We go out, and we leave something, we leave *hope*. We leave the memory. In the villages they can hold the memory. Dead, we are forgotten.'

The shame in her voice. 'I don't think I could live with it, me safe, the people who followed us abandoned.'

'We tried . . . You are a late bloody convert. We tried the only way that things get changed. Your way nothing changes. Your way is feeling comfortable gumming appeal envelopes and typing newsletters; lobbying politicians, and achieving sweet nothing . . .'

The whip in her voice. 'You bastard.'

'We tried . . .'

The shake in her voice. 'How do they know? How are they always with us, the helicopter?'

'I would have to sit down, and I don't have the time. Hell. I would have to analyse. I would have to think. I don't have the time. I don't know.'

The fear in her voice. 'When will they hit us?'

'They realize we are small. They will have seen from the air all the people that have left us. Perhaps tomorrow they will think we are ready to be hit . . .'

She helped him to push the cart and he laid the strength of his fist over her hand.

# 18

The sleeping bag, empty, was still in the floor area inside the hatch. There was no mattress, only the thickness of the sleeping bag to protect a man, asleep, from the riveted and ribbed flooring. Arturo came to the helicopter. He had, himself, used a collapsible bed in a two-berth tent, rested well. He ate a meat sandwich and held a polystyrene mug of thick coffee. He yawned and he stretched. He felt good. Around him was the clatter of the waking camp that was sited beside the wide road. He finished the sandwich and drained the mug. They were working fast around him to break the camp and load up the lorries. He started the routine, beside the helicopter, of his morning exercises, squats and thrusts and then a stampede of spot sprinting. Small groups of his men, those who would be lifted forward and into the ambush positions, were being briefed by their officers, as he had briefed the officers before crawling into his tent. The sweat ran on him. The men who listened to the briefings and who crouched around the maps cradled the weapons they would use; it would be close-quarters fighting, it would be short-range engagement . . . He saw the flier. The flier walked towards him and carried a collapsed entrenching spade and a roll of lavatory paper and a small towel and a plastic throw-away razor. He saw the grey tiredness of the flier's face and there were staunched cuts at the flier's throat and a place on his cheek, near to the scar, where the razor had taken the head off a healing mosquito bite. The flier came past him, did not acknowledge him, and loaded his kit into the helicopter. The early sun slanted on them, lit the grey of the flier's face.

Arturo slapped the pilot's back.

'I'm feeling good. Mr America, are you feeling good?'

Dismissive. 'Fine . . .'

'You had something to eat?'

'No.'

'Should you not have something to eat?'

The flier looked at him, drawn eyes. 'If I want something to eat then I'll find something to eat.'

Fuck him. If he did not want to eat then he would not be force-fed. If he wanted to fly on an empty stomach then he would not be begged to eat. A platoon of troops, thirty men, went past Arturo, going towards the first of the helicopters to have started up its engine, towards the slow warming swell of the rotors' swing. There was the young officer whose father had taught Arturo, the commissioned recruit, at the La Polvora training camp of the Kaibiles. There was the sergeant who had been with him in the first platoon to break the defences at Acul in Institutional Re-encounter '84. Those that had a free hand saluted him, most were too loaded by their weapons and their packs. Eager little bastards and ready to fight, ready to kill, the best . . . And this Arturo liked, they did not wear helmets, they wore proud the maroon berets of the Kaibil battalion, and they rejected the cumbersome movement-stifling flak jackets. The best . . .

'Shit faces, I want them alive . . . If I cannot have them alive then I want them dead . . . No fuck-up, no escape. They were against idiots when they were at Playa Grande and Nebaj and Santa Cruz del Quiché. Now, they face the Kaibiles. I want them so that they can be taken, first best alive, second best dead, through every rats' nest village in Quiché department. I want every man and every woman and every child in every village to see what has happened to those subversives when they met the Kaibiles. I want the spirit of rebellion beaten from every man and every woman and every child in every village. God go with you . . .'

The platoon being lifted forward would be divided into four sections. Four ways would be blocked. The lorries would carry the follow-up force that would trail the march, but it would be one of the four sections that engaged his enemy. The sections would be in position and he would be above where he could command and control and give the 'Contact' order. It was necessary to get the sections in early, far ahead of the march, so that surprise could be achieved. He had enjoyed making the plan.

Arturo teased. 'Which of you will it be that brings me the baby whore Ramírez? Alpha or Bravo or Charlie or Delta section? Which of you will bring me the Englishman with the fire? Which . . . ?'

They headed away from him, fast order and stamping their boots on the roadway, going for the helicopters.

He turned to the flier.

'We move in thirty minutes, right? What is your problem . . . ?'

He looked again into the dulled eyes, sunken.

'. . . Not the liberal shit. Do we find it *distasteful*? Are we fucking squeamish? They tried to destroy the country, my country. OK, I tell you something, Mr America, that may help you purge your liberal shit . . . It will not be the same again here. Too many commanders stood back. There are matters to be settled when this is over. Too many in the army hesitated. For me it is my country first, always my country, but it will be a new country where the old military are put to grass because they sat on their hands. You will be ready in thirty minutes?'

'Ready.'

'And tonight you will be back with your own people who will no doubt sympathize with you in your pain of having to work with Guatemalans . . .'

'If you'll excuse me, I'd like to be getting on with the flight checks.'

His pleasure at the anticipation of action was eroded. He did not know why the flier poured cold piss over him.

He was the back-marker.

The Canadian trailed the march. He maintained the link, just. Most times he could see them ahead of him, some of the times they were merged in the trees and he lost them. He did not think that it had been decided he should go back-marker but it was the way it had worked out. Gord was at the front. The plan had been explained to him the night before, and, God's truth, he had forgotten damned everything that had been told him. Just as, God's truth, it was his seventy-first year, and his memory was poor when he was tired. Tired? Damned exhausted. The hip hurt. He would have liked to have helped more, and he had taken one of the two machine guns from Gord and there must have been 250 rounds of belt ammunition, ball and tracer, wrapped round him. Couldn't have kept up the pace without the stick. The stick in his right hand and the machine gun across his left shoulder. They had explained the plan and all that the Canadian could remember was that he had to walk through this day and through another day, and he was not certain, damn it, that he could last . . . He did not stop at the rest halts. The rest halts were cut to three minutes in every sixty minutes. He caught them, each hour, at the rest halt, and when he caught them they were ready to move on. Hell no, no way he would hold them up . . . His mind meandered. There was a good Legion Club in Kingston, back up a side street from the lake. He might just get round to telling the guys a little of what had happened to just one veteran of the Cameron Highlanders of Ottawa. Might just tell Dave and Bill and Duggie and Hamish because they might be interested, because they had been there when the Falaise Gap was closed on 21st August in 1944. Wouldn't tell anyone else. Not the guys from 3rd Infantry or 4th Armoured, not the guys from Totalise and Goodwood and Atlantic, but he'd tell his good friends of Operation Tractable and the closing of the Gap what had happened to him in Guatemala. Be a hell of a job getting them to believe him . . . Wouldn't tell Miriam. No, not for Miriam to know. He'd tell Dave and Bill and Duggie and Hamish about the Englishman with the flame thrower . . . Sure as hell that hip hurt, and there wasn't the money now for the operation. His mind meandered on. Now, wait a minute, there was the little matter of the wicket gate at the back of the yard.

Before he went down to the Legion bar, the first time, he'd have the wicket gate painted for Miriam.

She might just skin him if . . .

'Would you kindly come this way, *sir*?'

The deference was a sneer.

He followed the customs service man. The Archaeologist was ragged-bearded and had collected no luggage from the carousel, and his passport looked as if it had been in the bath with him and the watermarked photograph was clean-shaven.

'Shouldn't take too long, sir. When we've cleared the flight through then we'll come back to you.'

They were in an outer office. There was a customs service woman behind him, black and big.

He croaked, 'How long?'

The customs service man had the passport and the AmEx plastic. 'This is standard procedure when a passenger has no resemblance to the passport photograph, when the passport is damaged, when the passenger is travelling into the country without baggage. I'm going to check back on your passport, sir, I'm going to check American Express, I'm going to check with University of Minnesota, when the flight's been cleared through.'

'May I, please, use the telephone?'

'No, sir.'

The outer door closed. He paced. The customs service woman stood in front of the outer door . . . Three hours? Four hours? Might hand him over to the next shift . . . The folded paper, Gord's paper, was in his breast pocket and burning it. He hadn't slept on the flight, across the aisle a baby had screamed continuously from Guatemala City to Houston. The door to the inner office was half open and there was a desk and a telephone on it . . . 'Do something more for me . . .' He had done nothing. Seeing the worn face and the exhaustion, and the trust. 'Do something more for me.' . . . He paced. She had a hell of a night stick, and she had the muscle to use the stick, but she didn't have a gun. He paced.

357

He went by the inner door. He darted inside.

The Archaeologist slammed the door shut on her.

He twisted the key and her shoulder hit the door. He rammed the bolt. The door shuddered, held.

The Archaeologist grabbed the telephone and it fell from the desk and clattered on thin-quality government carpet. He had the paper from his pocket. She was yelling and she hit the door again.

He dialled it like it was written down once he had the outside line tone. He knelt on the floor and punched the numbers.

International code, area code, exchange number, local number, and two shoulders hit the door and they were shouting for him. Local number ringing out . . . A woman's voice, crisp . . . An answerphone bleeping, last the long tone . . . Panic time . . .

The first splinter of the door. He tried to stay calm and read it like Gord had written it. The top hinge broke clear. It was the date and the time and the co-ordinates of the location. 'You made a good decision, bunking out. Gord, he'll be cold dead tomorrow, Gordon Benjamin Brown.' Pray fucking God you come through, Gord. He gave them again, date and the time and the co-ordinates of the location.

The message repeated over the telephone was '27–05–1509/9052'.

The door came in towards him. He had the paper in his mouth, and gulped. The customs service woman pulled the telephone cable from the wall socket. He swallowed. The customs service man had a revolver aimed on him.

He was handcuffed.

The customs service man said happily, 'You, asshole, are now in heavy trouble.'

Tom Schultz stayed cold.

As cold as when the weapons operator had hit the personnel carrier with the second TOW, the day before they were downed, and there had been a guy half out of the top hatch and waving a grey-white handkerchief when the second TOW had gone in. As cold as when he had come from the hospital to give the folded flag to the widow of the weapons operator at the small town cemetery and shaken the hands of the weapons operator's kids. As cold as when his father had told him, snivelling, that if the Revenue ever hooked into him then he was for the federal gaol at Marion in Illinois. As cold as when he had come home, where they had drifted to, Tacoma outside of Seattle, not announced, and found his mother being screwed hard by the gook from the gas station, and the dollar bills counted out to a hundred and left neat on the table in the hall. Staying cold was living with it, staying cold was survival.

The high sun seared through the Plexiglas of the cockpit shield. He had come across the desert, Gord, and risked living and surviving, Gordon Benjamin Brown, to lift out a pilot who was downed. He felt nothing of the rich warmth, stayed cold. Just another crap day's flying . . .

Arturo said into the microphone, '. . . Callsign Bravo section. It is yours. In your own time. They are yours, Bravo section. Out . . .'

. . . One man always had to fire first. One man would fire and that would be the signal, and the other men would follow . . .

They were among the old smoothed rocks that were lichen-covered and moss-coated. It was the absence of the birdsong that had alerted him. The big trees clung, thin-rooted, to the ground amongst the rocks. They were climbing, and the helicopter drone had dropped behind them. He was alerted because the happiness of the bright-feathered birds was gone from the forest. He had made the signals for care, caution, back down the march. No song from the birds, only the creak of the cart wheels and the whine of the wheelbarrow.

. . . One man always had to fire first, the law of the ambush . . .

Gord knew the sound. It was the sound from the man who fired first. The metalled click, the sudden movement ahead, the metalled scrape. The firing, the breech jam, the clearing of the breech. The man who fired first would be the man who had the best moment and the best aim and the best opportunity, and he had jammed. A second won, two seconds gained, three seconds achieved. Using three seconds, dropping behind the cart, and hoping, praying, crying that the men behind him would use three seconds . . .

The jam and the clearing of the breech of a lieutenant's Uzi machine pistol, close-quarters and point-blank weapon, was signal enough.

The shooting broke around Gord.

The hammer of the gunfire. The crack of the incoming. The howl of ricochets off the old smoothed rocks.

By three seconds, surprise had been lost.

Going through the routine that he had learned, and the bullets' flight above him and beside him. The firing ahead of him, and the firing of the machine guns from behind him. Heaving the firing lever. Flat on his stomach, reaching up, grabbing at the rusted arms of the cart and twisting them and jerking them so that the aim of the nozzle jets swayed across the rocks, among the rough of the tree trunks. Black oil squirting haphazard in front of him. Gord wrenched the ignition trigger. The fire flew.

The fire snaked. The fire leaped among the rocks and lingered on them, then burst forward. The fire splashed against the wide trunks of the trees, ignored them, then thrust forward.

Rich fire and black smoke cavorting ahead of him.

A wall of smoke and fire ahead of him.

A terror of hell in front of him, an inferno of smoke and fire, and all the time there was the hammer of the machine guns and the rifles on automatic behind him.

Ahead of him they had no target.

They had the fire and the smoke around them, and the fire caught them and the smoke choked them. Choking on the smoke, screaming, caught by the fire, a soldier ran towards them. The gunfire found him. Gord had his arm up, and he waved them forward from behind him. It was his training. If an ambush was broken then an ambush should be charged. The fire, and the terror of the fire, had kicked the hole in the ambush line. Precious seconds won and gained and achieved by the fire. He was bent behind the cart and he punched with the power of his legs to drive the brute forward, and he swerved the cart's arm, manoeuvred the brute so that the oil and the flame, the smoke and the fire, played over new rocks and new tree trunks.

Gord led the charge.

He turned once, fast. They were stumbling and careering after him. He saw Jorge . . . The Street Boy had the wheelbarrow . . . He saw Zeppo and Harpo and Groucho . . . Eff and Vee and Zed . . . Alex with the dog . . . It was stuck. The left wheel was blocked by a fire-scorched rock and a twisted tree root. He killed the firing lever and the flame died and the oil dribbled short. He had the cart clear.

He ran through the smoke, and through the burned undergrowth and he heard the stampede flight coming after him.

Gord shouted, 'Move it. They'll be behind . . . follow us. We've scattered them, they'll regroup, follow us . . . Hurry, hurry . . .'

Gord ran, driving the cart forward, until his lungs sobbed for rest.

He could not run. His hip would not allow him to run. The Canadian had the machine gun hooked under his arm and took the weight on his bent elbow, and he levered himself forward on the stick. He went through the settling smoke. He saw the soldier's face and it was the body of the soldier that was burned, and it was a young face. He had seen before the faces, in death, of young men that were unmarked except in terror. The ground around him was a carpet of guttering fire and it seemed that it was the cones from the high fir trees of the forest that burned the longest. He saw a soldier who seemed stuck with adhesive to a tree trunk, as if he had cannoned into the trunk and then the fire had caught them together and held them. He could no longer hear them ahead of him. He could not run and they were too far ahead of him. He was beyond the fire and the smoke was behind him. He knew what he would do. He lurched forward, went further, followed the thin wheel marks of the cart and the wide tread of the wheelbarrow, because he was not yet satisfied that he had found the place he looked for. He did not hear so well now, and it was worse after the gunfire, but he had heard clear enough what Gord had shouted . . . The enemy was scattered, would regroup, would follow . . . He could not run, and what Gord had said had seemed damn plain enough.

There was a place where two rocks were close together, big rocks, more than his own height, good granite rocks.

He went through the gap between the rocks and he sank down on his knees. It was a heaven to take the weight from his hip. He chucked the stick behind him, and he extended the bipod legs from underneath the barrel of the machine gun. The rocks gave him good cover and he had taken a position that gave him a fine view down the descent of the hillside and back towards the smoke and the small fires. He hooked the belts and bullets, ball and tracer, off his body and loaded the weapon. It would have been better if he had had the Street Boy with him to feed the belt, but he thought that he could manage alone.

He waited for the troops that had scattered to regroup and then to follow.

The Canadian thought of the Legion Club. He wondered what they would hear, Dave and Bill and Duggie and Hamish. He would have liked to have sat in the bar, been served lager beer by the steward, one last time. One last time he would have liked to have sat under the reproduction paintings of the Lancaster bomber and the Hurricane fighter. One last time he would have liked to have looked into the cabinets that held the old campaign medals and the faded ribbons. One last time he would have liked to have played cribbage with Dave and Bill and Duggie and Hamish.

He saw the first of the soldiers coming up the slope. He squinted down the barrel, over the V sight and the needle sight . . . Gord needed the time . . . He would have liked to have told Dave and Bill and Duggie and Hamish about the Englishman with the flame thrower, and about the young woman with

362

the dog, and about . . . There were three of them now, coming slow. The butt of the machine gun was hard against his shoulder and his finger was tight on the trigger, as it had been when the Cameron Highlanders of Ottawa had closed the Falaise Gap, 21st August in 1944. Of course, they would get round behind him, but not goddamn yet.

The Canadian fired.

It would be good if Miriam gave his medals to the secretary of the Legion Club so that they went into the cabinets on the wall, so that Dave and Bill and Duggie and Hamish could see them. There was the red streak of the tracer, one bullet in four.

They were still running. They were still gasping. They kept the pace.

Away behind was the clatter of the heavy machine gun.

The firing was faint, distant. The firing was short bursts, as the instructors taught on the range. Disciplined short bursts, not panic firing.

They were together. Gord looked at them, into their faces. He had run with the cart. He had not stopped, he had not checked. He had run for his life. He rounded on them.

'Didn't you watch for him?'

Jorge said, 'We were all fighting, Gord, it was not just you that was fighting.'

'Didn't you help him?'

Alex said, 'It is the pain of all of us, Gord, we are all responsible.'

He took the handles of the cart and heaved it forward, away from the diminishing sound of the short bursts of the heavy machine gun.

She came in through the front door of her flat, and she hung her anorak on the hook behind the door. She walked to the answerphone. She put it to Play.

She went into the kitchen. She hated to cook for herself. She was taking margarine from the fridge and a sliced loaf and a square of cheese.

'. . . Hello, my good friend, I'll be quite bereft when I lose your microchip conversation . . . It's confused down there. There's been an action, there are casualties, there's a follow-up sweep . . . My fellow's done rather well to have extracted that much . . . It may be all over, but then it might not . . . Can't tell you what I don't know . . . Don't you dare quote me, but I'm rather rooting for your man . . .'

There was a tomato in the fridge, shrunken like an old face. A cheese and tomato and diet margarine sandwich would be Cathy Parker's tea and dinner. She was cutting the tomato.

'. . . Fuck, a machine . . . Aren't you there? I was with Gord yesterday. A bad corner of Guatemala . . . It's his message . . . It's desperate for him. He needs wings. The Cubans brought him in, they have to bring him out. You're to fix it. Date is 27. Time is 0500 local. Place is 1509 stroke 9052. Christ, I don't know how you do that, get him out. Repeat, 27 hyphen 5 hyphen 1509 stroke 9052 . . .'

She heard the distorted thunder and then the call was cut.

She wrote it, 27-5-1509/9052.

She left the tomato and the cheese and the packet of margarine and the sliced loaf on the kitchen table. She left her front door wide open. She ran for the stairs.


They brought three stretchers from the forest to the cleared place where the helicopters had landed.

Behind the stretcher parties two soldiers dragged a body.

It had come over the radio that a gringo had been killed in the action.

He could just see the legs of the body that was pulled heavy through the long grass from the trees, and the big boots.

There was the fit. It slotted. The beacon signal was way ahead of where they had landed, six miles and might have been more. It made sense to Tom from what he had heard of the briefing by Kramer. Two hours of time had been won. Brown, Gordon Benjamin, would have been looking to win time. He knew they had used the fire and there had been the panic shouts on the radio, but then the fire had gone. It made sense that the flame thrower had been suppressed. But the guy had had a machine gun, and he had had grenades. Brown, Gordon Benjamin, would have stayed back. It had been all over their radio as they had circled. Alpha section joining what was left of Bravo section, then Delta section, then Charlie section. Then 1 platoon linking to 3 platoon and hooked up with the sections of 2 platoon. A shit of a firefight, running two hours, down below the tree canopy, played over the radio to them. One machine gun, and as many grenades as one man could have carried, and first a platoon tied down, and then three platoons held up. And all the time Arturo had been screaming for them to get him flanked, blow the bastard away. He wondered if he would recognize him. From the briefing, it fitted.

There was the boyish smile on Arturo's face and Tom tried to stay cold.

The briefing said that Gord would not have quit.

Tom followed Arturo towards the soldiers who dragged the body.

The briefing said that Gordon Benjamin Brown would have hung around.

They came to the body. The soldiers dropped the ankles of the body and stood back as if they feared their commander. Tom saw Arturo rock. He saw the smile wiped. He came to Arturo's shoulder and he looked down into the long grass, down through the blue and the gold of the wild flowers. A big man and an *old* man. A man who had lived his life. The body had been hit by many rounds of automatic fire, and it was scarred by the erratic pattern of grenade fragments. There was bright-green grass in the snow colour of the body's hair. He had never before seen living the man who was now the body, not when he had been pulled from the desert and into the Land Rover, not when he had shaken the hand and been helped into the casevac bird. The right hand of the body was locked in a closed claw fist and Arturo bent and prised it open and the folded cloth badge fell out from the grip, and Tom saw the badge that might have been worn on a veteran's blazer.

Tom stayed cold.

Just the once Arturo had rocked. He didn't swear and he didn't curse and he didn't stamp.

Arturo said quietly, 'Let's go flying again . . .'

Can't we do it?'

'Most certainly we cannot.'

'We have people in Belize, could put a helicopter in.'

'And start a war, no . . .'

Cathy Parker blazed, 'They've bugger all else to do . . .'

He had been about to go home. There was a nice little beat on the Wylye waiting for Percy Martins when he drove down to Wiltshire in the morning, and he needed the evening to prepare his flies and wax his lines. He had been into his coat when the front desk had rung upstairs, and he had said he would be there directly. She might have run all the way from Battersea, and across the bridge. He took her arm and manoeuvred her out through the swing door. They stood on the pavement.

'What would you have me do? Would you care to give me a pair of your knickers? Shall I send them recorded delivery to RAF, Belize City? Should they tie them to the radio aerial of a Lynx filled with desperadoes from the Special Air Service? Should we invade Guatemalan sovereign airspace and commence the War of Cathy's Knickers? . . . We will do what he asked us to do, and that, young lady, is a hell of a way over the top.'

He hailed a taxi.

Was the cabbie a complete fool? Didn't every cabbie in London know the new north London address of Cuba's delegation, moved from Belgravia back in the last year over the rotten matter of shortage of funds? He thought her a quite lovely young woman. He reckoned that if she had been in Belize, with or without her knickers, she'd have hijacked a bloody Lynx and God protect the sentry who tried to stop her. Quite lovely, and rather loving . . . He knew what they called him on the fifth floor, he had heard it through the door, the little creeps from their redbrick colleges called him That Pompous Shit . . . He would

366

not be pompous with Cathy Parker who was quite lovely, not be a shit with Cathy Parker who was rather loving. He felt a little younger, as young as he had been when he had presented a marksman's rifle to the former Prime Minister, and talked through the sniping of a Palestinian in the fastness of the Beqa'a valley of east Lebanon. And he would feel younger, too, when the word seeped down the antiseptic and plastic-coated corridors of Vauxhall Bridge Road that Percy Martins had tweaked the Yankee nose, prised open a Guatemalan gin trap, snatched back a rather useful young man.

He turned to her. Direct. 'Would I like him?'

She tried to smile. 'He's not easy.'

'What would I talk to him about?'

'He doesn't have small talk.'

'Him and me, train carriage, King's Cross to Edinburgh?'

'You'd need a good book, or a sack of newspapers. Wouldn't open his mouth.'

Trying harder. 'Could I take him fishing, take him to Twickenham?'

'If he went fishing it would be on his own. He reckons team sports are for inadequate people.'

'Hobbies . . . ? Is he a covert French polisher? Is he a dab hand oboist?'

It was a truer smile, but sad. 'Actually, there's nothing.'

'Forgive me, my dear, but what the hell was the basis of your relationship, if that's not overly impertinent?'

'Danger. The common bond was risk to life, limb, all that rubbish. I always felt so safe when he was watching for me. What did we talk about? Not a lot. Well, we talked technical, the job, personal security.' Her fingers pummelled a small linen handkerchief. 'He's not very good at talking, not very good at impressing strangers nor very interested.'

'So, when the danger ran out and he seemed rather boring, you ditched . . .'

'Something like that. I suppose he was useful when it suited me, useless when it didn't.'

'I think, my dear, old Rudyard captured it . . .

'I went into a public-'ouse to get a pint o' beer, The publican 'e
up an' sez "We serve no redcoats here."
    The girls be'ind the bar they laughed an' giggled fit to die,
    I outs into the street again an' to myself sez I:
    Oh, it's Tommy this, an' Tommy that, an' "Tommy, go
away"; But it's "Thank you, Mister Atkins," when the band
begins to play—
    The band begins to play, my boys, the band begins to play,
    Oh, it's "Thank you, Mister Atkins," when the band begins
to play.'

'. . . Most would say that I have absolutely no understanding of
the human race, but that prejudice is not entirely accurate. Well,
let's not look only at the dark side.'

They stopped. It was an unlovely street. Peeling facade, not
enough paint on the windows' woodwork, and the brass identi-
fication plaque needed polish and elbow effort. No, it had not
been his intention, but she seemed to be faster to her purse than
he was to his wallet.

She paid off the taxi.

He gave her a name.

'That's the man you want. Hidden away in the Military
Attaché's office, lowly title, but he's the intelligence guru . . . No,
no, I don't come in, no. Sorry, but it's up to you.' He had his
hand across his face. It went with the job, knowing which
window, above the Italian restaurant down the far side of the
street, housed the remote Five camera that surveyed the Cubans'
doorstep. He walked away from the camera. No bit of a woman
had ever made waves to save Percy Martins' neck, and no bloody
woman ever would. Better to let her have her head, but he could
not imagine that even the Cubans would be so stupid as to fly
into a roused hornet's nest in Guatemala. No, not even the
dumb Cubans . . . But kinder to let her have her head.

*   *   *

The coming engine drone, she heard the approach of the heli-copter.

She heard it and they all heard it. The helicopter was homing in on them from behind.

She was at the back and they had all stopped and they had all turned. All of their faces turned to her, shock and anger and despair, looking past her towards the sound of the helicopter . . . Bloody men, useless . . . They had just crossed a river. When it had been raining they would not have been able to make the crossing, but the water had gone down. They were all soaked to their waists and steaming in the day heat. She had crossed the river with Gord, helped him to get the cart across, and then gone back to help the Street Boy with the wheelbarrow. After the battle he was quiet, after the Canadian had gone it was as if the spirit had gone from Gord. He seemed, now, to sag in despair.

Bloody men. He had said he could not think. He had said he was too tired to think. Idiot bloody men.

She saw it on the faces of all of them, shock and anger and despair, as the helicopter quartered the airspace above them, closed in on them. Stupid bloody men . . .

She elbowed her way past them. She stood in front of them. The dog sat at her leg.

Alex snapped, 'Look.'

She took off her quilted coat. She took off her sweater and dropped it beside the quilted coat. She took off the once white T-shirt and it fell onto her sweater and the quilted coat.

'Idiots, look.'

She unlaced her boots and kicked them off. She bent and unpeeled her socks and threw them down. She unfastened the belt of her jeans and dragged down the zip and pulled the jeans off her thighs and shins. She looked them hard in the eyes. They were rooted. She pushed down her pants and wriggled them from her ankles.

'Fools, look . . .'

She stood naked in front of them.

'. . . And I am clean, and one of you is not.'

369

Only the sound of the approach of the helicopter.

She pointed to Gord. It was the order. The machine gun off his shoulder, the belt ammunition off his chest, the camouflage tunic off his body, and the shirt and the vest. The boots off him and the trousers and the socks, and the pants. She saw the pale of his body and the sores of the insect bites and the scars of the thorn scratches and the bare flatness of his stomach.

'Clean . . .' She pointed to Jorge. 'You, strip . . .' She fixed on the Street Boy. 'You, get on with it . . .' To the Indians. 'You and you and you. Best you can, help each other . . .'

And the one that Gord called Zeppo, and the one that Gord called Harpo. She looked into the face of the one that Gord called Groucho. She saw the pleading. All of them doing as they were told, bloody men. The clothes piling, the weapons heaped. The helicopter banked over them. She had the strength and she knew what she would find. She walked amongst them and some blushed and some turned away. Bloody Gord understood, and about bloody time that he understood . . .

The man that Gord called Groucho was the last.

Trembling hands at his coat buttons. Flickering fingers at his trousers.

The men had moved around him. They stood naked in a circle around Groucho. There was no escape for him. The shape protruded on his belly underneath his vest. She willed herself to watch. She felt the blow of the light wind on her breasts and the warmth of the sun on her stomach. The tears ran on Groucho's face. His trousers fell to his knees. The helicopter hovered over them. He pulled the vest so slowly up to his armpits. It was exposed. The thin strap, lying across an old appendix scar, had made a cruel weal against his skin. The strap held a small black painted box that was the size of a packet of cigarettes.

There was the cluster of naked bodies bent over Groucho. She turned away from the heave of the buttocks over Groucho, away from the pummelling fists.

Gord, savage and quiet, dressed.

Alex vomited.

# 19

On a string, like a grinder's monkey, they took Groucho with them. The string was to his bound wrists and there was a further length of string tied to each of his ankles that was enough to let Groucho take fast short steps, like a chained circus bear. They had been gone ahead for a half of the hour before the rest halt when Gord caught the group. Alex pushed the cart and the Street Boy had the wheelbarrow. Ahead of Alex and the Street Boy were Zeppo and Harpo and Groucho, and Harpo held the string. Eff and Vee and Zed kept the pace, and they would not last a great distance further, and struggled to help each other. Jorge, leading set the speed of the march. Gord caught them and he took the cart.

They would not do it without him.

When he rejoined them, when he took the cart handles from Alex, Groucho had turned. Gord had seen the face of Groucho. He had seen the split lip and the tooth gap and the closing puffed eye, and then Groucho had been jerked forward by the string. They, all of them, knew what would be done, and they would not do it without Gord.

Groucho had been one with them, he had shared with them and fought with them, and he belonged to them . . . Gord knew, they all knew, that sharing and fighting and belonging did not add to mercy . . . Groucho had been told the date and the time and the place, he could not be turned loose. They went forward. Gord checked his watch and saw the minutes that remained to the next rest halt . . . Groucho had whimpered it, while the vengeance beating of Harpo and Zeppo had split his lip and broken his tooth and closed his eye, the reason. For a daughter

371

that he had not seen for eleven years, for a young woman hanging by the ankle from a ceiling beam, he had broken the march, destroyed the dream. Gord had no thought of mercy.

The trees were thinner. The obstacles to speed were fewer.

Once he had shot a man in Ireland.

They had to cut round cleared fields where the land was bare and ploughed and waiting for the first sprout of the maize crop. They cut round the fields and they skirted the village. Dogs in the village barked and Alex had shifted the weight of the machine gun she carried so that she could rest her hand, soothing, on the nape of the neck of her dog. The trees were thinner because it was part of the forest where the people of the village would have come to gather wood, and where their pigs had routed out the undergrowth in the food search.

Once Gord had shot a man in Ireland. At the arms cache. In the dead of the night, after forty-two hours of waiting for him to come. The flare bursting light over the man bent over the excavated earth of the fox den where the RPG-7 was stored. A man frozen in shock as the flare had glowed above him. It had been the instinct of the man, for preservation, to throw down the pistol from his belt. Gord had seen him throw down the pistol. Gord had killed him, three aimed shots, three aimed hits. He had told the army investigators, and his corporal had backed him, and told the police detectives, that the pistol had spiralled away from the man's hand as the first bullet had hit him. What he had told the detectives and the investigators had gone onto the statement they had prepared for him, that he had signed. He had felt nothing, and taken a mug of sugared tea after the statement was signed, and gone back to his billet in the Lisburn barracks and slept well.

He could shoot a man, if it was expected of him, and feel nothing. Gord called the halt.

They sat amongst the thinned trees. He could shoot a man who had shared and fought and belonged, and who had destroyed the dream.

Jorge would not look at Groucho who had been the friend of his father. Jorge sat with his back to Groucho, and Harpo had let

372

go the string and put himself with Jorge and Zeppo. The Indians went into the trees and made their own group, and led the Street Boy with them.

Gord squatted on one side of Groucho, and Alex was on the other side of the man condemned. There would be three minutes for the rest halt.

Groucho talked.

'A rotten life, wasted. I don't know which was the greater waste, the life before Ramírez or the life with Ramírez in the triangle or the life of exile or the life of believing that we could win against them. You see, Gord, it was a terrible arrogance that made the life a waste. It was the arrogance of believing that a small and elderly man, a frightened man, could make his mark upon the world. I leave no mark, I leave no trace of my existence. At the ultimate moment, when I was challenged, I was just the small and elderly and frightened man, and I broke, and the delusion of importance that I had harboured was cracked. I was, as I had always been, nothing . . .'

The second hand of his watch raced, the minute hand jerked.

Gord had his arm around Groucho's shoulder and he gripped the sharp bone.

'. . . And nobody *cares*, Gord. It was left to me who is small and elderly and frightened, to try to shout in the night that there is injustice and evil in my country. Why don't they care, Gord? Where are they, those who should care? Why is it left to me who is weak to try to shout when those that have power do not care? The men who have power, how can they sleep in their beds and know that injustice is not punished, that evil is not checked? The great men in Washington and Moscow have abandoned us. The great men in Mexico City and London and Madrid and Paris have betrayed us. How can there be hope when the great men turn away, wash their hands, feel no responsibility? It is not right that only the small and the elderly and the frightened should carry the weight of the burden of responsibility. For them it would be so easy, for us it is so hard . . .'

The second hand moving and the minute hand jerking. Alex

cradled Groucho's head and held the cheek of his face against her chest, and gave him love.

'. . . I do not feel the fear, Gord, any longer. The fear is gone. I do not blame them because they beat me. They beat me because they would have done the same as I did, it was natural that they should beat me. I blame only the great men who do not care. We were out of our time, Gord. The new world of the great men is a world of self-interest, it is a world where the man who is small and elderly and frightened, and without power, can be ignored. I am of the old world where the struggle of man for his freedom is noble, and the repression of that freedom is heresy. Perhaps I do not wish to live any longer in the new world of the great men . . . Mine was only a small shout in the night and not heard. Do not let them sleep sweet. Wake the great men in their beds, Gord . . .'

The second hand had raced, the minute hand had jerked.

Gord called the end of the rest halt.

He went to Jorge and Jorge passed him the Kalashnikov rifle. He remembered the banter talk in the Land Rover, Frank and Vernon and Zachary. Always the joke talk, crap gallows humour, when the going was bad. He was never a part of the joke talk of 'Eff' and 'Vee' and 'Zed'. Zachary, 'Zed', had had the old book, dog-eared and dirt-stained, had it until the book had disintegrated but by then they had known the joke talk lines by heart. Always the joke talk lifted them when the going was worst.

*'Any club that would accept me as a member I wouldn't want to join.'*

Gord cocked the rifle.

Groucho ducked his head, exposed the back of his skull, and his eyes were open.

*'A man's only as old as the woman he feels.'*

Gord was close to him.

Alex pushed the cart away, followed Jorge and the group.

*'My mother loved children – she would have given anything if I'd been one.'* Thanks, Groucho. Thanks, Mr Marx. Thanks to

Francis and Vernon and Zachary for the crap joke lines when the going was worst.

Gord fired the single shot.

There was the clattered panic call of a pheasant in flight . . .

Tom had been asked, and he had given the advice.

'You tell them to stay back, stay right back.'

And it was the order that Arturo had relayed, that they should stay back, right back.

It had been more than a mile from the place that Tom was able to set down. There had been light scrub there and the troops had cleared an LZ for them. They were a mile from the beacon transmission point. They were guided from the LZ through the tree forest. He thought Arturo had been good. There had been commanders down in the Gulf who had snapped, gone haywire, when the balloon had punctured. Back in St Louis, the bossman on the surveillance team watching an out-of-state trafficker had blown his head when the team had shown out. There were some for winning and some for losing, and bawling for Mom didn't trip losing into winning. Arturo, from the air, had co-ordinated well the follow-up after they had cleared up the old guy with the badge in his hand. Hard for Arturo, when the ambush had failed, not to have blown his head or snapped. He'd done well . . . They reached the place.

So still and so calm and so silent.

They were good troops and disciplined. Bad troops would have gone right in for it.

It was slung from a tree branch. The strap was looped over the branch and the beacon box hung below. Too still and too calm and too silent. They all went on the course. Escape and Evasion. He had been on the one-week course a year and nine months before going down to the Gulf. Only half a day of the week had been about Evasion (Delay). Half a day given up to the tactic of delaying a follow-up force of troops in hostile territory. He pointed to the colonel's Uzi and he held out his hand for it. Arturo passed it. He armed it. He waved them all down and he lay on his stomach and he aimed at the black painted box. He fired . . . fucking missed. The echo of the shot died amongst the trees. On the ground, around him, the troops giggled, like that was good sport from a gringo. Tom was twenty-five paces from the tree. He fired again, and missed again. Arturo took the weapon. Arturo made the shot. It was as if the box had been kicked. The box, split open, leaped and fell and swung. So still. The giggle again around him. So calm. He had his hand on Arturo's shoulder, that he should not move. So silent. He counted.

The explosion came from across the path.

The blast hit their ears.

The shrapnel sang above them.

A good one from Gord, what he would have expected of Gordon Benjamin Brown. The fine string had been laid from the box and held taut up the strap and then hooked to the branch and then run down the tree trunk to a stone that weighted the string tight before the run to the grenade. It was pretty near to what they had taught at the half-day for Evasion (Delay) . . . Then watching Arturo. Arturo was on his hands and his knees and going forward and moving down the faint lines of the wheels' track.

It was a length of vine.

The vine was forty yards, near enough, from where the box had been hung. From where Tom was, the vine seemed to lie casual across the wheels' track. He went to Arturo who was kneeling short of the vine. Only when he was close to it could he see that the string was woven round the length of the vine. He felt the chill. No giggling now from the troops, no more fun from the gringo games, like they knew it was for fucking real . . .

Tom called for a length of rope, and when it was brought him, he tied the end of the rope to the vine. He crawled back, paying out the rope, never allowing tension in it. He saw they all lay on their stomachs. He jerked the rope.

The grenade blast gouged resined holes in the tree across the path, level with where a man's stomach would have been.

It was the right stuff, it was Evasion (Delay) done by a man who cared to be expert.

They went slow.

They found the body.

The dusk was coming to the forest trees. The presence of Gord chilled him. It was no place to be in darkness. He felt the power of Gordon Benjamin Brown. He thought of the string that had been wrapped to the strap and the string that had been gathered along a length of vine. He remembered when he had seen the face of the body, fear-filled, pulled onto the helicopter . . . the murdering bastard, Gordon Benjamin Brown . . . He was a part of it, dragged to it, Gord's war. He could not hide from it.

He shivered. He could see the wheel tracks of the flame thrower winding away into the trees. He thought that he had crossed the line. Searching for the new family had carried him somehow across the line, new loyalties claiming him.

'Let's get the hell out.'

Arturo said, 'Does he frighten you?'

'We'll go get the shit in the morning, and hit him.'

He wanted to be with her, close to her.

The dog was between them and the shoulders and the ears of the dog brushed against their legs.

He needed to know.

'You were wonderful with him. You gave him the strength. Because of you he went calm and he went proud. It was your strength, Alex . . .'

Her hand dropped to the dog's head. Her fingers locked in the coat of the dog's neck. He thought she choked. It would have been good for her if she had wept.

'. . . Where was the strength from, Alex?'

And again there was the head thrown back and the hair flying from across her forehead, and she blinked her eyes and seemed to cough. He thought that she had killed the chance of tears.

She said it flat. 'When I was thirteen, fussed over by Mummy, drooled over by Daddy, spoiled brat. Gymkhanas and Pony

Clubs. I had this little piebald, very calm. Round where we lived, Somerset, there was plenty of safe riding, off the road. I used to go out on my own, hard hat and jacket and blouse and jodhpurs, looking a proper fool. Are we getting there? Probably it was a rabbit hole. At the canter. Winston broke his leg. We were out in a hardwood plantation. It wasn't till dark that my mother went to panic state. There were five hours of darkness before I was found . . .'

He walked beside her, and took her hand.

'There was nothing wrong with me, just bruises. For five hours I held Winston's head before the torches came and the shouting. They didn't seem that bothered about Winston, and they wanted to take me away because it would be a long time before they could get a vet there to do the necessary. I screamed at them, every foul word that they didn't think their lovely little daughter, aged thirteen, would have known. It was put down to hysteria, but they backed off . . .'

His head was lowered. They went together, slow.

'I stayed until the vet came and put that sweet animal beyond pain . . . Bit young, don't you think, to lose your childhood at thirteen, yes? I loved that horse more than I loved my mother and my father . . . Well, that's a happy little story, isn't it?'

'Thank you for telling me, sharing.'

Alex laughed, shrill. 'Cliché of the day. You can buy strength, but at a hell of a price.'

When the sun was on the sea, slanting over the low islands of the Cayería las Cayamas, hovering above the slight waves, the signal reached the base.

The base commander read the signal that had been taken from the teleprinter, and he grimaced in surprise. He telephoned to the ministry, made it his business to speak personally to a major in air force intelligence to gain irrefutable confirmation of the order carried in the signal.

It was the dog day of the regime. It was the time when the regime bent to the circumstances of the new order. It was explained to him curtly ... Confrontation gone, independence lost, the knee bent ... a last throw. The base commander asked his orderly to bring him the pilot. Never again, not afterwards, the major had said, would such madness be repeated. The flight was ordered at the highest echelon of government. The final moment of madness from the 'old man' ...

After it was dark, after the sun had slipped on the Golfo de Batabanó, the orderly reported to the base commander that the pilot could not be found, gone fishing.

They made a camp by the swirl of a clean river pool.

Gord said they should all sleep.

They had no food.

Gord said that he would take the watch.

He started, alone, to refill the tubes on the cart.

Zeppo came to stand close to him, big and awkward. Harpo was behind Zeppo, hovering.

Zeppo said, subdued, 'I could not have done it, we could not have done it. He was our friend ...'

Gord scowled, gave them nothing.

'... I knew him, we knew him, like he was a brother. I feel the shame, we both feel the shame, because we kicked him and beat him when he was identified, that was what we did to our friend, our brother. You gave him love and we gave him nothing ...'

Gord stared back, brutal and cold.

'... Where he stood, I could have been standing, we could have been standing. We know that and we feel the shame ... We feel the greater shame because of what we have said to you, because we have not helped you. You have promised to take us out, and we believe you. We believe you because we understand that you are the only possibility we have of living ...'

Gord began, mechanical, to sort the tube lengths from the air cylinder in the wheelbarrow.

'... He spoke a great truth, the father of Rodolfo Jorge Ramírez, when he said that we should take a fighting man ... I ask for forgiveness, we ask for forgiveness.'

Gord was fastening the tubes.

They went away from him, clumsy and noisy, as the dusk darkness settled through the trees.

It was the birds that woke the Street boy.

There was the crashing of the birds in the trees above him and their screams. He could see the chase of the monkeys that had disturbed the birds. He loathed the place, and he had not slept as he did on the pavements near the big hotels of Guatemala City. The streets and the pavements and his friends, that was his freedom. The forest was his prison. He wanted again to feel the freedom . . . He had dreamed in the night of being with his friends and circling the tourists and watching for the opportunity, and he had dreamed of the excitement of running into the dark alleys behind the hotels when the police cars cruised by, and always in the dream he escaped from the police . . . They treated him like a child. The Street Boy did not believe he was a child. They treated him like a child and they had shielded his eyes when the man was shot dead. He pushed the wheelbarrow, he took his place, and they had no right to treat him as a child. He had heard the way that they talked, if the plane came, about a return to Havana . . . He thought Havana would be shit. From what they said, there was nothing for him in Havana, no tourists and no watches and wallets and no AmEx and Diners Club cards and no traveller's cheques. He craved the excitement again of hunting with his friends on the pavements of Guatemala City, and it had not been *excitement* when he had taken the wheelbarrow at the run through the ambush . . . No excitement, just terror, and he had wet his trousers as he had run, and he thought Gord knew that he had wet himself . . . They should not have shot the man. The man had been kind to him, the man had given him sweets and chocolate that had been taken from the camp at Nebaj and the barracks at Santa Cruz del Quiché. He would have much to tell his friends on the pavements of Guatemala City. He watched Gord. He was not sure whether Gord was awake or whether Gord slept. He would have liked to have taken Gord to Guatemala City . . . They would not let him go in the day, but it was not until he had dreamed that he had determined to break out from the prison that was the forest. They would not let him go because he knew the place where the plane would land and the time. The man who had given him the sweets and the chocolate had known the place and the time, and the man had been shot for his knowledge. He would go at the end of the day . . . and he would take the Kalashnikov with the folding stock. When he was back, on the pavements of Guatemala City, then he would show his friends the Kalashnikov and they would know that he spoke the truth of what he had seen.

Heh, a Kalashnikov would make him the king amongst his friends . . .

They found the pilot at first light on the beach.

He had made a fire between rounded sea-washed stones. The best fish that he had taken in the night, on a hand line with feathers, was the barracuda. He had made the spit, himself, in the garage behind his home, and he turned the gutted fish slowly over the wood fire and the smoke. It was what he always did when he went for the night's fishing, take the best and grill it for himself and eat it before going home with the rest of his catch. It was the best place to be, alone in the boat and out on the sea, away from the fantasy success of Havana, rubbish city.

He took the message.

The pilot was to report immediately to the base commander.

He finished turning the fish until the lifeless skin had peeled and fallen hissing into the fire. He ate the rich oiled meat of the fish until he was gorged. He threw what was left of the fish to the boldest gulls that had strutted close to him. He kicked out the fire. He checked the ropes that held the boat on the beach and then he went home and he gave his wife the fish that would be shared between his own household and his mother and her mother. His wife told him that she had heard that there was a shop in the old city, the rubbish city, that had soap. The pilot drove his wife to the shop and left her in the queue that had formed.

He reported to his base commander.

He was not asked, he was not permitted to evaluate the possibility of it, it was an order.

The day was tomorrow. The time was 0500 local. The coordinates of the location were 1509/9052.

It was found for him on the map, 1509/9052, at Canillá. It was not known what would be there . . . Landing lights? A grass strip? The military? How many to collect? There were no answers, the shrug of ignorance, but an order. The base commander was a Party member. The father of base commander had fought with the 'old man' in the Sierra Maestra mountains, and the uncle of the base commander had been with the 'old man' in the attack on the Moncada barracks at Santiago de Cuba. It would not have benefited the pilot to dispute a piss awful order. The pilot said that he would not require a navigator to fly with him, and that was his way of expressing an opinion on a piss awful order.

He went to the hangar.

She had not been repainted since he had brought her back. He walked in the darkened hangar around Echo Foxtrot. She was still black-coated and anonymous without markings. A beauty in her gaunt ugliness. He asked the supervisor of the maintenance technicians to work on the engines, and he asked for additional fuel tanks, and he told them at what time the work must be completed.

He went home again, to sleep. His wife was not yet back from the soap queue in the old rubbish city. The pilot would not tell her, when she returned, that he would be flying through the night into Guatemala.

He played good tennis. He came from the baseline to the net, and he could get back to take her lob when she retrieved his smash shot. He ran her ragged. When he played his best tennis, early in the morning after he had killed in the night, he had to scheme to permit her, at the end, to win.

The lieutenant, codename Benedicto, who had killed a young woman in the night with a pistol shot into the temple of her forehead, manufactured a twisted ankle as an excuse to lose. Only when he was losing, when the spark had gone from his game, did the crowd that had gathered start to disperse. Many had watched, but then there were many more back at the club than there had been the week before, back from Miami and Orlando, back from Houston, back from Los Angeles.

The fear of the rat mob swarming the streets of the capital city was buried, and he had played his part in the burying.

When she had taken the victory he walked to his fiancée and a warm smile played at his mouth, and he shook her hand in respect. It was what her father and mother liked to see as they took their breakfast against the plate window above the court. Only straggled ends now remained to be tied. The young woman had died because of what she had known and what she had seen and what she could have said. The lieutenant's was a war without surviving witnesses. Before he showered he went inside to the breakfast room and he took a glass of orange juice with his fiancée's parents, and he politely asked her father what was the price of beef up north in the burger trade.

Later, he would go back to the basement files of the G-2, Intelligence, and he would browse that he could better tie the ends.

They were supine. He thought none of them had slept well. He thought that in the quiet of the night they, each of them, would have lingered on the memory of Groucho, and Groucho's killing. No food for them. Again, Gord took charge.

They started beside the river. Gord led and they followed. He took them a full hundred paces up the bank of the river and he made the cart go through the ground where there was still wet mud from the old rain. The cart left good tracks on either side of their boot marks.

He waded into the water. The height of the flow was above his ankles and below his knee and the water washed the axle of the cart. He waved the Street Boy to follow him and the wheelbarrow made a boat, easy to manoeuvre. They came in after him. They dared not question him. He could see it in their faces, Jorge disputing the need for the cart, Harpo challenging the need for the wheelbarrow with the compressed air cylinder and the fuel, Zeppo ridiculing the further need for the fire . . . and they dared not speak it. The cart was his. The cart was power.

He stood in the water and they splashed around him and the dog careered after a floating leaf.

'I have to have the big effort. It is today, the next hour, that we either break free of them or we fail. I must have the big effort. I don't have the time, I don't have the patience, to explain everything that we will do . . . I have said that I will get you to a strip and if I have the big effort then I will achieve that . . . I have to hope that the plane will come to the strip, *hope*, but we will be there. If the plane comes then you will be going out. I don't care if you never walk, run, another yard after today, but you will walk today and you will run today. I don't care if you never lift anything again heavier than a beer glass, but you will lift weight today. I make a promise to you . . . If you don't want to run and lift weight today then go to the bank and sit on it and wait for the Kaibiles to come. And I promise, within twelve hours of them coming and taking you, you will be screaming for the chance to walk, run, and lift weight. For one more day we have to lose them, if we don't lose them . . .'

They depended on him. Gord was the straw they clutched at. They would follow him.

He dragged the cart wheels over the river stones and Zeppo helped him, and Harpo carried Gord's machine gun and Zeppo's machine gun, and Jorge directed the front of the buoyant wheelbarrow, and Alex carried Eff and Zed helped Vee. He took the cart down the river and they were straggled after him. Where they had gone up along the bank they now came down the river.

They were an hour in the river.

Gord called the rest halt.

They stood in the water and they gasped, and each of them had fallen, and each of them was grazed from the cold rock. Jorge was close to Alex. He said something to her, and there was a quiet smile on his face, and she laughed gently back at him. He could not hear what was said, what made her laugh. When had he last seen the quiet smile of Jorge? When had he ever heard the gentle laugh of Alex? They were the pretty young man and the pretty young woman. It was instant, the stab pain of jealousy . . . Alex had loved him and Alex had never laughed with him . . . It was a moment. He clawed the breath down into his lungs. The water was deeper. It was a place where a rib of stone ran into the flow of the river, cascading it. It was the stone that he wanted. All his strength to move the cart out of the river's flow and to draw it up onto the rib of stone, and again Gord's strength to help the Street Boy and Jorge lift the wheelbarrow onto the sliding surface of the stone. He told Alex, curtly, that first she must get the Indian onto the stone and then she must lift her dog onto the stone, the dog's footclaws must not scrabble in the bank of mud at the side of the rib of stone. They were gathered precariously on the stone and he snapped the instructions at them.

He would lead, and now he would carry Eff. Where his feet went their feet should go, exactly where his foot went.

Alex should carry her dog. The footclaws of her dog were not to touch the ground.

Jorge and Zeppo and Harpo were to carry the cart, 370 pounds' weight. The wheels of the cart were not to make tracks.

The Street Boy and Zed were to carry the wheelbarrow. Vee was to be at the back and what marks they left he should obliterate.

'Questions . . . ?'

Jorge asked, unsure, 'When will we know if we have lost them?'

Gord said, cruel, 'When the plane has landed, when there is no ground fire, when there are no helicopters, when the plane has lifted out, that is when we will know we have lost them.'

He loosened the straps of his backpack, so that it was low down over his haunches. He should have changed the field dressing and the face of Eff was greying and the breathing slower, and the flies swarmed at the wound. He heaved him up so that his belly was laid across the top of the backpack and he hooked his arms under the shoulder and under the groin of the man. It was the man who had brought the attaché case with the photographs into the bar beside the sea loch. It was the man who had smashed him down. 'What is the price of freedom? What is the cost of honour?' Gord swayed. He took the first step forward. Onto a stone. He staggered. Onto thin moss. Onto hard ground. Gord rocked. Onto a fallen branch that would not break. They followed him . . . He saw the pain of their faces as they cursed the dead weight of the cart . . . Stone to moss to hard ground to branch to stone . . . He was looking back. Vee was squatted on the rib of stone, one good leg, fuck knew what gangrene dirt was settling in one bad leg, and was wiping the stone dry with a cloth, like he was an old woman cleaning a front step.

Going slow, and going forward, and turning again and looking past them and seeing Vee spread dead leaves over each foot place.

There was a helicopter above, quartering and searching, but not the hound that tracks a scent. The helicopter had no trail to follow.

It was all that Gord could offer.

'I have lost them.'

Arturo said it into the face microphone.

Tom stared down into the tree canopy. Arturo had said it crisp. There were no excuses and no explanations. Tom raked the stretching tree canopy and saw nothing.

The distorted voice, 'Wait out.'

The Kaibiles had found the place where the group had slept, and they had found the track of the cart that carried the flame thrower, and the other wheel and foot marks. The Kaibiles had followed the trail along the bank of the river to the place where they had gone down into the water, and there they had lost the group.

Below him, under the trees and in the scrub, invisible from the air, were three companies of the Kaibil battalion. Below him, unseen from the air, was the struggling and running group . . . He thought of them in the Country Attaché's office. He wondered if they would have requested that another flier be brought in. He imagined them, the Intelligence Analyst and the Treasurer and the Chemist and the Liaison major from SouthCom, sitting with their coffees on the low easy chairs in the Country Attaché's room. And spread on the low table in front of their knees would be budget assessments and satellite telephone call intercepts and radio transcripts, and the big maps that marked the landing strips on the *fincas* that were red-ringed and believed to be transshipment points . . . They were irrelevant to Tom Schultz. He turned the bird. He went back over ground they had already quartered. Only his Huey bird in the air. As if he had made it his territory. Better alone. If there had been other birds up then the search would have been diffused and that way there was the probability of confusion. He had drawn the squares on the map and he worked over each square . . . They meant not a shit to him, the Country Attaché and the Intelligence Analyst and the Treasurer and the Chemist and the Liaison major from South-Com. He had tried to belong and he had failed . . .

The radio sparked in his ear.

'So, you have lost them, Arturo, brilliant, incredible. All shit promises, all shit talk. You asked for control, you were given control, and you have let them slip . . . You are all shit, Arturo. Should I, again, change the command of the battalion, Arturo? I have to go to the Chief of Staff, do I tell him Arturo is shit, should I tell him I was wrong to back you? Should I . . . ?'

Beside him, Arturo snapped the switch, cut the transmission.

. . . He had failed. They were irrelevant to him because he did not care whether Mother America was awash in smack, coke, crack. He did not care to fight a losing war against the dealers and the pushers and the traffickers of heroin, marijuana, cocaine . . .

Soft in his ear, Arturo said, 'Can you think like him? I cannot . . .'

He wanted only to hit the man. He hated the man. Each morning when he woke, faced another day, he thought of the man. The man dangled him. The man led him on a string. It was the same string that had fallen loose from the wrist of the body that he had seen. The man had the power over him, the man had saved him. He hated the man because the debt was unpaid, not even paid with a letter of gratitude.

'. . . think like him. What would he do?'

He hated the man that he thought of each morning when he woke.

Victory company and Defence company were held back from the river. 1 platoon and 3 platoon waited by the river. Alpha section of 2 platoon went upstream on the east bank of the river, and Bravo section went upstream on the west bank. Charlie section moved downstream on the west bank, and Delta section were downstream on the east bank. The men of each section crawled on their elbows and on their knees.

They moved as the order had been given to them from their officer in the helicopter. Their heads were inches from the ground. They were to lift each loose leaf. Their eyes squinted in concentration. They were to test each fallen branch. For twenty yards each side of the river, upstream and downstream, east bank and west bank, they searched.

There was a stone. Beside the small stone, under where the leaves had been scattered, was the mark of half of the heel of a shoe. The tooth grin broke on the muddied face of the soldier. He shouted. The corporal came to him. The corporal shouted for the sergeant of Delta section. The sergeant of Delta section shouted for the officer of 2 platoon. The officer ran across the width of the river.

\* \* \*

Arturo listening and first the smile and then the smile draining.

'It is the one mark. It is half of a shoe's heel. There are Indians with them, the vermin would wear shoes. But it is one mark. They can find nothing else . . .'

The sun was behind them. Tom stayed cold. The sun was dipping towards the Volcán de Fuego and the Volcán de Agua. He hated the man, cold hate each day that he woke, who carried the chit for the debt.

'Don't you have dogs? Can't you put dogs in? With dogs you can follow them through the night.'

'Was it convenient for you to come?' Percy Martins asked.

She shrugged. 'I'm here.'

'I'm not a popular man in this building.' He paused. 'You see, I'm out of my time. Well, it's not the occasion for me to be trawling for sympathy. What I'm trying to say, and it is remarkably rare for me, I am bothered about your man . . .'

He led her away from the front desk, away from the men who brought him the foul machine coffee, past the gum-chewing and leather-jacketed security fellows. They walked onto the bridge and the crowds of hurrying office workers and shop assistants flowed against them.

'. . . I couldn't abide to speak to that silly damn machine again. You want to know, my dear, what the news is. The news is both good and bad. No point gilding anything, too late for that, and you deserve to have it straight . . .'

She laughed, cold. She tensed. 'Let's get the good news out of the way.'

He tucked his gloved hand into the crook of her elbow, as if she was his niece. It was not important to her. She could smell the sharp marmalade on his breath and there were toast crumbs meshed in the brush of his moustache.

'Your message went through. Remarkable, but they haven't changed their cryptology for three years, doesn't give us any trouble. It went through verbatim . . . Can't say what they'll do with it at their end, Havana, but it was fine leaving us, right . . . ?'

He tried to make a little joke of it, and she thought he wouldn't have known a bad joke if it had bitten him. She could feel the clutch of his fingers on her arm. The pity of it was that she needed the old fart . . . It was ostentation, in her opinion, the way he smacked the tip of the furled umbrella on the paving. She took the big breath.

'And the bad news . . . ?'

He gabbed. 'They were ambushed. They were only a small group, when we last heard. They were ambushed by troops of the Kaibil battalion. They burned their way through. He has a flame thrower, it's a hideous weapon, and he scorched a path through the ambush . . . I've a very good man reporting to me, excellent contacts . . . He tells me there is a father and mother of an inquest in the High Command as to how your man was able to break the ambush. But that's not really the point, is it?'

She looked into the drawn face of Percy Martins, into the eyes that were furtive. The wind off the river snatched at his hair. 'What is the point?'

'They've had contact, the Kaibil battalion, and after contact there will be close pursuit. It will be close pursuit right to the landing strip. It will leave them vulnerable. Do I make myself plain, Miss Parker?'

She felt the shudder in her body. She took his hand from her arm, broke the grip. She strode away from him.

'Stay close to your telephone tomorrow, there's a dear girl . . .' His voice trailed behind her, died.

She walked the pavements, and once she slammed into the rubbish bin bolted to a lamppost . . . close pursuit.

She crossed the streets, and twice there was the bellow of a taxi's horn and the stretched scream of brakes . . . vulnerable.

She showed her ID to the Front Security.

She took the lift up.

She remembered him. Shy, not easy with her. Slow loving, not confident with her. She would never be so damn bloody stupid again. She remembered him in Ireland. The young Five girl who was winning the reputation and handling a player, and

390

becoming an item with the regiment man who usually seemed to work the duty for her field protection. Her Gord, hooked to her little finger. Tour served, gone home, back to paper-pushing before Mr Hobbes decided she was ready to be chucked over the water again. Gord, on the short leave, ringing and being invited to the Battersea flat. Not the way it had been in Ireland, because there was no danger in a bloody Battersea flat, no hazard, no need to shelter behind him when the secret fear caught her. Never be so damn bloody stupid again . . . Threw him out. Not returned the calls, recognized the handwriting on the envelopes and sent them back . . . Gone back to Ireland, the second tour and extended, put him out of her mind because that was the creed of Five . . . There were other *career* women at Five, hell's good careers and kicking the door down into the men's club and doing the job a hell of a sight better . . . and no man and no love and no babies . . .

She sat silent at her desk and the flow of the open-plan office moved around her, unnoticed.

He could see the village that was away at the far side of the landing strip.

They sat in the bush scrub where they could see the oil lamps and the big fire that burned in the heart of the village that was on the far side of the landing strip.

The Street Boy stood shy for a moment in front of Gord, and watched as Gord replaced the field dressing on the wound. He had the rifle that he wanted and two magazines, loaded, for it, and he had four hand grenades.

He said that he was going to look for apples, anything to eat, and none of them seemed to hear him.

The Street Boy left them.

# 20

They heard the throb beat of the marimba music, the honey-sweet rhythm of the muffled drum tips on the metal tubes.

They sat in the darkness and they listened and they watched.

They saw the dancing figures that were highlighted against the big fire burning at the heart of the village.

They sat in the darkness on the far side of the landing strip and the night dew cold cut at them and the hunger in their stomachs bit at them. When the wind gathered and came from the west across the landing strip they could hear the marimba music better, but Gord cursed the wind because it carried the smells of the pig that had been cooked over the fire for eating. They had not eaten, none of them, since the stampede run through the ambush, since they had discarded everything that might have slowed them. The dog, too, growled for food.

Zed said it was the Dance of the Bull. Vee said to Gord that the bull was sacred and prized for its strength and nobility, and Zed chuckled and said that the bull was valued for the wealth carried low under its back haunches. The figure of the prancing bull was against the fire and a great head had been made for it of cloth and painted wood and it leaped and charged and then backed away from the children. Gord watched the children. The children were decked for the fiesta, bright shirts and coloured skirts, and their cries of happiness came to him on the wind. In the shit corner of the shit country, the children scattered before the rush of the bull, shrieking in the fun of it, then rushed back as the bull retreated. He saw the floating movement around the bull of the taunting butterflies . . . If the plane came, *if*, and if they flew out, and if it were known to the military what strip they had used, then the village would feel the counterstrike. The homes of the children would be burned, the mothers of the children would be scattered, the fathers of the children would be shot . . . Gord watched the dancing of the butterflies around the bull, in front of the fire, and he heard the cheering of the mothers and the fathers as the children ran again from the charge of the bull, and the beat of the music grew.

Gord sat alone. He leaned his back against the cart and felt the harsh arms of the frame against his spine. He had loaded the tubes, slow but he had achieved it, and the fuel carried in the wheelbarrow was now exhausted, and he would have no further use for the air pressure cylinder. He sat alone but they talked to him in English so that he was a part of them. She was wonderful, Alex, and she was hunched among the low scrub bushes before the cleared area that led across to the goat-grazed landing strip, and she cradled the head of Eff, and Gord thought her as resolute as barbed wire. There were the soft and whispered voices of Jorge and Harpo and Zeppo. He was sorry that the Street Boy had gone . . . The dance was finished. The marimba music was lost. The children's voices faded. The bull was gone. The big fire in the heart of the village died.

Only the soft and whispered voices for company.

Later, he would make the fire heaps along the landing strip, when the village slept, when the butterflies rested, to guide the plane in, if it came.

Jorge talking fast. '. . . Go to Europe. Italy would be best. My sister is there, her husband would welcome me, her children would want to know me. I could stay with her until I was started. What I would like is to get the job of an auto salesman. Italy is best because then I could get the job of selling the Ferrari. It is fourteen years since I have seen my sister. I would sell the 512 TR model of the Ferrari. Think of the commission . . . It sells at 200,000 US dollars. If you sell it then you get to drive it. It has, do you know, 311 kilometres per hour top speed, zero to ninety-nine kilometres per hour in 4.8 seconds, that is just incredible . . . I think I will go to Italy and I think that I will sell the Ferrari . . .'

And what suit he would wear in Palacio Nacional, forgotten. And whether it would be the American Ambassador first, forgotten. And Gord's future . . . ?

Harpo said, '. . . Myself, Canada. The old guy, he said Canada was good. He said they have a big programme for refugees, and they give them good money. The cold is the hell there, but they live with it, I can live with it. On the west of Canada you can go out in a boat and you can catch the big Pacific salmon, wonderful fish. It is not bad when they pay you money so that each day you can go fishing in the Pacific for salmon. I think I would like Canada . . .'

And the charge with the machine gun on the gate of the camp at Playa Grande, forgotten. And Gord's future . . . ?

Zeppo said, '. . . I think I would try to get to Miami, but the bastard is getting there. I don't know whether I could manage the crossing, the open boat, bad currents. Perhaps they will let me go from Havana. I would like to have a coffee stall in Miami. Just like we were in Havana, there are so many refugees in exile in Miami, and they have to have a place to drink coffee and read the old newspapers. Make strong coffee, and take the money . . .'

And Gord's future . . . ?

And Alex's future . . . ?

The soft and whispered voices of the Ferrari salesman and the salmon fisherman and the bar owner played close to him. The village was silent and the lights had gone. A small crescent of the moon hung above the length of the landing strip. He stared down at his watch. Another hour to be killed before he could be certain that the village was settled, before he should go and make the fire heaps that would guide the plane, if it came.

And Gord's future . . . ?


The pilot walked down the line of them and he shook the hand of each of the base officers.

It was three minutes to midnight, three minutes to the time for the take-off.

394

The area of the apron in front of the hangar was bright from the high floodlights. He wore a woollen cap tight down over his scalp and a thick fleece-lined flying jacket over his one-piece fatigues and insulated long pants over his buttocks and thighs, and heavy boots that were proof against the cold in the goddamn Antonov. He could smile, dry, because every officer with the rank of major and above had stayed at the base through the evening and into the night, and then made a line so that he could shake their hands . . . Like none of the goddamn bastards ever expected to see him again. The base commander was last in the line. The pilot saluted, sloppy, and he shook the hand of the base commander, loose, and then he gave him his handkerchief and the loose change coins in his pocket and his air force ID and his gate entry card, and he gave him his wallet which had banknotes and the photograph of his wife . . . It was what he thought of a piss awful order.

He climbed up into the Antonov cockpit. He eased the flying helmet down over the woollen cap. He pulled the scarf up from his throat to cover his lower face. He gave the signal. The chocks were pulled away from the wheels. He turned the key, had ignition. The noise rattled around him, growing. The propellers spun.

The pilot took the Antonov out to the end of the runway. She seemed to him to be running sweet.

He could see the line of the officers watching and waiting, and behind the officers and standing in the open mouth of the hangar were the ground crew technicians who had worked at the engines. The pilot built the power.

The Antonov lumbered down the runway, along the channel of the blazing lights, and lifted.

He took her out over the sea.

He set the course.

He stood on a straight chair. Percy Martins manipulated the hands of the wall clock, put them back to Central America time. He checked at his wrist and made the final adjustment to the clock. It was seven minutes after midnight, Central America time. He stood down from the chair and went to the window and pulled the strings that lifted the blind. A pleasant start to the day in London. He craned his neck, pushed his nose against the glass, and saw a tug boat pulling a convoy of rubbish waste barges on the river. He had slept rather well because the easy chair in his office was expensive and comfortable, a perk that he had bullied from Property (Internal). He shaved with the electric razor gained from duty free in Athens, and charged on expenses, and now the subject of nitpick inquiry by Accounts. He assumed that he had slept rather better than that fine young woman, probably curled on a sofa with a travelling rug wrapped around her. He paced, restless and excited. Always the way he felt when a live mission was running . . . Shouldn't have been running, of course, no bloody authorization for sticking out his neck, but there were precious few on the Vauxhall Bridge Road, in the upper office suites of the building, who would dare play the heavy hand with Percy 'Sniper' Martins who had brought the head of a Palestinian killer to the Prime Minister's table . . . And about the right time to interfere finally.

Never best to give people too much time to ferret on a minor request. Too much time was too much doubt, and added to too much cock-up. He dialled. He estimated that the night duty man who picked up the telephone, Ministry of Defence (Intelligence), would be going off shift within the hour, would get the message passed fast enough to ensure he was not late home.

'Percy here . . . No, I have not yet died, and not yet been buried . . . Yes, I am alive and kicking hard. Small favour, Belize . . . Yes, Belize . . . Might be a flight coming across Belize airspace in three and a half to four hours' time. Won't have lights, won't have markings, won't respond to Belize control . . . Two favours, actually. Don't scramble for it, don't put the Harriers up, because its fuel will be on the edge and evasion will waste fuel. Second, do not inform our Yankee cousins of this flight, imperative you do not . . . Send it fast, there's a good fellow . . . I'm so grateful.'

It was as much as he could do, more than he should have done. He thought of the young woman with the answerphone, wasted in Five. He thought of the young man that she seemed to love, lucky devil, and there was work for him in Six. If the Secret Intelligence Service were ever again to make a mark, regain a trifle of independence from the Yankee cousins, then it would be on the backs of such young women and such young men, directed on operations by 'Sniper', of course. Just the fellow, just the ticket, he sounded, Miss Parker's Gord, for sniffing at the perimeter fences around the Ukrainian bases that held the nuclear warheads. The right sort of man to be up on the Turkish/Iranian border and supervising havoc in mullah-land. He'd march them into the Deputy Director General's office, craven creature, thought a real day's work was either sitting at a desk and studying altitude photographs with a magnifying glass or budget balancing with a calculator, and introduce them. He'd be back in harness . . . Blotted from his mind, unwelcome and unwanted, was the thought of close pursuit and an aircraft coming vulnerable to a landing strip. Fuck it and forget it . . . He *thought* he was secure in his employment whatever the outrage he caused on the upper-floor office suites of Vauxhall Bridge Road. The alternative to employment was compulsory redundancy, the voucher in the brown envelope, retirement to Motspur Park and the wife who ignored him and the son who rejected him. He would not go easy . . . It was the dream of directing field operations again that sustained Percy Martins.

He rang down to the front desk. Coffee, soonest, proper coffee.

The dogs had the scent trail.

They pounded on the scent foot marks, slobbering and snorting, hunting the trail.

The pair of bloodhounds had been flown in at the beginning of the evening from the headquarters of the Brigada de Investigaciones Especiales y Narcóticas, big beasts, the gift of the

Spanish Guardia Civil, black-and-tan-coated beasts. Two bitches, each weighing more than ninety pounds, each able to follow a scent that was more than a hundred hours old.

They had come across the river. They had been brought to the place where the imprint of a half of a shoe's heel had been found. The soldiers had stood back. The handlers had let the dogs circle the place. The scent had been found.

The handlers, experienced men, held the dogs on long leashes, and let them lead. The scent was made by men who had sweated hard, and left a good trail for the dogs to track. And easy for the dogs because the way that the men had gone was off the paths that were used by the people of the villages and forest people. One sweat scent for them to follow that was not confused. The pair of bloodhounds were the best, the passion of their handlers, young and strong dogs, and eager to please. The handlers slipped the dogs titbits of dried meat, and the dogs led them on and strained at the taut leashes. They had poor eyesight. Their world was a monochrome mess of shadows. They were at home in the blackness of the forest with their noses hovering above the ground on which men had struggled with heavy weights.

Behind the handlers were the troops of the Kaibil battalion. Slow going in the night forest and the dogs held back so that the troops could stay with them. It was past two. They used a compass to report back the direction that the dogs took them.

The generator gave the light to the lamp above the map.

Each time the call came, each time they gave the position, approximate because they had no landmarks in the night to relate to, Arturo made the crayon mark on the clear cellophane sheet over the map.

The line wavered. The line looped a village and skirted a cliff face and avoided cleared fields, but the line held. With his crayon he drew the first track of the line, joined the points.

Bad waiting. The camp on the roadside rested. A soldier coughed, a radio screamed in static transmission, a soldier tripped on a clattering rifle and swore, a jeep came and went. They were all waiting, and for him it was the worst. Past three . . . He would have them, find them, when the daylight came, if the dogs held the scent.

On the side of the landing strip away from the sleeping village, Gord gathered cut brush and light fallen branches. There was enough light from the crescent moon, barely, for him to see ahead and to see behind far enough to know where he had made the last heap of brush and branches, and under each of the heaps he forced what dried old grass he could find by touch.

He was near to the far end of the runway, had two more heaps to make, when she came to him.

She was quiet out of the darkness and she had drifted close to him before he started up. She was close to him, and her dog was beside her.

'Can I help?'

He was brusque. 'Anything that seems dry, scrub and brush and leaves and old grass . . .'

'For the aircraft?'

Bleak. 'There won't be a London omnibus coming this way . . . Christ, I'm sorry . . . to guide in the aircraft, if it comes.'

'You don't have to be sorry, not after what you have done for us.'

Savage. 'Are they still talking round the future?'

'It is only talk.'

'Shallow bloody talk. All right, fine, I had them wrong. I thought they were bigger . . .'

'Not fair, and it is all they have. It is all that is left to them . . . At the block, Jorge would have charged. You turned him. You made the big speech, "empty gestures" and "small victories". He would have charged their guns. You have to be fair, Gord . . . You have to have charity for those who don't have your strength, your purpose. He's honest and good and brave, Jorge is, so what does it matter if he's *shallow*? What is he left with, what are any of us left with? Please, Gord, try to be fair . . .'

He bent and his fingers groped for the loose wood and for cut brush, and his hands swept up the leaves that had been blown down by the winds and rain, and under the cut brush and the loose wood he reached for dried old grass. He made a great armful and carried it back to the line that he had made. He put his boot on the newest heap and carefully pressed it down, feeling the give, not so hard that he broke the branches and made noise. He touched her wrist. The rough fingers found her smaller and stubbed fingers.

'Thank you, thank you for being with us.'

She said lightly, 'Did I have the choice?'

'Thank you for your charity and your kindness and your love.'

'Speeches are the killer, silly boy. I don't need speeches.'

'When they had you . . .'

'Leave it, Gord.'

'When you were at Playa Grande . . .'

'Please, no.'

'When they held you at Playa Grande, when the interrogator had you . . .'

'It is gone, it is behind. I survived.'

'What did you learn of him, the interrogator?'

He heard the sharp breath drawn in. Her fingers were tight on his hand.

'Does it matter, what happened before . . . ? It was evil. It was wrong because it was not in anger. If you hurt someone and you are cold, if it is just work and routine to hurt someone and then to kill them, that to me is evil. I could not see him at first because the light was always in my face and he was behind the light. He had a beautiful voice. A clean and gentle voice. A soothing voice, lovely, and each time that he drew breath then he hit me. That was the evil, the beauty of the voice and the way he hit me. When the attack started, when they came shouting for him, when they opened the door of the cell, then I saw his face. It was their mistake that I saw his face. He was a young man, younger than you. He had eyes that were green-blue and deep. He had hit me and punched me and not a hair on his head was disturbed, and he had a moustache that could have been drawn by one pen stroke. Before they opened the cell door, before the light came on him, they called his name from the corridor . . . I was supposed to tell people who are in danger to have courage. I had no courage. He broke the courage in me. If you hadn't come, Gord, I would have told him everything that he wanted to know, I would have betrayed the people I loved . . . You called him Groucho, funny name, funny man, and he tried to tell you about the fear, and you shot him because he bent to the fear, as I would have bent to the fear. Would you have shot me, Gord . . . ? Would you have shot me, and justified it as *necessary*? Think of them, Gord, those that had the courage to join you, and then the courage to leave you and go home to be with their family, the Fireman, to be with their people, the Priest, to be with their friends, the little Street Boy. He will come for them, Gord, with his sweet silk voice . . . I don't want to talk of it ever again . . . They called his name, his name was Benedicto . . . Where there is no evil, if there is such a place, I want to find it . . .'

He kissed her, gently, brushed his lips on her forehead.

It was past four. He ruffled the neck of her dog.

Gord made the last heap of brush and branches and dried old grass.

The Antonov came straight in over the Cays.

If his navigation was correct then he was headed over Long Coco Cay. The pilot thought he had seen the white surf of Gladden Spit in the moon darkness, but it was difficult for him to be certain, navigating alone and flying Echo Foxtrot alone. If he was right then the light ahead, intermittent, was the lamp on the Bugle Cays, and after the Bugle Cays would be Harvest Cay and then the Belize shoreline north of Rocky Point South. It was a chance that the pilot took, to cross Belize, but it saved him fuel. It was a chance because they had the Harrier jets at Belize and they had the big radar dishes and they had the links with the fuck *yanquis*. He was low down on the water, and when he went by the lamp on the Bugle Cays then he would be at level height with the top of the tower. If he found the strip, if he could put down, if there was no ground fire, if they were there, then the going back would be easier because he thought that the Englishman would help him with the navigation.

By the pilot's estimate, he was on schedule.

The call came through. The radio was distorted. Hard for Arturo to hear the location message against the beat of the generator.

So tired. He wrote down the message. The tiredness ached in him. The map in front of him was blurred. He should have been sleeping, it should have been a lieutenant who monitored the radio, but a lieutenant might have let him sleep. He peered down onto the map. The symbols of the map and the contour lines rose to him and fell back. He ground the nails of his fingers into the palms of his hands. He squeezed the tiredness from his eyes. He made the mark.

He drew the line.

The line that Arturo drew bisected the ground between the village marked as Tzimatzatz and the village marked as Chuchucá. The line ran forward. The line, if extended, would reach the village of Canillá. The red circle symbol beside the mark of Canillá eddied and came again. He saw it and he lost it. The shiver in him. The cold trapped him through the weight of his camouflage coat and the thickness of his tunic top. The cold knifed the flesh on his spine. The red circle symbol was an airstrip.

He was shouting into the radio.

How far from the village of Canillá? Six miles.

When could they reach the village of Canillá? Not before 0630, maybe not before 0700.

What time was first light in this fucking place? About 0500 . . . The cold gripped him. He stared down at the red circle symbol that was an airstrip. Arturo ran. He weaved down the road, between the tents and the parked jeeps, past the sleeping soldiers, past the armoured personnel carriers.

He ran to the helicopter.

He ripped back the hatch door. He groped inside. He felt the sleeping bag. He shook the body frantic, in the sleeping bag.

'What the . . . ?'

'We have to go . . . *Now* . . . We have to fly.'

The drawled voice. 'Shit . . . Fly where?'

'Just fly. I'll tell you where to fly. Please . . .'

And the flier climbed down through the hatch door and stretched himself and yawned and belched, and walked to the ditch and bent and splashed water over his face, and stretched again. And the flier went with his torch and shone it up at the tail rotor, and then at the transmission of the main rotors. An agony for Arturo as the slow and precise flight checks frittered the minutes.

In the east there was the first smear of dawn.

He would hear it before he saw it.

On the horizon of the trees a fainter shade of grey made a knife ribbon across the blackness.

Gord wheeled the cart to the end of the line of the fire heaps that he had made.

There were birds calling now and a dog had started to bark in the village that was across the landing strip from them. When he reached them they were all sleeping. He moved quietly amongst them, and he woke each one of them. He moved amongst them for the last time. He shook each one and had his hand poised to slap over their mouth if they should cry out in the moment of waking. Jorge who wanted to sell Ferrari cars, and Harpo who wanted to catch salmon off the Vancouver coast, and Zeppo who wanted to open a coffee bar in the Little Havana of Miami, and Alex who wanted to run from evil, and Eff who wanted a doctor bad, and Vee who wanted a surgeon quick before the gangrene set, and Zed who . . . He woke them each in turn. Good men, and a good woman . . . He had tried for them, and he had failed for them.

Not a mosquito.

Gord strained to hear above the bird chorus.

Not a sweet honey bee.

Struggling to separate the sound from the barking of the village dog.

He knew the sound, the old engine's throb.

Coming slow and coming low, unseen but coming . . . They all heard it. They were around him, and Harpo took Gord's face in his hands and kissed his cheeks, and Zeppo pumped his hand, and the laughter came as tears in Jorge's eyes. Trying to be curt, hissing at them for quiet. They were to wait where they stood. No movement until the landing and then the taxi run. Eff to be lifted forward in the wheelbarrow, and Vee to be helped. Snapping the instructions . . . They all saw it.

A shadow, black, across the dawn light, grey.

Gord sprinted.

There was the high roar of the engine power as the plane banked, searching for the strip.

He saw the plane for a moment again, then lost it.

Down behind the cart. Jerking the lever. The fuel gushed. The black cascade was leaping forward into the dark. He hit the trigger ignition and the fire jumped after the cascade. A corridor of fire caught the line of the heaps he had made of cut brush and branches and old grass. The line blazed.

He stood. His hands rested on the handle of the cart, and he could hear the engines swarming to power for landing.

She came in quick, almost over him. She wavered above the end of the landing strip then dropped.

Gord watched.

She hit and she bounced and seemed to fly again, then dropped. She raced and bumped the length of the strip until the hammer of the reverse thrust trapped her. They were running towards the plane, whooping in their excitement, and Harpo led and Alex had the wheelbarrow with Eff slumped in it and the dog bounded beside her. The aircraft, night-black, slowed and stopped the forward run and began to turn, cumbersome, near to the trees. No slackening of the engine power. He could see the pilot with his face close to the cockpit window and see the hurrying gesture of his gloved fist that they should come faster.

Gord knew his mind.

The door was pulled open. The wheelbarrow was lifted inside. Jorge climbing in. The dog jumping. All of them crawling and pushing to win the way into the aircraft. Alex waving to him to come, from the hatch, frantic. He was at the far end of the strip and he stood with his hands loose resting on the cart's arm.

Gord saw the helicopter.

It was the flame that guided him.

Arturo was shouting, and he seemed not to hear him.

Tom was drawn to the flame line, the guide lights to a landing strip.

He was close to the tree canopy, and it had been shit flying off the instruments to get there in the darkness, until he had seen the line of fire. He was slowing the forward speed and dropping the altitude.

Arturo no longer shouted, Arturo pointed.

He had been taught to recognize aircraft, and he had seen the burned shell of the same aircraft type at the landing strip southeast of the *finca* Santa Amelia. Antonov, AN-2, designated 'Colt'.

Staying cold.

There was a drill for preventing an unarmed aircraft from becoming airborne.

Staying cold.

It would be the escape from the debt, the tearing up of the debt chit that hammered him every last goddamn morning that he woke.

They were all in the Antonov and the big brute was starting to move, and the door was open and he thought that he saw a woman in the hatch, the blonde hair of a woman. The routine was pretty damn simple against an unarmed aircraft. Tom scudded the bird low across the trees and across the cleared area until he sat above the runway . . . Arturo, dumb mother, hooked in at last, Arturo understood. No pilot would take off *through* a helicopter that hovered over him, that blocked his lift moment.

Arturo shrieked his happiness and he bounced in his seat, and he punched the cockpit air.

The oncoming path of the Antonov wavered, like the pilot was unsure, like the message had gotten to him. Going nowhere, nowhere fast. He thought, difficult to be certain, hanging over the strip, that the Antonov's pilot had the big shit doubt, would chicken. They'd all be hollering inside, all messing.

He would owe Gord nothing. It was the tearing up of the chit to Gordon Benjamin Brown. His sort of freedom.

He thought the Antonov was slowing in the take-off run.

The cockpit screen misted.

The curtain came up to the cockpit screen.

Diffused through the mist on the screen, Tom saw the fire pumping up at him, rising, falling back, rising further. The fire reached for him, groped for the mist on the cockpit screen.

He hit the left foot control pedal. He took the cyclic control stick into the pit of his stomach. Going for power . . . He felt the bird shudder as the Antonov went by them, airborne.

He turned his bird away.

Climbing beyond the reach of the groping flame. The debt was paid, forgotten.

He felt sick, small.


They held her in the hatch doorway.

She would have fallen.

The Antonov banked over the trees. Jorge had both his arms around her waist and his hands were locked together on her stomach. She didn't fight them. Harpo had one of her arms, and Vee hung on to her thigh. She saw him standing beside the cart, him a doll and the cart a toy, at the end of the runway.

He was standing with his arms folded, comfortable, and watching their going.

He, the doll, turned. He was walking for the tree line.

The cart, the toy, was clear in the grass at the end of the strip.

The Antonov straightened, to find its course, and she was thrown hard back onto the floor of the fuselage.

She sat on the floor and she held tight to her dog.

The thunder roar of the engines was around her.

# EPILOGUE

They stood amongst the stones.

Some of the stones were broken and some had toppled in the hurricane winds that hit the island most years, and the cemetery was a place of the past, of old dreams, and was not tended. It did not concern the authorities if stones were broken and had fallen, and if the weeds grew amongst the stones.

Jorge towered in front of the grave of his father.

It was the fifth time after their return that they had gathered in the cemetery, the second Friday of each month.

One of them, his father's friend, held the faded flag of Guatemala that hung lifeless because there was no wind. One of them, his father's friend, had in his hand the small bunch of flowers that would be laid on the raised earth before they left, and the flowers of the last month had been tossed aside onto the path, dead.

There had been more the first month, the first of the second Fridays, more who had known his father. The last two months it had only been the kernel of the group, those that had made the flight in and those who had made it out. Jorge said a few words, something about keeping the faith, something about hope, something about a return. The two men, fatter now, heavier now, their skin fleshed out to spread the lines at their throats, were on either side of him, and behind him were the three Indians. It was only on the second Friday of each month that he could take the time away from the big hotel at the Varadero resort where the Transtur buses brought the tourists that he waited on in the restaurant.

He laid the flowers that would be withered within a week, dead when he next returned to the grave.

She didn't fit. The police constable thought that she did not have the grey pallor of the rest of the bastards. All the police were in their public order gear. They wore the helmets with the visors, and held shields and batons, had the leg guards strapped to their shins. Too much colour in her face, too much weathering on her cheeks for her to fit, and her hair was bleached to soft corn.

She yelled, defiant, at the advancing police and bailiffs.

'Kaibiles . . . Kaibiles pigs . . .'

The police constable muttered to the colleague nearest, 'Silly bitch, privileged cow, should get off her arse and do something with her life, put something back. What's she on about?'

'God only knows, and He's welcome.'

They escorted the bailiffs into the shambles of old caravans and broken-down cars and Transits and trailers. The farmer was at the gate to the field and urged them on, shouted at them, to get the bastards out of his field. There was a dog, a big mature Alsatian, barking and leaping in the cab of the rusted Land Rover behind her.

'Kaibiles . . . Kaibiles shit . . .'

She was a full 200 yards from the nest, but she had the good binoculars from work.

It was the nearest Cathy Parker could be to him, to feel that she touched him. The two young birds, hatched in the late spring, five months old, thrashed in their first flight. She watched them. It was where he would have been, where his heart would have been. The birds flapped and screamed and fell and caught in the blowing wind that came from the west onto the upper rock slope of Sidhean Mor. She did not know whether he was alive or dead, captured or free, her answerphone had no message for her. She felt that she was with him.

High above her, where they would have seen her, were the soaring and circling parent birds.

\* \* \*

He stood at the back, he was behind the line of ranking officers.

The sun beat on him and there was no shade on the parade ground at the garrison camp. The sweat ran in the scar pit. He let the sweat lie in the pit of the scar and he stood hard to attention as the jeep that carried the casket went low gear past him. Tom was to attention and the ranking officers, bright in the best dress uniforms, medals catching the light, saluted the casket. It was a big casket, expensive dark wood. He could see it through the shoulders of the ranking officers and through the erect slow-marching soldiers of the battalion who flanked the crawling jeep. It wasn't funny, not funny at all, but he had to tighten the muscles at his cheek to mask the grin. A hell of a big casket, and a hell of a little of a corpse to stuff inside it. From what he had heard from the embassy people who had given their advice to the detectives from the Brigada de Investigaciones Especiales y Narcóticas, there were precious few pieces, small pieces, to go in the casket. Three pounds' weight of military explosive, a mercury tilt switch, battery circuit, a wired wristwatch for the connection, a magnet strapped to a plastic box, under the car on the driver's side, from what he'd heard, left the pieces few and small. The band played slow. The casket with the flag on it, and on the flag the maroon beret of the battalion, went by him.

He relaxed from the stiffness of attention. A private funeral afterwards. He would be away as soon as was decent. The Country Attaché was waiting on him, back at the embassy, would be kicking his heels for a lift to Flores up in the Petén. It was slow going out of the base, and he was held up in the queue of the staff cars as the military police shouted and blew their whistles and waved their white-gloved hands to give priority for the ranking officers to join the traffic flow. There was a small crowd outside the base gates. The crowd stood with expressionless faces. He had his window down to get the cool light wind into the oven interior of the station wagon. They were just a rubbish crowd from the shanty town beside the garbage dump. It was, at first, a growl of a shout. He saw a man in the drab uniform of a fireman. The shout might have come from him. The shout grew, sneering and mocking the closed cars of the ranking officers. He saw an urchin street boy. The shout, building, was the name.

'*Gord*, Gaspar . . . *Gord*, Gaspar . . . *Gord*, Gaspar . . .'

He threw open the door of the car. He piled into the crowd. The name beat in his ears. The face to the name was huge in his mind, what he had seen of the face below him, turning, then going into the trees. He had hold of the Fireman's tunic. The face was never forgotten. The crowd was all around him. The name was with him each morning as he woke. The Street Boy stared him out.

He shouted, 'He saved me, I saved him. Don't fucking think I couldn't have had him. He owes it all to me. I paid my debt. I don't owe Gord anything. We're level, me and Gordon Benjamin Brown. I turned away. He was dead without me helping him. Believe me, please, you have to believe me. I turned away to save him. I paid my debt . . .'

He was shouting into the silence around him as the military police pulled him back from the crowd.

He could no longer see the Fireman, nor the Street Boy.

It was only when Tom Schultz had reached La Aurora, met the Country Attaché, was changing into his flying gear, that he found that his wallet was gone from the inside pocket of his suit jacket.

He served, fast, an ace, and she was stretching and beaten. The lieutenant, codename Benedicto, had more time for tennis now. The game was not yet played long enough for him to have to manufacture the defeat, only the first set. He saw her pouted disappointment because she had not been into her stroke before the ball had passed her. He went to the back netting to retrieve a ball, to serve again. The court backed onto the car parking area that was set with trees and shrubs. He could see his own car, midnight blue, Peugeot 205 GTI. Her father had given him the car. The car shone in the morning sunshine. He bent to pick up the ball and when he straightened he saw the figure of the man beside his car, the back of the man, and the man walked away and the lieutenant did not see his face.

\*   \*   \*

412

After they had been to the grave, each second Friday in the month, they went to the café in the Campeche quarter at the south end of the Old City and the radio played Deep South jazz.

They would talk of the war and talk of the march and talk of the battles at Playa Grande and Nebaj and at Santa Cruz del Quiché. Just the three of them, talking and tapping their feet and drumming their fingers to the jazz music. The Indians did not come with them to the café in the Campeche quarter. *He* was not mentioned when they talked of the war and the march and the battles. They did not feel the need to talk of him, as if he had never been amongst them. It was good coffee, and it could be made to last until the dregs were stone cold, and then they would peck in their pockets for small change and linger with a second cup until it was the middle of the day and the table was required for eating.

When the news came on, after the jazz music, it was time for them to leave. As the news bulletin started, the owner of the café was at their backs, no respect, barking for them to be gone. They stood and they drained the cups the final time. It was after the sugar harvest production figures, and after the feature on the record number of visiting Mexican tourists. Jorge heard the name. The radio was always turned loud to beat the coughing pandemonium of the old buses on the street. He heard the name of the colonel and he heard the detail of the funeral. He broke from them. He wanted only to be back in the dim loneliness of the apartment he had shared with his father. The radio told of the visit to Havana of the Polish trade minister and his promise to buy more bananas . . .

They parted.

The one drove a cab, and counted himself lucky to have that work, and the other swept the floors of a hospital.

He would see them in a month.

Jorge crossed the street and climbed the stairs. He went into the apartment. He switched on the fan and he pushed aside the plates on the table from his breakfast and from his meal the night before . . . his eyes misted.

413

A cockroach scurried on the tiled floor.

His eyes were filled with the tears . . . The man was in his mind, the man who was not talked of, as if he had never been amongst them.

A cockroach ran from him and was ignored.

Jorge went into the bedroom and he knelt. He knelt beside the big bed with the iron frame and the sunken mattress that was stripped of sheets. He knelt below the magazine photograph of the stern jowl face of Leonid Brezhnev and against his arm was the low table on which was the mounted photograph of the young men smiling and holding the automatic rifles.

'. . . I will watch for you. Fire with fire . . . Take a fighting man . . .'

# THE OUTSIDERS

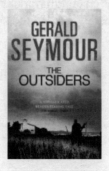

'Once again demonstrating his ability to probe the moral murki-
ness of the spy trade and create an absorbingly diverse ensemble,
Seymour crafts a sophisticated, reader-teasing tale.'
*The Sunday Times*

MI5 officer Winnie Monks has never forgotten the death of a young
agent on her team at the hands of a former Russian Army Major-
turned-gangster. Ten years later, she hears the Major is travelling to a
Spanish villa and she asks permission to send in a surveillance unit.

There is an empty property next door, perfect to spy from –
and as a base for Winnie's darker, less official plans.

But this villa isn't deserted: the owners have invited a young
British couple to 'house sit' while they are away.

Jonno and Posie think they are embarking on a carefree holiday in the sun.
But, when the Secret Service arrives in paradise, *everything* changes.

'Those [Seymour] sends off into dangerous territory are, in fact,
his readers. With each book, we enter a dangerous universe, and
are totally involved with utterly plausible characters, faced with
moral choices that are rarely straightforward.'
*Independent*

HODDER

# A DENIABLE DEATH

### AN EPIC NOVEL OF HIGH COURAGE AND LOW CUNNING, OF LIFE AND DEATH IN THE MORAL MAZE OF THE POST-9/11 WORLD.

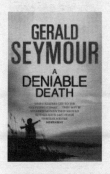

'Gerald Seymour is the grand-master of the contemporary
thriller and A DENIABLE DEATH is his greatest work yet.
Gripping, revealing and meticulously researched, this is a page-
turning masterpiece that will literally leave you breathless.'
Major Chris Hunter, bestselling author of *Extreme Risk*

YOU WATCH. YOU WAIT. THE HOURS SLIDE SLOWLY PAST.

A WHOLE DAY. THEN TWO.

YOU LIE UNDER A MERCILESS SUN IN A
MOSQUITO-INFESTED MARSH.

YOU CAN'T MOVE, LEAVE, OR RELAX.

YOUR MUSCLES ACHE FROM CLENCHING TIGHT FOR SO LONG.

IF YOU ARE DISCOVERED, YOU WILL BE TORTURED THEN KILLED.

AND HER MAJESTY'S GOVERNMENT WILL
DENY ALL KNOWLEDGE OF YOU.

'Great storytelling . . . you just have to read this novel . . . absolutely gripping'
*Eurocrime*

**HODDER**

# THE DEALER AND THE DEAD

## THE ARMS DEALER BETRAYED THEM.
## THE SURVIVORS WANT REVENGE.

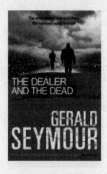

'*The Dealer and the Dead* is Seymour firing on all cylinders
and his rivals need, once again, to look to their laurels'
*Independent*

In a moonlit field near the Serbian border, Croatian villagers waited for an arms shipment that would never come. They
will never forget that night, or the slaughter that followed.

Eighteen years later, a body is discovered in a field, and with it the identity of
the arms dealer who betrayed them. Now the villagers can plot their revenge.

For Harvey Gillott, it was all a long time ago. But now the
hand of the past is reaching out across Europe, to Harvey's house in leafy England. And it's holding a gun . . .

'The final scenes are brilliantly orchestrated . . . Without doubt, *The Dealer
and the Dead* is one of the finest thrillers to be published so far this year'
*Yorkshire Evening Post*

**HODDER**

# THE COLLABORATOR

## CORRUPTION. BETRAYAL. REVENGE.

'A dense, intensely satisfying thriller from one of the modern masters of the craft, Seymour's latest novel will remind the world just how phenomenally accomplished a thriller writer he is.'
*Daily Mail*

Eddie Deacon has a new girlfriend. She's beautiful, clever and Italian.

And then she disappears.

What Eddie doesn't know is that Immacolata Borelli is the daughter of a merciless Naples gangster. She can no longer live with her conscience and has decided to collaborate with the police to bring down her own family.

But the Borellis will not lose their empire without a fight. They will use or destroy anything and anyone to prevent her from talking.

Including Eddie.

'Tight writing and meticulous research . . . Seymour paints the streets of Naples and their dark denizens with an artist's brush that lingers equally on the grime, the glitter and the blood'
*The Times*

**HODDER**

In the best books, the ending often comes as a shock.
Not just because of that one last twist in the tale,
but because you have been so absorbed in their world,
that coming back to the harsh light of reality is a jolt.

If that describes you now, then perhaps you should track down
some new leads, and find new suspense in other worlds.

Join us at www.hodder.co.uk, or follow us on
Twitter @hodderbooks, and you can tap in to a
community of fellow thrill-seekers.

Whether you want to find out more about this book,
or a particular author, watch trailers and interviews, have
the chance to win early limited editions, or simply browse
our expert readers' selection of the very best books,
we think you'll find what you're looking for.

And if you don't, that's the place to tell us what's missing.

**We love what we do, and we'd love you to be part of it.**

www.hodder.co.uk

@hodderbooks

HodderBooks

HodderBooks